M000303728

Mr.
Paddimir's
JUICE

TARAN A SCHILG

Mr. Paddimir's Juice

Copyright 2020 by Taran A. Schilg

All rights reserved. No part of this book may be reproduced, stored in a retrieval system, or transmitted in any form or by any means-electronic, mechanical, photocopy, recording, or otherwise-without prior written permission of the copyright owner.

This is a work of fiction. Aside from reference to known public figures, places, or resources, all names, characters, places, and incidents have been constructed by the author, and any resemblance to actual persons, places, or events is coincidental.

ISBN: 978-0-578-71440-0

Printed in the USA.

In loving memory of my dearest friend Silvia...
"Brave, Beautiful, Strong, and Courageous."
JUNE 9, 1972 – JUNE 6, 2020

One

E va rushed into Bertram's flower shop, the door slamming loudly behind her.

"Gertie, Gertie, do you have any flowers today?" she asked hastily, short of breath, her long blonde hair flowing behind her as she hurried toward the clerk's counter.

"Shhh, child, keep it down. Do you want me to get in trouble with Mr. Bertram?" Gertrude asked in a hushed tone.

"Oh, I'm sorry," Eva whispered, peering around the flower shop.

Gertrude Downing, also known as Gertie, had been a friend of Eva's mother, Margaret, whom everyone called Margie, since she was a child. Gertie had worked at Bertram's flower shop in Piccadilly for almost five years now. She was an attractive, thin, hardworking woman, with curly black hair that was tightly pulled back into a bun. Years of hard labor were etched into her worn face, much like the faces of many of the women Eva knew, including her mother.

"Mother's in a fuss—she's fresh out of flowers," Eva worried, wringing her hands.

"Well, I'm sorry Eva, but I just don't know how much longer I can keep giving you flowers for free," Gertie replied impatiently, a sallow look on her face.

Gertie desperately wanted to help little Eva and Margie Alderson, even though Eva wasn't really a little girl anymore. At sixteen, she was blossoming into a rather beautiful young lady. Her complexion was creamy and fair, her hazel-green eyes glistened, and her blonde hair was thick and wavy. She had a tall, slender figure like her mother and a sophisticated, long, pointed nose. Margie best keep a close watch over Eva, Gertie thought to herself.

The Aldersons had always been kind to Gertie but, since there was not much work to be had in London these days, she couldn't keep risking helping them.

"Mr. Bertram is starting to catch on and I'm afraid that I won't be able to give you flowers for much longer."

"I understand Gertie—just this one last time?" Eva pleaded, giving Gertie a pitiful look, her lower lip hanging down toward her chin. Gertie stood there for a moment, her hands on her hips and her mouth firmly pursed together. Staring at Eva she released a loud sigh.

"Oh, alright, here you go then," she said while shaking her head in dismay. Gertie gathered an assortment of primroses, green lavenders, carnations, and violets. She handed the flowers to Eva and carefully laid them in a large woven basket.

"Thank you, Gertie!" Eva exclaimed excitedly.

"Yeah, yeah. This is the last time, understand?" Gertie insisted harshly, wagging her finger as Eva briskly headed toward the shop door. Eva paused, turning at once, then deeply curtsied.

"Umble-cum-stumble!" she replied with a wink, then bounded out the door and down the busy street.

Eva skipped down Piccadilly joyfully, firmly holding onto the flower basket, when thoughts of her current situation rumbled through her mind. Suddenly, Eva's expression changed to a solemn stare and her skip slowed to a stop. Helplessly, she stared down at the hard clay road, a sinking feeling weighing down her chest. She began thinking of how her mother had been hawking goods for almost two years now, ever since Eva's father, Henry, had died in a factory accident. She knew it wouldn't be long until they would again have to find a way to obtain more items to sell at the market. They had never stolen goods before, but she wasn't sure how much longer they could continue down their current path before they would have to steal. A great many of the products people sold at the market were stolen. Eva was doing her best to help her mother keep her bearings, but making a living was becoming more complicated every day. The anxiety over not having goods to sell wasn't the only thing troubling Eva—she also missed her father most intensely. Slowly, she strolled down the street reminiscing about her father. She missed the way he would pick her up in his arms, swinging her around in circles while smiling at her. She missed playing games with him while mother fixed dinner. Most of all, she missed the way he would look at her mother and the way she would return his gaze. Seeing her parent's love for one another had always given Eva such a warm feeling in her heart. While standing in the street, Eva sucked in a deep breath of reassurance and sighed.

"We'll find a way, we always do," she said out aloud, reassuring herself as she hurried down the street and headed toward the Covent Garden market. When she entered the market, there were people scattered everywhere and multiple scents attacked her nostrils. The aromas of baked goods, fresh herbs, and livestock were mixed with the typical sewage stench emanating from the Thames. This particular blend of smells made Eva's stomach turn. She let out a deep breath and heavily pushed her way through the bustling crowd, skirting between venders and shoppers. The market was always busy—in fact, people would occasionally end up getting into fights or would trample one another. She had to be very careful as she squeezed herself through the thick crowd.

Eva anxiously searched for her mother, who was part of a group of ladies that the patrons referred to as the "flower women." Most of the men who purchased flowers from these women felt sorry for them, while the others bought flowers because they took an interest in one of the ladies. Eva's mother, Margie, always acted in a flirtatious manner toward the fellows but would never truly accept their advances. The truth was that Margie could have her pick of any man in town. She was tall and lean, with chocolate brown, wavy hair that she mostly wore in a loose bun with tiny curls that framed her face. Margie always carried herself with grace and elegance. She was a kind-hearted woman but with a bit of spunk in her as well, which Eva's father had always loved. Eva thought her mother was the most beautiful woman in London and admired her greatly. She wasn't sure whether her mother would ever love again and she believed that it was her duty to stick by her mother's side, being as helpful as possible.

Eva stood high up on the tips of her toes, trying to locate the flower women through the crowd. She was tall but didn't weigh much, making it easy for people to push and toss her to and fro. Soon, she reached the market section in which the flower women would usually stand when, unexpectedly, a large, distracted man bumped into her, flinging the basket from

8

her grip. She tumbled to the ground but no one paid her any attention. Feet were scurrying left and right around her, kicking and battering her in the process. Suddenly, Eva felt a massive blow to her head. Crying out in pain, she grabbed her head, feeling dizzy. The market surroundings melted into one another as her eyesight blurred and she began losing consciousness.

* * *

Eva was lying on cold, hard ground, when strong hands reached firmly underneath her body, scooping her away from the frenzy of moving feet. She blinked her eyes several times, looking around, trying to adjust her focus. Noises, which seemed to come at her from all directions, were subdued to a hum as a soft, deep tone left her rescuer's lips.

"Are you alright, my dear?"

Eva blinked rapidly, squinting as she glanced up at the man holding her tightly in his arms. She peered into his dark, wanting eyes and he stared back. The man's gaze was so intently and deeply fixed upon her eyes that she felt as if he were looking directly into her soul. He was a handsome man but there was something intimidating about him. His face was extremely sharp and she could see every line and detail of its structure. A fine, pronounced jaw and high-set cheekbones were framed by wavy, raven-colored hair that swooped to one side, caressing his brow. Light facial hair coated his upper lip and the ridge of his chin.

"Ye..ye..yes, sir," Eva mumbled, rubbing the back of her head. "Thank you, sir," she added politely while continuing to blink rapidly, still trying to regain her focus.

The man carefully set her feet first down onto the ground, making sure she was steady before fully releasing her from his grasp. Eva looked up at him as his penetrating eyes continued to stare back at her intensely. The man gave her a deliberate nod and smirked, holding the tip of his hat while bowing, his other hand gracefully placed behind his back. He continued locking his eyes onto Eva's for just a moment longer; then, he slowly turned and walked away.

Eva had never seen this man in the market before. She was sure she would have remembered him because there was something very intriguing about him. He wasn't like the other men that she had encountered in the market. This man wore a fashionable, long, black velour overcoat that was slightly open, showing off his coal colored shirt and black silk vest. He had a shiny burgundy tie wrapped around his neck, which tucked inside his shirt. A very tall, black top hat that looked practically brand new was perched on top of his head and he carried a very unusual golden walking stick. Eva had never seen such a satisfactory walking stick—it looked like it belonged to a prince. She continued watching the captivating fellow as he jaunted away, wondering why a gentleman like him would be in this stuffy, crowded market place. Unexpectedly, the man slowly turned his head and peered directly at her with a sly grin upon his face. At the sight, Eva's eyes widened and her heart began pounding. Again, he stared intently at her for an uncomfortable amount of time, as if he were studying her. Eva gasped and grabbed at her chest, trying to catch her breath, while he continued gazing at her. The man ended his look with a wink, then slowly turned back around and continued on his way.

Eva shook her head, holding her hands against her chest as she tried to regain her composure. She inhaled a deep breath, then bent down, wafting the dirt away from her challis skirt and pantalets. When she looked down at the ground, her face contorted in angst as she realized that she had dropped the flowers that Gertie had given her.

"Oh no, the flowers!" she exclaimed and began frantically trying to retrieve them from the dirt floor. There was no use, they'd all been trampled on and scattered into pieces. "Now, what am I to do? I can't go to mother with nothing in my hands, how will I tell her that I dropped the flowers?" she exclaimed aloud as tears filled her eyes.

Eva lowered her head and walked quickly back through the market toward the street. When she reached the entrance, she leaned against a brick wall and slowly sank to the ground, sobbing uncontrollably. For a while she hopelessly sat there, leaning against the brick wall, crying, and feeling sorry for herself as her head continued to throb in pain. A few minutes passed when she heard someone calling her name out from across the street.

"Eva, Eva!" the voice called.

She began looking around just as a stage coach dashed by, with horses galloping at full speed, lifting dirt all around her, and blocking her view. Eva squinted, letting out a few coughs while waving her hand around, trying to move the dust cloud out of her face, when she saw him.

"Georgie!" she cried out.

Georgie Thornber was Eva's oldest and dearest friend. He was a head taller than Eva and a couple of years older, with sandy blonde hair, big blue eyes, and a muscular build. There was something special about Georgie, almost as if a light were beaming within him—it always gave Eva hope. He also had a smile that could cheer anyone up in an instant. Eva's heart melted every time she would see one of Georgie's smiles. When he was nearby, she always felt safe. They had a unique connection, something so substantial that Eva thought it could never break.

Georgie was carrying several bags in his hands as he headed across the street toward her.

"Georgie!" she called out again as she rose quickly, wiping the tears from her eyes. She ran up to meet him, wrapping her arms around his neck as she embraced him tightly.

"Whoa, whoa, let me put the bags down first," he said, with wide eyes and a grin, but Eva didn't let go as Georgie placed the bags on the ground.

"Aren't you a sight for sore eyes," she replied and held onto him even tighter.

Georgie closed his eyes and embraced Eva, feelings flooding inside him. He missed her very much while he was away in the country and just the sight of her warmed his heart.

"Now, let me take a good look at ya," he said lightly, pushing her back a bit to get a better look. "You're as pretty as ever." He shook his head, his eyes bright eyes and his smile beaming.

"Stop that, Georgie Thornber! I barely recognized you, without street dust on your face!" Eva teased, tapping his arm as her face turned red as roses.

She had known Georgie for as long as she could remember. Their fathers were close friends and had worked together in the same factory. Ruben Thornber had moved his family into the city after losing his farm when Georgie was just a boy. After Eva's father's accident at the factory, Georgie's father ended up losing his job along with many of the other workers. Scotland Yard had investigated the incident and found that

12

there were too many men working in the factory as well as ill manufactured equipment. They also claimed that the area was too congested, forcing many of the men to leave.

Ruben, being a close friend of Eva's father, had found favor with the factory's owner, Mr. Lyons. Mr. Lyons knew of Ruben's experience working on a farm and recommended Ruben to be the new farming tenant at Magistrate Logan's country home in Oxfordshire. Georgie's mother and sisters worked on the farm as well, but Georgie stayed behind to help take care of his grandmother, Alice. She refused to leave London in her old age and had some money saved up that her late husband had left her. Georgie and Alice lived in the same lodging house as Eva and her mother, which was also owned by Mr. Lyons. Eva knew that Georgie had stayed in London to take care of his grandmother, but she didn't know that he had also stayed back because he wanted to be near her.

When Georgie was in London, he worked as a "growler" for a man named Mr. Gyles, taking care of horses and giving carriage rides to people around town. A few times each year, Georgie's dad would send for him to work as an extra hired hand on Magistrate Logan's farm during the sowing and harvesting seasons, earning extra wages. Georgie had been gone for two months this time and Eva was feeling a bit lost without him.

"So, how was your time in Oxfordshire?" she asked.

"Oh, you know, it's always great being out in the country and all, but I was ready to come back to see Grams—and you, of course," he replied coyly with a smile.

Eva blushed as her heart started beating a bit faster. "I was worried you might stay for good this time; it's been a whole two months," Eva said, distressed.

Georgie gave a half grin while nervously gazing at the ground. He bent down, grabbing hold of his bags.

"Let's move out of the street before we get run over by a growler," Georgie recommended and Eva helped him as they made their way out of the main street. They stopped near the edge of the market entrance and set the bags down.

"There was a lot more work to do this time around. Magistrate Logan acquired some new land next door. He also allowed me to work with his horses while I was there this time." Eva perked up, listening to him intently. "He had also just purchased a couple of ponies that needed to be broken in and asked if I could help," he continued, raising his chin high in the air. "The magistrate said he was very impressed with my skills!" he stated proudly, as Eva continued gazing up at him and smiling brightly.

"That's wonderful, Georgie!" she exclaimed, clasping her hands together. "You are so very good with the horses—you have a special gift, you know." She was grinning from ear to ear.

Georgie lowered his head slightly, blushing, then glanced back up at Eva with a smirk on his face. "There was one foal who gave me quite a bit of trouble. She sort of reminded me of you," he teased.

Eva looked up at him and noticed the playful grin on his face. She gave him a pout. "I hope I'm not that much trouble," she puffed, folding her arms and looking down at the ground.

Georgie gently grabbed her chin, giving it a little shake. "Of course, you're not. I'm just teasing you."

Eva looked up into his eyes. Her heart was pounding as feelings rose inside her. They had always been good friends but, over the last year, she had begun to think of Georgie as much

14

more than a friend and was hoping that he felt the same way about her. He gently released her chin, his eyes releasing hers.

"Oh, I almost forgot," he said, bending down and grabbing the large burlap sack. "This here bag is for you and Miss Marg. There's some fruits, veggies, and herbs in there for you to sell if you like."

Eva's eyes lit up as Georgie presented her with the sack.

"Oh my goodness, Georgie, aren't you a godsend!" she squealed excitedly, with a sigh of relief, tightly embracing him.

"Aww, don't mention it," Georgie said, closing his eyes and relishing having Eva in his arms.

Eva gently pulled away.

"I was just feeling sorry for myself before you arrived because Gertie gave me some flowers to sell and I got knocked down in the market, dropping them like a ninny," she said, exasperated, shaking her head. "Took a good kick in the head too." Eva rubbed the back of her head with her fingertips.

"It sounds to me like you were just being a bit clumsy," Georgie teased her with a smirk. Eva didn't reply, just rolled her eyes with a kittenish grin written across her face. "Well, I best be getting along to see how Grams is doing. I got some ingredients for her to make pies," Georgie added as he picked up the rest of his bags.

"Mmmm, I love Alice's pies—they're the best!" Eva closed her eyes and licked her lips as she thought about Alice's pies. Georgie glanced at Eva, then quickly turned his head away, hoping to restrain the feelings that rose within him at the sight of Eva licking her lips. He swallowed hard, then cleared his throat.

15

"So, I'll see you back at the house then?" he asked with a soft gaze.

"You can count on it!" she replied fervently.

Georgie smiled once more and Eva felt her insides swell within her as he walked backward while staring at her, giving her one more of his beautiful smiles. Oh, how his face shined, Eva thought, as her heart raced a little faster at the sight of him. She smiled back with a wave, then Georgie turned around and headed up the street toward Drury Lane. Eva turned back toward the market, inhaling deeply as she looked up at the market entrance. She felt that everything was going to be just fine now that Georgie was back in London.

Two

E va dragged the heavy burlap sack toward the market entrance. She used it to help push herself through the busy crowd, until she finally spotted the group of flower women standing at the back of the market. Ruby Dawson, Gladys Knightly, and Clara Simms were there.

Ruby was Margie's best friend. She had bright red, curly hair, which contributed to her given name, and crisp, green eyes. Her complexion was soft and peachy, with some freckles on her cheeks and nose. Ruby was known for having a temper and for making sharp, sarcastic comments.

Gladys Knightly was the oldest of the flower women and was short and stocky with salt- and pepper-colored hair. Gladys was very protective of the other flower women, seeing herself as the mother hen watching over her little chicks. She cared for the ladies but could also be a brute, standing toe to toe with any man in town. Once, a gentleman had bet Gladys that she couldn't carry his friend from the Covent Garden Market to Elephant and Castle street. She took the bet and won, making a pretty penny in the process.

Clara Simms was shorter than all the other ladies. She was in her late twenties and very pretty. She would often tell tall tales that affiliated her with the upper class and royalty, although everyone knew better. She had straight, dark blonde hair, large, brown doe eyes, and a tiny, well-proportioned figure. Many men were extremely attracted to Clara and she was highly responsive to their advances. She had a bewitchingly girlish way about her that was very enticing. Many of the women were jealous of Clara's beauty and the attention she would receive from the fellows. Nonetheless, the flower women still did their best to accept Clara and tolerate her snobbish ways.

"Blimey! There she is, Marg!" shouted Ruby as she pointed in Eva's direction.

"My goodness, child, what took you so long?" Margie questioned hastily.

"It's about time, I say. Did ye get lost, dear?" Ruby chimed in sarcastically.

"I'm so sorry, mother. The flowers Gertie gave me...well, I dropped them, here, in the market. This made me distraught, so I went back outside, feeling rather sorry for myself...when, you'll never guess who I saw—Georgie Thornber!" Eva ended, her voice rising excitedly.

"Oh, George is home!" Margie exclaimed, forgetting all about the flowers. "I was beginning to wonder if he'd stayed at the farm for good this time. The two of us would've had to keep watch over Miss Alice for the rest of her days."

Eva spoke up quickly, rather happy that her mother had forgotten all about the flowers, "I told him the same thing and he said that the magistrate had acquired more land and there was extra work to be done."

18

Gladys piped up, "Figures, we're out here, scrounging up enough to make lodging rent and the magistrate's purchasing more land?" She was clearly annoyed.

"Oh, I'm just glad he's home!" Margie breathed in a relieved tone, "Eva's been ever so bored without him." Then, she added, "I must say the news did brighten up my day a bit!"

Eva had a big smile on her face, her cheeks turning pink.

"So, what's in the bag then, girl?" Ruby sounded irritated, wondering why no one else had asked the same question. Eva rolled her eyes at Ruby, then perked up, showing her mother what was in the sack.

"Look what Georgie brought for us from the farm, mother!" Eva pulled out fruits and veggies from the burlap sack.

Margie took in a deep breath, "So no flowers to sell today, only beautiful fruits and veggies. I'll take it!" she chirped.

"I don't know, Marg. You might have to go stand somewhere else in the market. We are known as the flower women, you know. People come here expecting to find flowers," Clara chimed in, her nose high in the air, rolling her eyes. Clara had the most irritating, high pitched, nasally voice. Eva could barely stand listening to her sometimes.

Ruby moved closer to Clara.

"Well, I don't know, Clara, I've stood here before and seen you sell a lot more than just some flowers, you know what I mean? Maybe you shouldn't be standing here with us, either?" Ruby quipped in a brash tone.

Clara gave Ruby a "Humph," sticking her nose even higher into the air as she gracefully walked off a bit further away from the other women.

"Ah, don't mind her, Marg, she's just jealous. The poor girl's never had anything more to sell than herself and some flowers," said Gladys with a shake of her head and somewhat loaded sympathy. "Oh, here come some men heading our way," Ruby pointed out excitedly to the other women in a loud whisper, sticking her thumb out toward them expectantly. Clara heard Ruby and tiptoed back a bit closer to the other ladies.

"Alright, ladies, shoulders back, heads up, smiles in place," barked Gladys with military precision. All the ladies straightened up and put on their best faces.

"Well, hello there, Bert," Margie greeted one of the men, a flirtatious smile on her face.

"Good afternoon, ladies," Bert replied, taking off his black bowler hat while giving the ladies a courteous bow.

Bert was a regular customer of the flower women. He was a single, short, somewhat heavyset man, with light brown hair and an evident liking for Margie. He had an excellent job as a bank clerk but was also well known for his lousy drinking habits down at the pubs in the evenings.

"Oh, it's just Bert," said Clara with a disappointed sigh and rolled her eyes. She placed her hands around her waist, her flower basket hanging about her left wrist, her nose high in the air, and abruptly walked away.

Margie gave Bert a welcoming grin.

"What can we help you with today, Bert?" she inquired.

Bert shuffled nervously.

"Whatcha got there in the sack, Marg?" he nudged his head toward the burlap sack.

"Well, Bert, it just so happens that today is your lucky day! I just received some beautiful fruits and veggies from Oxfordshire, fresh off the coach!" said Margie with a proud look on her face.

"Oh, is that so?" Bert raised his eyebrows, looking somewhat surprised.

"Let me see here," Margie tapped her chin with her index finger and began rifling through the burlap sack. "It looks like I've got some nice rhubarb, blackberries, apples, currants... What's your pleasure, Bert?" Margie looked up at Bert with a grand, expectant smile.

Ruby leaned toward Margie, placing her hand up to hide her mouth. "I'm pretty sure it's you, Marg," she whispered in a hushed tone out of the corner of her mouth, a devilish grin on her face.

The other women burst out laughing. Margie gave Ruby a light backhanded slap on the hip and spoke through her teeth with a fake smile on her face.

"Cut it out, Rube, I'm trying to make a sale here."

Ruby giggled and backed up, covering her mouth with her hand. Bert glared at Ruby and lifted his chin high into the air while clearing his throat.

"I think I'll take some of those apples you got there, Marg," stated Bert, ignoring Ruby's smart remark.

"Alright then, how many would you like?" Margie questioned.

"Uh, let's see. How about five apples?" he queried, rubbing his hand against his whiskers.

"Sounds just right to me!" Margie replied with a genuine smile on her face, happy to be making a sale. "That'll be ten pence."

Eva handed her mother a brown paper sack, which she generally used for flowers. While Margie filled the bag with shiny red apples, Bert removed his hat, sticking it under his arm. He reached into his pocket and pulled out a handful of coins, shuffling through them with his fingers until he found ten pence.

"Here you go, Marg," he said, handing her the money.

"Much obliged," she replied with a nod, taking the coins from his hand.

"So, Marg, have you heard about the circus coming to town this weekend?" Bert asked as he placed the remaining coins back into his pocket. He grabbed his hat from under his arm and began rustling it nervously with his hands.

"Why, yes, I did see some signs up around Piccadilly. Are you planning to attend this weekend?" Margie asked politely, trying to make small talk.

"Well, um, yes, actually, I purchased two tickets for Saturday afternoon." Bert swallowed hard and began to sweat. He looked as if he might become ill.

"Oh, I'm sure you'll have a wonderful time," Margie replied, handing Bert the bag with apples. He fumbled around, trying not to drop the bag along with his hat. He was looking down uneasily, slightly rocking back and forth.

"Well, Marg, actually, I was wondering if, maybe, you, um, would like to join me? You know, at the circus. It's some fellows from America, supposed to be quite the show," Bert asked, gazing wide-eyed at Margie, a hopeful expression on his face.

Margie's eyes widened in surprise and she smiled politely as she spoke, "Bert, it is mighty kind of you to ask; however, our friend George has just come back to town and—"

"Oh, of course, Marg," Bert interrupted, "I completely understand, yes, of course, you're busy. I'm sure…," his words trailed off nervously and a disheartened look rested upon his face. There was an awkward pause for a moment, as Bert fiddled with his hat.

Margie felt sorry for him. "Well, of course, I could go with you, perhaps just as friends?" she suggested, a sympathetic look on her face. Ruby gasped loudly, leaving her mouth gaping wide.

Bert perked up, his eyes once again growing wide with excitement at Margie's acceptance of his invitation.

"Well, that would be quite nice, you know, just as friends, of course," Bert nodded, a satisfied look resting on his face. "Why don't I meet you out in front of the circus on Piccadilly at, say, around half past six?"

"That sounds lovely, Bert," she agreed, giving him a pleasant grin.

"See you on Saturday, then, Marge." Bert turned and looked at the other flower women. "Ladies," he nodded, placing his hat on his head, a broad smile on his face. He turned with a little skip in his step and walked down through the market, head held high.

Margie rubbed her forehead and looked down at the ground. Ruby walked over to her, shaking her head from side to side.

"Good job Marge, now you've done it! He thinks he's got a chance wit' ya!" Ruby exclaimed.

"I can't believe you said yes!" Gladys burst out, a confused look on her face.

Eva couldn't believe it either; she knew her mother had no interest in Bert Darby.

"I felt bad for him. I didn't know what else to do. You saw the look he gave me. He looked so pathetic." Margie's mouth twisted in a distasteful grimace.

"Well, just don't be shocked when he shows up at the circus comin' off a bender!" spouted Ruby.

"Oh my," Margie touched her cheek, "I certainly hope he doesn't show up intoxicated." She sucked in a deep breath. "It's been so long since I've courted. I'm not even sure if I remember how it all works." There was a bewildered look on her face.

"Courting!" shouted Ruby. "You're not courting Bert, Marg! You're just going to the daft circus with him, for goodness' sake! Courting, she says!" Ruby's face turned bright red. This always happened when she started to lose her temper.

"Calm down now, Ruby, before you've gone lost the plot," said Gladys.

Ruby huffed, "Fine then, Gladys, you talk some sense into her!" She waved her hand and walked away to calm down.

"All the men in London and you decided on Bert Darby?" Gladys questioned Margie shaking her head.

"I really don't understand what all the fuss is about. It is only the circus and I did say we were only going as friends. I know he's a bit of a slosh, but he's not a bad fellow. He's always been kind to us," replied Margie, sounding as if she was trying to convince herself.

"My, my, did I just overhear that someone's going to the circus this weekend with Bert Darby?" Clara snubbed.

"Oh, here we go," Gladys said, rolling her eyes.

"Yes. I would appreciate it, Clara, if you kept your opinions to yourself this time," Margie said in the flustered tone. Clara stuck both hands out in front of herself defensively.

"I'm not trying to start anything, Marg." Everyone knew that wasn't true. "It just so happens that I will also be attending the circus this weekend. I've been called on by the Archbishop of York's nephew, Marcellus Pascoe." Clara started dancing around, clapping her hands together enthusiastically.

"Is that so, Clara? How fortunate for you, dear," Margie spoke sarcastically, a loathsome look on her face.

"In fact, I had a new dress made for the occasion," Clara squealed with excitement.

Eva rolled her eyes and Margie gave her a blank stare.

"Oh brother," sighed Gladys. "You never did have the knack for keeping your trap shut, have you, Clara?" Gladys shook her head. Clara lifted her chin high, sliding both hands around her waist from the top down to her skirt.

"Anyway, I best be getting on, I have plans for the evening. Good day, ladies." Clara waved her hand slightly and walked away with her head held high.

Ruby rushed back over to the flower women, waving her hands frantically. "You're not going to believe what I just heard!" she shouted.

"I thought I sent you to go calm down, Ruby?" Gladys inquired in a peevish tone, placing her hands on her hips.

"Never mind calming down, I just got some news..." Ruby's voice trailed off as she watched Clara walking away. "Where's she off to, it's the middle of the day?" she asked.

"Never mind her, what is it that you've heard?" asked Gladys with anticipation.

"Well, I was told by Sissy Crainer, you know the woman that sells baked goods down that—"

"Yes, yes, we know who she is," Margie said, trying to rush Ruby along.

"Well, she said that Lucious Paddimir was at the market today."

"Lucious Paddimir!" Margie gasped.

"Well, that's most surprising. People don't usually see him out, especially during the day. He usually only comes to town in the evenings, if you know what I mean," commented Gladys, raising her brows.

"Why is that?" Eva inquired. All three women began glancing at one another nervously but said nothing, so Eva asked again, "Why is it that he usually comes to town only in the evenings?"

Ruby replied quickly, trying to sound clever, "Oh well, I don't know, dear, maybe he's one of those, what are they called?" Ruby began clicking her fingers, thinking, as the other ladies gazed at her, confused. "Oh bother, you know, one those people that only come out at night and bite necks?" The ladies gave Ruby a distressed look. "You know what I'm talking about—vampires!" Ruby gushed. "Yeah, that's it, maybe he's a vampire!" Ruby had a big smile on her face, looking quite pleased with herself, as if she had come up with a viable answer. The ladies just stood there, astounded.

Gladys shook her head. "Well, a vampire of sorts, I would say," she huffed.

"Shhh, thank you very much, Ruby, for making my daughter think there are vampires on the loose! That's all I need to deal with now!" Margie whispered, exasperated with Ruby.

"What? I was only trying to help! I thought it was better than telling her the truth! What do you want me to say, Marge? That he's a dodgy, tot-huntin' scoundrel, only out for—"

"Ruby!" Margie interrupted, shouting, an indignant look on her face. Margie breathed deeply, calmed down, then turned to Eva. She spoke quietly and calmly to her daughter. "The truth is, dear, we don't actually know that much about Mr. Paddimir, other than that he is usually spotted around town in the evenings and that he makes quite of bit of money selling that famous juice of his," Margie explained.

"Oh, so, he sells juice?" Eva piped up. "Well, perhaps he was just in the market today to sell some of his juice?" she proposed excitedly, "And suppose people prefer his juice at night before bed? That could be why he usually only comes to town in the evenings?" she further suggested, a look of satisfaction on her face. Eva was proud to have she answered her own question.

Gladys slowly walked up to Eva, shaking her head as she patted her on the back. "You're probably right dear, I'm sure he just came to the market to sell some of his famous juice." Gladys winked at Ruby and Margie behind Eva's back.

The ladies quieted down and let the discussion end since Eva seemed to be satisfied with the answer she proffered herself.

Half-past six came and the flower women packed up their goods for the day.

"Well, I'm off to bemuse myself at the pub. Would anyone like to join me?" Ruby asked with a sigh, as she gathered her items together.

"I'm afraid I must go home today, Rube," replied Margie.

"Ohhh, have to start planning for your big evening with Bert, eh?" Ruby chuckled sarcastically.

"No, Georgie has just returned and I'm sure Eva is aching to visit with him," Margie answered.

"Oh, yes! I want to hear all about his time in Oxfordshire!" Eva exclaimed excitedly.

"I'm also going to have to pass, Ruby. I have to get home to Mr. Knightly—he hasn't been feeling very well lately," Gladys added, gathering her belongings with a worried expression on her face.

"Give Charlie my regards, Gladys," said Margie with a grin.

"Will do Marg. Well, I'm off, ladies, night." Gladys began walking through the market, waving her hand. Ruby and Marge stared at Gladys as she hobbled away. Ruby placed her hand on Margie's shoulder.

"She sure is a bit off," Ruby teased, shaking her head and grinning as she stared after Gladys.

"Really, Rube, the things you say," Margie replied, shaking her head with a smirk. The rest of the ladies gathered their belongings and went their separate ways for the evening.

Margie placed her arm around Eva. "Are you ready to head home, dear?"

"You betcha, I can't wait to see Georgie," Eva responded with an ache in her voice, grinning from ear to ear.

"Well, then, I think we are going to have to work together to get this bag to the lodging house," said Margie. The two of them picked up the large burlap sack filled with produce and headed out of the market. They entered the street just as the sun was setting on the far side of the road. Bursts of red, orange, and pink mixed together across the pale blue sky. Margie let out a sigh and shook her head.

"It sure is beautiful. It seems as if the sun is touching the earth. Makes you feel hopeful, doesn't it?"

"Sure does, Mum," Eva replied, inhaling a deep breath and thinking about Georgie. She squinted her eyes as she gazed out toward the deep sea of colors that were making their way across the London skyline.

Three

T he last bit of sunlight was sinking into the ground just as Margie and Eva stepped onto the first row of their lodging house's porch stairs. The sizeable Victorian brick home was in decent condition in comparison to most of the other lodging houses. Mr. Lyons, the owner, had recently renovated it, desiring to acquire a more significant profit from the tenants, but his plans changed when the factory accident occurred. Mr. Alderson's death at the factory had moved Mr. Lyons to graciously offer Margie and Eva to stay at the lodging house at a much lower rate. While they still had to pay a small amount for their rent, Margie was nevertheless grateful to Mr. Lyons for providing them with a decent place to live, under the circumstances.

Eva did not feel the same way. She harbored deep resentment in her heart toward Mr. Lyons for her father's death. According to the newspaper, several pieces of machinery at the factory had not been up to code and it had been overcrowded with workers. Mr. Lyons had been aware of these problems but did nothing to resolve them. Eva felt that Mr. Lyons allowed them to stay at the lodging house in order to lessen his own guilt over her father's death. Times were very difficult for most Londoners and Eva's mother would tell her to count her blessings because things could be much worse for them. Hence, Eva tried to do so despite her feelings toward Mr. Lyons.

The ladies stood on the porch step, exhausted from carrying the burlap sack from the market. The weight of the sack had caused their walk home to take much longer than usual. Although they'd moved it slowly, the bag felt heavier with each step they took. By the time they reached the lodging house, their arms were worn out.

"Alright now, we have to get it up into the house. So, on the count of three, we'll head up the porch. Alright?" Margie said with a heavy nod.

"Okay, mother, you count," Eva replied with a huff.

"Alright then, ready...one...two...three," her mother said, as they held the sack, ready to drag it up the stairs. At that moment, Georgie came hurrying out of the lodging house's front door.

"Need some help, ladies?"

Before they could answer him, he grabbed the bag and lifted it over his right shoulder in one scoop. Looking back at Eva and Margie, Georgie gave them one of his grand smiles and Eva smiled back as her insides welled up at the sight of him. Eva had noticed that Georgie's skin had become tanned from working outside for months and she thought it was a good look on him. She remembered how, as childhood friends, they would often chase the mice around the lodging house and run through mud puddles together. Things were different between them now and Eva was developing deeper feelings for Georgie every day—however, she was too embarrassed to tell anyone about them. She would often secretly envision the two of them being married and having a home of their own one day. The thought of it made her heart race and cheeks blush.

31

"Oh, thank heavens for you, George. You saved us twice today, you know!" Margie exclaimed, raising her arms in the air and releasing a life-saving breath.

"All part of the job, Miss Marg!" Georgie climbed up the rickety porch stairs and headed up into the foyer through the front door. "I'm going to leave the bag here next to the door and I'll bring it over to the market for you in the morning," he stated and laid the bag next to the front door.

"Oh, you're a godsend, George!" Margie gave him a big kiss on his left cheek, making both his cheeks turn bright red while he sported a proud, childish grin. Eva stared at him, beaming from ear to ear. She could feel her heart beating faster, just gazing at him.

"I can't thank you enough, Georgie, for everything you have done for us today," Margie gushed with a pleased look on her face, shaking her head from side to side.

"Well, there is something you ladies could do for me," he said, eyebrows raised and voice heightened in expectation.

"What is it, George?" asked Margie.

"Anything for you, Georgie," Eva stated proudly.

"I say, why don't you two lovely ladies join Grams and me for some homemade pies this evening?" Georgie was desperately hoping they would say yes. He needed to talk to Eva about something and didn't want to put it off any longer.

"Sounds amazing and its definitely too tempting an offer to turn down," Margie exclaimed.

"I'll say, fresh pies and your company, of course," Eva spoke excitedly, a coy smile on her lips.

"Alright then, see you ladies in, say…" Georgie glanced down at his watch, "a half-hour?"

"Absolutely, see you then!" Margie replied.

Margie and Eva began heading upstairs when, out of the corner of her eye, Eva noticed that Georgie was watching her. She stopped for a moment on the stairs and gazed over at him, causing their eyes to meet. Georgie's gaze did not leave hers and he continued looking at her most intently. Eva spoke up, hesitantly, in a soft voice.

"See in you in a little while, Georgie."

There was no smile on his face as he continued to pensively gaze up at her.

"Goodbye, Eva."

Eva jolted back a little, puzzled by his remark. It was very odd for Georgie to behave in such manner. Their eyes remained locked on one another a few seconds longer and Eva's heart pounded more quickly with each passing moment. Suddenly, Margie yelled down the stairs.

"Hurry up, Eva, we have to clean up a bit before we go over to Alice and George's!" Startled by her mother's voice, Eva pulled her eyes away from Georgie's and glanced up the stairwell.

"Coming, Mum!" she called out in an exhausted tone. When she turned back to look at Georgie, he had already vanished down the corridor toward his lodging room. Eva was puzzled by what just happened and began to wonder whether something might be wrong.

* * *

After freshening up, Margie and Eva went down to Alice and Georgie's for dinner. Eva could smell the freshly baked pies as soon as she entered the corridor that headed toward Alice and Georgie's lodging room. The aroma was intoxicating. It had been so long since Eva had a fresh, hot pie. Margie knocked loudly on the door, waited a bit, then knocked again. Alice was hard of hearing and it took her some time to make it to the door.

"Come in, come in!" she called through the closed door.

Margie opened the door, peeking inside the lodging room.

"I'm sure you know by now, ladies, you're welcome to come right in!" Alice spoke in a loud but sweet tone. She was seventy-one years old, but Eva thought she looked closer to ninety. She was a short, white-haired lady with a slight hunch and she always smelled like rosewater, which she made herself. Alice had become somewhat of a grandmother to Eva over time, especially since she had not had the pleasure of knowing her own grandparents. They had all passed away when she was very young and Eva had, secretly in her heart, adopted Alice as her own.

"Have a seat, have a seat, ladies," said Alice in her usual loud but sweet and shaky voice. She waved her hand as she walked around the kitchen. "I've been slaving away at the stove since George returned earlier today. I wouldn't want any of the goods that he brought back to go to waste."

Eva and Margie sat down at the small wooden dining table. It was a dark chestnut color and looked like any other table except for its claw-style feet. Alice and Georgie's living quarters were very humble, to say the least. Alice had pictures covering the walls of their main living area. There was an array of small knick-knacks scattered throughout the room, which she had either collected or inherited over the years. White, handmade doilies rested on all tables. A brown chesterfield sofa, with matching chairs, and a flower-patterned chaise lounge resided in the corner. Eva loved coming over and relaxing on the chaise lounge, pretending to be Queen Victoria while enjoying a cup of tea and some of Alice's homemade pastries lying on the small side table next to her. She would sit and imagine the day away until Alice would summon her out of her glorious daydreams to help with chores around the house.

Alice began setting plates of food on the dinner table. The meal consisted of some sliced cheese, fruit, boiled potatoes, and an assortment of individual-sized pies. Eva reached out to take a pie but Alice quickly grabbed her arm and then loosened her grip to a gentle touch.

"Mind your manners Miss Eva, we must first wash up and say grace," Alice corrected, gazing down at Eva.

"Oh, I'm sorry, Alice, I forgot," Eva apologized in slight embarrassment, her head bending down with a sallow look on her face.

"Now, there, there, it's alright, dear." Alice gave Eva a side hug, then Eva rushed over to the washing area and began to clean her hands. Margie followed her to do the same.

"Where has George gone off to?" Margie inquired with a raised voice as she scrubbed her hands in the washbasin.

"Oh, you know George, always rushing off to help those in need. Mr. Roberts asked him to help move his bath near the fireplace. You would think that man was just waitin' for George to come home so he could have a hot bath in front of the fire!" Alice said harshly while rolling her eyes. Margie and Eva giggled and then, once again, sat at the table.

The lodging house was divided into three living spaces. The third space, upstairs near Margie and Eva's room, consisted of just one room that was occupied by an older gentleman called Mr. Tom Roberts. He lived across the hall from Eva and Margie. Mr. Roberts mostly kept to himself and lived alone. He was bald, had a gray beard, and was an attractive man for his age; however, whenever Eva saw him, he always seemed to have a sour expression on his face. Eva was a bit frightened of him, but Georgie had told her that Mr. Roberts wasn't a mean fellow, just a very serious one. He had worked at "James Smith & Sons" for many years, selling umbrellas and walking sticks to the upper class.

Georgie burst through the front door, out of breath.

"Sorry I'm late, ladies." He hurried over to the basin to wash up before dinner.

"So, how is Mr. Roberts doing?" Alice asked in a slightly irritated tone.

"Oh, he's doing just fine. It was good to see him again," replied Georgie, plopping down in the seat next to Eva. She looked over at him, hoping to connect eyes again but Georgie didn't even glance her way. He gave Margie a big smile and Eva thought that was odd.

"May I say grace? I'm starved," he asked, kindly.

"I'm sure you are, boy! Go ahead," Alice replied and slowly sat down at the table.

They all held hands, bowed their heads, and closed their eyes, except for Eva—she watched Georgie as he prayed. Georgie spoke slowly and his eyes were tightly shut, as if he was being very intentional about the words.

"God bless the food and Grams who prepared it. God bless Miss Marg and Miss Eva. Thank you, Lord, for them all, Amen." The prayer was simple and sweet, yet Eva could sense Georgie's heartfelt sincerity while he spoke it.

"Well, now, help yourselves," Alice said, anxiously waving her hand.

Everyone started grabbing the pies and reaching for the food. Eva took a big bite of the vegetable pie; the warm, crispy morsel melted in her mouth.

"These are amazing, Alice!" she exclaimed.

"Oh, they are delightful as usual," said Margie.

"Thank you, ladies, it's a lot of work but, in the end, I always enjoy making them," replied Alice, a smile on her wrinkled face as she spooned out some potatoes.

"So tell us, George, how was your time in Oxfordshire?" Margie asked before taking another bite of pie.

"It was nice seeing mum and pop, of course, as well as being out in the country! Got to love that fresh country air!" he said with a broad smile while inhaling a deep breath. He had a very fulfilled look upon his face, which worried Eva.

"Oh, I'm sure it's nice out there, with the wide-open spaces," replied Margie. The thought of being out in the country, away from the smells and noises of the busy city sounded nice to Margie. Eva didn't want to talk about the country any longer. Listening to Georgie, she could tell how much he enjoyed being in Oxfordshire and even the possibility that one day he would leave her for good made her nervous.

"How was your journey home?" she asked, trying to get Georgie's focus back on the present.

"It was decent, I suppose. I took the carriage back with the magistrate, which makes for a long journey. He was coming back to London for a few weeks and apparently wanted to have his carriage with him." Georgie sighed, looking down. "The trip gave me a lot of time to think about things, though," he said, nodding his head as his eyebrows lifted high. The manner in which he responded made it seem as if he carried the weight of the world upon his shoulders.

"Seems to me that you have a lot on your mind?" Margie inquired.

Georgie kept his face turned toward his plate, then nervously moved his eyes up to his grandmother. He shoveled some food into his mouth, while his leg began tapping rapidly under the table. No one said anything and Eva knew something wasn't right—but didn't understand why Georgie wouldn't just say what it was.

Finally, Alice exclaimed, "Go on now, boy, out with it!" as she nudged him on the arm. "He's been a bundle of nerves waitin' to tell the both of you," Alice spouted.

Margie and Eva looked at one another concerned.

"Well, Georgie, what is it already?" Eva asked in an interrogative tone. She knew something was wrong and her heart was pounding so hard in her chest that she thought everyone at the table must be able to hear it.

"Well, Magistrate Logan likes my work ethic and has offered me the stable master position at his farm. This afternoon, I went down to the court and accepted his offer."

Eva felt the blood drain from her face.

"But you said just today that you couldn't leave Alice?" she piped up in a worried tone.

38

Georgie swallowed hard. He wasn't lying—he did come back to help take care of his grandmother, but she had insisted that he takes the position in Oxfordshire. Alice looked over at Eva.

"I'll be just fine," she said, shaking her head. "George needs to do this so he can make a life for himself, instead of staying around here taking care of his old grandmother," she claimed assuredly with a slight laugh.

"So it's final, then, this is what you truly want to do?" Margie inquired.

Georgie hesitated. He believed that this would be the best way for him to make enough money so that he could eventually marry Eva and they could start a life together.

"I...I think this is the best thing to do, Miss Marg, yes," he replied sympathetically, knowing that they would miss him and that he would miss them in return. He looked up at Eva's worried expression and could tell that she was not happy about the news. He noticed that she was pressing her lips together tightly, which she always did when she was nervous or upset.

Georgie wanted to tell Eva how he felt about her, but he didn't think that the timing was right. He needed to have more money saved up so they would have a good start to their marriage. He also needed more time to finish fixing up a small shed on the magistrate's property. Georgie was hoping to turn the old shed into a lovely home for the two of them one day. He desired everything to be perfect and in place for the beginning of their life together, before he was ready to tell her.

Eva stared vacantly across the table, feeling as though breath had been knocked out of her. Margie saw Eva's expression.

"Well then, George, we're so happy for you!" she piped up quickly, smiling as she quickly reached across the table to tightly grab hold of Eva's hand. She knew Eva was extremely disappointed by the news and was trying to console her without making a scene.

"Isn't that right, Eva?" asked Margie with a nod, indicating to Eva that she should show support for Georgie's decision.

Eva didn't know what to think. This was something she had feared, something she had dreaded—and now it was coming true. Georgie was Eva's only true friend and, just when she thought they were beginning to become fond of one another, he has decided to leave her? Eva's head began to spin and the pie that had tasted so wonderful only a few moments earlier ended up being a big lump right in the middle of her throat. She had lost her appetite, swallowing the rest of the pie while doing her best to prevent tears from welling up in her eyes.

Eva stared down at her dinner plate with no expression upon her face. Everyone at the table could tell that she was not pleased about Georgie's decision, but she didn't care. Suddenly, Georgie secretly grabbed Eva's hand under the table and began rubbing his thumb softly against the top it. She quickly sat up in her chair, extremely surprised by Georgie's affectionate gesture. The soft graze of his thumb against her skin caused perplexing feelings to stir within her. She knew things were changing, but she wasn't exactly sure in what direction they were moving. There were so many feelings swirling inside her as Georgie held her hand, but it seemed as if he didn't want anyone to know. Eva wasn't sure what this meant since he was leaving her to permanently go to Oxfordshire. Perhaps he was feeling bad because he knew how greatly she would miss him.

After dinner, Alice invited them to sit on the sofa for some tea and conversation. Eva declined, her emotions overflowing after the news that Georgie was moving away to the country. Alice and Margie discussed some local events they'd read about in the newspaper, while Eva and Georgie pretended to be listening to the conversation. So much was going through both their minds. To Eva, the small talk felt unnecessary. All she wanted to do was go somewhere she could be alone and let the tears flow. Occasionally, out of the corner of her eye, she would catch Georgie watching her but, whenever she would look over at him directly, he'd quickly turn his head away. Why did he seem troubled? Did he desire her approval? Well, he wasn't going to get it, Eva thought to herself.

Alice spoke, trying to engage Eva and Georgie in the conversation.

"So, what are everyone's plans for the weekend?" Alice's hands were folded as she glanced around the room.

"Mum is going to the circus with Bert Darby this weekend," Eva said in a snarky tone.

Georgie livened up a bit. "Oh, really? Miss Marg, that sounds like a real good time," he said excitedly. Eva rolled her eyes.

"Say, I have an idea, why don't the two of you go together. I'm sure you would have a splendid time!" Margie suggested smiling ear to ear. The thought of going to the circus with Georgie caused Eva to perk up a bit. She thought she might be able to convince him to stay in London. Georgie spoke up quickly but hesitantly.

"Well, actually, I can't go this weekend. Mr. Gyles asked me to help move some horses that had sold outside of London. I thought it was a good opportunity to make some extra money, so I accepted the offer."

Eva's smile quickly turned into a scowl and she peered at Georgie from across the room.

"That's fine. I wouldn't want to go anyway!" Eva shouted rudely, crossing her arms. "It's just a dumb circus with fat elephants, filled with a bunch of flaming nobs!" she exclaimed harshly, lifting her nose up in the air.

"Eva!" scolded Margie. "It's not like you to say such things."

Margie looked at Eva with disappointment. Eva stood up at once and bolted out the front door, embarrassed by her behavior. Georgie quickly glanced at the two ladies, then ran after her.

"Eva, Eva, wait!" he cried out as he rounded the corner of the corridor and found Eva sitting on the staircase, weeping while covering her face.

Georgie slowly walked over and sat down next to her. Clutching his hands together, he placed his forehead against his knuckles and rested his elbows upon his knees.

"Oh, Eva," he sighed.

She sobbed harder at that and tears ran down her cheeks, landing on the stair steps below. She thought she might make a puddle, so she quickly began wiping her face. Georgie carefully placed his arms around her shoulders, bringing her firmly to his chest. Eva closed her eyes tightly as her face was pressed up against him. She could feel the movement of his body while he breathed in deeply, trying to calm his nerves. Georgie began gently rubbing Eva's shoulders, doing his best to console her and, at that moment, Eva relished her proximity to Georgie. She wished that the moment would never end and desperately desired for him to kiss her and tell her how much he loved her.

"Eva, I won't be gone forever, I promise," he whispered softly in her ear.

Once again, tears began welling up in Eva's eyes. She was crying so hard that she was unable to speak and began sucking in gasps of air in between her cries.

"It wasn't an easy decision to make, you know, but the offer was just too good to pass up. When I'm the stable master, I'll have better pay than I would just working as a growler. I wouldn't disappear for good, you know, just for a while to save up some money—then, I will be back to see you," Georgie paused, gathering his words to try to say something that would bring solace to Eva. "You and Miss Marg could come visit me in Oxfordshire. A trip to the country would be nice, right?"

Georgie kept talking, trying to convince her that he was making the right decision but, in reality, he was trying to convince himself. He was hoping that he was doing the right thing by working hard and saving enough money before asking Eva to marry him. Georgie desired to be a good provider and to become the man that he felt Eva deserved.

Eva looked up at Georgie helplessly; her eyes were red and swollen. The sight of her caused Georgie's heart to melt. He gazed down at her, softly lifting her face into his strong hands as more tears fell from her cheeks. Eva stared hopelessly into Georgie's eyes.

"Oh, Eva, I…" his words trailed off as he shook his head and began wiping Eva's tears away with his thumbs.

Watching her filled with so much emotion caused Georgie's eyes to fill up as well. His heart was breaking for her and he wasn't sure how to make it any better. Oh, how he wanted to tell how much he loved her and why he was really going to Oxfordshire! He wasn't just going to make a life for himself—but to create a life for both of them. As much as he desired to tell her, there was something inside him that prevented him from doing so. In that moment, he realized that he was afraid. He thought that Eva would maybe immediately want to go with him to Oxfordshire, which he wasn't prepared for, and he also feared that she might not feel the same way about him. He knew Eva loved him as a friend, but he wasn't positive that she would want him as a husband.

Georgie leaned his face in, close to Eva's, softly whispering while gazing into her eyes. "I am so sorry. I never intended to hurt you, but—" he stopped speaking abruptly, choked by the emotions that were once again welling up inside him.

His hands were trembling as he continued to hold Eva's face. He glanced down at her lips, desiring more than anything to kiss her gently but, instead, he leaned forward, placing his forehead against hers. Eva could feel Georgie's hot breath against her skin, which sent tingles down her body. Feelings that she didn't quite understand were coursing through her and, at the same time, she could sense Georgie's own frustration with himself. At that moment, Eva realized that he didn't want to leave her but that he had to leave her. He needed the stable master position for his future. Eva did not want to keep him from what would be best for his life, so she pulled herself away from his arms. Standing up in haste, she quickly wiped the tears from her face.

Eva finally felt that she understood Georgie's predicament and kindly said to him, "Thank you for having us over this evening. Everything was delicious. Would you please thank Miss Alice for me and tell her that I am sorry for my behavior?" Then she quickly ran up the stairs, leaving Georgie behind on the stairwell, alone.

Four

The cold March wind blew harshly against Eva's face as she walked toward Covent Garden in the late afternoon on a Tuesday. Three months had passed since Georgie moved to Oxfordshire. Eva still couldn't bear to think about him leaving or her eyes would tear up in an instant. Oh, how her heart ached for him to return to London. She had felt foolish for the way she behaved, refusing to even set eyes on him before he left for Oxfordshire. The last time she saw Georgie was on that stairwell after dinner on the evening that he revealed he was moving away to become the stable master on Magistrate Logan's farm. Somehow, she had managed to avoid him, even at the lodging house, during those last few weeks. She would leave the house after Georgie left for work in the morning and would return before he would arrive in the evening. When he would come to her room wishing to speak to her, she would refuse to see him. Now, she wished that she could have those two weeks back to spend as much time with him as possible before he left town.

"Boy, I'm stubborn as a mule," she whispered angrily to herself as tears began rolling down her cheeks. She quickly wiped them away from her face as the bitter wind blew against her skin, causing it to chafe.

Eva had treated Georgie very poorly but, despite her actions toward him, Georgie continued to be extremely kind to both her and Margie. He sent them goods from the farm every couple of weeks and was basically providing for them since there were no other goods for them to sell. Georgie also wrote letters to Eva, which she refused to read. She wasn't particularly good at reading and it was too difficult for her to hear how well he was doing in Oxfordshire without her. She had envisioned a future for the two of them but Georgie obviously didn't feel the same way. Her heart would break every time she thought about him and even selling the goods he sent them felt wrong. Eva believed that Georgie was sending them goods because he felt guilty over leaving her. She was convinced that he knew how she felt about him and, in Eva's mind, his moving away was his way of taking the easy way out rather than telling her that he only cared for her as a friend.

This winter had been wretched. People were starving and going into workhouses. Families were separated and there were people found frozen to death in the morning hours not having found a warm place to go to at night. These were terrible times, Eva thought to herself and, just when she didn't think things could get any worse, her mother had fallen in love with Bert Darby. No one could believe that Margie was fond of the plump drunken soul. He was able to hold it together through the day and to keep his job at the bank but, after completing his working hours, he would drink the night away. Eva couldn't understand what her mother saw in Bert. He wasn't a bad man, but he wasn't a great man like her father either. Eva's father, Henry, had been soft, kind, and debonair. He had been extraordinarily handsome and tall, the kind of man that Eva thought any woman would desire. Bert, on the other hand, was short, round, awkward, and always tripping over things. Eva's head began to feel dizzy when she thought about everything that was changing around her—however, for her, life seemed to be standing still. Everyone else was moving on with their lives, without her, and she felt left behind. She tried hard to fix her thoughts on something else. She worked hard to think of anything that would bring her hope but nothing came to mind. There was no hope anywhere, she thought to herself.

Eva arrived at Covent Garden half an hour before noon. There weren't many people at the market that day, so she quickly made her way through the small crowd.

"There's Eva!" shouted Gladys to the other ladies. Margie lifted her arms and let out a big sigh.

"Where have you been?" she demanded in a frustrated tone.

Eva refused to respond or even look at her mother. Ignoring Margie's question, she walked over and began chatting with Clara.

"What's gotten into that one lately?" Gladys whispered to Margie and Ruby.

"It seems she got the morbs ever since that friend of hers left town," replied Ruby with a shrug.

"Yes, of course, she misses Georgie, we both do, but she's also upset over the fact that I'm still courting Bert. What's so wrong with the fact that I might actually be happy for once in two years!" Margie yelled out the last part loud enough for Eva to hear her. Eva rolled her eyes in response to her mother's comment. Gladys gave Ruby an odd look with a raise of her eyebrows, then turned and walked away. The truth was that all ladies felt that Margie was selling herself short by her involvement with Bert.

"So, Marg, how serious are you? You know, about Bert?" Ruby asked inquisitively.

"Well..." Margie trailed off, contemplating her relationship. She had never actually thought about the future but had only been enjoying having some companionship for the first time since Henry had passed away. "We've been courting for about three months now, so I would say things are pretty serious," she finally said, realizing how long her and Bert and been together.

"Hmmm," replied Ruby, gazing upward, her index finger tapping her chin, "I'm sorry, Marg, but I just don't get what you see in the man." Ruby shook her head.

Margie turned harshly and looked Ruby directly in the eyes, "What I see is a man with a good job who treats me fairly. I would say that, in this day and age, that's something hard to come by." Margie paused for a moment, glaring at Ruby and Gladys. "I don't have to explain anything to anyone. My choices are mines to make—if you don't like them, Rube, then I would kindly ask you to put a cork in it!" she retorted and strutted off in a hurry.

"Why, I never," gasped Ruby, placing a hand over her heart, offended by Margie's comment.

All the flower women gathered together after Margie hastily walked off.

"What's gotten into Marg?" asked Clara snootily.

"I don't know. I think she's lost her marbles. Marg always had good sense but what's happened to her lately?" asked Ruby.

"Well if you ask me, she's forgotten the way things were and she's tired of the way things have been, so she's taking what she can get," said Gladys with raised brows.

"But she could do so much better than Bert Darby," stated Clara with a distasteful look. All the ladies were taken back by Clara's somewhat thoughtful response, so she quickly added, "I mean, she's not going to marry a duke or anything, but she's definitely too good for Bert Darby." All the ladies nodded their heads in agreement.

"What are you all talking about!" Eva shouted. "You all stand here, day in and day out, with nothing to show for yourselves. If mum's happy, she's happy, and that's all that matters, I suppose!"

Eva ran off to the corner of the market, crying. She was tired of crying and of the hopelessness that enveloped her. Gladys walked over, kneeling next to Eva. Gladys' knees cracked and her face grimaced as she lowered herself down onto the floor.

"There, there, dear girl. I know things have been difficult lately. In fact, they have been right awful for quite some time. But things will change Eva. Life is always changing and you're growing up. Many girls your age are going to school, working, or even marrying. It's high time that you help Marg, instead of being a hindrance to her, dear." Gladys made a sad face realizing that Eva was hurt by her words, but she wanted to be honest. Eva was no longer a little girl, after all. "We all love having you here, Eva, but have you thought about finding a way to make some money on your own?" Gladys questioned, placing her hand on Eva's shoulder, trying to comfort her.

The thought of working made Eva sick to her stomach. She knew she must do something but, without any education, what could she do?

"What am I supposed to do when not even mum can get a job that pays decently? If it wasn't for Georgie sending goods and Mr. Darby picking up the financial slack, I'm not sure what we would do Gladys," Eva blurted out in a worrisome tone.

"Well, maybe Mr. Lyons could find you a job somewhere or, perhaps, you could work for Mr. Bertram with your mum's friend Gertrude?" Gladys suggested and Eva perked up.

"That's a great idea, Gladys! I'm going to go to Mr. Bertram's right away." Eva leaned over, giving Gladys a big kiss on the cheek as she popped up on her feet. "I'll be back in a flash." Eva winked at Gladys and started off when, suddenly, she stopped and turned around slowly. "Thank you, Gladys, for being there for me," she said, smiling.

Gladys gave her a big, goofy grin, then Eva turned around and began walking away.

"Hey, Eva," hollered Gladys behind her in an exasperated tone, "you mind helping me up, dear?"

"Oh, of course! I'm so sorry," Eva replied, turning around and helping the worn woman to her feet.

Eva arrived at Mr. Bertram's flower shop around three o'clock. The doorbell dinged as she entered.

"Be with ya shortly," Gertrude said without looking up to see who was at the door, busily arranging a bouquet of flowers. Gertrude was positioning some long-stemmed Japanese quince, along with winter-flowering cherry blossoms and yellow mahonia's. The colors were vibrant and complemented one another well, Eva thought to herself. She stood in front of the counter with a big broad smile on her face.

Gertie spoke as she turned around, a "How may I help you?" leaving her lips. Suddenly, the tone of Gertrude's voice change mid-sentence.

"Oh no, Eva!" she shouted, shaking her head. "I've got no flowers for you today or any day for that matter," Gertie sputtered, quickly walking out from behind the counter, picking out more flowers.

Eva's smile turned into a frown.

"That's not why I'm here, Gertie," she replied in a low, frustrated voice.

"Then what is it you're after?" Gertie spoke as she walked back over behind the counter and continued arranging the flowers.

"Well, actually, I was wondering if Mr. Bertram needed some help around here?"

Gertie looked up at her slowly and glared. "You after my job, girl? After all I've done for you and Marg!" she said angrily.

"No, no, Gertie!" Eva said defensively. "I was just wondering if you needed help, and if Mr. Bertram might be hiring for odds and ends, that's all!" Eva was angry that Gertrude would accuse her of wanting to take her job.

"Oh," replied Gertie, slightly embarrassed, "Well, I'm sorry to say Eva but, unfortunately, there's no extra work around here. Mr. Bertram isn't hiring, dear."

Eva released a loud exasperated sigh and shouted, "Bollocks!" then quickly headed for the door.

"Eva!" Gertrude called after her, surprised by the girl's response, but Eva didn't look back, she was too upset to care. She exited the flower shop with her head hanging down as feelings of hopelessness began gripping her once again. Anxious thoughts were spinning in her mind like a carousel out of control. There was no one to help her, no one who cared for her or comforted her any longer. She was officially on her own.

Slowly, she strolled down the street, not paying any attention to where she was going when she walked right smack into a man's chest.

Eva didn't even bother looking up at him but mumbled a sad "I'm sorry sir" and continued on her way, her head still down. A pleasant voice spoke up behind her.

"Well, my dear, we meet again."

Eva quickly looked up at the man and was immediately ensnared by the darkest, most bottomless eyes she had ever seen. She felt she was swimming in their vibrant glow. The smell of the man's cologne made Eva's insides feel warm and was a breath of fresh air in comparison to the typical foul stench of the streets.

"I'm... I'm so sorry, sir," Eva spoke nervously, not taking her eyes away from his.

"I would say this is fate, wouldn't you?" he asked, suggesting that Eva had met him before that day. Eva stared at the man for a moment, realizing who he was, but unsure whether she should let him know that she recognized him.

"I'm sorry, sir, but I'm not sure we have met before?" she inquired kindly.

"Oh, now, I am hurt," the man replied, placing his hand on his heart and pouting a little. "I nearly saved your life the last time we ran into one another," he stated.

Eva suddenly changed her tone, as if she just now realized that this was the man who had picked her up in the middle of the market when she had nearly been trampled some months ago.

"Oh...oh my," Eva said, embarrassed, as she touched her brow, "How could I have forgotten you? Yes, you did quite save my life that day in the market. Thank you again," she said with great appreciation for her rescuer, as she remembered the day.

"The name is Lucious Paddimir," he bowed and a tipped his hat.

Eva knew the name—she had remembered the flower women gossiping about him that day in Covent Garden.

"How do you do, Mr. Paddimir. My name is Eva...Eva Alderson," she smiled, nodding her head in return.

Lucious carefully stole Eva's right hand, bringing it up to his lips. Ever so gently, he kissed her hand while he continued to stare deeply into her eyes. Lucious' kiss took Eva's breath away, sending tingles through her body, and she suddenly felt warm. He was quite forward, she thought to herself. Lucious slowly brought Eva's arm down while intertwining his fingers with hers; then, gradually caressing them, he soothingly released her hand. Eva looked down, gazing at her hand, which continued tingling from his touch. She wasn't sure what to think of Lucious Paddimir; men didn't usually show affection in public, especially not to her.

"I welcome you to call me Lucious," he said, once again placing his hand upon his chest and nodding slightly. He had a peculiar smile on his face that seemed to fit him just right.

"Alright, then, Lucious," Eva said breathily, smiling coyly. She realized Lucious did not seem to be in a hurry and she wanted to take her time with him as well. There was something very intriguing and alluring about him.

"Say, I know this is sudden—and a bit out of the ordinary—but I have some people coming over to my house this evening; a party of sorts. How would you like to join us?" Lucious asked, giving Eva an inviting grin.

"Uh, umm," Eva spoke nervously and began gazing anxiously around the street, surprised by his confident advance toward her.

"Is there something wrong, dear?" he inquired.

Her eyes quickly looked back at Lucious, "Well, it's just...I...don't..." The words trailed off.

"Oh, of course," Lucious interrupted coolly, "I should have known that a beautiful woman like you would already have plans for the evening. Silly me," he remarked while shaking his head, appearing to be slightly embarrassed.

"Well, that's not exactly what I—" she was about to explain when he interrupted her again.

"Oh, good, so you don't have any plans for the evening?" A satisfied grin rested on his face and his eyebrows lifted in expectation.

Eva stood there silently, looking helplessly into Lucious' wanting eyes. Waiting for a response, he once again gently grabbed her hand and began smoothly rubbing her palm with his thumb. Lucious was staring so profoundly into Eva's eyes that she felt as if she was in a trance. Her heart was racing and feelings that she couldn't explain were coursing through her body.

She was trying to find the words to reply when a "No, not at the moment" came coolly out of her mouth. She was shocked by her own response but didn't show it on her face. Eva continued staring, fixated onto Lucious' wanton eyes, and gave him a flirtatious smile in return.

"Excellent," he said soft and slow. "My carriage will pick you up at half-past seven. I'm very much looking forward to becoming more acquainted with you, Miss Eva Alderson."

Lucious leaned over once again, kissing Eva's hand this time while closing his eyes as if he were savoring the moment. She watched most intently as sensations billowed inside of her. He slowly opened his eyes, locking them with Eva's and, with another leering grin, turned and walked down the street. Eva watched him walk away, swinging his cane about as her heart continued pounding in her chest. She sucked in a few deep breaths and noticed that his attire was rather expensive. She wondered if he might be wealthy, judging by the fashionable way he was dressed when, suddenly, it dawned on her.

"Wait!" she shouted.

Lucious stopped and turned around slowly.

"You don't know where I live," she yelled over the noisy sounds of the street.

Lucious raised his voice, "Don't worry, my dear. I'll find you, Eva Alderson, you can count on it." He tipped his hat once more with a mysterious smile, then winked and walked away.

Eva stood still for a moment, running through her mind everything that had just occurred. She was contemplating how she had arrived at Mr. Bertram's flower shop looking for work and left with an evening engagement? What would her mother think? More importantly, what would she wear? Eva's clothes were hardly fashionable. She would have to borrow something from her mother. Thinking of her mother reminded Eva of what the flower women had said about Lucious Paddimir that day in Covent Garden. They had spoken about him as if he were a horrible man. Gladys mentioned how he did not come out during the day and something about a rare juice that he sold? Eva had run into him, twice, in the middle of the day. The only information the flower women had was gossip and not fact, Eva thought to herself. Ruby had even referred to him as a vampire.

"Preposterous!" Eva said aloud, rolling her eyes.

Lucious didn't seem dangerous at all to her. He was charming, gentle, sophisticated, and very attractive. He was nothing like they described. In that moment, Eva decided that her mother mustn't know who was throwing the party she was attending that evening.

When she arrived at the lodging house, her mother and Bert Darby were laughing and drinking together on the sofa in their sitting room. Margie never drank much before meeting Bert but now it was a nightly occurrence for the two of them. She told Eva that if Bert could afford it, then why not? Margie had changed upon developing a relationship with Bert. He was kind enough but an entirely obnoxious side of him came out when he drank. He would speak loudly and make rude comments about people. What was worse is that Eva's mother would join him. Eva figured that her mum was just trying to make Bert feel like he belonged.

"Well, hello there, Eva!" Margie thundered.

Eva didn't reply, she was peeved to see them drinking and laughing together.

"Oh, are you still sore at me?" Margie asked, rolling her eyes and looking at Bert.

Eva stopped and stared at her mother.

"No, actually, I'm not. In fact, I have plans for the evening. I will be leaving around half-past seven," Eva spoke proudly, strolling toward the bedroom.

"Oh really, who are you going out with, the Prince of Wales?" Bert asked in a teasing manner. Margie and Bert began laughing loudly at his remark and Margie was waving her hand, motioning him to stop.

Eva let out a flustered sigh, "Actually, I met a very nice gentleman today outside of Bertram's flower shop who invited me to join him and some friends for a party this evening."

Margie sat up on the sofa.

"And do I happen to know this nice gentleman you are referring to?" she inquired while taking another sip of her beverage.

Eva paused for a moment.

"No, I don't think you've ever met him," she answered nervously, unsure whether her mother had ever met Lucious.

"Well, I'm not sure I want you going out with a strange fellow," Margie replied in a concerned tone.

"Oh, Marge, lighten up, the girl's sixteen after all. I think it would be good for her if she found some mates of her own. Don't ya think?" Bert said, nodding his head.

Eva was surprised to hear Bert taking her side.

"Well," Margie paused, "I suppose your right. Meeting some people your age might just be what you need right now. Especially since George—" Margie caught herself, knowing she shouldn't mention Georgie's name or else Eva would become greatly upset.

The room went silent for a moment and Eva bit her lip, mainly because Lucious was probably closer to her mum's age than her own. Breaking the silence, Eva spoke.

"I will need to have something nice to wear. May I borrow something of yours, Mum?" she asked with hopeful eyes.

"Yes, of course, dear, just be sure not to spill anything on it," Margie replied, wagging her finger as Eva ran over to her excitedly.

"Thank you, Mum!" she exclaimed, wrapping her arms around her mother and kissing her on the cheek.

Margie blushed, then placed her hand on Eva's and began patting it.

"Now, you best go along and figure out what you'll be wearing this evening," she said, holding back the tears in her eyes. Margie couldn't remember the last time Eva had given her a hug, let alone kissed her on the cheek. She had been very distant these past three months.

Eva strolled into the bedroom, knowing exactly what dress she wanted to wear that evening. Opening the wardrobe, she pulled out a red satin Christmas gown that her mother had worn to a party some years ago. This dress was Eva's favorite. She had tried it on many times over the years and, usually, it would hang loosely around her tiny physique. Eva put the dress on, doing her best to button the back buttons on her own. Gazing at herself in the mirror, she was quite pleased with how the garment finally fit her body perfectly.

Eva had a tall, lean figure, but all the right womanly features flawlessly filled out the dress in all the right places. The gown was a ruby-red color and hung off her shoulders, exposing her light, pale skin. A tightly fitting bodice wrapped around Eva's waist with smooth, white pearls running along the neckline. The skirt was tiered and had ruffles bouncing down. Tiny red bows were intricately placed around the skirt and across the back buttons. Underneath, the dress had a hoop cage causing it to flare out. Eva also put on her mother's long white gloves and matching red heels. She looked at herself in the mirror, admiring her own beauty. This was the first time in her life that she didn't feel like a little girl but like a woman. She felt excitement and anticipation for the evening shooting through her entire being while, at the same time, her hands were trembling from nerves.

Eva asked Margie to help her with her hair. Margie twisted Eva's hair up into an exquisite do and then placed a beautiful silver butterfly hairpin on the side, making sure it stayed in place. Margie's mother had given her the hairpin when she was a young lady and she thought it was time to pass it on to Eva.

"You look absolutely lovely, Eva. My little girl has officially grown into a beautiful woman," she said proudly.

Eva turned around and smiled at her mother.

"Thank you for doing my hair, Mum."

Margie smiled in return, placing her hands on Eva's shoulders.

"Please be careful tonight, dear. Now, you're certain that these are good fellows and that you'll be safe?" she asked, concerned.

"Yes, mother, I will be fine. I promise," Eva replied reassuringly.

"Would you like Bert and me to walk you where you need to go?" Margie asked.

"No, he is sending his carriage to come pick me up," Eva replied, turning away from her mother. She didn't want to have to explain anything else. The fewer questions her mother asked, the better, she thought to herself.

"His carriage?" Margie exclaimed, surprised. "That's very kind of him." There was some apprehension in her voice. "So, who is this gentleman? I don't think you mentioned his name?"

Eva looked up at Margie nervously, pressing her lips together.

"Oh, didn't I? Well, his name is Luke," Eva replied, trying to sound sure of herself.

She did not want to give Lucious actual name, fearing her mother would become suspicious that it was Lucious Paddimir.

"Luke, you say?" Margie asked questionably, knowing that when Eva pressed her lips together, she was hiding something.

"Yes, Luke Paddington, I think he said something about attending King's College," Eva responded, trying to sound confident even though she was lying.

"Oh...alright then, I guess he sounds like a good chap," Margie replied, nodding her head, taking Eva at her word. Eva felt horrible for lying to her mother but if Margie knew the truth, she wouldn't let her go to the party.

The carriage pulled up exactly when Lucious had said, at half-past seven. Eva had been watching out the bedroom window, waiting for the carriage to arrive.

"It's here, Mum!" she called out as she rushed over to the mirror to take one last look at herself. She inhaled deeply as she ran her hands down the tight bodice of the dress, then headed out the bedroom door. "Goodbye, mother," Eva called with a wave as she briskly made her way to the lodging room door.

"You be back by eleven sharp, Eva," Margie commanded.

"Yes, of course, Mum," she replied. Closing the door behind her, Eva headed down the stairs and outside to the carriage.

She shyly strolled up to the carriage, where a man was waiting for her next to the carriage door. Eva cautiously walked up to the man while doing her best to remain confident.

"Good evening, Miss. My name is Archibald Sunders and I will be driving you this evening to Master Lucious' home."

Archie was a tall, extremely thin man who was probably in his mid- to late-forties. He had dull black hair and was extremely pale.

"Yes, sir," Eva replied with a shy nod.

"Good, then let's be on our way. Also, Miss, please call me Archie," he said with a nod as he extended his hand to help Eva into the carriage.

"Thank you, Archie," Eva nodded nervously, placing her hand in his she stepped up and into the carriage.

Eva settled into her seat and realized that it was somewhat difficult to see where they were going in the dark, especially through the small carriage windows. Soon, she heard the reigns slap against the horses back and, with a loud neigh, the carriage began moving forward. Now that she was actually sitting inside the carriage, her nerves began taking over and her stomach started to turn. A part of her wanted to tell Archie to take her back home but another part was excited to see Lucious. She was wondering who exactly this sophisticated, mysterious man, Lucious Paddimir, was and why he was interested in her? The more Eva thought about it, the more excited she felt. As the journey continued for a while, she pretended that she was a princess in a fairytale, out on a grand adventure to meet her Prince Charming. Regardless of her inner struggle, Eva knew one thing for certain—that this would be an evening she would never forget.

Five

T he carriage ride continued for what seemed like forever. Eva started feeling a bit frantic. Where was this man's house? Where was Archie taking her? They had been driving for quite some time.

"Archie?" Eva called out the side window, loud enough for him to hear her over the trotting horses.

"Yes, Miss?"" He replied, looking back at the carriage.

"Exactly how much farther until we reach Lucious' home?" she asked, trying not to sound too anxious.

"Don't worry Miss, we'll be there very soon."

Eva nervously rubbed her white gloves together while attempting to look out the carriage window to see whether there was a house in sight. Suddenly, the carriage rounded a corner and she saw a building that looked like a palace—all lit up from the inside out. Eva gasped and covered her mouth excitedly.

"Is that Lucious' home?" she asked Archie.

"Yes, Miss, we have arrived," he replied.

When the carriage pulled up to the stately country house, Eva immediately heard music playing from the inside as well as people talking and laughing loudly. There were several odd smells—smoke, food, and spices—coming from inside that made Eva's nose tingle. The carriage door opened, allowing the light from the house to enter it.

"Welcome to Liberation Hall, Miss Alderson," Archie said coolly, with a nod, as he helped Eva exit the carriage.

There was a drunken man, left of Eva, flirting with two women while smoking a pipe.

"Well, hello there, Miss," he spoke loudly, wobbling around, giving Eva a toothy grin and a nod.

The ladies smiled and politely curtsied. Eva nodded back, hoping the uncomfortable feeling she felt inside was not reflected on her face. She was afraid but wanted to remain composed and was beginning to wonder what she had gotten herself into by coming here this evening. Her mother had warned her about Lucious, but he seemed so sweet to her every time they interacted. Also, he *did* nearly save her life.

"This way, Miss, Master Lucious is awaiting your arrival," Archie said, taking Eva's hand and guiding her over to the front door.

The door gaped open, allowing the cool night breeze to enter the busy house. Eva walked in alone through the doorway threshold. She had never been in a mansion. The grand entryway had marble floors and moldings everywhere. Paintings and expensive artifacts were intricately placed throughout the sizable manor. There was a beautiful, curved staircase made of dark wood, which elegantly led up toward the most stunning crystal chandelier Eva had ever seen. Gobs of people were standing around talking noisily. The sound seemed to echo throughout the entire large estate. Eva looked straight ahead and saw Lucious speaking with some of his guests. He looked so dashing in his distinguished suit. It was a short, black, tailored smoking coat with an elegant matching bowtie, but no walking stick accompanied his attire this evening. Their eyes locked and Lucious politely excused himself from the guests he was speaking with, strolling over to Eva quickly and taking her hands. He gently kissed the top of her gloved hand, sending tingles down her spine again.

"Eva, I've been anticipating your arrival all evening!" he spoke powerfully so that everyone in the vicinity could hear him. Still holding her hand, he backed himself away from her, taking a good look at her entire form. "You look exquisite, my darling!" he stated emphatically.

Eva felt her face light up and knew that it must be bright red from embarrassment. She gave a polite smile and curtsied. Suddenly, Lucious swiftly pulled her into his body, wrapping his right hand around her waist, while his left hand was still holding tightly onto her right. Raising their hands together into a dancing stance, he brought his head close to her left cheek. She could feel his hot breath against her skin, which sent sensations down her neck. She closed her eyes while breathing heavily; her heart pounded in her chest. Lucious was unpredictable but confident, which was all part of the intrigue.

Whispering in her ear most delicately, his breath caressed her skin, "You look absolutely delicious tonight, Eva."

Eva stirred within and a bead of sweat began to form on her forehead. She had never felt this way before. Lucious frightened her but he also fascinated her at the same time. When he held her in his arms, she felt power radiate from his being, bringing a sense of safety and security to Eva, which were both comforts that she had not felt in a long time. She opened her eyes and realized that there were several people in the room watching them. Everyone at the party openly admired Lucious, gazing at him with eyes of wonder as if he truly was a prince.

Lucious pulled himself away from Eva while still holding her hand tightly and began promenading her around the house, introducing her to all his friends. Eva was astonished to find that there were well-known artists, writers, and even some aristocrats from London's high society attending the affair. She noticed that many of the women were wearing a much looser style of clothing than the typical Victorian fashion dictated. Some of them had blouses on that hung well below their shoulders, brightly colored and mismatched, with slacks that bagged out like bloomers. Eva then turned toward the drawing room and gasped when she saw something most astonishing— an artist was painting a nude woman right out in the open. People were standing around, watching as the artist composed the woman's physique on the canvas. Eva felt flushed, covering her face and quickly looking away. She had never experienced anything like this in her life. Lucious noticed that Eva appeared to be embarrassed and uncomfortable.

"Are you alright, my dear? Perhaps you would like to go somewhere quieter?" he asked, bending down so he could gaze into her eyes.

"Yes, I think I would like that very much," Eva spoke with confidence, although she felt flustered. She didn't want Lucious to think of her as a child but as a woman who was mature enough to engage in festivities at his home.

Lucious walked Eva back outside, where it was calmer. Everyone who was outside earlier must have made their way inside the house because now they were alone together. He released Eva's hand and began pacing while inhaling deep breaths of the crisp, cool air. The tone of his voice became grave and his hands were clasped behind his back.

"Eva, Liberation Hall is a place where people are free to be themselves, without the staunch English lifestyle hanging over them like the gallows. Most of the people here need a place to go, a place to be themselves, without feeling looked down upon or outcast. There is no judgment or discrimination here at the Hall. This building is a place in which everyone can receive what they most desire. You may call it whatever you like, but I simply believe that it's the way life was always meant to be lived—freely, as one will."

Lucious strolled over to Eva, taking hold of her hands. He gazed affectionately into her eyes. They were standing so close that Eva could feel his warm breath against her face.

"I know what people say about me, Eva. That I'm a scoundrel, a dishonest scalawag of sorts, but I'm only really guilty of giving others what they truly desire. Offering them the world they hunger for. I allow them to enjoy their lives. And I ask you, Eva—is that really such a crime?" he spoke softly, leaning his head toward Eva's and passionately pressing his lips against hers, sending a rousing shock through her body.

His hand glided, slowly, from Eva's back down to the bodice of her dress. Lucious held onto her hips tightly, pulling her even closer to himself. The moonlight beamed through the trees and, at that moment, it felt as if time stood still. An extended few seconds passed before Lucious gently pulled himself away. He looked down, taking Eva's hands and intertwining his fingers with hers. Gazing back up, he looked affectionately into her eyes.

"Unfortunately, I mustn't keep my guests waiting," he said softly.

Eva breathed deeply, trying to regain her composure as she looked for words.

"Oh...oh yes, of course, Lucious."

He kissed her on the forehead and she closed her eyes, relishing the feel of his lips against her skin. Then, hand in hand, they walked back inside the house.

After re-entering the foyer, Lucious led Eva down the broad corridor to the left, where there was a massive table filled with hors d'oeuvres. The scent of food caused Eva's stomach to rumble. She suddenly realized she was starving but, instead of leading her to the appetizers, Lucious escorted her toward a group of people standing in a circle, drinking, and talking.

"Eva, I would like you to meet an excellent friend of mine, Miss Claudia Jones."

A tall, slender, dark-skinned woman turned around and smiled at Eva. Claudia's raven black hair was wrapped into an elegant bun on top of her head. She was wearing a long, loose-fitting golden dress that was cut low around the brassiere to show off her bosom. Claudia's eyes were a light grey-blue color and Eva thought that Claudia was the most beautiful woman she had ever seen.

"How do you do, Eva. I have heard so much about you. Lucious hasn't stopped speaking of you since he arrived back from town this morning. You must be an extraordinary woman to have caught his attention," Claudia spoke with enthusiasm and smiled at Eva. Then, she gazed over at Lucious and gave him a somewhat distasteful look.

Eva noticed Claudia's exotic accent right away.

"It is very nice to meet you as well, Claudia."

"You can call me Dia," Claudia interrupted.

"Your accent is unique. You're not from London?" Eva questioned.

"Oh no, I am from a tiny island in the Caribbean called Barbados. Have you heard of it?" Claudia asked.

Eva felt foolish; she had not heard of Barbados.

"I have heard of the Caribbean but not of Barbados, I'm afraid."

Claudia touched Eva's shoulder and leaned in closer.

"You would love it, Eva. Barbados is a paradise—crystal blue waters, palm trees coating the island, warm sunshine on your skin, and sand as white as English faces." Claudia let out a slight laugh, then took a sip of the sherry she was holding in her hand. "Oh, I miss it terribly," she said with an ache in her voice.

Eva glanced to her left and realized that Lucious had vanished. She anxiously began searching the room for him when Claudia noticed.

"Oh, don't worry about Lucious, he does this sort of thing often. He's very good at disappearing," Claudia said, tipping her head and raising her eyebrows. She took another sip of sherry and Eva chuckled uncomfortably, assuming that Claudia was making a joke.

"So, what do you think of Liberation Hall?" Claudia asked, waving her glass and glancing around the room.

"Well, it's very different from any place that I've seen before. Even though I have seen a lot of unusual things growing up in London, I've seen nothing quite like this," Eva replied, shaking her head and looking up toward the glittering ceiling.

Claudia laughed again.

"Sweetheart, you haven't seen anything yet!" she exclaimed, touching Eva on the arm. Her laughter continued as Lucious returned, holding a beverage in one hand and a plate of food in the other.

"Lucious dear, Eva was becoming a bit worried about you taking off like that and not saying anything." Claudia tapped his shoulder, giving him a coy smile.

"Well, I wouldn't want my guest of honor to starve to death, now would I, Dia?" Lucious responded with slight exasperation in his voice, then turned to Eva.

"Sustenance for you, my love. I'm sure you're absolutely famished."

Lucious handed Eva the beverage and proceeded to pick up one of the canapés.

"Escargots a la Bourguignonne," he said as he raised the hors d'oeuvre toward Eva's mouth. Eva could tell that Lucious desired to feed it to her.

"Oh, alright," she muttered hesitantly.

"Now, open wide. Trust me, you'll love it," Lucious said, looking up at Claudia with a devilish smirk. Claudia rolled her eyes and took another sip of sherry.

Meanwhile, Eva had closed her eyes, opening her mouth just wide enough to allow Lucious to feed her the delicacy. She wasn't exactly sure what she was eating, but it delighted her taste buds.

"Would you like another bite, love?" asked Lucious, smiling.

Suddenly, Claudia piped up before Eva had a chance to respond.

"Are we in love already Lucious, darling? Oh, how very quickly we fall in and out of love."

Claudia released a stifled laugh, then gave Lucious a hard look while taking another sip of her sherry. Lucious glared at her, a fake smile resting on his face.

"Perhaps you've had enough of that sherry for the evening, Dia, dear?" Lucious sounded irritated.

Claudia rolled her eyes, crossed her left arm over her right, and proceeded to drink even more while gazing around the room. She was clearly annoyed. Eva felt awkward watching Lucious and Claudia's interaction. She began to wish she could excuse herself when Lucious promptly changed the subject.

"Why don't you try some punch, Eva."

Eva quickly took a sip of the red concoction, hoping to distract everyone from the previous conversation.

"Mmmm, it's delicious. Thank you, Lucious." The punch was very sweet but very strong, making Eva feel a little dizzy.

"So, is this the famous juice you sell in town?" Eva asked inquisitively.

Claudia let out another peal of laughter; however, this time, some of the sherry was still in her mouth, getting caught in her throat and nearly choking her.

"Are you alright?" Eva inquired as Claudia coughed, her brow lined with concern.

Lucious rolled his eyes and began gazing around the room. Claudia coughed a bit more and then took another sip of sherry.

"Yes, dear, I'm fine," she responded, waving her hand expeditiously as if she were waving Eva away. "Well, if you will excuse me," she continued, raising her head high in the air, abruptly pushing herself past both of them and sauntering to the other side of the room.

They both watched Claudia as she walked away.

"May I?" Lucious asked warmly, taking the punch from Eva's hand and placing it, along with the plate he was holding, on a nearby table. Grabbing both of her hands, he brought them up to his chest.

"I apologize for Claudia's behavior. We were an item some time ago and, occasionally, she reveals how difficult it has been for her to accept that we are no longer together. Especially when I invite a beautiful young woman, such as yourself, to one of my parties at the last minute." Lucious paused for a moment, then leaned closer to Eva.

"She knows I am quite taken with you, Eva," he said, staring affectionately into her eyes. Lowering their hands, he continued to speak, "Claudia and I are still friends, however, and I have great respect for her. She will always be a part of my life. I hope you can understand that?" Lucious asked with a bit of a pout.

Eva said nothing in return. Lucious switched his gaze from Eva to across the room, where Claudia was standing, and Eva followed his gaze over to Claudia. Feelings of inadequacy began to flood Eva now that she was aware of the fact that Lucious and Claudia had most certainly been intimate with one another.

Lucious brought Eva's chin up, forcing her to look him in the eyes once again.

"Are you alright, love?" he asked.

Eva nodded somberly. Lucious brought Eva's chin to his carefully. Tilting his head, he leaned in and kissed Eva's lips ever so softly. She closed her eyes, savoring the moment. After a few seconds, she pulled away smoothly. Lucious spoke tenderly.

"I only have eyes for you, Eva."

Eva's heart began pounding again; she could feel it resounding powerfully in her chest. Then, she noticed that some of the guests were watching and talking about them, but Lucious didn't seem to care, which comforted Eva. He just kept his eyes on her the entire time.

"And no, this isn't the juice I peddle at the market, but we will be getting to that later," Lucious said, giving her one of his flirtatious winks and a sly grin.

After Eva devoured the last of the hors d' oeuvres, Lucious began showing her around the house again, describing the art and fixtures as they went along. The house contained numerous diverse rooms, each with its own distinctive theme. One unusual room was the smoking room in which both men and women inhaled tobacco-like substances out of large vessels that Lucious referred to as *hookahs*. He had purchased the devices while visiting India and fell in love with their design. The different smoke aromas filling the room caused Eva to feel a bit nauseous. After exiting the smoking room, they entered a much larger section of the house, where there was live music and dancing.

"This is the ballroom," Lucious stated.

The ballroom was hot and stuffy, people were scattered from wall to wall, and Eva felt like she could hardly breathe.

Pretty much everyone in the room seemed to be three sheets to the wind and the music consisted of several red-headed, bearded men playing fiddles and a tambourine. Eva had heard this music before, playing late at night in the summer when the lodging house windows were left open. She knew that this sort of music was often associated with pubs and establishments of ill repute. While they walked through the room, Lucious clapped loudly to the music. He was grinning from ear to ear, joining in with his guests, although he looked a bit out of place, she thought.

Lucious gazed over at Eva and noticed that she seemed overwhelmed by all the celebrations around her. Hastily, he grabbed her hand and decided to leave the ballroom at once.

"I have something I want to show you," he said, his face lighting up with excitement.

He led Eva down a narrow hallway to the far end of the house. The sounds of music and people talking grew more distant as they continued further down the small corridor. Eva felt apprehensive but, inhaling a deep breath, she reassured herself, certain that Lucious would not harm her. Finally, they came to a room draped by a red velour curtain that looked somewhat cryptic.

"Ah, yes, last but not least—the famous Paddimir Juice Room."

Lucious bowed and put his hand out, allowing Eva to walk through the curtained doorway. The room was quite large in comparison to some of the others she had seen earlier. Several red velvet, French-style settees covered the area. The juice had an odd stench that seemed to saturate the room. Eva thought it smelled similar to the cough medicine that her mother would give her when she had the croup. Overall, it was tranquil enough, although it was strange that people were lying around everywhere. Many were slumped over sofas with dazed looks in their eyes. There was a sizeable bar, where barrels lined the wall, and there was a door with a large lock on the outside. The environment made Eva feel uneasy. Something wasn't quite right about this, she thought to herself.

The juice had a rich, vibrant, saturated red color and there were crystal decanters filled with the brew sitting all over the coffee-colored bar with matching crystal glasses.

"So tell me about the juice, what's it made of?" Eva asked inquisitively.

"Ah, ah, ah, but isn't that the question, Eva?" Lucious teasingly responded, while wagging his finger at her.

He walked over to the bar and picked up one of the sparkling crystal decanters, turning it in different directions and watching the candlelight reflect through its beautiful crystal edges. The red liquid sloshed around inside the bottle.

"That, my dear, is what everyone wants to know, but what no one will ever find out," he said as he continued examining the decanter.

Eva was beginning to feel nervous. Lucious' demeanor had changed from flirtatious and charming to austere. Gazing at the decanter intensely, he seemed to be in a far-off, distant land. Then, swiftly, he broke his pensive gaze and quickly returned to his bewitching self.

"Shall we go mingle?" he proposed, looking up at Eva with a smile and raising his eyebrows as he pointed toward the doorway.

He led her back through the velour curtain and out to where most of his guests were gathered. She thought about how it must be getting late and asked Lucious for the time. He pulled out a golden pocket watch from his front jacket pocket.

"It is almost half past midnight, love."

Eva gasped.

"Oh my, I must be getting home. My mum will be awfully worried about me," Eva said frantically.

"Yes, of course, I will summon Archie to take you home right away. We certainly don't want your mother to be worried. She may never allow me to see you again," he added with a mischievous grin.

Eva bit her lip and nodded in agreement. She knew her mother would most definitely never allow her to see Lucious again, especially if she knew what she had encountered this evening.

He walked her to the front of the house, then went to fetch Archie and the carriage. Eva sat down on the front porch, thinking about everything she had seen and experienced that evening. Most of it made her feel slightly distressed, except for Lucious—he was alluring and kind and obviously fond of her, but she wasn't certain that she could get used to this way of living. When Lucious returned, he saw Eva sitting on the step, shivering in the cold.

"My goodness, you're freezing. Here, take my jacket."

Lucious removed his overcoat and placed it around Eva's shoulders and, as he did so, he kissed Eva lightly on the lips.

"I certainly hope to see you again soon, Eva," he said, smiling and gazing intensely into her eyes.

The look in his dark eyes, as he stared at her, caused Eva's heart to pound harder. She was becoming very fond of Lucious, although something about him frightened her. She thought that, possibly, it was his power and influence that intimidated her. This time she leaned into Lucious and sweetly pecked him on the mouth.

"You can count on it," she replied coolly, a flirtatious smile on her lips. Her eyes glistened as she stared up at him wantonly.

Lucious gave a slight laugh.

"You could, possibly, have a profound effect on me, Miss Eva Alderson."

They were both admiring one another when they heard the horses coming around the corner of the house.

Lucious helped Eva up from the step, taking her into his arms.

"How about next time we meet in a more intimate setting? Say, tomorrow evening at Rêves? Archie and I will pick you up at half-past seven?" he asked enticingly.

Eva's eyes lit up, "Rêves! That's one of the most fashionable restaurants in London!" she exclaimed.

Lucious started laughing, "Yes, I know love, only the best for you."

He leaned in, giving Eva one final, passionate kiss. She reluctantly pulled away.

"Thank you for a lovely evening, Lucious," she said politely.

"And thank you for coming to my small intimate gathering," Lucious replied, sarcastically.

They both laughed lightly and Lucious helped Eva into the carriage, taking back his jacket.

"Until tomorrow, my love," he said as he closed the carriage door.

Eva nodded through the carriage window, giving him a coquettish grin as the coach took off into the cold black night.

Six

The next morning, Eva was woken by her mother, who stood over her as she lay on her cot in the sitting room. "Eva, Eva, wake up, dear. I have to be getting to town. I want to hear all about the party last night."

Margie was shaking Eva mildly, trying to get a response from her.

"Hmmm...what?" Eva mumbled, rubbing her eyes and yawning.

"I want to hear all about last night," Margie said in an exasperated tone.

"Mum, I'm knackered. I'll tell you all about it later," Eva responded groggily, still rubbing her eyes.

"Oh, alright," Margie agreed, finally giving up, "but I want to hear every detail. By the way, you didn't arrive home until well past one o'clock, missy." Margie was clearly annoyed.

"I'm sorry, mother, but..." Eva hesitated, sitting up on the sofa. "Luke doesn't exactly live here in the city. He has a house in the country and it took some time to get home last night," she explained.

"Oh, really? Interesting," Margie said suspiciously. "But you had a nice time, you say?" she inquired, hoping that Eva had made some new friends.

"Yes, it was marvelous, but I'm very tired now and I will tell you all about it later," Eva brushed her off and Margie sighed.

"Alright, you go ahead and sleep, dear."

Margie was about to leave Eva alone when Eva spoke, remembering that Lucious had invited her to dine with him that evening.

"Oh, I almost forgot. He's taking me to Rêves this evening for dinner!" Eva exclaimed.

"Rêves? This evening you say?" Margie asked enthusiastically yet with a questioning note.

"Yes, Mum. Why—is an extravagant dinner out at Rêves too good for us?" Eva responded in a snarky tone.

Margie peered at Eva.

"No, I just don't want to see you get hurt, that's all."

There was a moment of silence, then Margie decided to say what was on her mind.

"To be honest with you, Eva, this Luke sounds a little bit too good to be true."

Margie tried to say it while also considering Eva's feelings, but she was concerned for Eva's well-being and didn't want to see her daughter get hurt. This boy, Luke, seemed to be moving rather quickly, Margie thought, calling on Eva two nights in a row and taking her to a fancy dinner. She knew that Eva was a bit naïve when it came to the world. She was a dreamer who often had her head up in the clouds, believing in fairytales and happy endings, but Margie knew that that was not reality. She had always tried to keep Eva as sheltered as possible, but now she feared that it would end up hurting her more in the end.

Eva didn't respond to her mother but stared coldly out across the room. She knew her mum was right, Lucious did seem too good to be true. Nevertheless, Eva felt that she had to give him a chance. She also knew that her mother could never know the truth about who was courting her. Eva's young life had been filled with much pain thus far and Lucious made her feel special. Regardless of the outcome, Eva desired to see more of him.

After several moments of silence, Margie continued.

"I care about you, Eva. I hope you understand," she said with heartfelt distress.

"I do understand, Mum, but you also have to know that I am a woman now and it's time that I experience life the way I choose, even if I'm wrong. It's still my choice," Eva told her mother.

Margie was surprised by her daughter's response. Eva had always been so child-like and now she was talking about how she was a woman and about making her own choices. Margie wasn't used to this side of Eva. At the same time, she also knew that Eva was right. She had to experience life for herself, even if her time with this Luke fellow ended with heartbreak and disappointment.

"We'll talk more about this later. You get some rest now," Margie said, patting Eva on the arm.

"Thank you, Mum," Eva replied.

Margie stood up from the sofa and began heading for the door when Eva spoke again.

"Oh, and just so you know…" Eva paused and Margie turned around looking at her intently. "I'm delighted, Mum, for the first time in a long time," Eva said sincerely with hopeful aspiration in her eyes.

"I'm so glad to hear that, dear." Margie gave Eva a kind smile but, inwardly, she was distressed about the decisions her daughter was making. Margie had mother's intuition and something didn't feel right about Luke.

"Oh, Eva, will you please go visit Miss Alice today and make sure she's doing all right? It's been a while since I checked in on her," added Margie.

Eva had only seen Alice in passing these last few months when Margie would go visit her. Alice would open the door to let Margie inside and Eva would give her a quick wave, then step out of sight. The last thing Eva wanted to do was spend time with Alice. It was hard enough being at the same lodging house, which held all her memories of Georgie, without also going to his former lodging room. Eva was trying to move on with her life, but it was difficult for her. She was beginning to fall in love with Lucious, but she was still in love with Georgie. Perhaps a part of her would always be in love with him.

"I don't want to go over there," Eva pleaded.

"I think it would be good for you and I know Alice is missing you something terrible," Margie replied.

"Please, don't make me go, Mum!" Eva begged her mother.

"Don't you miss Alice? You can't stay away forever," Margie questioned.

Eva was going to try to stay away for as long as possible, but maybe her mum was right, perhaps it was time for her to see Alice.

"Oh, alright!" she responded indignantly. "I will do my best to check on Alice today, but I'm not going inside for a visit. I'll stop by at the door to make sure she's doing fine," said Eva wearily.

"Thank you, Eva," Margie replied, a grateful look on her face.

* * *

Later on that day, Eva finally managed to pull herself away from her warm, cozy cot, deciding to get cleaned up and check on Miss Alice. She wandered out of the lodging room and down the corridor to the bath. Eva and Margie were very fortunate—most lodging homes didn't have indoor plumbing. When Mr. Lyons renovated the house, he added running water and flushing toilets. Margie and Eva's bath was in the upstairs corridor, although only Margie and Eva used it. Mr. Roberts refused to share a toilet and bath with women and opted for a tub in his room and the old outhouse in the back instead.

Eva finished washing up and dressing for the day. She peered in the mirror, combing out her wet hair as drops of water dripped onto the floor. Staring at herself in the mirror, she couldn't understand what Lucious saw in her; she was just an ordinary girl. She knew that there was a natural beauty about her, but Lucious could have any woman he desired. So why was he fond of her? The inadequacy Eva had felt the night before was bubbling up inside her once more. She stared at her reflection in the mirror, frowning as tears began filling her eyes. Her mother was right, what was she doing? How was this wealthy, sophisticated businessman ever going to love an unfortunate, poor, simple girl like her? She had nothing to offer him in return. She had no dowry and she wasn't educated. The only thing she knew how to do was keep the house, but Lucious already had servants. They had nothing in common, except their apparent attraction for one another. Eva contemplated not showing up for their engagement that evening, but then she thought that Lucious might come to the house to fetch her. The last thing she needed right now was her mother finding out where she had been or who she had been with. She made up her mind that this would be the last time that she would ever see Lucious Paddimir, no matter how he made her feel when she was with him.

Eva left her lodging room and headed downstairs to Alice's. Before knocking on the door, she inhaled a deep breath and then exhaled it slowly to prepare herself for a conversation with Alice. She knew that Alice was bound to mention Georgie and she did not want to hear about him right now. She gave the door a few hard knocks, making sure Alice could hear them, then waited a few moments for Alice to come to the door. When it finally opened, Alice's eyes grew wide at the sight of Eva.

"My, if it isn't Miss Eva! You're a sight for sore eyes. I certainly didn't expect to see you today. Come on in, dear." Alice motioned Eva to come inside the lodging room, but Eva stayed frozen at the door.

"Alice," Eva spoke up loud enough for her to hear, "I can't stay today. I just wanted to check in on you to make sure you're doing all right?"

Alice turned around and hobbled back over to the door.

"Won't you stay for just a bite of pastry and a spot of tea?" Alice beckoned.

"I'm sorry, but I just don't have the time today." Eva tried to sound convincing. "Is there anything you need?" she asked.

"No, no, I'm fine," Alice huffed. "I did, however, receive a letter from George a couple of days ago. He says you're not returning any of his letters?" Alice asked, troubled.

Here we go, Eva thought to herself, releasing an annoyed sigh.

"I just haven't had a chance to read them, that's all," Eva rolled her eyes.

"Oh, alright, then. I understand, you're still cross with him, yeh." Alice started nodding her head. She knew exactly why Eva had not read Georgie's letters.

"It's, it's just...It's complicated, Alice," Eva said exasperated.

"Ah, I see. I really think you should read his letters, dear. You may be surprised by what they say," responded Alice in a mild, beseeching tone.

"You mean, he's sorry? I gathered that already," Eva stated indignantly.

"He's more than sorry, Eva," Alice allowed her words to trail off, "but that's not for me to say, you should really hear it from George. I told him I'd stay out of it and that's exactly what I'm going to do." Alice sounded slightly annoyed with herself for saying too much, then gave Eva a sad look as she noticed tears rolling down Eva's cheeks.

"So, how long does he plan to stay in Oxfordshire?" Eva asked, big-eyed, wiping the tears away from her face.

"Well, he says he's going to be there for about a year, dear, but that he has a plan that he's working on—and I think you'll be pleasantly surprised when you read those letters," Alice explained.

Georgie wasn't planning to return for a whole year! What if he came back with a wife? Eva was angry and heartbroken. She believed that, had Georgie loved her the way she loved him, then he would have stayed in London to be with her.

"You let Georgie know that if he really cares for me, then he'll come home now!" Eva responded bitterly, pointing aggressively to the ground.

Alice became very quiet, shocked by Eva's response. Eva had grown a bit of a temper over the past year.

"I don't think you're giving him a fair chance, Eva. You're stubborn and, if you continue this way, you'll lose in the end," Alice responded angrily, shaking as she spoke, her cheeks turning red.

Eva was offended by Alice's response. She knew that Alice was honest and could come across harsh, but her words really hurt this time.

"Good day, Alice," Eva said harshly, then stormed off down the corridor.

"Eva, wait! Eva!" Alice called out.

But Eva continued down the hall and rushed back up the stairs.

"Well, I never. Good riddance, I say!" spouted Alice as she slammed the door.

Eva climbed the stairs, sobbing and vigorously wiping the tears away from her eyes. She was tired of this lodging house and the people in her life. She wanted to start a new life away from this place. She changed her mind—if Lucious could give her this opportunity, then she would do whatever it took to be with him in order to get a fresh, new start.

She strode furiously toward her lodging room door and nearly tripped over several boxes that lay in front of the doorway. The boxes were white, with delicate navy blue ribbons tied around each one. She looked up and down the corridor, trying to see who had left the packages, but there was no one in sight. They must have arrived while she was downstairs with Alice. The top box had a card attached to it with Eva's name written on it. Pulling the card off the box, she entered the lodging room, leaving the door wide open, and immediately searched for a letter opener. Slashing the envelope open, she carefully pulled out the card.

All it said was: "To my love, Eva, the most enchanting woman in all of London. Signed, Lucious Paddimir."

After reading the card, Eva walked back out into the corridor, astonished that Lucious had sent her gifts. Excitedly, she began picking up the boxes two at a time, carrying them into the lodging room. She laid them out on the table, opening the smallest box first. She carefully untied the dark blue, silky bow and gracefully removed the box top, pulling back the tissue paper. Eva's eyes lit up—it was a small bottle of French perfume. She proceeded to open the bottle and place small drops on the inside of her wrists. She waved her hand back and forth, wafting the scent toward her nose. An aroma of roses, lavender, and sandalwood graced her senses. She thought the perfume smelled exquisite. Placing the fragrance down on the table, she began to open the second box.

Lifting the lid off the box, her eyes grew wide.

"Oh my!" she gasped.

The box contained a gold, girandole style necklace that was encrusted with tiny blue topaz jewels. The jewels covered the entire piece. Its most prominent feature was one large topaz stone, which was encircled by several small, white diamonds. Eva held the necklace up to her body; looking down, she could barely see the tiered treasures lightly caressing her neck. Her heart raced and she was overwhelmed by Lucious' generosity toward her. This was too much, she thought. She placed the necklace back into the box and walked over to the water basin. Drawing herself a glass of water, she drank it down swiftly. What would her mother think? This man was giving her elaborate gifts and she barely knew him.

Eva took some time to calm herself down from the excitement and delight she was experiencing, then decided to open the third box. She lifted the box top, pulled back the tissue, and feasted her eyes upon a beautiful, black, velvet cape that was laid out there together with an attached bonnet to keep her warm. Eva thought about last evening and how Lucious had noticed that she was shivering while she waited for the carriage to arrive.

"He is so thoughtful," She said aloud and rubbed her palms against the soft velvet fabric.

The cape had a velour ribbon in front, holding it in place. She wrapped the cloak around her shoulders and closed her eyes, feeling how cozy and warm it was against her skin. Then, she noticed a pair of long, white gloves, covered with embossed flowers, sitting at the bottom of the box as well.

Eva placed the gloves on her hands and began opening the fourth box, which contained a pair of golden, velvet court shoes with a diamond buckle on top of each. She tried on the shoes and found that they fit perfectly. How did Lucious know her shoe size? Eva wondered but, as quickly as the thought came to her mind, she promptly pushed it away. She didn't want to know how all this was possible—she just wanted to enjoy the moment.

Finally, she opened the last box. Inside was a stunning sky-blue gown that perfectly matched the topaz necklace. The dress was made of silk satin and had a bustle, with tiers flowing down the skirt. Beautiful, white lace highlighted the open neckline of the dress and its bell-shaped wrists. Small pieces of lace adorned each skirt layer, draping elegantly toward the floor. Eva grabbed the dress and headed toward the bedroom. Holding the extravagant dress up to her body, she gazed at herself in the mirror. She couldn't believe that such a dress belonged to her. Eva never thought anyone would ever buy her such beautiful things and felt overwhelmed to have received such elaborate gifts from Lucious. She stared at herself in the mirror and decided that she was going to take Lucious' advice on life. She would allow him to give her the experiences she desired, the life she hungered for, and would relish spending the evening with him.

Eva began preparing herself for her engagement with Lucious, hoping to be finished before her mother arrived home. She knew that she would have to explain the new garments and didn't want to have that discussion until after she returned home for the evening. She was frenzied with excitement, sensing the romance that awaited her. All she could think about was Lucious, his smile, the way he held her in his arms, his soft kisses on her lips. This moment was the most exhilarated Eva had felt in her entire life.

She was finishing styling her hair when there was a knock on the bedroom door.

"Eva, we need to talk. Please open the door," Margie asked, sounding discouraged.

Eva released a frustrated sigh. "I have to finish getting ready, Mum," she called out.

"We really need to talk. I just visited Alice and she told me about your tiff today. I'm really worried about you, Eva." Margie sounded desperate.

Eva exhaled deeply and walked over, opening the bedroom door. Margie grabbed ahold of Eva, without even looking at her attire, and embraced her tightly. Then, she pushed Eva back, placing her hands on her shoulders, gazing most seriously into her eyes.

"Eva, I'm not entirely sure how to deal with all that you're going through right now. You've been upset for the past few months and now you're beginning to lose your temper. I want to help you, but I need you to talk to me," Margie pleaded, looking at her with heartfelt concern.

Suddenly, she gazed down, noticing Eva's attire, and her eyes grew wide. Staring at Eva, her mouth flung open and her demeanor changed.

"What are you wearin', girl?" she asked in a vexed tone. "Where did you get the money for all these trappings?" Margie grabbed Eva's dress contentiously. "You didn't steal these, did you?" she asked, indignantly, clasping Eva's necklace in her hand and giving it a hard, cold stare. Margie's cheeks were burning red with anger. "Eva, you tell me right now—where did these things come from?" Margie stomped her foot in outrage.

"They came, they came—from Lucious. He sent them to me as gifts!" Eva spoke sharply, then quickly put her hand to her mouth, realizing she had just given away his real name.

"Did you say Lucious? I thought you said you were seeing a boy named Luke?" Margie inclined her head toward Eva, a fierce look in her eyes.

Eva's eyes grew wide and her lips were pressed tightly together. She finally spoke.

"I am going out with a boy named Luke mother. I just accidentally said the wrong name," she began backing away from Margie, letting out an uncomfortable laugh, but Margie could tell she was lying.

"Eva Ann Alderson, you tell me the truth right now! Who have been you seeing?" Margie asked forcefully.

Eva began moving her hands wildly, trying to calm her mother down.

"Alright, alright, Mum." Eva inhaled a deep breath then calmly explained, "I've been seeing a man named Lucious Paddimir. He is kind, gentle, and generous. He cares for me, Mum, and I care for him as well. He bought me these gifts and had them sent to the house for me to wear this evening." Eva's confidence rose as she spoke. "What's so wrong about that?" she asked her mother, genuinely perplexed.

Margie stared at Eva in astonishment. She couldn't believe what she was hearing.

"What's so bad about that, what's…what's so bad?" Margie was shaking her head back and forth wildly, placing her thumb and middle finger on the ridge of her nose. She looked down at the ground, trying to regain her composure. Margie placed her hand back down at her side and brought her eyes to Eva's, giving her an intense stare.

"Eva, men don't just buy elaborate gifts for girls they'd met the day before on the street!" she said harshly.

Eva stood there silently; she could tell her mother was terribly angry.

"He wants something from you—if you haven't already given it to him," Margie waved her hand, tears gathering in her eyes. "Eva, I'm worried about you!" she said, sounding frightened. "Lucious Paddimir has the reputation for being a gal-sneaker, amongst other things. And there's certainly something not right about that 'juice' he sells!" she exclaimed, shaking her head and waving her finger.

Margie placed her hands on her hips and continued shaking her head back and forth.

"You're going to have to send all these items back to him and you're certainly not going with him anywhere—not this evening and not ever again!" Margie shouted, pointing at the garments. Then, she sharply turned and began heading out the bedroom door.

"You can't tell me what to do! I'm a woman now and if I want to see Lucious Paddimir, then I will see Lucious Paddimir, even if you don't approve!" Eva shouted back at her mother.

Margie slowly turned around; this time, her mouth gaped open. She was shocked by Eva's response.

"Excuse me?" she glared.

"I'm keeping the garments, Mum, and I'm going out with Lucious tonight—and there's absolutely nothing you can do to stop me!" Eva stated emphatically, lifting her chin high into the air.

She walked over to the mirror hastily and finished putting final touches to her hair, then dabbed a little of the new perfume onto her wrists and neck. She placed the cape around her shoulders, tying the ribbon tightly around her clavicle. Last, she carefully put the new, white gloves on her hands.

Margie stood in the bedroom doorway, staring helplessly at her daughter as she dressed for Lucious Paddimir. Her eyes began to fill with tears and she didn't know what more she could do. Eva wasn't a child anymore. She couldn't just pick her up and bend her over the knee, give her a few whacks on the bottom, and send her off to bed. Oh, how she wished Henry were here. He had a way with Eva and she always seemed to revere him more than her mother. Tears now spilled over and began flowing down Margie's cheeks.

Eva looked at her mother, noticed that she was crying, and raised her chin even higher into the air. Her mother's emotions would not interfere with her decisions, she would not allow it. She walked over to the doorway and spoke confidently.

"I want you know that I'm not trying to hurt you, Mum. I know you're only trying to protect me, but I have to do this for myself. I hope that, one day, you will understand."

Margie had no words to mutter. She wiped the tears from her eyes, staring down at the ground, shaking her head, and feeling powerless and defeated. Margie stepped out of the doorway, allowing Eva to walk across the threshold. The only thing she could think to do was pray that Eva would be all right, but she had a gnawing feeling in the pit of her stomach that something terrible was going to happen.

"I think I will wait downstairs for Lucious to arrive," Eva said and headed for the lodging room door.

"Eva, wait!" Margie called out.

Eva turned around harshly, peering hostilely at her mother. Then, she noticed how tired and worn her mother looked, the difficult years wearing on her face. Eva started to feel guilty for her behavior but still didn't want to change her mind about seeing Lucious. She sucked in a deep breath and raised her chin a little higher.

"Yes?" Eva inquired.

Margie rushed over to her daughter and wrapped her arms around her. She kissed her cheek while tears continued rolling down her face. She was looking at Eva softly.

"I love you."

Eva's demeanor lightened and she began to feel her own emotions build within her.

"I love you too, Mum," she replied softly.

Margie gave Eva one more strong hug.

"Please be careful tonight," she said as she held onto Eva firmly.

"Yes, mother, I promise. I'll be fine," Eva assured her.

As Margie released her from her grasp, Eva gave her mother one last smile and then turned and walked out the door.

Seven

E va eagerly awaited Lucious' carriage to arrive, pacing back and forth restlessly in the foyer of the lodging house. She continued recalling the quarrels she had earlier that day with both Alice and her mother. She felt terrible about the way she had talked to Miss Alice. Her mother was right, her emotions were profound lately—but she didn't know how to sift through them all on her own, let alone how to try to explain them to her mother.

After a while, she decided to stop fretting over her problems and focus on thinking about Lucious instead. Eva was growing very fond of Lucious Paddimir and knew that their relationship was moving quickly. She didn't care. Lucious was the first person, in a long time, who seemed to take an interest in her and to think about her needs and desires. Eva looked down at the dress he had purchased for her. She pressed her hands against the satin silk fabric, hoping she looked flawless for him. After all, he had taken time out of his busy day to purchase these lovely items for her and she didn't want him to be disappointed in her appearance. Eva suddenly realized that she was going to have to converse with Lucious for the entire evening. This rendezvous was not like the party last night, where there were other guests to commandeer his attention elsewhere. She wondered what they would talk about with one another and fervently hoped that she wouldn't say something foolish again, recalling her question about the juice from the previous evening.

Eva closed her eyes, inhaling deeply and trying to calm her nerves. She could feel her heart beating rapidly in her chest. When she opened her eyes, Lucious' carriage was pulling up in front of the lodging house. Sucking in one final breath, she gracefully sauntered toward the carriage, making sure her posture was perfect. Eva assumed that Lucious would be watching her as she made her way.

"Good evening, Miss Eva," Archie greeted her with a nod but without any expression.

"Good evening Archie, it is nice to see you again."

He nodded once more as he opened the door to help Eva inside the carriage. She immediately noticed that Lucious was not inside and began to feel apprehensive.

"Archie? Where is Lucious?"

"Oh, he got tied up in town, Miss, but he will meet you at the restaurant."

Eva nodded, then stepped into the carriage, a bit disheartened by Lucious' absence.

As the carriage made its way through town, Eva felt butterflies in her stomach. She had walked past Rêves on several occasions and had always wondered what it was like to be a patron, but she never thought that she would actually have the chance to find out for herself. The carriage arrived in front of the restaurant. Eva's hands were trembling and excitement filled her. Lucious was waiting for her, just as Archie had said. The carriage slowed to a stop and Lucious opened the door.

"Eva!" he gasped at the sight of her.

Her eyes widened, unsure whether his response was good or bad.

"You look absolutely ravishing, my love." Lucious grabbed his chest dramatically.

Eva smiled brightly, pleased by Lucious' response, then allowed him to help her step out of the carriage. Lucious locked eyes with Eva, entrancing her with his gaze. He paused for a moment, then gently lifted her hand to his lips, delicately kissing it. Eva's breaths began to shorten and new sensations moved within her. Lucious lowered her hand, winking and flashing her one his charming smiles.

"Shall we," he asked, holding out his arm for Eva to take. She did so tenderly and they entered Rêves together.

The atmosphere in Rêves was utterly charming. Rich, mahogany wood lined the doorways and paintings covered every available space on the walls, except for a few randomly placed trophy antlers. There were golden gas lamps and candles lighting up every room, releasing a soft glow throughout the entire restaurant. Burgundy velvet banquettes and chairs sat underneath beautiful wooden tables. Eva was doing her best to take it all in, as Lucious quickly led her through the restaurant to a small stairwell in the back. He took her up a flight of rickety stairs to a beautiful, breathtakingly adorned room, where there was only one small table.

Eva's eyes lit up as she absorbed the atmosphere surrounding her.

"Oh, Lucious, this is exquisite!" she exclaimed.

"I'm so happy you are pleased, my love. I hope it's alright that I requested a private room for just the two of us this evening.

I didn't want it to be so terribly loud and overwhelming as it was last night," Lucious responded, sounding proud of himself.

Before now, Eva could only have imagined a place such as this one. The walls were entirely encased by dark, mahogany wood and trimmed with gold edging. There were elegant mirrors and paintings of famous patrons, as well as golden gas lamps covered by red shades with fringes, lining the wood walls. Their table was covered with a beautiful white linen tablecloth. Gold-laced porcelain china with cherry accents, matching the burgundy velvet chairs, was carefully arranged on top. A large, golden candelabra was lit in the middle of the table and a centerpiece displayed flawlessly bloomed, ruby-red roses. The ambiance was utterly romantic, Eva thought.

A man was awaiting their arrival. He was of medium height and looked to be about the same age as Lucious, although he was bald in the front, with reddish hair on the sides of his head, as well as a fluffy red mustache. He motioned over to the table and began pulling out the chairs.

"I hope everything is to your liking, sir."

"Yes, Anvil, everything looks splendid," Lucious replied, pleased.

Eva began removing her cape and gloves.

"Why don't I help you with that."

Lucious walked over to stand in front of Eva. Looking into her eyes, he gently pulled on the velour ribbon, loosening it from around her neck. His fingers lightly grazed her skin. Eva sucked in a deep breath, finding the action slightly titillating. Lucious had a satisfied look on his face as he removed the cape from her shoulders and handed it to Anvil. He motioned toward the chair with his hand, welcoming Eva to take a seat. She sat down carefully, ensuring that she maintained her posture as Lucious helped scoot her chair closer to the table.

Once they were both seated, Anvil brought out a silver pitcher of water and filled up their water glasses.

"The usual, sir?"

"Yes, thank you," Lucious replied.

Anvil scurried off right away, leaving the two of them alone in the private room.

"At last, here we are, Eva." Lucious released a sigh of relief while adjusting his jacket. He then placed his hand over Eva's, staring affectionally into her eyes. Eva thought that she could get lost in Lucious endearing brown eyes and her heart began pounding.

"How do you like the gifts, love?" Lucious asked, smiling and looking at the necklace he had purchased for her. Eva touched the chain.

"Oh, they are all so lovely Lucious, thank you. But it's too much," Eva spoke honestly but graciously, trying not to offend him. Lucious gazed back up and leaned in closer.

"But I want to spoil you, my darling," he said, kissing Eva gently on the lips and sending tingles down her body. Pulling away, Lucious intertwined his fingers with hers. "I say, I think I did a splendid job—you look absolutely radiant."

Eva gave him a coy smile and blushed.

Anvil re-entered the room with a bottle of wine in his hand. He proceeded to pour it into their crystal glasses. Lucious lifted his glass and took a sip of the wine.

"Mmmm…marvelous as usual. Go ahead and taste it, Eva," Lucious insisted.

"Well, I don't drink wine that often," she commented, nervously.

Eva had never really had any alcohol, except when her mother had allowed her to taste the rum punch last Christmas. And the punch she had at Lucious' party the previous evening, of course. Lucious leaned in toward Eva once more, resting his hand upon hers.

"It might help loosen you up a bit," he whispered, winking.

Eva let out a nervous laugh, then took a sip of the wine. Her eyes widened—it tasted awful to her, but she didn't want to hurt Lucious' feelings.

"It's wonderful," she lied with a smile.

Anvil came back into the room again, holding two bowls of soup.

"I hope you like game soup, Eva," Lucious said with anticipation.

"It smells delightful," she responded.

The soup consisted of a hearty broth, bits of pheasant, onion, carrots, and celery. Eva took a spoonful, bringing it carefully to her mouth, working hard not to spill anything on her new dress. She spooned the soup into her mouth and found that it was the most delectable soup she had ever tasted. She closed her eyes, savoring its flavor.

"You like?" Lucious asked inquisitively.

"Yes, it's absolutely delicious," Eva assured him.

"Good, it's one of my favorite dishes," Lucious stated, looking satisfied. He placed his spoon down beside his bowl. "So tell me," Lucious went on, inquisitively looking at Eva with one of his usual, forward, flirtatious grins. "Who is Eva

Alderson? Other than, of course, the woman who has stolen my heart?" He took a sip from his wine glass as he waited for her to respond.

Eva perked up, surprised by his question. She did not know what to say, so she gave him a kind but nervous smile. She thought about how nothing was exciting in her life. What was she supposed to tell him? That her mum was a Covent Garden flower woman, that her best friend moved to Oxfordshire to work on a farm, and that he was the best thing that has happened to her in a long time?

Eva's eyes were wide and darted anxiously around the room. She did not move her head and was trying not to look at Lucious directly. She had been concerned about having to converse with him and her worries were becoming a reality. Her heart raced and she could feel the blood flowing rapidly into her cheeks. Lucious continued to stare at her, waiting for a response, so she decided that she should probably answer him.

"Well, there isn't much to know really, I suppose. I grew up in London and have lived here my entire life with my mother and father...until," Eva swallowed hard and paused, "he passed away, about two years ago now."

Lucious gave Eva a sympathetic look and began rubbing the top of her hand.

"I'm so sorry, love. Would you mind telling me how it happened?" he asked, sounding genuinely concerned about her feelings.

Eva explained what happened to him very slowly, staring into the distance as she did so, remembering her father's death.

"Well, he worked at a factory and something went wrong with a piece of machinery. A large heavy beam fell, injuring some of the men and killing two of them, one being my father." She looked down at her plate as feelings churned inside her. She was embarrassed to tell Lucious the story of her father's death and she didn't like talking about the event.

"Oh, Eva, I am so sorry for your loss," he said, trying to console her.

Eva continued staring at her plate and Lucious gently picked up her chin, making her look him in the eyes. Eva saw much love and concern for her in his eyes and decided to continue.

"Well, now it's just me and mum and..." she inhaled deeply while repositioning herself in her chair. Suddenly her demeanor shifted from sorrowful to confident. She looked him directly in the eyes and spoke forthrightly.

"To be honest, I really don't want to talk about me. My life really isn't all that exciting and...well, it's pretty much downright boring. That is, until I met you," she added, a kittenish grin splattered across her face. She was proud of herself for being honest with Lucious and he smiled heartily in return.

"Well, then, let's make a toast." Lucious held his wine glass high into the air, "To new beginnings and non-boring lives. May you live a life, Eva, that brings you everything your heart truly desires," he stated confidently, giving her a wink, and then took a sip of his wine.

"I'll drink to that," she agreed and proceeded to take a large gulp of the wine.

The two of them continued talking and Eva found herself enjoying Lucious' company. She was beginning to feel more comfortable around him as he told her stories of his extravagant travels around the world. Lucious had met kings and sultans on his journeys, searching for the perfect ingredients to create his juice. He explained to Eva how his juice helped people forget their worries and how he was making the world a better place. She found it surprising how easy it was for her to talk to Lucious and how many exciting stories and adventures he had to share. He was very warm, welcoming, and non-judgmental, which allowed Eva to feel at ease with him.

Meanwhile, Anvil continued bringing course after course—meats, potatoes, pies, and puddings. Eva was stuffed but hated wasting food with so many people starving on the streets of London. Finally, however, she decided she couldn't eat another morsel, just as Anvil entered the private dining room again. This time he was accompanied by two other waiters and they began serving the last course—consisting of cheeses, nuts, and fruits—and poured fresh wine into new wine glasses. Eva looked at the hearty spread in dismay. Lucious noticed the strange look upon her face.

"Is everything alright, love?"

Eva glanced up at him. "I'm sorry, Lucious, but I couldn't possibly eat another bite," she said apologetically.

Lucious smiled at Anvil. "I'm afraid that we have filled Miss Alderson to the brim, Anvil, so to speak," he noted.

Anvil nodded, "Will that be all then, sir?"

"Yes, of course, add it to the tab and I will pay at the end of the month, as usual," Lucious replied.

"As you wish, sir," Anvil replied.

Lucious rose from the table and helped Eva up from her chair. Looking at her intently, he spoke while holding her hands.

"So, Eva, what did you think of Rêves?"

Eva looked at him, wide-eyed.

"I don't think I've ever been served that much food in my entire life. It was all so delicious. Thank you for bringing me here tonight, Lucious," she replied kindly.

Lucious leaned closer to Eva, caressing her hand.

"Yes, well, there's plenty more where that came from love, as well as gifts for you. See, Eva, when you're with me, you are treated as nobility." He bowed, kissing her hand and continuing to stare into her eyes. "I have a few more surprises for you tonight."

Eva began looking around the room.

"Oh, they're not here love. In fact, there's something I want to show you," Lucious gave Eva a flirtatious grin and raised his brows. He had a scandalous look upon his face.

Eva smiled kindly in return, wondering what more Lucious could possibly have planned for her. She couldn't imagine a more romantic night than the one she had already experienced.

"Shall we go?" Lucious asked her as Anvil handed their coats to him.

Once again, he helped Eva with her cape. Placing the garment around her shoulders, he tied the ribbon around Eva's neck, then ran his hands along her clavicle bone up to her shoulders, placing them securely on her waist. Closing his eyes, he bent down and kissed Eva passionately. She closed her eyes and kissed him in return, as rousing sensations coursed through her body. Lucious continued moving his hands down, around Eva's hips and thighs, then he carefully pulled away a few moments later, his hands once again on her waist.

"Ah, I've been waiting to do that all evening," he said with a pleased look on his face.

Eva smiled back, her breathing labored and her head spinning. She wasn't quite sure whether it was from the kiss or the wine. Lucious took Eva's hand, leading her back down the staircase, out a back doorway, and into an alley.

"Shouldn't we go to the front, where the carriage is waiting?" she asked uneasily, looking around the dark alley. Eva wasn't usually allowed to walk on the streets after dark. Her mother had always said how dangerous it was in London at night.

"No need to worry, dear. I'm right here," Lucious said, grabbing hold of Eva tightly. "I won't let anything happen to you. Besides, I already sent Archie away for the evening. I thought it would be nice for us to walk to our next location alone. It's only a couple of blocks from here," Lucious assured and quickly led her out from the alley and into the open street.

Eva felt safe with Lucious, believing she had nothing to fear when she was with him.

Eight

Rain started falling during the chilly London night.

"Oh bother, it's beginning to rain," Lucious said, annoyed. "I'm afraid we're going to have to make a run for it—it's not much farther from here." He looked down at Eva.

"Oh, these shoes, I'm afraid I can't run." Eva glanced down at her brand-new heels but, before she had a chance to say anything else, Lucious scooped her up in his arms. Holding her tightly, he quickly headed down the walkway.

Eva laughed. "Lucious, you can't carry me the whole way!" she exclaimed.

"I most certainly can," he assured her, smiling from ear to ear. "Besides, it's right up here."

Lucious hurried, carrying Eva just a little longer, then he carefully placed her feet on the ground.

"Just like the first time we met," he said, grinning while rubbing his hand against Eva's. She noticed that they were standing in front of an apartment building.

"Lucious, this is someone's terraced house?" she questioned, confused. She couldn't understand why Lucious would bring her to someone's home so late at night.

"This isn't just someone's house, Eva. This is my house," he said with a tantalizing grin.

Eva was perplexed. "I can't just go into your home with you, alone, what will people think?" she spoke frankly, glancing around the street to see whether anyone was watching them as the rain continued beating down harshly.

Suddenly, Lucious leaned into Eva forcefully, pushing her up against the brick wall of the building. He pressed his body firmly against hers and began kissing her aggressively against the wall. After a few seconds, he pulled away slightly, only inches away from her face and stared seriously into her eyes.

"I don't know whether you noticed, Eva Alderson, but I don't give a damn what anyone thinks about me," he said sternly. Then, again leaning into Eva, he kissed her for a few moments longer while Eva stood very still, shocked by his unpredictability. He loosened his grip, fiercely looking into her eyes.

"What do think people are thinking now, Eva?" he asked her, an enticingly devilish grin residing on his face. Eva's heart was pounding as she looked up at him wide-eyed. Lucious started laughing, then backed away from her and began searching for the house key in his pocket. He grabbed Eva's hand and tugged her along.

"Hurry, before we both catch a cold," he said, pulling her into his house, closing the door, and locking it behind them.

"So this is it, my London home," he said confidently, as he removed his top hat, and placed it on the coat rack next to the door.

Eva glanced around. It was pitch black, except for a few candles lit here and there. Lucious bent down and pecked Eva on the cheek.

"See, that wasn't so bad and no one even noticed, probably." He let out another laugh, slinging his scarf and coat over the rack. Eva was still taken aback by Lucious' intensity outside and decided that it was best to remove her cape herself this time. She quickly untied the ribbon and handed the cloak to Lucious so he could place it on his coat rack. Lucious gave her a slightly disappointed pout.

"Allow me to show you around a bit," he said, rubbing his hands together while walking down the narrow corridor, past a small kitchen on the right. The kitchen was open to the rest of the house, similar to Eva's lodging room. A dining table stood in front of the kitchen, leading to a sitting area that allowed for only one sofa, two chairs, a small coffee table, and two side tables. Eva saw a fireplace lit against the back wall, where the chairs were stationed.

"Yes, it's not very large, but it's enough to get me by while I'm here in London."

Eva nodded her head in agreement.

Lucious pointed to the door on the opposite side of the corridor, away from the rest of the house.

"This door here leads to my housemaid's—Mrs. Martindale—quarters. I assume she has already retired for the evening."

He quickly walked back down the corridor toward the front door as Eva tried to keep up with him. Lucious turned around, taking Eva's hand in his and leading her up the stairs. He peeked back at her while raising his eyebrows up and down wildly. Eva chuckled, knowing he was acting silly. Once they arrived to the top of the stairs, Lucious brought her to the far left of the staircase.

"This is a guest room; however, there are no lanterns in there so, of course, you can't see anything," he stated, then lead her rapidly to a door on the right of the guest room. "Here is the guest bath, annnnndddd"—Lucious turned quickly, dragging Eva back over to the right of the stairwell, where there was just one door—"this is my bedroom, of course."

He presented the room to her as he leaned over the threshold, smiling widely. Turning the knob while still looking at Eva, he allowed the door to swing open on its own since he was still leaning over the doorway.

The room was filled with candles and there was a lit fireplace in one corner. Eva could smell Lucious' cologne; it's fragrance filled the entire room and smelled heavenly. There was a large bed to the right, with nightstands on both sides. Lucious walked across the room quickly, opening another door.

"This door leads to the ensuite bath."

Then, walking back across the room toward the other side of the bed, he opened another door.

"And, last but not least, the wardrobe."

He opened the door, then shut it quickly, acting silly once again.

"So, there you have it, Eva, my London home. I hope it meets your approval," he said, bowing deeply, then walked back toward Eva rubbing his hands together.

"Oh yes, it's wonderful Lucious. I've never seen a terraced house of this size," Eva stated. The truth was that Eva had never been in a terraced house before at all, everyone she knew lived either in lodging homes or slums.

She stood in the doorway awkwardly and began looking around the room anxiously, rubbing her hands together.

"Perhaps you would like a nightcap?" Lucious offered, pointing to a small bar next to the fireplace in his bedroom. Eva hesitantly nodded her head to signal a yes because she wasn't sure what else to do or say. She felt uncomfortable standing in a man's bedroom. There was a small table, with two bistro-style chairs sitting on the far side of the wall in front of what looked like a window, although a large velour curtain covered it. Eva walked over and sat down in one of the chairs. Lucious poured them two glasses of what Eva thought was sherry and handed one to Eva.

He sat down on the large bed in the middle of the room and began patting his hand, summoning Eva to come and sit next to him. Eva's heart raced nervously, as she continued to stay where she was, frozen in the chair.

"Won't you come to sit next to me, Eva?" Lucious asked enticingly. "Those chairs aren't the most comfortable," he noted.

Eva nodded her head cautiously and slowly stood up, walked over to the bed, and sat down next to Lucious. Knots were forming in her stomach and she was feeling very restless. She was beginning to understand that Lucious probably desired more than she was willing to give him and this made her extremely concerned.

"Lucious, what are we doing here?" she asked him quietly, gazing around the bedroom apprehensively. Instead of answering, he offered.

"Why don't you have some of my juice, it will help you feel more relaxed?"

He dipped his chin, looking at Eva gravely. She leaned toward the glass slowly. The juice had a medicinal smell mixed with oddly scented herbs. Lucious' eyes were fixed upon her intently as she took a tiny sip of it. Eva's face distorted when she tasted its repulsive flavor, which was like wine but more bitter and much stronger. After swallowing the distasteful concoction, she pursed her lips together and licked them, trying to remove its essence from her mouth.

"So, this is the juice you sell, then?" she asked hesitantly, thinking of how foolish she sounded last evening when she had asked about the juice.

"Yes," Lucious replied coolly. "Go ahead, have another sip," he suggested, once again watching Eva as she took a deeper gulp of the juice this time, trying to please him. "Very good," he said smoothly.

After the second taste, Lucious removed the glass from Eva's hand, placing it on the side table next to his bed.

"My juice has profound effects on people, Eva. They purchase it in troves, you know. I spent many years traveling the world, finding the right spices and herbs to create the perfect elixir," he stated emphatically.

Eva began to feel unsteady; colors were appearing before her eyes, swimming all over the room.

"Are you alright, my love?" Lucious asked, placing his hand on Eva's. She looked down at it.

"I...I feel strange," she replied.

"It's alright. It's just the juice beginning to work, that's all," Lucious said, trying to sound comforting. Eva kept opening and closing her eyes for some time, hoping that the colors would fade away soon.

"I see different colors swirling all around you, Lucious," she said, sounding concerned.

"Don't worry that will end soon and then you'll notice that every cell in your body is fully awakened to all its senses. You'll begin to feel things you've never felt before Eva," Lucious said excitedly and began to remove Eva's gloves carefully from her hands.

Eva felt warm sensations moving through her hands and arms as Lucious removed her gloves, placing them on his nightstand. While Lucious was near his nightstand, he discreetly pulled something out of one of the drawers. He moved back, leaning in closer to Eva. He took hold of her bare hand and spoke softly.

"Ah, that's better," he said and began rubbing Eva's hand. She felt sensations coursing through her body wildly, which were now extremely heightened by the juice she had consumed.

"I have something to ask you, Eva," Lucious stated tenderly yet seriously.

Eva noticed that Lucious seemed somewhat nervous, which was unusual for him.

"Yes, Lucious, what is it?" she asked, as her head began to clear somewhat. Although she felt a little dizzy, she was feeling a bit more like herself again. Eva realized it was the first time since entering Lucious' bedroom that she was unafraid of the situation at hand. Lucious was right—the juice made Eva's mind feel light and airy, while everything that touched her body felt more intense.

"Eva, what I'm about to ask you may seem...well, odd, and presumptuous. But I'm the kind of man who goes after what he wants and what I want, Eva, is you."

Lucious leaned in even closer and his breathing was a bit labored as he spoke.

"I know that this is all very sudden, but I have something for you."

He pulled out a small black box from behind his back. Eva's eyes grew large, staring at the black jewelry box and not knowing what to say. Lucious slowly opened and presented it to Eva. Inside, the box contained a golden ring with a large ruby stone that was surrounded by white diamonds.

"Eva, this is a promise ring. I give you this ring, promising to love and provide for you always. You will never want for anything, ever again. I have all the money I could ever need or desire, but the one thing I don't have, the one thing that is missing from my life—is you, Eva." Lucious paused, looking deeply into Eva's eyes.

"I want you to know tonight, this very night, that I want you. I hope that you want me in return. I will spoil you rotten and treat you like a princess. Everything that belongs to me will also be yours. However, if you accept this ring and my heart, you must know that I can never marry you. This ring seals us together but, because of my business and reputation, I am not a man who is able to marry. I hope you can understand," Lucious nodded his head.

Eva continued staring into Lucious' intensely captivating, dark eyes.

"If you accept this ring, you may not go back to the life you lived before. By accepting me, you are choosing my life—with me and only me. Eva, you will become mine."

Lucious took Eva's hand, kissing it while gazing into her eyes lustfully. Speaking in only a whisper, he said, "I love you, Eva."

Eva felt such intense sensations flowing through her body, but her mind was very muddled. Numerous thoughts were rumbling around in her head but the juice prevented her from being able to think straight.

"Lucious, I don't know what to say," she replied, a distressed look on her face.

"Say yes to me, Eva, say you'll be mine." Lucious was trembling as he slipped the ring on her finger. Eva looked down at the large jewel resting on her hand. She was in awe of its beauty.

Slowly, Lucious reached up, removing the butterfly hairpin that was holding Eva's hair in place. Wavy, blonde tendrils began flowing down around Eva's face, shoulders, and back. Lucious ran his fingers through Eva's hair, then gently caressed her face. Holding her chin ever so delicately in his hands, he brought her mouth to his, kissing her tenderly. Moving his hands down Eva's body carefully, he firmly grasped her waist, eagerly laying her down upon the bed. He leaned over her and the kisses that started out soft and gentle were now becoming more intense, matching his rising passion. He unbuttoned his shirt and began removing his clothing while gently pulling his lips away from Eva's.

Lucious was kissing her chin, working his way down her neck and clavicle. Eva's eyes were closed and she relished Lucious' mouth against her skin. He swiftly picked her up in his arms, moving her to the top of the bed and placing her head on the pillows. His lips continued kissing her mouth while his hands skillfully removed her clothing. His fingers traced down Eva's body, feeling every curve of it. They were passionately kissing and Eva was grabbing his shoulders.

Suddenly, a surge of pain shot through her entire body. She gasped, crying out in pain and digging her fingernails into his back. The pleasure she had felt just moments earlier had turned into extreme discomfort.

"Oh, Eva," Lucious moaned heavily in her ear.

He kept driving his body against hers and, with each thrust, Eva ached more. She wanted it to stop, finally fully realizing what they were doing. This wasn't how it was supposed to be. *This can't be happening, what have I done?* Eva thought to herself, as tears welled up in her eyes, her heart sinking deeper with each passing moment, fully aware now that she had given herself to Lucious Paddimir.

Lucious released a loud groan as he thrust himself powerfully into Eva's body one last time. She tightly shut her eyes, trying to breathe through the suffering. Finally, Lucious stopped and stared down at her fondly, while his body still trembled. He was breathing heavily as he was trying to catch his breath. He kissed Eva gently on the lips; then, speaking softly into her ear, he muttered, "I love you."

Eva pressed her lips together, biting down hard. She looked up at Lucious, giving him the best smile she could muster.

"I love you, too," she replied, even though she was not entirely convinced in her heart.

"I'm going to go freshen up," he said, kissing her once more before he walked quickly over to the ensuite bath and closed the door behind him.

Eva lay there, staring at the ceiling above for a few moments. Her body was in shock, traumatized by the whole experience. What was she going to do? What if Lucious didn't live up to his promises? She would be ruined. Eva held her hand up in the air, looking at the crimson-red rock, trying not to cry. She pulled back the blankets on the bed, covering her nakedness. Turning over on her side, she faced the room and wrapped her arms around herself, hugging tightly. Eva had never felt more alone than she did at that very moment. Her heart was breaking, for she had disappointed everyone who loved her, including herself.

Lucious returned to bed, lying down, covering himself with blankets, and curling up behind Eva. Placing his arms around her, he hugged Eva's waist and held her firmly. She could feel his body pressed up against her. Lucious kissed her cheek.

"We should probably get some shut-eye, love."

Eva didn't respond. Lucious caressed her face with his finger.

"You're alright..." he stated.

Eva nodded her head.

"Don't worry, it will get better, I promise," he murmured, leaning over her to blow out the candle lying on the night table next to her side of the bed. Eva closed her eyes tightly, feeling wholly disheartened.

"Oh, I almost forgot." Lucious grabbed the glass of juice from the nightstand. "You'll want to drink some of this; it will help you sleep."

Eva took the glass from Lucious. Sitting up, she took a large swig of the juice. Her face contorted with disgust and she shook her head from side to side.

"Don't worry, the taste of the juice will improve as well," he said, smiling.

Eva looked over at Lucious, lying next to her. Her wavy, flaxen hair was hanging around her face perfectly. Lucious locked his eyes with hers.

"You're so beautiful, Eva," he told her, leaning in and softly kissing her on the lips. Eva felt her heart melt a bit at Lucious' words. She may not love Lucious now, but perhaps she would learn to one day. Eva smiled, then placed the glass down on her nightstand. Lucious leaned over, blew out the candle on his nightstand, then once again wrapped his arms around Eva's body.

He whispered in her ear, "Goodnight, love."

Eva paused for a moment, trying to settle into the bed.

"Goodnight, Lucious," she replied.

As she lay in Lucious' arms, the juice began to relax her and she fell asleep quickly.

Nine

The next morning Eva woke up and tried to open her eyes. She winced and grabbed her forehead, which was throbbing in pain. Lying there for a moment, she realized that her hands were trembling, that she was sweating, and that her heart was racing. Eva didn't know what was happening to her body. Sitting up quickly, she let out a groan, still holding her head, for the pain was so intense. After sitting up for a moment, she soon realized that her head wasn't the only part of her body that ached. The awful, burning sensation from last night continued into the next day. Quickly, Eva's heart sank as she remembered what happened last evening and realized that she was still in Lucious' bed—a quick glance over to where Lucious had lain on the bed last night revealed that he was gone. Frantically, while remaining in the bed, she began searching the room for him. Squinting, she noticed that the ensuite door was open, so she assumed that he wasn't in there. Perhaps he was downstairs? Eva's eyesight was a bit blurry, but she thought she saw a white, silk robe laid out at the bottom of the bed. Reaching out in haste, she grabbed the robe and wrapped it around her body. She stood up slowly, her entire being shaking. She walked over to the bedroom door, feeling like she might faint from the pain at any moment. Opening the bedroom door gingerly, she tried not to make a sound but the door began to creak. Closing her eyes and gritting her teeth, she hoped no one would hear that she had opened the door.

Suddenly, a woman's voice called out from downstairs.

"Miss Eva, is that you?"

The woman knew her name? Eva could hear the woman coming up the stairs and she quickly jumped back into the bed, covering her head with the blankets. The woman knocked twice, then burst through the bedroom door.

"Ah, good morning, Miss Eva, my name is Mrs. Martindale. I am Master Lucious' maid and he has informed me that you will now be staying here with us."

Eva's eyes widened and she slowly uncovered her head to look up at Mrs. Martindale.

"There you are, dear."

A loud, short, chubby, grey-haired lady was standing in the room dressed in a maid's outfit, holding a tray in her hand. She walked over, setting down the plate of breakfast foods onto the small bistro table across the room. Proceeding to talk to Eva while opening the curtains, she pulled back the heavy shades to allow sunlight to enter. Eva shaded her eyes against the sudden appearance of sunlight because her head was still pounding. Mrs. Martindale took no notice and rambled on.

"So, just a few things you should know. If you should need me, just pull the bell rope on Master Lucious' side of the bed and I will be at your service. Master Lucious requested a poached egg, dry toast, and a pot of tea to be brought up to you this morning, but if there is something else more to your liking, don't hesitate to ask. Would you like me to draw you a hot bath, dear?"

Eva looked up at Mrs. Martindale with a dazed expression on her face. Mrs. Martindale stood there expectantly, waiting for an answer.

"Oh, well, I suppose," Eva said, removing her hands from her face. She glanced down at the bed, noticed that there were spots of blood on the linens, and rapidly moved the bedsheets around, looking at the blood-stained mess. Eva didn't understand, she wasn't menstruating. It suddenly dawned on her that the blood must be a product of her intimacy with Lucious. Her heart sank and she was utterly mortified by what she saw. It must have shown on her face because Mrs. Martindale spoke again.

"Oh, and don't worry about the bed linens, dear, I'll get the blood out," she said with a wave of her hand, as if it was no problem at all.

Eva looked up at Mrs. Martindale, a horrified look on her face and her mouth gaping open, but the older woman was already heading to the ensuite to draw Eva's bath.

Eva could hear Mrs. Martindale turn on the bathwater and rummage through some items in the ensuite while talking to herself the entire time. Eva pressed her hand against her head; she still couldn't think straight. Looking down at her hands, she saw that they were trembling profusely. She felt terribly anxious and was beginning to have chills. Mrs. Martindale walked back into the bedroom.

"I laid out everything you'll need for your bath, dear. There's soap, washcloth, towel, and comb...oh, and a brush. There are also other toiletry items that you might want in the drawers." Wobbling over to the wardrobe, Mrs. Martindale opened the door. "In the back here, behind Master Lucious' suits, there are plenty of dresses for you to choose from. I'm sure you'll find something in your size." Turning sharply, she headed across the room.

"Here, in the chest of drawers, you'll find undergarments and unmentionables; that sort of thing," Mrs. Martindale continued, giving another wave of her hand. She hurried back into the ensuite, shut off the running water, then quickly wobbled out and headed toward the bedroom door.

"I turned on the geyser to heat the water for you." Standing at the bedroom door, she glanced around the room one last time and sighed, "Well, I think that's all. If you need anything, just ring the bell." Giving a closed mouth grin, she exited the room just as quickly as she had entered it.

Eva sat there for a minute, rethinking everything Mrs. Martindale had said to her. Then, she tried to move her body and sluggishly placed her feet on the floor. Eva desperately wanted this horrible feeling to go away. Her entire body was beginning to tremor forcefully and she felt nauseated.

Suddenly, Miss Martindale opened the door again, popping her head back inside the room. Eva jumped and gasped, grabbing at her chest.

"Oh, I almost forgot, Master Lucious says to make sure that you drink some of that juice. Oh, and..."—she finally slowed her speech down a bit and gave Eva a soft smile—"he also says to tell you that he loves you. You must be a special one, indeed." With another goofy grin for Eva, she raised her eyebrows and quickly closed the door behind her.

The juice, Eva thought, *that must be what is making me feel this way.* She lifted her hand, which was shaking uncontrollably, and reached toward the glass that lay next to her on the nightstand. Drinking just a few sips of the juice, Eva began feeling better. Lucious was right; she was getting more used to its flavor. Eva's body began to relax, the chills left her, and calm and relief washed over her body.

Eva lay back down on the bed, allowing her head to clear. As she rested, she became fully aware of the void she felt in her heart. Looking over to where Lucious had lain, she placed her hand across the bed and realized that she wanted to be near him. A part of Eva felt like it was missing without Lucious being present. She wondered…was this love? This feeling was different than the way she felt about Georgie. Sure, she loved Georgie and would miss him when he was in Oxfordshire, but her life would go on even when she was a bit depressed without him. With Lucious, on the other hand, the feeling was something that Eva had never felt before. She was empty without Lucious near her and all she wanted was for him to hold her in his arms—but he wasn't there. What was it that Claudia had said? That Lucious is good at disappearing. Why didn't he say goodbye this morning? Eva only knew that she now had a newfound longing in her soul for Lucious and the feeling frightened her.

Taking in a deep breath, she decided that she should bathe before the water had completely cooled. She slipped carefully into the warm tub, which helped sooth the discomforts of her body. She washed with the soap that Mrs. Martindale had laid out for her and began recalling everything that Lucious said last evening. Eva thought of how her mum must be worried sick because she had not returned home last night. She missed her mum something terrible and was regretting the argument that they had yesterday. Oh, how she wished that she could turn back time. She began sobbing and her tears dripped down from her cheeks and chin to merge with the bathwater below.

Eva removed herself from the tub, drying off with a towel. She tied the robe tightly around her body and gazed into the mirror, thinking how everything had changed since the same time yesterday. She was truly a woman now and there was no going back. Eva sank onto the floor and began crying once again. The tears didn't stop falling until she started to feel sick to her stomach.

She looked down and noticed that the trembling had begun again and that the cold sweats were returning. She quickly ran over to the nightstand, grabbing the juice glass. She tipped the glass upside down—but the juice was all gone. Lucious must have more in here somewhere, she thought, as she hurried over to the bar in the bedroom. Bending down, she began rifling through various liqueurs. After picking up and examining several different bottles, she found that none of them contained Mr. Paddimir's juice. She let out a loud sigh of frustration, then grabbed her face in despair and began sobbing loudly again. She wanted it so badly, she figured that she must be addicted to the juice—her mother had been right about that as well. Eva was crying and shivering uncontrollably. Wiping her eyes with her hands, she looked up and noticed a silver flask sitting on top of the bar. She closed her eyes, breathing deeply, hoping that the vial contained some of the juice.

Eva did her best to open the flask since her hands were shaking wildly. She inhaled the contents of the container and exhaled a sigh of relief—it was definitely the juice. She drank a hefty swig of the pungent liquid and then another one, until she could feel her nerves calming. She was relieved as she felt her body relax and her heart rate slow down. She shook her head. *How am I going to live this way?* she wondered to herself.

After she sat on the floor for a while, Eva decided to try and find the strength to stand, although she was still somewhat dizzy from the juice. She made her way to the wardrobe, looking at what items were available for her to wear. She thought it was odd that Lucious would have women's clothing in his closet but assumed that they belonged to family members.

She opened the wardrobe and found Lucious' exquisite, tailor-made suits hanging in the first row. Eva grazed her fingers along their luxurious fabric and held one of the sleeves up, bringing it close to her face and breathing in its scent. She could smell Lucious on the garments, which brought comfort to her. She was missing him hopelessly and wondered how she could miss someone so much after only knowing him for a few days.

Eva sighed and decided to try and find a dress that would fit her. There were several dresses of different colors and elaborately fashioned styles in the wardrobe. She hoped to find one that fit her as perfectly as the blue dress that Lucious had purchased. Glancing down at the racks below, Eva spotted an assortment of beautifully adorned boots and pumps. Picking up a white leather boot, she noticed it was her size and that it looked as if it had never been worn. Thinking that was odd, she reached up, taking hold of one of the dresses and noticed that the dress was her size as well. In that moment, Eva realized that all the dresses and shoes were made to fit her.

"How on earth did Lucious know my dress and shoe sizes?" she asked aloud and resolved to ask him about the clothing at some point.

Eva decided on a lovely chartreuse green day dress that settled off the shoulders. The sleeves were tight and short, but Eva felt it would be suitable for wearing inside the house without a scarf. She turned to lay the dress out on the bed but hesitated as she remembered the soiled linens. Looking at the bed, Eva was confused—the linens were now fresh and clean. Realizing that Mrs. Martindale must have come in and changed them while she was in the bath, Eva's cheeks turned red and she felt embarrassed remembering the blood-stained sheets.

Walking over to the chest of drawers, she opened the top one and began searching through the undergarments. Eva found a diverse number of unmentionables, some in styles she had never seen before. There were many corsets, some of which were made of satin, with lace trimmings and looking highly provocative. Eva chose a simple white corset and bloomers and began dressing, but realized that the corset was rather difficult to tighten on her own. She thought about it for a moment, then decided to summon Mrs. Martindale for help. She inhaled deeply and tugged hard on the rope. After a moment, she heard Mrs. Martindale tromping up the staircase. Eva paused, prepared for the older lady's bold entrance this time. Mrs. Martindale knocked twice on the door before barging in.

"What can I do you for, Miss Eva?" she asked and curtsied.

Eva looked over at her, wide-eyed.

"I was wondering if you would help tighten my corset?" Eva asked shyly.

"Well, of course, Miss." Mrs. Martindale started bustling across the room, when she stopped, staring at Eva. She had a surprised look on her face and asked, "Is that what you plan on wearing under your dress, Miss?"

Eva looked down nervously at herself, wondering what was wrong with the undergarments she had picked out.

"Wouldn't you like something a little more...*séduisant?*" Mrs. Martindale suggested.

Both women paused for a moment and Eva scratched her head.

"Well, is there something else you have in mind?" Eva asked in a slightly testy tone.

Excitedly, Mrs. Martindale hobbled over to the chest of drawers quickly. Rifling through the undergarments, she pulled out a red satin full-bodied corset, adorned with black lace edging.

"Well, if I looked like you and were dressing for Master Lucious I would pick something a bit more like this."

Mrs. Martindale proceeded to hold the corset up to her chest and began looking down at herself. Eva's eyes widened as she quickly bit her lip, trying not to laugh out loud. The corset was nearly three times smaller than Mrs. Martindale. Eva watched as she continued holding up the seductive corset next to her plump figure. Looking down at herself, the old woman was grinning from ear to ear and nodding her head, looking quite pleased with herself.

"Ah, yes, that looks very..." Eva's words trailed off. She just stood there staring at Mrs. Martindale, biting her lip so hard and doing her best to refrain from laughing.

"Alright then, time to choose. What's it going to be?" Mrs. Martindale asked, still holding up the corset.

Eva rubbed her chin, pretending that she was contemplating which one to choose.

"I'm definitely going to have to go with the red corset with black lace," she replied, nodding her head assuredly.

"You can't go wrong with it, Miss. You just can't go wrong," responded Mrs. Martindale in agreement. "Well, let's get you dressed then," she continued, releasing a sigh.

Eva quickly changed from the plain corset into the seductive one Mrs. Martindale suggested. She held tightly onto the bed pole while Mrs. Martindale gave the corset strings a good tug, eliciting a cough from Eva.

"You alright, dear?" Mrs. Martindale asked.

"Yes," Eva replied, squeezing her eyes closed while trying to breathe deeply.

Mrs. Martindale pulled the strings even tighter.

"Uh, I can barely breath," Eva squeaked while sucking in small gasps of air.

"It's good then!" Mrs. Martindale piped up, nodding her head as she tied the corset in place. She stood back, taking a good look at Eva. "Hmmm...you look so thin," she said with a distasteful look on her face.

Eva stared down at herself in a concerned manner, sliding her hands from the top of her waist down to her hips.

"Is this how it's supposed to go?" Eva asked.

"Hold on," Mrs. Martindale replied.

Walking back over to Eva, she stuck her hands down the top of the corset, pulling Eva's bosoms up. Eva let out a shocked gasp and her jaw dropped as she looked at Mrs. Martindale in great surprise.

"There, that's better," Mrs. Martindale affirmed with a smile, nodding her head. "You've got to prop them up a bit, dear," she spoke while motioning with her hands.

Eva looked at her, appalled.

Mrs. Martindale then placed the chartreuse green dress over Eva's head and Eva stretched her arms through the armholes of the dress. Mrs. Martindale buttoned up the back of the dress while Eva stood, gazing at her reflection in the full-length mirror and moving the dress from side to side.

"That's a beautiful dress, Miss Eva, excellent choice, indeed," Mrs. Martindale approved. "Let me know if you want help with your hair, Miss," she added with a bright smile.

Eva turned around quickly.

"Umm, yes, that would be wonderful," she replied, smiling back.

Mrs. Martidale was beginning to grow on Eva. She wasn't sure how she had felt about her earlier in the morning, barging into the bedroom unannounced—but now, after getting to know her better, she reminded Eva of a blend between Gladys, Alice, and her mum. She felt comforted by having Miss Martindale in the house, giving her a helping hand. She didn't know that living with Lucious included a lady's maid, although Lucious did promise her that she would live like the nobility.

Mrs. Martindale placed final touches on Eva's hair.

"There you go now, Miss. I say, you just might be the loveliest lady in all of London. I can see now why you caught Master Lucious' eye." Mrs. Martindale gave her a wink and made a clicking noise by sucking her tongue against the roof of her mouth.

Eva smiled politely, "Thank you, Mrs. Martindale, for everything." She genuinely appreciated the older woman's help.

"You're very welcome, Miss." Mrs. Martindale gave Eva a nod and a slight curtsy, then headed toward the bedroom door.

"Oh, Mrs. Martindale!" Eva called out.

"Yes, Miss?" she turned around and asked.

"If I may ask, what is your Christian name?" Eva inquired.

"My name is Bertha, but Master Lucious doesn't like me to use my Christian name around the house." She shook her head with a distasteful look on her face.

"Oh, I see," replied Eva. "Well, Mrs. Martindale it is then," Eva agreed.

"Yes, Miss," the woman replied with a nod, then left the bedroom closing the door behind her. Eva understood why Lucious didn't want to use Mrs. Martindale's Christian name; she couldn't imagine Lucious calling any woman Bertha. She looked down at the ground and let out a good laugh.

*　*　*

The morning had started out roughly for Eva but, by the end of the day, she was feeling somewhat satisfied. She was beginning to imagine herself living in the terraced house with Lucious, picturing them both dressed up in their fashionable wardrobes, going out to exquisite restaurants and extravagant parties. There was only one thing causing Eva to feel sorrowful and that was the fact that she missed her mother. She would have to try to talk Lucious into allowing her to send her mother a letter, at the very least, letting her know that she was all right. Eva wanted her mother to see that she was doing fine but, looking down at the flask, she had to ask herself whether that was actually true. Eva unscrewed the cap off the wretched juice flask and took another large sip. She was doing her best to make sure that she avoided feeling foul. When Eva drank the juice, it was easier for her to feel normal again but, at the same time, it also desensitized her to the things that happened around her.

Eva walked over to the large bedroom window and gazed out into the dreary London day. Mrs. Martindale barged through the bedroom door.

"I just came to fetch your breakfast tray," she said as she headed across the bedroom. Mrs. Martindale stopped and stared at the tray. "Why, you haven't even touched your breakfast and it's nearly dinner time, dear," she said, hobbling over to the table and picking up the tray.

Eva ignored her comment.

"Do you think Lucious will be home soon?" she asked in a yearning tone.

"Ah, well, it's hard to say when Master Lucious will come through the front door, but it could be any time now." Mrs. Martindale felt a bit sorry for Eva. "Why don't you come downstairs, Miss, and wait for him there. You've been cooped up in this bedroom all day."

Eva agreed and followed Mrs. Martindale down the stairwell. They entered the sitting area and Eva noticed that Mrs. Martindale was setting out the china for dinner.

"Would you like me to help you?" Eva inquired and motioned her hand toward the china on the tables.

"Oh, no dear, you're a woman of leisure now. Why don't you go sit in the chair by the fire and have a cup of tea," Miss Martindale suggested.

Eva didn't want to sit down and have a cup of tea; she wanted Lucious by her side. Just then, Eva heard the front door swing open wide. Rushing over, she was pleased to see Lucious tapping the rainwater out of his umbrella in the doorway.

"Lucious!" Eva exclaimed excitedly.

Running over to him, she wrapped her arms around his neck and then, grabbing his face, she firmly pressed her lips against his. She pulled away slowly, looking up at him and beaming from ear to ear. Lucious looked down at Eva, smiling, then glanced out the front door.

"Say, Eva, you might want to close the door before showing so much affection, who knows what people might think?" he teased, giving her a wink and one of his devilish grins.

"Oh, stop it, you!" Eva tapped his chest. Releasing him from her grasp, she turned to close the front door.

"Well, hello, Miss Martindale," said Lucious loudly as he leaned his umbrella against the wall.

"Master Lucious," she replied from across the room with a nod and slight curtsy.

Lucious hung his top hat and wet overcoat on the rack, then turned to Eva and wrapped his arms around her waist, kissing her intensely. Eva delightfully returned the kisses.

"I say this is the best welcome home I think I've ever received," he spoke loud enough for both women to hear while his arms remained around Eva's waist.

"Mrs. Martindale, why is it that you've never welcomed me home this warmly?" he said teasingly.

Mrs. Martindale blushed, giving him a bashful smile and a wave of her hand. Eva let out a giggle and Lucious took her hand, walking over to the table with her.

"Dinner smells delicious," he stated emphatically as he pulled out a chair for Eva and helped her scoot in closer to the table. Then he sat down beside her.

Mrs. Martindale brought the newspaper over to Lucious.

"Your paper, sir," she said with a curtsy.

"Thank you kindly," Lucious responded with a smile.

He unfolded and fanned out the newspaper. Eva sat at the table, moving around in an unsettled manner, and Lucious glanced over at her.

"Is there something wrong, love?" he asked, somewhat annoyed.

"Oh, no, there's nothing wrong," she replied.

Lucious nodded his head in agreement but continued watching Eva out of the corner of his eye as he turned the pages of the paper. Eva kept twitching and moving about while sitting in the chair. Lucious stopped and looked over at her once more.

"Then stop fidgeting already."

Eva sat straight up and did her best to stop moving. She rolled her eyes, leaning over toward Lucious.

"It's this blasted corset; it's itchy," she whispered, as she wrinkled her nose and scratched at her chest.

Lucious gave Eva a sly smirk.

"Which one are you wearing today, love?" he inquired, turning the pages of the paper.

"The red one with the black lace," Eva whispered.

"Mmmm...I can't wait to see it later," he said, with a naughty grin, placing his hand on Eva's.

Eva gave him a coy smirk.

"Oh, and I have a story to tell you that goes along with the corset," she whispered excitedly, "it's most funny." She glanced over at Miss Martindale.

Lucious smiled back, squinting his eyes at Eva, "What exactly did you do all day?" he inquired.

Eva smiled, looking down at her plate and adjusting her napkin.

"Wouldn't you like to know," she flirted, glancing back up at Lucious.

Lucious stared at Eva with a slightly confused smile on his face, as if he were trying to figure her out. He continued flipping through the paper but then decided to set it down, pulling a flask out of his coat pocket. Opening it, he offered Eva a drink. She looked at the container. She didn't want a sip of the juice but she needed it. Taking the flask from Lucious' hand, she took two quick swigs of the liquid and then handed the bottle back to him. He also drank some of the juice, after which he placed the flask back in his jacket pocket.

Mrs. Martindale walked over. She carried a large pot and set it down on the table. The pot contained roast beef with potatoes and carrots. Walking back to the kitchen, she then carried in a basket of homemade biscuits with butter and a tea tray. Finally, she set a bottle of Bordeaux on the table.

"Beautiful choice, Mrs. Martindale," Lucious said happily.

The juice certainly did not interfere with Lucious appetite—he forked a large helping of the roast onto his plate, then filled the rest of it with potatoes and carrots. Eva was starving; she hadn't eaten all day. Now that Lucious was finally home, her appetite had returned. She didn't want to make a pig of herself, so she took a small portion of the roast, then spooned a few potatoes and carrots onto her plate. Picking up a biscuit, she placed a generous amount of butter on top, while Mrs. Martindale poured some wine into their glasses.

"I hope the breakfast I sent up to you this morning was alright?" Lucious asked, looking over at Eva.

Eva's body stiffened.

"It was very thoughtful of you," she responded politely.

Mrs. Martindale interjected.

"She didn't touch her breakfast, nor her lunch either. This is the first time she's eaten all day."

Eva felt like Mrs. Martindale was tattling on her. She gazed down at her plate, blushing. Lucious gently took hold of Eva's chin, bringing her face up to look into his eyes.

"Eva, you must eat love, you need to keep up your energy," Lucious spoke in a concerned tone, then gently released Eva's chin from his grasp.

"Oh I will, I just wasn't very hungry today is all. We had such a heavy meal last evening," Eva replied, trying to sound convincing.

Lucious nodded his head in agreement. Mrs. Martindale was standing in the kitchen, rolling some dough and Eva looked over at her, frowning. Mrs. Martindale saw Eva's face and quickly put her head down as she continued working.

When they finished eating, Lucious took Eva by the hand and strolled over to the small sofa in the sitting room. They sat down on the couch and he gave her a coquettish grin, as if he were expecting something from her. Sighing, he picked Eva's legs up and placed them over his lap, causing Eva to lay back onto the sofa pillows. She readjusted herself, placing her hands across her waist. Lucious grabbed her right hand, intertwining their fingers with one another.

"Ah, that's better. Now, tell me all about your day," Lucious inquired.

"Well, there's not much to tell really. I woke up just as Mrs. Martindale barged into the bedroom door this morning," Eva said, slightly irritated, rolling her eyes.

Lucious let out a brief laugh. "Go on love," he urged, intrigued.

"I took a bath, then decided to find a dress in the wardrobe and found this beautiful green gown," Eva said, looking down at her dress smiling.

"I say it's quite lovely on you and brings out those dashing green eyes of yours."

Lucious grazed Eva's forehead with his finger, sending tingles down her spine. She wanted to ask Lucious how he knew her dress and shoe sizes but refrained from doing so; she didn't want to dampen the mood.

Eva sat up on the sofa a bit. "Lucious, I have something I want to ask you." She gazed down at their hands hesitantly, moving her fingers through Lucious'.

"What is it, love?" he asked. Eva was nervous and her hands were slighting shaking. "I..."

Lucious gently lifted Eva's chin, forcing her to look him in the eyes once again.

Inhaling a deep breath, she asked, "I was wondering if you would allow me to go home, just one last time, to say goodbye to my mum?" She looked sadly at Lucious.

He sat up straight, clearing his throat. "Oh Eva, I wish I could, but I'm afraid there's just no way that would be possible," he responded, after a moment's pause. "See, I'm certain your mother would not approve of us."

Lucious looked at Eva sympathetically. Tears began welling up in her eyes. She pressed them together tightly, causing the tears to roll down her cheeks. Lucious leaned in, wiping the tears away from her face.

"Do you think she would approve of us?" he asked, pretending to be sincere.

Eva shook her head no.

"No, I didn't think so," he continued, raising the intensity of his voice. "She will force you to stay away from me, Eva, and she will never allow you to see me ever again! Is that what you want? You want to never see me again? What about our promise to one another?" Lucious gazed down at the ruby ring he had given her and gently grazed it with his finger.

Eva also looked down at the ring and, after a moment, she nodded her head in agreement. "You're right, I can't go back to see her—but, could I perhaps write?" Eva looked up at him, hopeful.

Lucious inhaled a deep breath and let it out. This showed his evident agitation with her but, realizing she wasn't going to relent, he agreed.

"Alright, alright, you may write to your mother and let her know that you are safe—but you may not tell her your location. I don't need her coming to find you and take you away from me." As he spoke, Lucious looked deeply into Eva's eyes and kissed her hand.

"Thank you, thank you, thank you!" she exclaimed, ecstatically grabbing his face and kissing it all over.

Changing the subject, Lucious asked with intrigue, "So, what's this now about your corset?"

Eva giggled, leaning closer into Lucious. She spoke in a whisper, "Well, I picked out a simple corset to wear and rang for Mrs. Martindale to come help lace it up for me. When she walked into the room, she saw the plain corset and asked: 'Is that what you plan on wearing under your dress, Miss?'" Eva imitated, making her voice sound high pitched and dramatic like Mrs. Martindale's. "I asked if there was something else she had in mind and she said: 'If I looked like you and was dressing for Master Lucious, this is what I would wear.' Then she pulled out the red satin corset with the black lace edging."

Eva hit Lucious on the chest with the back of her hand as she laughed silently. She gave him an overly dramatic, seductive look and pointed over to Mrs. Martindale. Lucious' eyes grew huge as he glanced at the older woman with a frightened look on his face then, gazing back at Eva, he let out a quiet laugh.

"That's not all," Eva continued to speak, "she proceeded to hold the corset up to her body and it was nearly three times too small. It looked absolutely ridiculous." They both let out peals of laughter, causing Mrs. Martindale to inquire, loudly, from the kitchen.

"What are you two snickering about over there?"

Eva looked at Lucious as she pressed her lips tightly together, trying not to make a sound. Lucious put his index finger up to his mouth, motioning for her to be quiet while smiling at the same time.

"We best go upstairs," he suggested and Eva nodded her head in agreement.

Lucious picked Eva up from the sofa and they headed upstairs. While they were leaving the room, Mrs. Martindale gave them both a distasteful look and continued kneading the dough. Lucious carried Eva up the stairs and entered the threshold of the bedroom, closing the door behind them with his foot. He laid Eva down on the bed.

"Stay right there," he softly commanded. Removing his jacket, he hung it on the hook attached to the bedroom door. Walking over to the bed, he straddled Eva, gazing down at her wantonly. Lucious gently wiped her hair away from her face and began kissing her passionately. He slid his hand up under her dress, but Eva gently pushed him away.

"What's wrong, love?" he asked with a puzzled look on his face.

"Lucious," Eva said, removing herself from under him and sitting herself up on the bed. She brushed out her dress with her hands and Lucious sat up as well.

"What is it, Eva?" he asked, looking perplexed.

"I know what you want from me. I want to be with you as well, but I'm not sure my body can handle that sort of thing right now, after last night."

Lucious lifted his chin and brought it back down.

"Ah, I see," he murmured as he began rubbing his chin, obviously contemplating something. "Well, there are ways for us to enjoy one another without being fully intimate," he suggested, a seductive smile spreading across his face. Eva gazed at him, confused. Lucious patted her hand, realizing she had no idea what he was referring to. "No worries love, I will teach you everything you need to know."

Ten

Georgie shouted as he shot up in bed, abruptly awoken by another terrible nightmare. Inhaling deeply, he tried to catch his breath as he rubbed his forehead. Beads of sweat were running down his face and the bed linens were completely soaked. This night was the third night in a row that Georgie had the same, horrifying dream—Eva, helpless and lost in the woods, crying out his name in need of help. He saw himself searching for her, wandering aimlessly through the thick, black forest, when, suddenly, a blood-curdling scream resounded. The dream would then switch to Eva, who was being ferociously attacked by several carnivorous beasts—a lion, a bear, and a pack of wolves—but he was unable to find her. He would wake up calling out her name. Georgie knew something was dreadfully wrong. He could feel it, deeply, in the pit of his stomach. Walking over to the water basin, he splashed some cool water on his face, drying it off with a towel. He decided, then and there, that he must go back to London to make sure that Eva was all right.

Georgie had written to Eva several times since he moved, explaining how much he loved her, but she had not written to him in return. He firmly believed that she felt the same way about him, even though Alice had sent letters saying that Eva was still distraught with him for leaving London. On several occasions, he had contemplated going back, taking Eva into his arms, and making his intentions known to her. He wanted to be with her so much it hurt, but he was trying to do the right thing and not give in to lust and temptation.

Georgie dressed himself, then walked out to the horse barn even though it was still the middle of the night. He had to finish all his duties before catching the morning train. Georgie fed the horses, allowing them to eat while he cleaned their saddles, bridles, stirrups, and bit harnesses. After the horses finished eating, he let them out to pasture to roam while he raked out the dung and then swept and washed every stall. Bringing the horses back in, he checked all their hooves, making sure no foreign materials affected their footing. Next, he brushed their coats using a curry comb and then a whale brush, making their coats shine. He cleaned their ears, eyes, and noses with a moist sponge and applied oil to their hooves and tails. Georgie usually performed these tasks twice a day, along with conducting the training of the horses and cleaning any carriages that might be filthy. Once he finished his duties for the morning, he set out to find his father and let him know that he was going back to London to check on Eva.

The sun began rising over the tree line, creating a beautiful array of colors that washed over the morning sky. Georgie walked through the open fields breathing in the fresh country air. Oh, how he loved it out here—but he loved Eva more. He wanted Eva to marry him and to build a life together with her at the farm in Oxfordshire. He could envision the two of them walking through the countryside, laughing, and holding hands.

Georgie headed toward the barn in which the farm equipment was kept when he spotted his father lying on the ground underneath the thresher.

"Hello, Pop!" Georgie called out while he was still a little ways off.

Mr. Thornber looked over at Georgie, pulling himself out from under the thresher. He stood up, wiping his hands with a cloth.

"Well, hi there, George!" Mr. Thornber yelled back. "What can I do ya for, son?"

Georgie inhaled deeply, wiping his brow with a handkerchief.

"I had another nightmare about Eva," he said, looking concerned.

"So, you are going back to London, then?" his father asked.

"I've got to," Georgie shook his head. "Somethings not right, I can feel it." Georgie pointed to his gut with his thumb.

His father nodded his head, "You gotta do what you gotta do. You need to be at peace."

"I need someone to cover for me while I'm gone," Georgie stated, searching for suggestions.

"Well, Mr. Hammond's been looking for some extra work. I'll see if he'll fill in for ya. Either way, don't worry about it, just go make sure Eva's doing fine," Mr. Thornber assured him.

"Thanks, Pop," Georgie nodded, turning and walking back toward the cottage.

"Hey, George!" Mr. Thornber called out.

Georgie turned back around.

"I sure hope everything is alright with Eva!" he said with a sympathetic look.

"Me too, Pop!" Georgie yelled back, then headed toward the main house to get cleaned up and catch the morning train.

* * *

Georgie stepped off the train and the foul stench of London immediately attacked his nostrils. He shook his head from side to side and a distasteful look appeared on his face as he gazed around, taking in the city atmosphere. He began making his way toward the lodging house but decided to stop by Covent Garden first to see whether Eva was there. Walking through the market, he couldn't see Eva or Margie anywhere. He visited all the places they would typically be but did not find them. Finally, he spotted Margie's friend Ruby.

Georgie walked over to the flower women.

"Hello ladies, I'm George Thornber," he said, placing his hand upon his chest. He removed his hat as he spoke politely to the ladies. "I'm looking for Eva or Miss Margie Alderson."

Clara squeezed herself tightly between Georgie and Ruby, pushing Ruby out of the way. Ruby made a sucking sound and looked at Clara abhorrently, then glanced over at Gladys. Georgie backed away from Clara.

"Do you mind, Clara?" Ruby asked, annoyed.

"Well, hello there, George," said Clara in her high pitched, nasally voice.

"Hello," he said kindly with a nod, but he was put off by Clara's forwardness.

"We're not sure where Eva is—" Clara replied gazing at him wantonly.

"Or Margie, for that matter," Gladys interjected, looking miffed with Clara.

Georgie had both a concerned and curious look on his face.

"They haven't been around all day?" he questioned.

"Not for days, actually," Gladys replied, shaking her head.

The flower women began looking at one another, wondering how much they should say. Ruby moved closer to Georgie so that no one in their vicinity could hear her except for Georgie and the other flower women.

"Truth is George, Eva went missing about three days ago. Margie's been in a state, out looking for her everywhere since then," Ruby confided, shaking her head with a grievous look on her face.

Georgie turned white as a sheet and feelings of panic and dread began to rise inside him. Inhaling a deep breath, he cleared his throat, rubbing his hand through his hair. He was trying to remain calm and speak evenly as he continued asking them questions.

"What do you mean, Eva's been missing for three days? Miss Marge doesn't have any idea where she might be or who she might be with?" Georgie asked, extremely concerned.

The flower women began looking back and forth at one another with troublesome expressions upon their faces. Georgie could tell that they knew something from their reaction, but that they didn't want to say it.

"Look, ladies, if you know anything, you've got to tell me," Georgie said firmly, waiting for a response.

Gladys finally spoke up, "Margie said that Eva had told her she was courting with a fellow named Luke."

Georgie closed his eyes as he felt a pang hit his gut, but he continued listening to what Gladys had to say very carefully.

"The following day, Eva received several expensive gifts from this so-called Luke fellow and, of course, Marg was concerned and demanded to know where the gifts came from. Well, Eva let it slip that she was actually seeing Lucious Paddimir. She left that evening, going with him to Rêves for dinner—and no one's seen her since." Gladys shook her head as tears filled her eyes. "I'm just so sick over it. She could be anywhere," she added, becoming choked up and placing her hand over her mouth.

"Pull yourself together, Gladys," said Ruby, gently elbowing Gladys in the side. "Look, you've got to help her, George. You gots to find her. You're Eva's best friend, she'll listen to you," pleaded Ruby.

Georgie felt like the wind was knocked out of him. He didn't know how nor even where to begin, but he was going to find Eva at all costs.

"Thank you, ladies," he replied, nodding, then turned sharply, slung his bag over his shoulder, and began running through the crowded market place.

Georgie ran all the way to the lodging house, entering through the front door. He threw his bag on the foyer floor and continued up the stairs to see whether Miss Marge—or possibly Eva—was at home.

"Miss Marge, are you in there? Eva... Margie...?" he shouted, beating on the door. There was no answer. He hurried back down the stairs, heading toward his grandmother Alice's lodging room. He began beating on her door, calling out.

"Grams! It's Georgie!" He could hear Alice's muffled voice through the door.

"George, is that you?" she asked as the door swung open.

"Grams," he said, giving her a great big hug and sounding somewhat relieved.

"Oh, George, thank heavens you are here. Things are terribly wrong, son, so terribly wrong," Alice sounded most disturbed.

"I know Grams, I stopped at Covent Garden to see whether Eva was there and Margie's friends told me that she's gone missing."

Georgie entered the small lodging room and began pacing back and forth while rubbing his hands through his hair.

"I don't know what to do. I've got to find her—but how?" Georgie sounded a bit frantic as he continued pacing the room.

"I just wrote to you yesterday, telling you what happened. Margie was so upset, Georgie. She said she went to Scotland Yard and they did nothing for her." Alice shook her head. "They said they would let her know if someone fitting Eva's description turned up," Alice choked, as tears filled her eyes. "Georgie, I'm afraid of what could happen to her. This Lucious Paddimir is a bad fellow, the worst kind." Alice sat down in the chair, shaking her head.

Georgie crouched down, on his knees, in front of Alice's chair. He picked up both of her hands and looked her in the eyes.

"I'm gonna find her Grams. I'm gonna find Eva and bring her home," he stated, fully convinced.

Alice patted Georgie on the hand. "I sure hope so, son, I really do," she replied as tears filled her eyes.

Georgie stood up at once and began pacing back and forth while thinking out loud.

"I need to find out more about this Lucious Paddimir," he said.

Alice perked up. "Perhaps you can go to Magistrate Logan, he might have some information about this fellow," she suggested.

"That's a great idea, Grams," Georgie said, looking at Alice with hope in his eyes. "He's in town right now, too, and I have favor with him. I believe that if he knows anything, he'll tell me," Georgie said, nodding his head, relieved to have somewhat of a plan. "I'll be back with Eva, Grams," he promised, bending down and kissing his grandmother on the cheek.

He went to stand up but Alice firmly grabbed his arm. Georgie knelt back down in front of her chair.

"Now, you listen to me, George, you have to make sure of something."

Georgie nodded his head, listening intently to what his grandmother had to say.

"You have to decide right now whether you can love Eva despite where she's been, what she's done, and who she's been with—or even how she treats you when you find her. Decide now that, if you go after her and are able to bring her home, you won't hold any of it against her but will love her unconditionally to the end. Can you do that?" Alice asked, looking Georgie directly in the eyes.

He knew what Alice was saying and what she was suggesting. He didn't know much about Lucious Paddimir, but he had a pretty good idea of what he wanted from Eva. His heart ached as he stared back at Alice.

"I love Eva with every morsel of my being and I will love her until the day I die. So, no matter what she's done, where she's been, who she's been with, or how she treats me when I find her, I will love her forever, Grams." Georgie paused. "So, the answer is yes. Yes, I can do that," he replied in agreement with a look of complete unconditional love and sincerity in his heart.

Alice knew he meant what he said.

"Good. Now, go out there, find Eva, and bring her home," she said, confidently. "Oh, and George, be careful," Alice continued, looking at him worriedly.

"I will, Grams," he replied, gave her one his bright smiles, and another kiss on the cheek, then headed out the front door.

* * *

Georgie arrived at the magistrate's office and hurried up to the clerk sitting at the front desk.

"I'm looking for Magistrate Logan?"

The clerk pointed to the front door through which Georgie had just entered. He looked in that direction and saw the magistrate walking with a group of men on the walkway.

"Thank you," Georgie replied with a smile and a nod. He ran out the front door, catching up with the magistrate.

"Magistrate Logan!" he called out, removing his hat from his head.

The magistrate stopped and turned around, looking to see who called out his name.

"George? I thought you were in Oxfordshire, at the farm?" He was surprised to see him in London.

"Yes, sir, I was, but I have a friend who's gone missing and I thought you might be able to help," Georgie said, breathing heavily and trying to catch his breath.

"Oh, I'm very sorry to hear that. What is it that I can do for you?" the magistrate inquired.

"Well, I need some information about a man named Lucious Paddimir."

The magistrate's eyes grew large and he motioned the other men to continue walking without him. He waited for them to walk some distance ahead before answering Georgie.

"What is it, exactly, that you wanting to know about Lucious Paddimir?" asked the magistrate most inquisitively. "You think he might have your friend?"

"Yes, sir, I think that he might," Georgie replied with a nod.

The magistrate paused for a moment, contemplating his next words, "What does your friend look like, George?"

Georgie's heart raced as he began thinking of Eva.

"Well, she's tall, blonde, beautiful, with green eyes," Georgie replied, a twinge pulling at his heart, thinking of how he might never see her again.

"I see," the magistrate responded, shaking his head. He did remember a girl fitting Eva's description attending Lucious' party a few nights back. Magistrate Logan didn't want to give Georgie too much information about Liberation Hall, since he was ashamed to have partaken in some of the activities there himself.

"Well, the only thing I can tell you about Lucious Paddimir is that he has a home outside the city, called Liberation Hall.

It takes over an hour to get there by carriage. But that is all I know."

"Thank you so much, sir," Georgie replied with a look of gratitude and a nod.

"You're welcome. Oh, and George," the magistrate added.

"Yes, sir?"

"Lucious is a mighty and persuasive man. He has many allies everywhere, so please be careful," Magistrate Logan emphasized his words and gave Georgie a solemn stare.

Georgie nodded his head, swallowing hard, then turned and went his way.

Eleven

The sun was peeking through a gap between the dark velour curtains, causing a ray of light to shine down onto Eva's face. Stirring in the bed, she covered her eyes with her hands, trying to keep the sunlight at bay. Suddenly, a feeling of fear gripped her and she frantically reached across the bed, worried that Lucious might not be there again. Reaching over, she felt his bare chest exposed above the covers. Letting out a sigh of relief, she scooted nearer, curling up next to Lucious and resting her head against his chest. She could hear the rhythm of her lover's heart beating. Closing her eyes, she inhaled a deep breath, cherishing the moment while she listened to his heart pound within his body. Eva softly rubbed her face against his warm skin, breathing his scent in deeply, which sent pleasant sensations tingling down her body. She wished that this moment could last forever.

Lucious woke as he felt Eva brushing up against him. He let out a soft groan, readjusting his position, and wrapped his arm around her as he watched her nuzzling his chest. She was undeniably beautiful—there was no question about that, Lucious thought to himself.

"Good morning, love," he murmured, smiling down at Eva while caressing her back with his fingertips.

"Good morning," she replied as she climbed up, laying her face down next to his and gazing into his eyes.

"How are you feeling this morning?" Lucious asked, grazing his hand along her side.

Eva had not intended to be intimate with Lucious after her experience the previous night but, as one thing led to another, Eva's body relaxed and allowed her to enjoy being with him.

"I feel absolutely wonderful," she stated, looking at him affectionately.

Lucious smiled widely. "Good, very good. Perhaps we could have an encore this morning, then?" Lucious grabbed Eva's hip and moved her even closer to his body. "But then I really must be getting ready. I have an extremely busy day ahead of me," Lucious added gently, lifting Eva's chin and bringing her mouth to his own.

Eva moved her mouth away from Lucious' and quietly asked, "What exactly are you doing when you're out all day?"

Lucious sighed and explained, "Well, love, I own several business establishments throughout London. So, I make my rounds, visiting each one daily. I deal with employees, clients, problems, and I also check my books to make sure that none of my clerks are stealing from me. That's all really, it's rather dull."

Eva nodded her head, then noticed that her body was beginning to tremble and a cold chill was moving through her. She breathed in deeply.

"I think I need a sip of the juice," she said, then reached over and grabbed the crystal glass containing the famous elixir. Sitting up in the bed, she took two large gulps. The juice felt as if liquid love was spreading and coating her insides. She crawled back over to Lucious and handed him the glass, offering him some juice. Lucious took two full sips as well and, immediately, the feeling of euphoria began flowing through his body. The juice always made him feel invincible, like he could conquer the world. He set the glass down on his nightstand, then forcefully grabbed Eva, leading them to intimate pleasures.

Afterward, Lucious amorously looked up into Eva's eyes. She smiled at him, laying her head upon his chest. He could feel her long, blonde waves softly grazing his skin. He lightly caressed her back while staring up at the ceiling and thinking about how he had created the most exceptional job in the world for himself. Eva looked up at him, lightly touching his chin with her finger to get his attention.

"I love you, Lucious."

Lucious, truthfully, felt nothing of the sort in return but knew that he must play along.

"I love you as well," he replied fondly, but a cringing sensation resided in his gut. They lay there for a while, cuddling in one another's arms, until Lucious patted Eva softly on the hip.

"Unfortunately, I really must be getting ready and going about my day."

Eva frowned as she moved over, allowing Lucious to exit the bed. He put on his robe, then went over to the wardrobe, picked out some clothes, and walked into the ensuite bath. A little later, he came out and walked over to Eva, who was still lying in bed. Sitting down next to her, he leaned over and kissed her.

Releasing her mouth, he spoke tenderly, "I have to go now."

Eva gave Lucious a disappointed pout. She didn't want him to leave—just the thought of him being away for the day made her heart hurt. She nodded, her head knowing that he must go take care of his businesses. Lucious stood up and walked out the door, quietly closing it behind him.

He ran down the stairs quickly, making his way over to the coat rack and picking up his overcoat. Slinging it around his shoulders, he buttoned it up. Lucious then grabbed his golden cane and headed out the front door. The carriage was already waiting for him on the road. Archie came walking around the back side of the carriage.

"Good day, sir," he said, tipping his hat.

"Good day, Archie," Lucious nodded in return.

"Where would you like to go today, sir?" Archie asked stoically.

"I think I will stop by Scotland Yard on the way to Liberation Hall—but be sure to drop me off at the back door. I wouldn't want anyone to see me entering the station," Lucious said assuredly.

"As you wish, sir," Archie replied with a nod as he opened the carriage door.

The carriage arrived at Scotland Yard a little after noon. Archie dropped Lucious off in an alleyway behind the police station, just as he requested. Lucious glanced around before entering through the back door; then, he crept down the corridor until he arrived to Inspector Blake's office. Lucious tapped on the door with his cane.

"Come in," a gruff-voiced man called from behind the door.

Lucious entered the inspector's office. "Good day, Blake."

The inspector stood up immediately.

"Lucious, what on earth are you doing here?" he asked, surprised.

"I just came by to check and see how things are going with Mrs. Alderson?" Lucious inquired.

"Humph, that crazy old bat. She's here day in and day out driving us all mad looking for that daughter of hers," spouted the inspector, extremely frustrated.

"Yes, that's what I was afraid of," Lucious brought his hands up to his mouth in a prayer stance. "I can't have her making an entrance now, bilking up my plans. I have men arriving from abroad for Eva's debut in a couple of weeks and I need you to continue putting her off," he insisted earnestly.

"Well, that depends..." the inspector gave an evil smirk, leaning back in his chair and tapping his fingers together. "It's gonna cost you," he said most seriously.

Lucious gave him a brazen stare, "Ah, yes, I thought as much."

Lucious pulled out a bag of coins from his coat pocket and tossed it across the room toward the inspector without warning. The bag smacked Inspector Blake right in the chest. He looked up at Lucious and glared.

"This will have to do," Lucious said with an indignant expression. "You will no longer receive any more currency from me. If you desire extra payment, you will have to come to the Hall...for Katrina, perhaps?" Lucious suggested with a sly smirk. "I know you fancy her."

The inspector swallowed hard, giving Lucious a sharp look. "Is that all?" he asked, highly annoyed.

Lucious nodded, turned, and opened the door. He glanced up and down the hallway in both directions before exiting, making sure he was not seen.

The carriage pulled up to Liberation Hall later that afternoon. Lucious let himself out of the vehicle, walked up the front steps, and entered the house. Removing his overcoat, he handed it, along with his cane, to one of the manservants standing at the mansion's entrance.

"Master Lucious," the manservant nodded.

"Curtis," Lucious nodded in return.

Lucious turned toward the drawing room just as Claudia was entering the foyer.

"Ah, Dia, you're looking swell, as usual."

Claudia nodded without an expression on her face. Lucious picked up her hand and kissed it gently. Claudia rolled her eyes and her body shuddered in response to his touch.

"Shall we..." Lucious motioned his hand toward the drawing room.

After entering the room, he sat down in a chair, picked up his pipe from the side table, and placed it in his mouth. Claudia walked over to him with a match, lighting his pipe for him. She shook the match and put it in the ashtray on the table, then sat down on the sofa across the room from Lucious. He removed the pipe from his mouth, blowing some smoke into the air.

"Well, Dia, we have much to discuss regarding next week's debut. Have you, as of yet, received any offers for Eva?" Lucious asked, sticking the pipe back into his mouth.

Claudia nodded. "It looks as if you're going to get your money's worth with this one. I received an offer yesterday from a banker, bidding one hundred pounds. Just this morning, another letter came, from a viscount, for one hundred and fifty," Claudia replied.

Lucious lifted his chin high into the air, blew out another puff of smoke, a delighted look upon his face.

"Yes, yes...very nice, indeed. I knew Eva would be worth my investment and, with things going this way, I could receive up to three hundred pounds for her just on her debut night alone. If I play my cards right, not only would I get full reimbursement for my "wooing" expenses but bring in a surplus right away." Lucious released a hearty laugh, shaking his head with a great, big smile on his face. He was so pleased with himself.

Claudia closed her eyes, repelled by Lucious' comments. Pulling herself together, she let out a sigh and asked, "How are things going in London?"

Lucious crossed one leg over the other and removed the pipe from his mouth, blowing a puff of smoke into the air. "Well, you know, Eva's definitely in love with me. She'll do anything I ask of her"—he looked over at Claudia with a proud grin on his face—"and she's becoming rather good in the bedroom, I might add." He raised his eyebrows and inhaled a deep breath. "Yes, Eva has been plucked, primed, and is now ready for service." Lucious smiled as he placed the pipe back into his mouth.

Claudia swallowed hard and put her arm across the back of the sofa. She was doing her best to compose herself and not allow Lucious' crude comments to get the best of her.

"Yes, I heard that you've been enjoying playing house in London with Eva," she responded smugly.

Lucious glared back at her with a cold, hard stare. Standing up from his chair, he placed the pipe down on the table and walked across the room to Claudia. She sat straight up on the sofa, gazing at Lucious with fear in her eyes. He sat down next to her and placed his arm along the back of the couch behind her.

"If by enjoying myself you mean banging Eva day and night, then yes...I've quite enjoyed myself," he said, nodding his head while looking intently at Claudia, an arrogant smile plastered across his face.

He leaned in closer to Claudia, grazing his nose against her jawline while breathing on her neck. Claudia grabbed at her throat, sucking in a breath. Lucious repulsed her and the thought of him taking advantage of that young girl made her sick to her stomach. When he looked back up at Claudia, his eyes were black as coal.

"Don't forget the first rule of Liberation Hall, no judging... Dia...dear," Lucious said harshly, then stood up expediently and walked out of the room.

Claudia breathed in deeply and gazed out the drawing-room window, shaking her head. She inhaled another deep breath as she tried to regain her composure. How she despised working for Lucious—but he frightened her. She had seen what he was capable of doing to hurt people. He was an extremely evil man, the worst kind. Lucious was incapable of loving anyone except himself. Claudia had seen many girls fall into Lucious' trap over the years—one of them being herself. He was smart and devious, he knew how to choose the right ones: beautiful, lonely, poor, and, usually, either without parents or with parents who didn't care they were missing. He had debated whether or not Eva was a good candidate because of her mother, but

Eva's beauty far outweighed any expense that he would have to endure to keep her mum at bay. Lucious' hunch had proven right—Eva was going to make him a fortune. Claudia released another sigh; she hated seeing these young girls become Lucious' assets.

Suddenly, Lucious popped back into the drawing room, causing Claudia to jolt out of her thoughts.

"Forgot my pipe," he said with a smile. Walking over, he picked up his pipe from the table and placed it back in his mouth. He inhaled a puff from the pipe while squinting and allowed the smoke to flow out of his mouth slowly. "Oh and, by the way, I'll be staying for dinner this evening," he added, trying to annoy Claudia.

"Won't Eva be waiting for you?" she asked coolly, hoping he would return to London.

"Eh," Lucious responded with a dismissive shrug and proceeded to leave the drawing room.

* * *

Eva sat anxiously by the front window, waiting for Lucious to arrive. She looked up at the clock on the wall, which read nine o'clock. *Where is he?* she thought to herself.

"Miss Eva, why don't you come eat some dinner," Mrs. Martindale called out. The old woman came wobbling around the corner, looking for Eva. She watched Eva waiting there by the window for Lucious and it made her frown. Eva looked over at her.

"I just don't understand, where he could be?" she said, greatly troubled about him.

"It's hard to say, Miss. Master Lucious is a very busy man."

Eva looked back out the window.

"I'm going to clear the table—are you sure you don't want something to eat?" asked Mrs. Martindale again in a somewhat begging tone.

Eva shook her head "no" while still gazing out the front window.

"Oh, alright, then," Mrs. Martindale sighed, then hobbled back over toward the kitchen and cleared the table, putting all the food away.

Once she was finished, she came back to Eva, who was still sitting by the window.

"I'm turning in for the night, Miss. Is there anything I can get you before I go to bed?"

Eva looked down at the flask of juice she held in one hand and the letter she had written her mother in the other. Lucious had promised her that he would personally mail the letter himself. She looked back out the window, shaking her head and letting out a sigh.

"Alright then. Goodnight, Miss."

Eva said nothing in return. All she could think about is how she had feared this would happen. She had worried that Lucious would leave her just as Georgie and her father had done. Eva felt sick inside as she curled up with her back pressed against the wall, holding her knees up to her chest. The gas lanterns on the street were reflected in her eyes while she gazed through the window and tears began running down her face. She hated this feeling—didn't he miss her as much as she missed him?

Lucious quietly opened the front door to the terraced house around midnight. He silently walked in, removing his overcoat and hanging it up on the rack along with his cane. Turning around to lock the door, he noticed Eva lying by the front window, asleep on the floor. The moonlight shined down on her, causing her flaxen hair to glisten in the light as a letter to her mother and a flask of juice lay by her side. He let out a slight laugh, shaking his head. He walked over to the items, picked them up from the floor, and placed them in his suit jacket pocket. Then, he carefully picked Eva up from the floor and carried her to the bedroom, laying her gently down upon the bed. Eva nestled herself up against the pillows making a slight moaning sound.

Lucious walked over to the bar and poured himself a glass of juice, taking a few sips of his own poison. He set the juice down on his nightstand and began removing his coat jacket when he suddenly remembered the letter that Eva had written to her mother. Pulling the letter from his coat pocket, he proceeded to open it up and read its contents. Quickly, Lucious realized that Eva could barely write and that her spelling was atrocious. He thought about how desperate she must have felt in order to take the time to write this letter to her mother. After seeing her handwriting, it was possible that it had taken her most of the day to accomplish this task. Lucious was frustrated by the message and the inability to read Eva's handwriting fully. He tore the letter into pieces, which he then threw into the lit fireplace. Afterwards, he removed the rest of his clothing, slipping into the bed and under the covers.

He moved closer to Eva and began kissing her face and neck, waking her from her slumber. Eva sucked in a deep breath and looked groggily over to see Lucious staring down at her.

"Lucious," she said softly. Smiling, she gazed up into his eyes.

"Yes, love," Lucious spoke tenderly in return, looking at her as he caressed her face with his fingers.

"I didn't think you were going to come home. I was scared, Lucious, that you had disappeared."

He let out a short laugh. "Don't be silly, I'm not going anywhere."

Eva sat up in the bed, rubbing her eyes. She grabbed Lucious' hands and held them up near her chest.

"You have to understand something," she said solemnly.

Lucious looked at her, wondering what she could possibly have to say.

"My father left for work one day and never returned home. I don't do well when people leave me." There was a sad look in her eyes.

"But I'm not leaving you, Eva. I just had to work late that's all," Lucious said as he gazed fervently into her eyes.

"Please, I beg you, don't ever do that again. Promise me that you'll tell me from now on what time you plan to return home and then do so, promptly," she pleaded.

"Oh, course Eva, I promise," he responded in a loving and sincere tone, although he didn't mean a word of it.

Twelve

The next morning, Lucious and Eva were eating breakfast downstairs at the dining table. Lucious was reading through the morning newspaper, when he abruptly folded it in half, quickly sticking it into his suit jacket. He called Mrs. Martindale and she hurried over to the table.

"Yes, Master Lucious?" she asked, giving a nod and curtsy.

"Eva and I will be going to Liberation Hall for the weekend. We will need you to pack our belongings for us," he commanded.

Eva could hear the intensity in Lucious' voice.

"Right away, sir," replied Mrs. Martindale and hobbled speedily up the staircase.

"Eva, you may want to go up and show her what you would like to bring with you," Lucious suggested as Eva took a sip of tea.

Placing her cup down on the table, she tried to lighten the mood.

"Yes, Master Lucious, sir," She replied sarcastically in a high-pitched voice, looking over at Lucious with a smirk.

Lucious didn't seem to be amused; he continued staring out across the room, deep in thought. Eva cleared her throat and scooted her chair away from the table. She walked behind Lucious, placed her hands on his shoulders, and bent down, kissing him on the cheek. Lucious looked over at her, patted her hand, and smiled. Eva let out a sigh.

"I'm heading upstairs now," she said.

"Alright, love," he replied, paying her no mind.

Eva started making her way toward the staircase when Lucious called out.

"Eva!"

She turned around, looked at him, and hoped that he was going to give her some attention.

"Make you sure you pack some of those deliciously scandalous corsets," he said with a devilish grin and a wink.

She nodded, giving him a coy smile, then headed upstairs to help Mrs. Martindale.

Lucious and Eva rode in the carriage, making their way to Liberation Hall. He did not seem like himself the entire day. He was quiet and tense, instead of his usual flirtatious self. He was also not attentive to Eva and she knew that something was wrong. They were sitting side by side in the carriage, holding hands, when she turned toward him and poked her head out in front of him, trying to get his attention.

"Are you alright?" she asked.

Lucious was staring out the carriage window. He glanced over at her.

"Oh, yes, love, sorry. I just have a lot on my mind, is all," he replied.

163

"Yes, I can see that," she frowned, slightly irritated.

Lucious sighed and turned to Eva.

"You're right. I'm sorry, love." He looked deeply in her eyes, kissing her tenderly on the lips.

"Now, that's better," she said with a kittenish grin.

Lucious licked his lips, then took both of Eva's hands. "Eva, there are a few things I have to inform you about concerning Liberation Hall."

She looked intently at him, waiting to hear what he was about to say.

"You know, I don't stay at the Hall all that often anymore because most of my business is done in London and well..." Lucious tilted his head, "part of what keeps Liberation Hall running is the fact that I allow several individuals to stay at the house full time. One of those individuals is Dia."

Eva sat up straight in the coach seat. "Oh, I see," she replied, looking down at her lap.

"Claudia has lived there for many years now. It is more her home now than it is my own. She helps manage certain jobs around the house," Lucious said while rubbing Eva's hand, trying to soften the blow.

"Like a wife?" Eva pipped up, looking at him contemptuously.

Lucious leaned in closer to Eva, lowering his chin; he looked deeply into her eyes.

"Like an assistant," he replied with certainty.

Eva paused. "And there is absolutely nothing at all between you and Dia any longer?" she asked, waiting to see how Lucious would respond.

"Oh, God, no…" Lucious retorted, rolling his eyes.

Eva was taken back by his quick response, but it convinced her that Lucious was telling her the truth. She softly nodded her head in agreement while letting out a soft sigh.

Lucious smiled as he patted her hand. "There's also something else." He swallowed hard.

What else could there be, she thought?

"A few of Dia's friends live there as well?"

"Friends? What sort of friends?" she questioned, puzzled.

Lucious looked up without moving his head, pretending to recount the names of the women who lived there.

"Well, there's Marissa, Katrina, and Bethany," he said, looking back at Eva.

"They're all lady friends?" Eva sounded surprised.

"Yes, well, you know how Queen Victoria has lady companions…it's sort of like that," Lucious replied with a shrug.

Eva nodded her head, although she didn't like the thought of Lucious being at the Hall with all these women. Nevertheless, she had realized that she had no authority to demand otherwise, it was Lucious' home.

While they were still on their journey to the Hall, Eva suddenly remembered the letter that she had written to her mother the day before. She turned and looked at Lucious.

"The letter—I wrote a letter to my mum. I was holding it last night while I waited for you to return home. Did you see it anywhere?" she asked anxiously.

"Oh, yes!" Lucious eagerly replied. "It was lying on the floor next to you, so I picked it up and placed it in my jacket pocket for safekeeping." Lucious patted his chest. "This morning, while you were still upstairs, I gave it to Mrs. Martindale to post in the mail."

"I thought you said you would mail the letter yourself?" Eva asked, slightly annoyed.

"I was going to, love, but I knew I wouldn't have the time to take the letter in today and thought it would be best for Mrs. Martindale to do so—that way your mum receives it right away."

Eva let out a sigh of relief, nodding her head. She was relieved that the letter had been mailed. She inhaled deeply and leaned back, relaxing against Lucious' chest. He wrapped his arms around Eva, a devious smirk playing on his face.

The carriage turned a corner and went down a lane, at the end of which stood Liberation Hall. Eva had never seen the Hall in daylight and it looked much larger than she remembered. The carriage pulled up in front of the mansion and Archie opened the door, helping Eva out. Lucious followed, taking in a deep breath of the fresh, country air. Eva looked at the front steps leading into the house, reminiscing about her first kiss with Lucious. She thought about how much had changed in less than a week since she had first come to the Hall. Lucious took Eva's hand and they entered the house together, Archie following behind them with their luggage.

"Well, here we are again," Lucious spoke, smiling at Eva.

Eva looked around the foyer, taking in her surroundings. She felt like she was seeing the Hall for the first time. Claudia hastily rounded the corner of the corridor.

"Ah, Claudia," Lucious called out.

She slowed her pace upon seeing Lucious with Eva at the Hall. She had not expected them today.

"You remember Eva Alderson," Lucious introduced, motioning his hand toward Eva.

Claudia nodded and replied, "Of course, how lovely to see you again, Eva."

Eva nodded politely in return.

"I wasn't expecting you today, Lucious," Claudia stated.

"Something came up and I had some business to attend to here at the Hall," Lucious said, looking somewhat irritated.

Claudia squinted, wondering what could possibly have gone wrong.

"Curtis, please go fetch Nancy and have her show Eva to the room in which she will be staying while at the Hall," Lucious commanded.

"Yes, sir,"

Curtis looked like he was only a little older than Eva. He was about the same height as Lucious, with soft brown hair, brown eyes, and a healthy physique. Eva looked up at Lucious, confused. She moved to stand in front of him so that Claudia couldn't hear her speak.

"I'm not staying in your room with you?" she whispered with a frown.

Claudia turned her head away, realizing that Eva didn't want her to hear what she was saying. "I'm going to go to the study, if you'll excuse me," she interjected, then turned and walked out the foyer, heading down a corridor to the right of the staircase.

Lucious took both of Eva's hands. "You most certainly can stay in my room while you are here, Eva," he stated. "However, since there are plenty of rooms at the Hall, it's nice for everyone to have their own room in case they need some personal space."

Eva nodded her head in agreement. She also understood that it was probably better, for the sake of appearance, for them to have separate rooms.

Nancy, the lady's maid, arrived to the foyer.

"Nancy, would you please show Miss Alderson to her room and unpack her belongings."

"Yes, sir," Nancy replied with a nod and a slight curtsy.

Nancy was incredibly petite with dirty blonde hair and dull brown eyes. She was a rather plain-looking girl in her late twenties.

"Oh, please also show Miss Alderson where my room is as well," Lucious added while nodding his head.

Nancy gave a Lucious another nod, then waited for Eva. Lucious leaned down delicately, kissing Eva's lips.

"Go on now. I'll come up and check on you later when I'm done in the study. It probably won't take any longer than a half-hour," he said, motioning for Eva to go upstairs.

She frowned, then followed Nancy up the staircase and into a room directly across the balcony.

"This will be your room, Miss, and here across the hall is Master Lucious' room." Nancy pointed toward a door diagonal from Eva's bedroom.

It's not too far away, Eva thought.

Then, Nancy led Eva back into her room, which was reasonably large. The bed was up against the wall on the left side of the door. A chest of drawers was across the room, adjacent to the bed. There were two doors on each side of the chest; one door led to an ensuite bath and the other to the wardrobe. A fireplace was located on the far side of the room, away from the door. Dark green velour curtains were hanging on both sides of the windows and the bed sported a matching green flower-patterned bedspread. Two night tables were located on both sides of the bed, each with beautiful bouquets of white hydrangeas and red roses in crystal vases on top.

"This is quite lovely," Eva commented.

"Would you like me to unpack your belongings for you, Miss?" Nancy asked and Eva nodded.

Eva sat down on the bed, breathing in deeply, then walked over to her bag just as Nancy was hanging up some of her dresses in the wardrobe. She reached in, pulled out a flask containing the juice and removed the cap. She took several gulps of the juice while Nancy wasn't looking. Eva was drinking more substantial quantities of the juice every day. She placed the top back on the flask and lay down on the bed, closing her eyes as a feeling of ecstasy came over her, making her feel awake, as if her body was coming alive. Eva thought it was strange how the juice made her feel better and better each time she took a sip. She yawned, once again closing her eyes, tired from staying up late the previous night waiting for Lucious to come home and ended up falling fast asleep on the bed.

* * *

Lucious watched as Eva followed Nancy up the staircase, then expediently walked out of the foyer and down the corridor to his study. Claudia was sitting at his desk on the other side of the room, waiting for him. Lucious closed the French doors behind him and turned around, peering at Claudia.

"Dia, dear...Did you happen to see the London newspaper this morning?" he asked, holding his hands in a prayer stance, sounding calm but exasperated.

Claudia shifted back and forth in the movable chair.

"No, I haven't. Now, will you tell me what's wrong already?" she asked, annoyed.

"Take a look for yourself."

Lucious pulled out the newspaper from his coat pocket and threw it down on the desk in front of Claudia. Claudia picked up the paper and began unfolding it.

"Page three," Lucious stated while walking away from the desk to pace back and forth.

Claudia opened the paper, turning to page three. She read the title aloud, "Missing Girl, Mother Accuses Juice Man."

Claudia let out a quiet laugh. "Well, I've seen catchier titles," she replied.

Lucious turned around, slamming his fists down on the desk and yelling in her face.

"This is serious, Dia!"

She jerked back, away from him, closing her eyes.

Claudia took a few breaths, then spoke, "Lucious, it's not as if you kidnapped Eva; she has willingly 'chosen' to go with you. You, technically, haven't done anything illegal."

"That's not the point, Dia. The point is that this looks bad for business, all around. I don't need people questioning my methods!" he shouted at her, then leaned into her face. "I need you to...fix...this." He emphasized the last three words.

"Me?" Claudia placed her hand up to her chest. "What am I supposed to do about this?" She couldn't believe that Lucious was making the newspaper article her problem.

"Isn't there someone at the newspaper that you're blackmailing or have on your payroll?" Claudia asked, annoyed.

"Yes—and I'm going to kill that editor!" Lucious yelled, slamming his fist on the desk.

Claudia's eyes grew wide and as she backed away from him. She couldn't be sure whether Lucious was just saying things in anger or whether he was serious.

Lucious leaned against the desk, his hand on his head. A moment later he turned and bent forward across the desk, glaring at Claudia, his face only inches away from hers.

"You're going to go to London and you're going to make this right," he spoke slowly and emphatically. Then he abruptly turned and started walking away from the desk.

"Do you have any suggestions?" Claudia asked loudly as Lucious headed toward the door.

"I don't know, Dia," he continued walking away while frantically waving his hands. "Go sleep with someone, the entire newspaper staff for all I care. Perform some services and take the girls with you. Just do whatever you have to do to get the story retracted!" he yelled, slamming the office door behind him.

As Lucious entered the corridor, he paused for a moment to regain his composure. Straightening his jacket, he inhaled deeply, then continued down the hallway.

Lucious soon arrived at Eva's door giving it a gentle tap.

"Eva," he called out lightly, then slowly entered the room.

Looking over to the bed, he saw Eva spread out across it, a flask of juice lying next to her. A feeling of panic overtook him. He rushed over to check her pulse. Touching her wrist, he let out a heavy sigh of relief. She must be tired, probably from being kept awake for many nights by him, he thought to himself.

"That's all I need now, you dosing on me," he muttered under his breath sarcastically.

Lucious looked down at her, lying peacefully on the bed. How beautiful she looked when she was sleeping. He carefully picked her up, placing her head on the pillow and curled up next to her. Lucious wrapped his arms around her and she released a soft groan of pleasure, smiling as he held her firmly in his arms.

"Hello," she said softly.

"Hello, love," he said, smiling back at her.

Eva turned back around, closing her eyes and falling fast asleep in Lucious' arms.

Claudia was heading up the staircase toward her bedroom. As she walked through the corridor, she passed Eva's bedroom and quickly glanced inside the room. What she saw made her stop short. Turning around, Claudia did a double take and peeked into Eva's bedroom again. She couldn't believe her eyes—Lucious was cuddling with Eva on the bed. His arms were tightly wrapped around her and he seemed to actually be enjoying himself. Claudia had never seen Lucious do such a thing before; at least not in the middle of the day and for no clear reason. She watched them for a few more moments while hiding behind the door. Then, closing her eyes, she turned and walked away.

Thirteen

Georgie was walking up a dirt road, heading toward another small village. He had been searching for Eva on the outskirts of the city for three weeks straight, asking people whether they knew or heard anything about either Lucious Paddimir or Liberation Hall. The only information he had received thus far was from a fellow a few towns back. The man had told him about Mr. Paddimir's juice concoction, which was sold on the streets of London. This juice was known for causing people to feel euphoric, while desensitizing them to what was happening around them at the same time. The drug was costly and highly addictive. Georgie shook his head, thinking about it; he was worried sick about Eva. The only thing he could figure was that Lucious must have drugged Eva with this juice, causing her to go home with him.

His eyes began to fill with tears—how could he have let this happen? He blamed himself for leaving Eva in London. He knew she was fragile, especially since her father had passed away but he had genuinely thought that she would wait for him. He had been saving money for a while and almost had enough to give their life together a good start. The magistrate was impressed by Georgie's work and he was settling into his position quite well. He knew it wouldn't have been much longer before he would have been able to come back for her, to ask her to marry him. The wait, however, was too long for Eva. She needed someone to love and care for her and Georgie wasn't there.

All these thoughts rushed through Georgie's mind, causing him to release a loud cry. He dropped to his knees and began weeping.

"What have I done!" he cried aloud.

If he couldn't find Eva, he would never be able to live with himself. He was supposed to protect her, to be there for her, and he had failed to do either. He planned on never giving up until he found her. After a few desperate minutes, Georgie inhaled a deep breath, wiping the tears from his face and picking himself up from the ground. Dusting off his trousers he kept walking toward the village up ahead.

Georgie was tired, dirty, and hungry. He had been walking from town to town and sleeping on the streets like a vagrant. He had mostly been eating foliage that he found by the road on his journeys between villages. When he would spot a fresh body of water, he would drink, clean up, and change his clothing— but it was more than a week now since he had been able to change his garments. Every once in a while, he would find a pub and pay for a cheap meal, but he didn't know how long it would take him to find Eva and didn't want to waste his limited resources. Georgie thought that maybe it was time to go back to London to check in with Alice and Margie, as well as to get a fresh change of clothes. However, he didn't want to relent. He had a feeling, deep inside, that he was getting closer to finding her and didn't want to quit now.

Georgie walked into the town pub to finally get some actual food to eat in order to maintain his strength. Sitting down at a rickety, old, wooden table, he placed his face in his hands.

The owner of the pub walked up to him, "Good day, what can I get ya?"

Georgie slowly looked up at the man.

"Oh boy, you sure look like you could use a pint," the owner said, taking in Georgie's haggard appearance with an unpleasant look on his face.

Georgie shook his head.

"I'll take some water and whatever this will get me," he shoved a coin across the table toward the man.

"Well..." the man scratched his head, "that'll get you some bean soup and a slice of bread, but that's about it," he added with a shrug.

"Then that's what I'll have, sir," Georgie replied kindly, once again resting his head in his hands. He couldn't stop thinking about Eva and could feel that it was urgent for him to find her quickly.

The man came back to Georgie's table, carrying a plate of fish, some potatoes, a hearty helping of cheese, and two slices of bread.

"Here ya go," he said, setting the plate down in front of Georgie.

Georgie looked up and saw the food—it looked mighty good, he thought to himself, but he couldn't afford this meal.

"I'm sorry, sir, but I think you're mistaken. I ordered the bean soup," Georgie said, gazing up with a half-grin.

"Oh, I know you did," the man smiled, "but you looked so pathetic that I decided to give you a better meal, on the house. So, eat up, before I change my mind."

Georgie perked up, "Thank you kindly, sir!"

He gobbled up the plate of food. It almost felt like too much food since he had eaten so little over the past few weeks. Despite feeling full, he ate every last bite because he did not know when he would have another decent meal. The pub owner came over again.

"How'd ya like the food?" he asked somewhat sarcastically as he gazed down at Georgie's empty plate.

"It was mighty fine, sir, thank you again. I really appreciate it," Georgie replied with heartfelt gratitude.

The pub owner pulled out a chair and sat down at the table with Georgie.

"You look like you've hit some hard times boy, what's the story?" he inquired.

Georgie looked up at him with tears in eyes. The man raised his eyebrows, taken aback by Georgie's emotions. Georgie felt silly for crying, but he couldn't help himself. He was grateful for this man's generosity toward him but he was also constantly thinking and worrying about Eva. He quickly wiped his face with the back of his hands.

"A friend of mine has gone missing. I'm afraid she's in terrible trouble," Georgie explained, looking distraught.

The man sighed with a dismal look on his face.

"Well, that's a shame," he responded, shaking his head. "What makes you think she's in trouble?" he asked.

Georgie paused for a moment, thinking about Eva.

"The man who has her, well, he's a nasty man, that much I do know," Georgie said with great conviction.

"So, you know who's got her, then?" the man was surprised.

Georgie looked down at the table, taking in a deep breath and nodded slowly.

"Yes, but I can't find the place where he's keeping her. I have the name of where he lives, but no one's been able to tell me the exact location," explained Georgie with frustration in his eyes.

"What's the name of the place, then?" the man asked inquisitively.

Georgie looked gravely into the pub owners' eyes as he replied, "Liberation Hall."

The pub owner paused for a moment, rubbing his tongue along the back of his teeth and squinting. He was thinking hard.

"You know, I think I've heard of that place," he said, covering his mouth with his hand. He was trying to recall where he had heard the name.

"You have?" Georgie perked up, listening intently to what the man was about to say. The pub owner was staring across the room.

"Yah, that's right. Some chaps came into the pub not too long ago. I heard them talking about a place called Liberation Hall and it piqued my interest. I thought it was an odd name for a hall," the man said, shaking his head.

"Do you remember if they said where it's located?" Georgie asked, silently praying that the pub owner would know the location of the house.

"Lemme think," the owner replied, still rubbing his chin with his hand. Suddenly, the he burst out, "Shepperton! Yah, that's it, that's what one of the fellows said, that the house was in Shepperton, along the Thames," he spoke quickly, nodding his head with excitement.

178

Georgie's eyes grew large. "God bless you, sir!"

He grabbed the pub owner's hand, shaking it aggressively, overjoyed by the new lead. He wasn't sure if it was accurate, but it gave him hope that he might find Eva soon.

Georgie quickly rose from the chair, grabbed his bag, and headed for the door.

"Where do you think you're going?" the pub owner called out.

Georgie turned around nervously, looking at him.

"I was going to go to Shepperton, sir," he replied.

"This time of night?" the pub owner asked with some surprise. "The sun's setting and Shepperton's nearly eighteen miles from here. That'll easily take you seven, maybe eight hours on foot and that's without stopping," the man said with a shrug.

Georgie thought that if he walked all night, he could get there by morning, but the man continued, "And, to be honest with you, boy, you look like you could use a bath and a good night's sleep. I've got an extra room upstairs—it's yours for the night if ya like."

Georgie thought about it. The offer was tempting—it would be nice to get some proper rest and possibly a warm bath, but he was too anxious to reach Shepperton.

"I appreciate the offer, sir, but I really have to be going," Georgie insisted.

"Alright then, at least take some food wit' ya," he started walking back toward the pub's kitchen and Georgie peered at him, surprised by his kindness.

"Sir, why are you being so kind to me?" Georgie inquired.

The pub owner turned around and looked at Georgie.

"Well, I suppose my son would've been about your age now…Had his sweetheart gone missing and he was out looking for her—I sure would hope that someone would've been kind of enough to give him a helping hand." There was a sorrowful smile on his face.

"I'm sorry for your loss, sir," Georgie said somberly.

"Life goes on, I suppose," the pub owner sighed. "Lemme go pack you some grub," he insisted, walking back through the kitchen door.

Georgie decided he should wash up and, after doing so, he returned to the pub's dining area. The owner had prepared a basket for him that was filled with sandwiches, cheese, and some warm bread.

"Gully, thank you so much, sir. I'm much obliged," Georgie replied, extremely grateful.

"You're welcome. Say, I didn't even catch your name?" the owner inquired.

"George Thornber," he replied.

"The name's Will, Will Bartly."

"Thank you again, Mr. Bartly, sir," Georgie held out his hand. "You've once again given me hope."

Mr. Bartly shook Georgie's hand. "I hope you find your friend, George," he said with a nod.

Georgie smiled and headed out the pub door, making his way toward Shepperton.

Fourteen

Two weeks had gone by since Lucious and Eva came to Liberation Hall. Lucious had first told her that they were only staying for the weekend but then changed his mind. Eva enjoyed living in the large spacious mansion but missed having Lucious all to herself. She had treasured their time alone in the terraced London house, when it was just the two of them, which had made their relationship feel more authentic. She also missed Mrs. Martindale; the chubby old lady had been like a mother to her even though she knew her for less than a week. Thinking about Mrs. Martindale led Eva to reminisce about her real mother. She wondered whether her mum had received the letter she had written to her and whether she was doing all right without Eva in her life. She hoped that her mother wasn't angry with her for running off with Lucious. Eva knew that, despite what she had done, her mother missed her and she also missed her mother very much in return. Sometimes she would cry at night after Lucious had fallen asleep, thinking about her mum. Eva believed that one day they would see each other again, perhaps when she was older and Lucious trusted her to return to him.

Spring was approaching and, when the sun was shining brightly, Eva would go out behind the Hall. Bringing a blanket, she would lie on the ground and soak up the warm sunlight. Sometimes, she would pretend that Georgie was lying next to her. She could see them joking and laughing together; then, opening her eyes, she would realize it was all in her imagination and would feel sad, missing her friend again. Sometimes, she wondered whether Georgie even cared that she had left home and whether he also missed her. Eva realized that a part of her must still love Georgie even though he didn't feel the same way about her. She often missed his warm smile, the fun they had together but, most of all, she missed the light that he carried inside him. Eva hadn't seen such a light in a long time. The people living at Liberation Hall were kind enough, but they didn't have any light inside them. Lucious, at times, seemed to have light in his eyes—but Eva had also seen great darkness in them, too.

The Hall was rather busy on most days and nights. There always seemed to be men coming and going for various reasons. Occasionally, businessmen would stop by to speak with Lucious but, most of the time, they called upon the ladies of the house. Eva knew that all the women who lived at Liberation Hall, except her, were seeing multiple men. When she asked Lucious about it, he reminded Eva that Liberation Hall was a place of freedom, where people could be themselves without judgment. Men would arrive in the middle of the night and disappear at the other the end of the corridor not to be seen again until morning. The thought of it all made Eva shudder, although she was beginning to adapt to the environment more and more with each passing day.

Eva also felt more comfortable around Claudia as time went by. The jealousy she once felt toward her had dissipated as she realized that nothing was going on between her and Lucious. Their interactions with one another were only business-related and, at times, they seemed like they could barely stand one another. Eva did wonder whether Claudia was jealous of her relationship with Lucious, just as he had claimed the night of the party.

Overall, Claudia was very respectful toward Eva, doing her best to make sure she was comfortable. She was also helping Eva learn how to be the mistress of the house. Lucious had asked Claudia to teach Eva proper etiquette and art, as well as to work with her on her handwriting and spelling. Eva understood that if she was to take over running the house eventually, she would need to learn everything she could from Claudia. She also needed to know how to converse with the businessmen who came to the Hall.

That very evening Lucious was hosting a party of sorts for several of his business colleagues. He said that some of them were coming from as far away as America for the event. He told Eva that she had to look her very best and that this was the most important occasion of the year. Lucious also made clear what he expected of Eva throughout the evening. She was supposed to make the men feel comfortable by talking and flirting with them. Claudia had taught Eva how to be coy and coquettish, making the men feel desired, which would apparently guarantee that they had an enjoyable time. She also said that their appearance didn't matter. Eva was instructed to be equally affectionate toward each of them—especially if they took an interest in her. Despite her lessons, Eva was still nervous about talking with wealthy, prestigious men. Claudia told her that it was sometimes better to flirt with her eyes and to lightly caress their arms than to speak, especially if she didn't know what to say.

Eva was getting ready for tonight's event. Lucious wanted to make sure Eva looked most desirable and had a unique dress made for her for the occasion. He surprised her with it the night before, telling her that he had another gift for her to commence the evening. Eva gazed at herself in the full-length mirror, knowing she looked stunning in the pale pink gown. The gown was cut in the princess sheath style, with a sloping neckline that was adorned with embroidered lace around the shoulders. The skirt had tiers that were covered with matching embroidered lace and beading, white bows flowing down the train. Nancy had dressed Eva's hair by curling small sections of it with a hot iron and then placing the curls intricately on top of her head so that tendrils flew out, bouncing around her neck. She'd left some of the tendrils out, near Eva's ears and forehead, to dangle gently against her face. Nancy had also lightly applied some rouge to Eva's cheeks and lips, offsetting her creamy complexion against the light pink gown. Eva had never felt more beautiful than she did that evening.

As the time for the arrival of the guests drew near, Lucious knocked on Eva's bedroom door. She poised herself, inhaling deeply before allowing Lucious to enter the room. Lucious opened the door and, upon seeing Eva, he was taken back by her beauty.

"Eva, you look categorically ravishing this evening."

Lucious meant every word he said. He gracefully picked Eva's hand up, delicately kissing her while relishing the moment. She gave him a coy smile, her neck turning red and matching the rouge on her cheeks. Lucious felt an unexpected twinge of jealousy hit him, realizing that he would not be spending the evening with her. He took a deep breath and cleared his throat to regain his composure. He had to remember that tonight was about business, not pleasure.

"Shall we have a drink before heading downstairs?" Lucious suggested.

Eva shyly nodded in agreement.

He took her hand, leading her to his bedroom. He walked over to the bar, pulling out two crystal glasses and looked back at Eva, noticing that she was rubbing her gloves together nervously.

"Are you feeling alright, love?" he asked while pouring the juice into the glasses.

Eva looked down at the floor. "I'm just a little nervous, I suppose," she replied, swallowing hard.

"Oh, you're going to do just marvelous. You've been preparing all week for tonight," Lucious spoke dramatically, pulling a bottle of clear liquor from the bar cabinet. "Perhaps I should add something a bit stronger to the juice to relax you even more?"

His words were more of a statement than a question. He poured some of the clear liquor into the glasses, knowing that he needed to be very careful. Lucious wanted Eva to be relaxed but not intoxicated. He also didn't want her to overdose, which could happen by mixing too much alcohol with the juice.

Lucious turned around, carrying the glasses across the room toward Eva while gazing at her wantonly. Handing her the drink, he lifted it high into the air, saying emphatically, "To us, Eva. Cheers, love!" clanking his glass against Eva's.

She smiled, then nodded, drinking some of the juice. Immediately, the feeling of tranquility began to take over her body. She leaned into Lucious, placing her arm around his waist under his suit coat. The touch of Eva sent shocks through Lucious' body. She looked up at him seductively, reaching her face up to his. Lucious bent down, lightly touching his lips to hers. He embraced her, deeply kissing her mouth, then forced himself to release her from his hold.

Eva could hear the guests arriving in the foyer.

"Shouldn't we be getting downstairs?" she asked.

"Haven't you ever heard of being 'fashionably late?'" he winked at her. "Also, I have something to give you first."

Lucious opened one of the chest drawers and pulled out a square-shaped velvet box. He walked over to Eva, who was breathing heavily at the sight of the box. She was thinking that Lucious might propose to her tonight. Even though he said he would never marry, Eva had secretly been hoping that he would change his mind. Lucious brought the box over and opened it, revealing a diamond chandelier necklace. Eva sucked in a loud breath, her mouth hanging open in complete astonishment at the sight of the sparkling jewels.

"May I?" Lucious asked.

Taking the necklace from the box, he placed it on Eva's delicate neck. She touched the ornament dangling from her clavicle, then reached up to Lucious and firmly grabbed him, pulling him toward her and kissing him aggressively. She detached her lips from his while looking at him amorously.

"I love you, Lucious Paddimir."

Lucious smiled, kissing Eva once more before preparing to head downstairs.

Claudia knocked on the door while Lucious and Eva were still fixated on one another.

"Come in," he called.

Claudia opened the door, "Lucious, your guests are waiting." She looked over at Eva and nodded, then walked out the door.

"You ready, love?" Lucious asked.

Eva nodded her head yes, taking in a deep breath as they joined arms. The juice had calmed her but she was still somewhat nervous when they headed downstairs. Leaving the bedroom, they turned the corner and stepped out, standing at the top of the staircase. Eva saw about ten to twelve men gazing up at her.

"Miss Eva Alderson and Mr. Lucious Paddimir," Curtis announced while they stood at the top of the staircase for another moment.

Lucious glanced over at Eva and said, "See, they can't take their eyes off of you...but I really can't blame them." He gave her a pleasant grin.

Eva smiled back at him and, together, they promenaded down the staircase.

Fifteen

E va's début had begun and Claudia had already explained the process to the men before Lucious and Eva came downstairs. When each of the buyers had finished their opportunity to evaluate Eva, they would decide whether or not they wished to place a bid for her. Then, when they were ready to make an offer, they would go to Claudia and give her their price. Claudia would keep track of all the offers made throughout the evening and, once she had received all bids, the two highest bidders would be escorted into Lucious' study to negotiate the price further. The only exception to the rule were the men who had met Eva before her début evening, had already taken an interest in her, and had placed their bids before this evening. These men had already started the bidding process. Now, on début evening, the price would continue to rise. Once Lucious receives the final highest offer and payment, the winner would then get to spend the night with Eva in her bedroom. A part of the allure for these men was the game of it all, seeing who would win the evening with Eva. Lucious had a reputation for supplying the most beautiful and well-trained women in all of London. The men were guaranteed to get their money's worth when purchasing a woman from Lucious Paddimir.

There were many occasions when suitors would return to the Hall having fallen in love with one of the women. When this occurred, the suitor would be able to fully purchase his lover at an extremely high price from Lucious and the woman would become the suitor's full-time, personal courtesan. The suitor would then provide a private home for the woman, taking care of her as his mistress. Lucious' ultimate goal was to make the most out of his investments. There had also been several cases when a woman was highly prized by several men and, consequently, Lucious had refused to sell such women because of the continual profit that they brought him. When Lucious did allow a woman to be purchased and taken away from the Hall, he would then find and groom another new, young girl to replace the one that had been sold.

Two hours had passed and the evening was going splendidly—nine of the men had already placed bids on Eva. She was doing beautifully, flirting with all the men, captivating them. Lucious wasn't too worried going into the night. He knew that Eva was delightful to be around when she was just being herself—and the juice helped as well. Lucious pulled out his pocket watch to look at the time and walked over to Claudia.

"Five minutes left and then we'll need to go through all the offers," he whispered to Claudia.

She agreed and walked to the other side of the room, continuing to accept bids.

Lucious was approached by his American acquaintance, a Mr. Reginald Wittaker. He walked up to Lucious, holding a cigar in his hand. Lucious looked down at the cigar, giving him a distasteful look.

"Quite a nice a place you got here, Lucious," said Mr. Wittaker.

Lucious nodded. He didn't want small talk, he wanted offers.

"And what about Eva?" Lucious inquired, gazing over to where she was standing.

"Well, that's why I came over here to give you my offer," Reggie stated, taking the cigar out of his mouth and blowing a puff of smoke into the air.

"I don't handle the offers, Dia does. I thought this had been explained," Lucious said, irritated, glancing around the room.

"Do you always let your women do your work for you, Paddimir?" Reggie said, letting out a slight laugh.

Lucious glared at him.

"What's your offer?" he asked stoically.

"Four hundred pounds," Mr. Wittaker responded smugly.

Lucious nodded and began walking toward Claudia when Mr. Wittaker stopped and grabbed his arm.

"We need to talk about shipments," he said.

Lucious looked down at Reggie holding his arm. He took Reggie's hand and gruffly removed it from his body.

"Come back tomorrow and we'll talk about the shipments. Currently, I have other business to attend to. If you'll excuse me," Lucious said indignantly, then walked over to Claudia.

He looked across the foyer, watching the attendees fawning themselves over Eva.

"Remind me why I invited that fat, blasted American?" he asked Claudia, annoyed.

"Because he's filthy rich and just happened to be in London," Claudia responded as she gazed out at the room.

"Oh, yes, that's right," he said, a snarky expression on his face. "I'm about to close the biddings, Reggie just bid four hundred, what's your highest bid?"

Claudia looked at her note pad.

"Sir Patrick, with three hundred and twenty-five pounds," she spoke softly, looking out at the foyer and trying to be discreet.

Lucious closed his eyes and exhaled a sigh of dismay. He did not want Reggie Wittaker to win the bid for Eva but, with such a significant difference in offers, he wasn't sure he would get a better one. Just then, Lord Manchester approached Claudia.

Speaking very quietly, he muttered, "Five hundred quid."

Lucious eyes grew large upon overhearing the Baron's offer. Once Lord Manchester walked away, Lucious closed his eyes, grinning from ear to ear and released a sigh of relief.

Claudia leaned over to him.

"Do you want me to bring Mr. Wittaker and Lord Manchester into your office to re-negotiate offers?" Lucious said nothing. He didn't look at Claudia but simply shook his head.

"I thought as much," Claudia agreed. She knew how much Lucious detested Reggie.

Lucious had never received four hundred pounds for a girl, let alone five hundred. He didn't even know that Lord Manchester had that kind of money to spend on a prostitute. Lord Manchester was in his mid-sixties and, typically, didn't attend Lucious' soirées. He had lost his wife a few years back and was probably looking for some companionship. Lucious had been surprised that he accepted the invitation to the début but was now relieved that Reggie did not win the bidding. Lucious strolled over to Eva and took her firmly by the hand, moving swiftly, excited by his earnings. Eva looked at him, surprised.

"It's time for us to go upstairs," he whispered in her ear. She smiled, thinking he meant that the two of them were going to retire, together, for the evening. They warmly thanked all their guests for attending the party, then Lucious escorted Eva up the stairs to his bedroom.

"I can't tell you how proud I am of you, Eva! You were splendid, absolutely splendid!" he exclaimed, kissing her on the hand.

Eva blushed, smiling coyly. Then, she grabbed Lucious around the neck, pulling him down to kiss him—but Lucious stopped her, pulling her hand away from his neck instead.

"We need to talk, Eva," he said, leading her over to the bed and sitting down. "Here, why don't you have some juice?" Lucious handed her the glass of juice laced with the liquor from earlier in the evening.

Eva had an extremely concerned look on her face. Lucious had never rejected her advances before and she was wondering what was wrong.

"I have a problem, Eva."

Eva looked at him intently, waiting for him to continue.

"I owe someone money. You know Lord Manchester?" Lucious asked.

"Yes, from tonight. He seems like a very kind man. He recently lost his wife," Eva commented with compassion.

"Ah, yes, a very kind man," Lucious said somewhat insincerely. "However, I don't have the money to pay him right now," he continued.

"Oh," Eva was surprised because he always made it sound as if he had plenty of money.

"I mean, I do have money—it's just currently tied up in some investments," Lucious explained, looking at Eva strangely.

"Why are you telling me this, Lucious?" she asked.

"Well, because Lord Manchester said that he is willing to trade with me instead of taking the money that I owe him."

Eva looked at Lucious, confused.

"What sort of trade?" she asked.

Lucious looked at her very seriously.

"Well, you," he said nervously.

She looked at Lucious, perplexed.

"What do you mean, me?" she asked, insulted.

"He said that if he could spend the evening with you, then he would clear my debt."

Eva's heart dropped; she couldn't believe what she was hearing.

"Lucious, this is absurd, you're certainly kidding," she laughed uneasily.

Lucious looked at her most gravely, shaking his head.

"No, Eva, I'm most certainly not kidding." He gave her a hard stare.

"Well, I'm not doing it!" she shouted, standing abruptly and heading toward the door, when Lucious grabbed her arm and pulled her back down on the bed. He proceeded to take her other arm, forcing her to lie down. He straddled her, leaning his face into hers.

Staring down at her for a moment, he spoke softly yet anxiously, "Eva, please don't do this to me. I love you. I love you so much—this hurts me more than it hurts you." He began kissing her on the neck and face.

She was turning, trying to get away from him.

"I thought you loved me, Eva, I thought you said that you would do anything for me," Lucious said as he began to cry. Releasing Eva from his grip, he put his head on her chest.

Eva was confused. She hesitantly placed her hands down on his back. She had never seen Lucious cry before and it was hurting her heart to see him like this.

"Well, take back the necklace you gave me tonight. Here, you can have it back—that should help you pay him," she said and began removing the necklace that Lucious had given her that evening.

"Now you're rejecting my gifts?" Lucious asked, insulted. "Eva, you're breaking my heart." He let go of her abruptly, moving away from the bed to stand in front of the lit fireplace. "The necklace isn't worth as much as I owe him," Lucious said sadly, pretending to wipe his eyes.

Eva stood up from the bed, breathing heavily. She waited a moment, then walked over to where Lucious was standing. She placed her arms around Lucious from behind and began lightly rubbing her hands on his chest.

"We'll think of something," she said, trying to console him.

Lucious turned around, looking down at her firmly.

"I have already thought of something Eva—you," he said brashly. He stared helplessly into her eyes. "It's only one night," he said, pleading.

Eva saw how desperate he looked and it caused her eyes to fill with tears. She glanced down at the ring he had given her.

"All right," she said sorrowfully, wanting to please him.

"Oh, Eva, I knew you'd come through for me." Lucious leaned in, kissing her.

She kissed him back passionately, letting him know how much she loved him. Lucious detached his lips from hers. Eva pulled away, walking over to the side table. She picked up the glass of juice laced with the liquor. Sitting down on the bed, she drank the entire glass in one go. A calm came over her and the concoction relaxed her but she was still upset by the entire ordeal. Lucious walked over and sat down on the bed next to her. He placed his hand over hers.

"Do your best to enjoy yourself tonight, love—just think of me," he quipped, kissing her hand.

She gave him an unpleasant look, pressing her lips together tightly. She was beginning to feel nauseated. At that moment, someone knocked on Lucious' bedroom door.

"Come in!" Lucious called out.

Claudia poked her head in the door.

"Lucious, are we ready?" she asked.

"It's time, Eva." Lucious nodded his head.

Eva looked at Lucious and then at Claudia.

"This was all your idea, wasn't it?!" Eva yelled, marching over to Claudia, pushing her in the chest.

Claudia leaned away from Eva.

"I have no idea what you're talking about, Eva," Claudia replied, offended.

"This was all your idea, me sleeping with Lord Manchester to pay him off!" Eva yelled in Claudia's face.

"No, this was not my idea," Claudia said calmly and assuredly, shaking her head.

"Eva, keep your voice down," Lucious corrected her firmly.

Eva realized that Lord Manchester was probably waiting for her in her bedroom. They all stood there silently for a moment, saying nothing. Lucious turned to Eva.

"Now, Eva, Dia is going to explain a few things to you and you're going to listen and be kind to her," Lucious said, speaking to Eva as if she were a child. He grabbed ahold of both her hands. "I love you, Eva, and I'm proud of you. You're a very mature woman to be doing this for me."

Eva looked up at him longingly, tears flooding her eyes. Oh, how she wished he would change his mind. Eva loved Lucious and wanted to please him—and if this would please him, then this is what she was going to do.

"Come into my room, Eva, I will help you get ready," Claudia said.

Lucious bent down, kissing Eva one last time. She gazed up at him, distressed, then walked out of the bedroom and down the hall to Claudia's room. Claudia turned and gave Lucious a peevish look, shaking her head. Lucious shrugged, raising his brows with a pleased smirk on his face. Claudia took Eva to her bedroom, which was on the same side of the hall as Eva's room. Her door sat diagonally in the opposite direction from Lucious' bedroom door.

They entered the bedroom.

"Now, there are a few things that you need to know before you see Lord Manchester. The first thing, Eva, is that this man is part of the royal hierarchy. It's essential to respect him and you'll do exactly as he desires. I'm assuming Lucious has shown you everything that you might have to...perform...this evening?" Claudia cleared her throat as she looked at Eva regretfully.

The look on Eva's face was very disheartening. Claudia remembered having the same look the first time Lucious had schemed her into sleeping with another man for money. Eva continued staring down at the floor. The coloring of her face had turned somewhat yellow and she looked like she might be ill.

"Now, moving on. For your safety, it's imperative that you wear a contraceptive," Claudia said adamantly.

Eva's eyes shot up, an anxious look on her face.

"What's a contraceptive?" Eva asked timidly.

This poor girl's mother had taught her nothing, thought Claudia.

"Well, it's something you wear to keep you safe," Claudia said, glancing down as she picked out a nightgown for Eva to wear. "From certain diseases, as well as to guard you against having a child."

Eva's eyes grew large and she was rapidly shaking her head no. She wasn't saying no to the contraceptive necessarily but the entire situation.

"If you ever expect to be with Lucious again, then you are absolutely required to wear one of these. He insists, Eva," Claudia said firmly.

Eva once again lowered her head, looking back down at the ground, and said nothing to Claudia.

"Alright, let's freshen you up. There's also a new nightgown here for you to wear."

Eva felt dizzy, her heart was racing. What was happening? What was she doing? She wondered why everything was happening so quickly. Claudia helped Eva undress and put on the light pink, silk nightgown. She then applied more rouge to her cheeks and lips, trying to bring some color back into Eva's face. She pulled the pins out of Eva's hair, loosening her curls around her shoulders and back. Then, she had Eva apply perfume to her neck and wrists. Last, she explained how Eva should use the contraceptive.

Preparations complete, Claudia stood back and looked at Eva.

"Other than the expression on your face, you look absolutely beautiful."

Eva's eyes were vacant. "I think I need some more juice," she said.

Claudia released a frustrated sigh, "Eva, you can't keep Lord Manchester waiting. Besides, Curtis has put a mobile bar in your room in case Lord Manchester desires a drink. Alright, it's time to go now."

Claudia opened the door. She had learned from Lucious that she couldn't give the girls enough time to think about what they were doing; she had to keep things moving along so they didn't change their minds.

Eva turned around, looking back at Claudia, "Do I knock?" she asked.

"He's not in there, Eva. I'll send him up once you're positioned in your room," Claudia snapped.

Eva nodded her head and started walking toward her bedroom.

"What am I supposed to do when he arrives?" Eva whispered, asking Claudia as she was beginning to descend the staircase to fetch Lord Manchester.

"Do whatever comes naturally," Claudia whispered back, frustrated.

Eva thought that this request was going to be extremely difficult since there was nothing natural about what she was doing, but felt she had no choice. She entered her bedroom, positioning herself on the bed like she would for Lucious. Feelings of regret were rising within her. She thought she might be sick. Eva inhaled several deep breaths as she waited for Lord Manchester to arrive when there was a knock on her door.

"Come in," Eva called, trying to sound confident.

She seductively posed herself for Lord Manchester as he entered the room. Upon seeing Eva lying alluringly across the bed, the Baron stopped and stared at her for a moment, leaving the door gaping open. After a few moments, Eva spoke in a loud whisper, pointing to the door.

"The door Lord Manchester," she said, motioning with her hand for him to close it behind him.

"Oh," he said, nervously shutting the door.

Eva's heart was pounding hard in her chest; she thought it might explode.

The Baron stood awkwardly in front of the door, looking unsure of what to do.

Eva thought he seemed to be more nervous than she was— if that was even possible.

"Perhaps you would like a drink, my lord?" Eva asked with a nod.

Lord Manchester paused. "Yes, perhaps I will have a drink," he replied.

Eva suddenly realized that it was her job to make the drink for the Baron. She rose from the bed and gracefully made her way across the room to the mobile bar.

"What would you like to drink, my lord?" she asked.

He cleared his throat. "Please, just call me Charles," he insisted.

"Alright then, Charles," she nodded, smiling.

"I'll have a brandy," he stated.

Eva retrieved a glass from the bar and poured some brandy into it. She then handed the glass to him, gazing at him coquettishly.

"Do you mind if I have a drink, too?" she asked.

"No, of course," he said, waving his hand toward the bar.

Lord Manchester looked around the room for a chair. Realizing there were none, he went over and sat down on the edge of the bed. Lucious had purposely removed the chairs from all the girls' rooms so the patrons would have to sit on their beds. This ensured that things moved along swiftly.

Eva poured herself a glass of Paddimir's juice. Taking several gulps, she began to feel euphoria course through her veins.

"You were quite thirsty," Lord Manchester noted.

Eva wiped her mouth gently, realizing that she probably hadn't look very ladylike as she gulped down the juice. She gingerly set the glass down on the mobile bar, then sauntered over to Lord Manchester, sitting close to him on the bed.

Lord Manchester cleared his throat and moved around a bit, looking down at the proximity of their bodies.

Eva thought that he seemed most uncomfortable.

"I'm afraid, I've never done this before," he paused timidly, "acquired a woman that is."

"Well, that makes two of us," Eva replied and snickered, then quickly covered her mouth, realizing that she probably shouldn't say such things to the Baron.

Lord Manchester laughed, "Well, I supposed that's true." He lightened up a bit.

Eva smiled at him and was relieved that he was not offended by her comment.

"Well," he continued, "it being your début and all, I'm sure..." his words trailed off.

Eva gave him a blank stare. She had absolutely no idea what he was talking about, so she smiled and nodded, just as Claudia had taught her. Then, she leaned closer to him, trying to respond the way she would if he were Lucious.

Eva gently removed the drink from Lord Manchester's hand, then crawled across the bed to lay the glass down on her nightstand. She crawled back over to him while gazing at him enticingly. She positioned herself next to him on the bed once again, looking into his eyes as she lightly caressed his hand. Lord Manchester's breath was taken away by the touch of Eva's hand against his skin and he breathed in deeply. She gazed deeply into the Baron's crystal blue eyes as they stared back at her wantonly.

He was quite attractive for an older man, Eva thought. She was beginning to look at him differently than she had earlier when they'd first met. Eva sat up on her knees, leveling her face with his; then, leaning in, she softly kissed his lips. She could sense his hesitation as she kissed him, but it wasn't long before the Baron gave in, kissing Eva in return. She gently pressed her hand against his chest, causing him to lie down on the bed. After a few moments, Lord Manchester gently pulled himself away from Eva. He was staring up at her, his breathing labored.

"Is everything alright, Charles?" she asked, smiling, while lightly rubbing her finger along his chest.

He perked up. "Oh yes, everything is fine," he said to reassure Eva. Then, after a moment, he nervously spoke, "It's just that I haven't been with anyone since my late wife."

Eva realized at that moment that the Baron was a lonely man looking for some companionship and was, perhaps, missing his wife.

"When did she pass?" Eva inquired.

"Oh, it's been close to two years now," he answered, pondering.

Eva thought how that was nearly the same amount of time since her father had passed away.

"I'm very sorry for your loss, Charles," she said tenderly, looking down at him.

"Thank you, Eva," he replied affectionately, gazing into her eyes.

She leaned back down toward him, delicately taking his face into her hand, and kissed him deeply once again. She continued with Lord Manchester, feeling that it was her duty to comfort and please the lonely soul and help him find solace in his time of need.

* * *

Once Claudia had sent Lord Manchester up to Eva's room for the night, she walked down the stairs and over to the drawing room. Pouring herself a drink from the bar she found Lucious already residing in the room, sitting in his chair, and smoking his pipe as he waited for her.

"Well, Claudia, congratulations are in order. We've done it again!" he exclaimed proudly, a smug look on his face.

"Yes, Lucious, we've done it again," she said unenthusiastically, rolling her eyes. They had once again succeeded in ruining another young girl, she thought.

Claudia walked over to the sofa and sat down across from Lucious.

"Oh, I'm utterly exhausted," he groaned, leaning his head back against the chair. "Can you believe we made five hundred pounds this evening...in one evening?" Lucious looked up at her shaking his head in disbelief.

"Well, you did always say that Eva was your golden goose," Claudia said as she took a sip of her drink.

"Yes, but I had no idea that it was going to be that much. I only hope he walks away fully satisfied. My reputation is built upon the satisfaction and discretion of my customers," Lucious said, inhaling another puff of smoke and then blowing it back out, slowly, into the air. "I mean, if you think about it, he's really the perfect match for Eva's début. Losing his wife and all...she's probably feeling sorry for him. Eva's so good-hearted like that," Lucious said cheekily, crinkling his nose while inhaling another puff. "I mean, how hard could it be to satisfy the old man? He probably hasn't been with a woman since his wife died. I wouldn't be surprised if he pounces on her as he walks through the door. That randy, old codger," he scoffed with a mischievous smirk and placed his pipe back into his mouth.

"Oh, Lucious, will you shut up already!" Claudia spouted at him angrily.

Lucious looked over at her, smiling.

"What's wrong, Dia? Don't have the stomach for it anymore?" He was giving her a devilish grin as the smoke leaked from his mouth.

Claudia inhaled intensely, shaking her head in disgust.

"Say, Claudia," Lucious leaned in toward her with a sly look, while remaining in his chair, "why don't we, for old times' sake, go upstairs to my room and celebrate our conquest?" Lucious asked, gazing at her seductively.

Claudia swallowed, trying to keep the vomit from climbing up her esophagus. She gave him a loathing look in return.

"I'd say that I think our time has passed, Lucious," she spoke with conviction. "I suggest that you go elsewhere in search of company this evening."

Rejecting his advances, she crossed her legs and turned away from him. Lucious was furious at her rejection—he peered at her, while leaning back in his chair and taking another puff of smoke.

"You're right, Dia, you probably wouldn't be able to satisfy me, anyway. As long as you've been around, you're most likely all loosey-goosey..." Lucious scoffed back, staring at her sardonically.

Claudia could feel the heat rising in her face. She wanted to come across the room and choke him but she breathed deeply, instead, composing herself. She smiled.

"You're the one to talk, Lucious. I'm surprised your knob hasn't fallen off after all this time!" she said hostilely, setting her glass down on the side table as she stood up at once with her head held high. She started walking away but then turned back around and said, "Oh, and Lucious, I will need the payment for those transactions in London. You know, taking care of your little newspaper debacle." Her tone was haughty as she walked out of the drawing room.

Lucious glared wrathfully across the room, puffing on his pipe. Once he finished smoking, he placed his pipe down on the table and went upstairs. Upon reaching the top of the staircase, he gazed over at Eva's bedroom door. Quietly he walked up to the door, leaning his ear toward it to hear what was happening inside the room. He listened for a few moments, then let out a disappointed sigh as he was unable to hear anything. He continued down the left side of the corridor in search of a companion for the evening.

Sixteen

The next morning, Eva turned in her bed to lie on her side when she heard someone moving around in her ensuite bath. Pausing, she remembered how Lord Manchester had been with her during the previous evening. She quickly turned to grab the juice she had poured after they had been intimate and drank the rest of it in haste. She lay back down on the bed, unsure how she felt about last evening. A part of her felt used and ashamed, yet another part of her believed that she was helping both Lucious and Lord Manchester. Charles was a kind, gentle man, and she could tell that he missed his wife.

Lord Manchester walked out of the ensuite, fully dressed. He stood there, awkwardly, in Eva's bedroom. She rose from the bed not wanting to see him standing there, uneasy. Her nightgown flowed across the floor as she walked through the room toward the Baron. She took both of his hands, looking deep into his eyes.

"Well, I have to be going," he said, gazing down at Eva.

She nodded her head, then reaching up she pecked him softly on the lips. Lord Manchester closed his eyes, savoring Eva's kiss.

"Would it be possible to see you again next week?" the Baron asked nervously.

Eva was surprised by his advancements but tried not to show it on her face—she didn't want to hurt his feelings.

"Well, I don't know? You will have to talk to Lucious," she said, believing that he would inform Lord Manchester that she would not be able to see him again.

"Yes, right, of course," he said in agreement. "Well, good day, Eva." He stood there for a moment gazing at her, then hesitantly took her hand, brought it up to his mouth and kissed it.

She smiled back at him pleasantly. "Good day, Charles," she murmured.

Lord Manchester nodded and then walked out her bedroom door.

Eva looked up at the ceiling, inhaling and then exhaling deeply. She realized that tears were rolling down her face. Wiping them away, she walked over to the bell to ring for Nancy. She grabbed her robe, wrapped it around herself, then lay back down on the bed. Placing her hands over her face she began to sob. Eva wasn't sure whether she was crying for herself or for Lord Manchester. He must have been terribly lonesome to ask Lucious for her instead of payment.

She was also contemplating her relationship with Lucious and how she hoped that this wouldn't change things between them. She loved him so much, but now she had been with another man. Lucious had agreed to the arrangement, but she didn't know if it would eventually change his feelings toward her. Eva lifted herself from the bed, walked over to the mobile bar, and poured herself another glass of juice. Drinking the entire glass in one gulp, the ache she felt began to dissipate.

Nancy arrived knocking at the bedroom door.

"Come in," Eva called.

"Would you like me to bring you some breakfast, Miss," Nancy asked.

"No, thank you. Actually, would you please draw me a bath?" Eva asked, sounding distressed.

"Yes, Miss," Nancy nodded.

She went into the ensuite to prepare Eva's bath when Eva realized that the contraceptive was still inside of her. Nancy returned from the ensuite.

"Your bath is filling up. Would you like me to set out your clothes for the day, Miss?"

"Yes, thank you, Nancy," Eva nodded.

The girl laid out Eva's garments, while Eva hurried into the ensuite bath to remove the contraceptive. Claudia had explained to her the night before everything that she was supposed to do in the morning. Then, Eva stepped into the bath, allowing the warm water to wash over her body. She imagined the bathwater cleansing her inside-out, removing the filth from her physical body along with the shame that was beginning to permeate her soul. Eva wrapped her arms around herself, feeling that there was a great void deep within her. It was an emptiness that was even deeper than the one she felt when Lucious was not with her. This void settled in the pit of her stomach, like a lump of coal, yet the numbing juice withheld the pain from rising.

Lucious was in the dining hall, eating his poached eggs and dry toast, when his American acquaintance, Reginald Wittaker, arrived.

"Reginald Wittaker is here to see you, sir," Curtis announced.

Lucious released a sigh of exasperation.

"I forgot that that old pillock was coming today," he said, patting his mouth with his napkin and throwing it down on the table as he stood up.

Lucious met Reginald in the foyer.

"Ah, Reggie, good to see you as always," he gave him his best fake smile.

"Lucious," Reggie responded smoothly in a proud tone.

"You are here to discuss shipments?" Lucious inquired.

"Amongst other things," Reginald spoke while his eyes continued shifting around the room as if he were looking for something.

"Why don't we go back to my study?" Lucious suggested, motioning with his hands to show the way. He thought that Reginald was acting rather suspicious.

Lucious closed the study doors behind them.

"What can I help you with, Reggie?" he asked while walking over to the chairs. Lucious put his hand out, welcoming Reginald to take a seat.

"I need another shipment of the juice; it's selling like hotcakes in New York. Also, I want to begin expediting it to other states."

Lucious cleared his throat. He was thrilled that the juice was beginning to take off in America but didn't allow it to show on his face.

"How many crates would you prefer to add to your current order?" Lucious spoke, crossing one leg over the other and placing his hand on his chin, his elbow resting on the arm of his chair.

"Well, I was considering somewhere around two hundred," Reginald stated confidently. "However, I would like to negotiate the price. If I'm doubling my order, then I want a discount," Reginald demanded smugly.

"What kind of discount were you thinking?" Lucious was rubbing his chin, contemplating what Reggie was about to say.

"Thirty percent off the current price," replied Reginald, sitting up straight in the chair.

"Oh no, no, no, that's not going to happen," Lucious scoffed, shaking his head. "No, the best I can offer you is ten percent. Any more than that and you will begin cutting into my juice creation costs."

Reginald gave Lucious a hard stare. "Okay, ten percent it is."

Lucious smiled widely and began to stand up from his chair. He was pleased that the negotiations had gone expediently, allowing Reginald to leave soon.

"There's something else I would like to discuss with you, Lucious," Reginald piped up while motioning Lucious to sit back down in the chair.

Lucious slowly sat down, looking at him intently, waiting for what he was about to say.

"My offer still stands for the girl."

Lucious gave Reginald a side glare.

"Four hundred quid?" he questioned.

Reginald nodded in agreement.

"Well, you do understand that Eva is still resting this morning from last evening's rendezvous. You will have to return later," Lucious said, rubbing his chin and contemplating the money he would be making on Eva.

"I'll be back around ten o'clock this evening," nodded Reginald and walked out the study door.

Lucious sat there for a moment rubbing the whiskers on his chin, his typical, devilish grin spreading across his face. His expression changed when he realized that he was now going to have to convince Eva to sleep with Reginald Wittaker. He knew it was probably going to be much more difficult to persuade her this time.

Eva did not leave her room the entire morning. Lucious took out his pocket watch; it was nearly half-past twelve. He decided that he should go upstairs to check on her. He approached the top of the stairwell when Eva exited her bedroom.

"Eva!" his eyes lit up at the sight of her coming out of her room. "It's good to see you up and around this afternoon."

Eva turned toward Lucious but kept her head down. He walked over, grabbed ahold of her hand, and lifted her chin to look her in the eyes. When Eva looked at Lucious, it made her heart ache. She just wanted things to go back to the way they were before coming to Liberation Hall. Lucious could see the sorrow in Eva's eyes.

"I'm sorry, love, was it just awful?" he said, pretending to pity her.

Eva stood in silence for a moment.

"I would like to go back to London," she stated firmly.

"I'm afraid we can't do that Eva, I have to stay here for now," Lucious replied.

"Then send me without you," she said with longing in her eyes.

Lucious humphed, "You don't want to be with me?" He acted as if he were insulted.

"Of course, I want to be with you." Eva placed her arms around Lucious, hugging him tightly. "I just want to go back to London, to the way things used to be when it was just the two of us," she pleaded.

Lucious wrapped his arms around Eva, knowing that she was very fragile right now. He didn't want to start an argument in the corridor.

"Why don't we go into my room. I have something I want to discuss with you."

Eva followed Lucious into his bedroom and he closed and locked the door behind them. She walked over, sitting down on the bed while Lucious walked over to his bar.

"Eva, I have some very distressing news for you, perhaps I should get you a drink," Lucious spoke while pouring Eva a glass of juice.

She couldn't possibly imagine what could be worse than last evening's news—when he had asked her to sleep with Lord Manchester.

"What is it Lucious, just tell me," she demanded, annoyed, closing her eyes.

Lucious sat down, handing Eva the beverage. She took a few sips of the juice, allowing it to calm her mind. Then, Lucious took the glass from her and set it down on the nightstand.

"Well, I first want to say that Lord Manchester was very pleased upon leaving this morning. He had such a wonderful time that he has requested to see you again next week," Lucious said, patronizingly peering at Eva as if she had done something wrong.

Eva's heart began to race. She was worried that he was upset with her.

"Lucious, I was only doing what I thought you wanted me to do. I didn't know that he would want to come back!" she exclaimed worriedly.

Lucious leaned in closer to Eva, his demeanor changing slightly.

"I told him that the same time next week would work out perfectly."

Eva's eyes grew wide; she was stunned by Lucious' response to Lord Manchester.

"What?" she said breathily, peering at him bitterly. "If he was so pleased this morning, then why is he coming back next week? He has received his payment!" she shouted, standing in haste.

Eva was furious with both Lucious and Lord Manchester—they were both using her for their arrangements and she wasn't going to tolerate it any longer. "This is absurd! I am not sleeping with Lord Manchester…again!" Eva yelled as she headed toward the door.

"Eva, calm down and get ahold of yourself," Lucious demanded firmly, trying to make her feel stupid for being upset with him.

Eva was breathing heavily as she walked back over to Lucious. Bending down, she looked him fiercely in the eyes. "I understand that Lord Manchester is lonely and misses his wife, but he's not going to use me as his companion on the side!" she commanded, then once again began heading toward the door.

Lucious stood up, grabbing her arm, pulling her back down on the bed.

"Let go of me!" she spouted.

Eva was trying to tear herself away from Lucious' grip.

"We must keep Lord Manchester happy, Eva, or he could ruin me if I don't live up to my side of the agreement," he pleaded.

"You said it was for one night only. You said you loved me, Lucious. If you love me... then, please, don't make me do this again...please!" Eva began crying, her body slowly relaxing as she rested her head on Lucious' shoulder.

Lucious knew that his game was getting old and he was honestly tired of playing the charade. He decided it was time to inform Eva of his real intentions before she did something he would regret.

"Well, that's the funny thing about love, Eva, to one person it can mean one thing and to another person it can mean something entirely different," he said jeeringly.

When Eva looked up, Lucious had a great, big smile on his face.

"What?" Eva muttered, shaking her head in disbelief.

"I'm afraid I'm not who you think I am, love." Lucious' rich, dark eyes suddenly turned black as midnight.

"What are you talking about, Lucious!" Eva was breathing heavily and fear began rising inside of her.

"I don't actually own businesses all over London. Well, I do...they're just not exactly reputable, as they say."

Eva's body was in shock; she couldn't move as she waited for what Lucious was about to say next.

"Eva, I own the most sophisticated, high-class brothel in all of London. It's called Liberation Hall and you, Eva, are one of its harlots—who now belongs to me—and I can do with you whatever I desire."

Eva felt like the wind had been knocked out of her. She backed away from Lucious, squinting and shaking her head relentlessly. She couldn't believe what he was saying to her.

"So, so, this is all a lie...us...we're a lie?" Eva was rapidly pointing back and forth between the two of them, her heart racing, realizing what he had done. "Lucious, you never really loved me, it was all trick?"

Eva tried to break away from Lucious' grip, but he grabbed her even tighter, pulling her down, forcing her to lie on the bed. He turned his body toward Eva, straddling her to keep her from getting loose.

"Get off of me! Get off me Lucious, let go of me!" she yelled.

Lucious just stared down at Eva, laughing at her.

"Oh, I do try to love Eva, as best as I possibly can but, as Dia will tell you, I am absolutely incapable of truly loving anyone. Well, other than myself, of course. I'm so sorry...

love." Lucious was patronizing her with a big, devilish grin on his face.

Eva began screaming, trying to fight back.

"Help me! Help me, please!" Eva was trying doing her best to get away from Lucious, but he was holding her down with great force.

Lucious leaned closer to Eva's face.

"Also, Reginald Wittaker has purchased you for this evening. I expect you to do your best for him." His black eyes were vicious as they glared down at her.

"I won't do it! You can't make me, Lucious!" Eva yelled in his face.

Lucious began squeezing Eva's arms tighter while digging his knees into her thighs.

"Ow! Stop it, Lucious, please, you're hurting me!" she cried out in pain and fear swelled in her chest. She knew that Lucious was much stronger than her and that he could injure her severely.

"You think this hurts? You haven't seen anything yet, love."

Lucious drove his knees deeper into her thighs. He was gripping her wrists so tightly that she could almost feel her bones bending beneath her skin. Eva gasped for breath as Lucious lay down on her, pushing his weight into her body. He leaned his face into her nose, speaking very slowly while peering into her eyes.

"Mr. Wittaker has come a very long way and has paid a considerable amount of money just to bong you, my dear. So, you're going to give the old chap exactly what he desires. And if I find out that you didn't, then I will make your life a living hell. That includes every person that you have ever cared about—starting with your dear old mummy."

Eva's eyes widened and she began to weaken, tears streaming down her face as she realized the truth of Lucious' words.

"And if you ever try to escape me, I will find you—just like the first time." A heinous smiled covered his face.

Eva remembered how Lucious had told her that he would find her the very first time his carriage had picked her up from the lodging house. She closed her eyes tightly, feeling like her entire world was caving in. She knew that Lucious was right, that he would find her and that she would never be able to escape him. She had freely given herself to him and was now trapped in his cage, known as Liberation Hall, with nowhere else to go.

Lucious Paddimir owned her.

Seventeen

Georgie had walked most of the night, doing his best to make it to Shepperton by morning. He had almost reached the town just as the sun was getting ready to rise when his legs started giving out on him. He knew that he couldn't go any further and decided to rest for a while on the side of the road. He opened the basket that William Bartly, the pub owner, had given him and pulled out the last bit of food. After he finished eating, he fell asleep, with thoughts of Eva racing through his mind even as he slept.

Georgie could see Eva in a beautiful green field, touching the wildflowers and running barefoot through the meadow. She would look back at him, smiling, while she continued sauntering along the foliage when, all of a sudden, something would catch her eye, causing her to stop dead in her tracks. There was a pack of wolves approaching and surrounding her. Georgie could see their teeth snarling and growling as they waited for the perfect opportunity to attack. He desperately tried to get to her but couldn't move closer—there was an invisible wall separating him from Eva and the wolves. All at once, they ambushed her, knocking her down to the ground, until all Georgie could see were the wolves tearing the flesh from Eva's body.

He awoke shouting, "Eva!"

He realized, upon waking, that it was just another nightmare. Shaking his head, he inhaled deeply, trying to awaken himself fully. He pulled out his handkerchief from his pocket and wiped the sweat from his face. Sitting there for a moment, he looked down at his watch to check the time. He had slept for nearly four hours and it was already nine o'clock. Rising from where he was lying down, he tried to get up but his legs wouldn't move; they were too exhausted from the journey.

"Come on, old boys," he said out loud, hitting his legs trying to get them to go.

He tried bending them so he could stand, but they were too stiff and sore and there was no budging them.

"Dang it," Georgie said aloud, slamming his hand on the ground in anger.

He leaned back on the rock and began praying that his legs would move again soon. He let out a despairing sigh; he was probably still another three or four miles away from Shepperton. Then, once he arrived in the town, he still had to find Liberation Hall.

Georgie continued hitting and rubbing his legs every few minutes, trying to get them to loosen up. He was starting to get some movement, although he was in terrible pain. Looking down at his watch, he realized that two hours had passed since he first tried to stand. Highly motivated, he finally stood up, holding onto the rock he had rested his head upon and began slowly taking steps, crying out in pain during the process. He began making his way to go pick up his bag, thanking God for each step that he was able to take. He slung the bag over his shoulder and left behind the basket that William Bartly had given him.

Georgie walked up the road toward Shepperton, hobbling as he made his way. A few minutes later, a wagon came down the road behind him and suddenly slowed to a stop.

"Whoa…whoa," the driver called out, causing the horses to halt. "Hello there, are you heading into town?"

Georgie looked up at the man. "Yes, sir, making my way to Shepperton," he replied.

"Would you welcome a lift?" the man asked.

Georgie's eyes lit up. "That would be swell, sir, thank you." Georgie first slung his bag up onto the wagon and then he tried lifting himself onto the platform, but he was too weak and his legs were extremely stiff.

The man watched as Georgie struggled to pull himself up onto the wagon.

"Here, let me give you a hand," he said, putting out his arm and allowing Georgie to use him for leverage.

Georgie grabbed the man's hand, pulling himself up while letting out a loud groan. The man gave Georgie a sideways look as he settled himself into the wagon. Clicking his tongue, the man patted the horses with the reins and the wagon began moving down the dirt road.

"The name's Dr. Edward Kenny," he said, looking over at Georgie while he continued to hold the reigns.

"George Thornber. Nice to meet you, Dr. Kenny, sir. Thank you, again, for the ride."

Dr. Kenny was a stately man in his forties, dressed very nicely for being out so far outside of London. He had dark brown hair, brown eyes, and a thin, pointed nose.

"So, what brings you to Shepperton?" asked the doctor.

Georgie inhaled a deep breath, then let it out slowly. He had told the story about Eva so many times now. But he would continue to do so if it would help him get closer to finding her.

"Well, I have a friend who's gone missing, around three weeks ago now. I've been following a trail that has led me here, to Shepperton," Georgie explained while rubbing his thighs.

"Have you been traveling on foot this entire time?" Dr. Kenny asked, astonished.

"Yes, sir, I have."

Georgie turned his head away, looking out toward the woods they were passing by. The man stared at Georgie in disbelief.

"Well, no wonder you are hobbling the way you are. Don't have a horse to ride?"

Georgie looked over. "No, sir, not one of my own, although that's what I do. I'm the stable master at Magistrate Logan's farm in Oxfordshire," Georgie said.

Dr. Kenny gazed over again at Georgie, raising his eyebrows in question.

"You came all this way from Oxfordshire?" Dr. Kenny asked in disbelief.

Georgie let out a laugh, knowing that the doctor was implying that he had walked from Oxfordshire to Shepperton. Georgie thought that, given the distance he had walked, he might as well have walked from Oxfordshire.

"No, sir, I took the train to London. It was there that I found out that Eva went missing. Since then, I have been searching for her outside of London," Georgie nodded.

"Oh, I see, so it's a lady friend who's gone missing then?"

Georgie didn't say anything. Doctor Kenny looked over at him with a grin.

"I'd say, if you've been searching for a lady friend for the last three weeks on foot, you must certainly be in love, bloke." The doctor let out a slight laugh.

Georgie looked over at the doctor. "Yes, sir, I certainly am," he nodded, most seriously.

"So, what makes you think she's in Shepperton?" Dr. Kenny inquired.

"Well, I know the man who's taken her."

The doctor glanced over, listening intently.

"His name's Lucious Paddimir and I've been told that his home is somewhere around these parts."

Dr. Kenny turned his head back to the road and didn't say anything for a moment.

"Yes, I know of Lucious Paddimir," he spoke solemnly.

"You do, sir?" Georgie asked, hopeful.

Dr. Kenny slowly nodded his head, continuing to stare forward, down the road.

"I've seen what his juice does to people. The drink should be illegal, it puts people in the most disturbing states." The doctor shook his head, a distasteful look on his face.

Georgie swallowed hard and said nothing in return. His heart began pounding at the thought of what could be happening to Eva. Dr. Kenny looked over at Georgie, seeing that he was concerned and decided to change the subject.

222

"Say, George, I have a cottage that no one is staying in at the moment. Perhaps you would like to bunk there, while you search for your friend?"

Georgie looked over at the doctor, his eyes wide.

"Yes, sir, I would appreciate that very much," Georgie spoke with much gratitude.

"If you wouldn't mind, I would also like to take a look at your legs," the doctor said, looking down at Georgie.

"That would be fine with me, sir." Georgie gave a nod, still rubbing at his thighs.

Dr. Kenny looked over with a pleased grin, then slapped the reigns on the horses causing them to trot faster.

The wagon pulled up to a beautiful, Edwardian style home that had a long picket fence lining its drive. Georgie's eyes lit up at the site of the doctor's property.

"This is a very nice home you have here, sir," he said.

"Thank you. I grew up here. It was my father's and he passed it down to me," Dr. Kenny replied and smiled proudly.

The wagon pulled up in front of the house and out ran three young children yelling, "Papa...Papa!" There were two older boys, probably seven and nine, and a little girl around five years old.

"Oh, come here, you!" Dr. Kenny called out as he jumped down from the wagon.

The children tackled the doctor, hugging him fiercely, and the little girl grabbed his leg. He bent down, picking her up.

"This here is Suzie. Will you say hi to our guest?"

The doctor looked down at the little girl as she shyly glanced over at Georgie out of the corner of her eye.

"Hello," she said, leaning her head into her father's shoulder.

"And over here are Brant and Douglas—this boy here is George Thornber."

The two boys walked over to the side of the wagon, where Georgie was sitting. They nodded, sticking out their hands toward him in a confident manner.

"How do you do, Mr. Thornber," they both greeted him assuredly.

Georgie smiled, leaned out from the wagon, and firmly shook the boys' hands. He was impressed by their hospitality toward him.

"How do you do," he replied kindly in return.

"Boys, help us grab the luggage and head inside the house," Dr. Kenny commanded. The little boys ran around to the back, pulling the bags off the wagon and carrying them inside the house, while he set Suzie on the ground.

"Now, let me help you get down from there, George."

Dr. Kenny came around to the side of the wagon on which Georgie was sitting. He moved Georgie's legs closer to the edge of the wagon, then allowed Georgie to hold onto his hand as he helped him stand on his feet. Georgie had a grim look on his face as he stood up. He slowly stepped down from the wagon, landing on the dirt drive and letting out another groan. He nearly fell but Dr. Kenny was there to catch him.

"Yes, it seems that your legs are extremely strained not only from all the walking but also from dehydration and malnutrition. I will have to examine you to make sure that there's no serious damage."

Georgie closed his eyes and gave him a heavy nod; then, Dr. Kenny helped Georgie into the house, holding his arm.

"Lillian!" Dr. Kenny called out.

A woman of medium height, with dark hair and light brown eyes, came around the corner, drying off her hands with a dishtowel. She had a joyous look on her face at her husband's arrival.

"Oh, darling, how I've missed you," she said warmly, giving Mr. Kenny a peck on the lips.

A pang hit Georgie's heart while he watched how delighted Mrs. Kenny was to see her husband. He remembered how excited Eva was to see him whenever he would return from Oxfordshire and was hoping that one day soon she would be happy to see him again.

"And who do we have here?" she asked cheerfully.

"This here is George Thornber. I told him that he could stay in the cottage for a few nights, while he searches for a friend who's in town. He also needs to let those legs of his have a good rest and heal a bit." Dr. Kenny pointed down toward Georgie's legs.

"Of course, the cottage is all ready for company but, first, why don't you come sit in the kitchen and I'll get you both some dinner. I'm sure you're starving after your long journey from London," replied Mrs. Kenny.

The men followed Lilian into the kitchen, sitting down at a small wooden table. Dr. Kenny pulled over a chair and grabbed a pillow from another room, using it to prop up Georgie's legs.

"There you go," he said. "Elevating your legs should allow them to get better circulation, helping to decrease the swelling."

Georgie nodded. "Thank you kindly, sir, for everything."

Dr. Kenny smiled. "You're welcome, George."

Lilian brought Georgie a glass of water and he drank it all at once. She looked over at the doctor, surprised by Georgie's thirst, then poured him another glass of water and began preparing leftovers of roast beef, vegetables, and Yorkshire pudding. The smell of the food made Georgie's mouth water.

"How was your seminar in London, dear?" Lilian asked while heating the roast on the stove.

"It was most fascinating. We studied germs and bacteria and how they are linked to diseases. I love learning about science," he said, looking over at Georgie while eagerly sharing what he had learned. "They're saying that certain bacteria and organisms cause specific types of infectious diseases. There is one doctor who is actually working toward finding the causative agents for cholera and tuberculosis, which could lead to creating cures!" Dr. Kenny exclaimed.

"Oh, that would be wonderful!" Lillian placed her hands on her cheeks. She almost seemed more enthusiastic than Dr. Kenny about the seminar.

"Lilian wanted to be a doctor, but her parents frowned upon the idea," Dr. Kenny explained.

"So, now I live vicariously through Edward," Lilian piped up, shaking her head.

Georgie wasn't paying any attention to their conversation; he was staring out the kitchen window, thinking about how Eva could be nearby.

Dr. Kenny looked over, noticing that Georgie was lost in his thoughts.

"Lilian dear, George's been searching all over the countryside for weeks now looking for his friend. A young lady, who has gone missing, and his journey has led him here to Shepperton," Dr. Kenny explained.

"Oh, my," gasped Lillian. "Do you have any idea where she might be in Shepperton?" she asked, sounding concerned as she whisked the eggs for the Yorkshire pudding.

Dr. Kenny cleared his throat, trying to get Georgie's attention. Georgie looked up.

"Oh, I'm sorry, I was…" his words trailed off.

"That's alright. You probably have much weighing on your mind," Dr. Kenny replied, then continued, "Lilian was just asking if you know where she might be…Eva, is it?"

"Yes, sir, her name's Eva." Georgie looked up at Lillian. "Ma'am, I strongly believe that she's being kept at a house here in Shepperton, named Liberation Hall."

Lilian immediately stopped whisking the eggs and quickly turned around, looking at Georgie.

"Oh my," she said once again, this time clearly shocked and highly concerned.

Georgie could tell by her reaction that she knew something about Liberation Hall. He gazed at her anxiously, waiting to hear more, but Lilian turned back around and once again began rapidly whisking the eggs. He then looked over at the doctor, waiting for a response. Dr. Kenny moved around nervously in his chair, looking back at Lilian.

"Please…If you…Doctor, if you know anything, please tell me," Georgie pleaded.

Dr. Kenny hesitated, then finally began to speak.

"Well…some time ago, a woman showed up to our house in a carriage. She was of African descent…and she had an accent; definitely not English," he said, shaking his head. "She pounded on the door in the middle of the night and had a young girl of nearly fifteen or sixteen waiting in the carriage…the young girl was in terrible pain." Dr. Kenny let out a sigh of anguish as he recounted the event. "The girl's name was Lila. She had been heavily drugged…and the woman asked us to take care of her, then left in a hurry with a man, driving off in the carriage. When we brought Lila into the house, she was writhing in pain. Apparently, she had been with child and to terminate it…she had…"—Dr. Kenny looked down at the table, tears filling his eyes—"used a device of some sort, causing herself to miscarry. Something went wrong and the baby had not entirely exited the poor girl's body."

Georgie's eyes grew large and he was beginning to feel ill. The doctor went on.

"We tried to save her, but…by the time they brought her to us…there was nothing more we could do," Dr. Kenny said, shaking his head.

Lilian turned around, tears streaming down her face. "The only thing the poor girl kept saying was Liberation Hall… Liberation Hall," Lillian spouted.

Dr. Kenny looked at Georgie with devastation in his eyes. "I'm so sorry, George, if this is where your friend was taken."

Georgie began breathing heavily. He felt lightheaded and thought that he might pass out. He continued staring down at the table and all he could think about was Eva—how he needed to get her out of that house and away from that wretched man! Georgie began to try to move from the table.

"George, you must sit down," the doctor insisted, worried about his legs.

"I have to find her…I have to find Eva," Georgie said anxiously as tears began welling up in his eyes, but he couldn't move his legs. He slammed his fist down, rattling the contents on the table. "I'm sorry, I'm so sorry," he said as he scrambled to wipe up the water that spilled on the table with a table cloth.

Lilian covered her mouth with her hands; her heart was breaking as she watched this poor boy in so much pain. She walked over to him, placing her hand on top of Georgie's shoulder. He looked up at her, tears making their way down his face.

"We will do whatever we can to help save your friend, George." Lillian looked down at him wistfully. Dr. Kenny nodded his head in agreement.

"Thank you, thank you both," Georgie said, looking back and forth between the two of them, as Dr. Kenny placed his hand on top of Lilian's.

"First, though, you have to get yourself well. You will be no help to Eva in your current condition, I'm afraid," said Dr. Kenny shaking his head.

Georgie agreed because he knew that the doctor was right.

"Directly after dinner, I will set you up a hot bath with some salts that will help relax your muscles. Then, once you're dressed, I will examine you. Hopefully, in a couple of days, along with plenty of rest and proper nutrition, you'll be able to go out and find your friend, but I insist on lending you one my horses." Dr. Kenny gave Georgie a raise of his eyebrows.

"Yes, sir," Georgie concurred.

Georgie didn't want to wait for days before he could go out and search for Eva when he was so close to finding her now. But he also knew that his legs needed to heal. The story about Lila made him sick to his stomach every time he thought about it—how could someone force a young girl to do something like that to herself?

What kind of man am I dealing with? he wondered. Georgie only knew one thing—that he was going to find Eva and set her free.

Eighteen

Eva reached over and picked up the glass of juice that was sitting on her nightstand. She looked down at the lush liquid, remembering how she had once hated its taste but, now, she couldn't imagine living life without it. Lucious had told her that Liberation Hall was a place of freedom, where people could have what they truly desired, but Eva had never felt more trapped and restrained in her entire life. She brought the glass up to her lips, took a few sips, and instantly felt the rush of relief come over her body. The juice seemed like freedom but wasn't, not really—it was just an unrelenting chain that kept her tied to Liberation Hall and Lucious.

Eva sat on her bed, looking down at the dark black and blue bruises on her forearms. She knew that everyone in the house could see them, too, but no one dared say a word. She sighed. Hearing a knock at the door, she thought it was her lady's maid and called out, "Come in, Nancy."

When the door opened, Lucious was standing there, holding a small black box.

"Good morning, love."

Eva tensed up at his entrance. Since the day of the incident, she had not felt the same around Lucious, although she couldn't help that a part of her still loved him. He had always been unpredictable but, after seeing the vicious side to him, she now feared being close to him.

"I have something for you."

Lucious excitedly presented her with the box he held, while gazing down upon her amorously. He opened the box, revealing a beautiful, teardrop, sapphire ring inside. The stone was much larger than the ruby promise ring he had given her that first night at the terraced house—a deep blue rock, in a silver setting, surrounded by white diamonds. Lucious retrieved the ring from the box and placed it upon Eva's ring finger, where an engagement ring would be worn.

"I hope you like it. I picked it out myself when I went into London yesterday."

Eva's eyes were fixed on the ring; she stared numbly at its brilliant elegance.

"It's wonderful, Lucious," she politely replied.

Lucious let out a humph. "It's more than wonderful, Eva. I have never chosen a more exquisite ring for anyone—but, if you don't want it, then I'll simply take it back."

He began trying to remove the ring from her finger and Eva could tell that he was offended by her response.

"I'm sorry Lucious, you're absolutely right—it's the most beautiful piece of jewelry I have ever seen in my entire life!" she said, looking up at him joyously, trying to console him.

Eva feared that she would anger Lucious and did not want to upset him in any way.

His demeanor lightened. "That's better," he said coolly.

"I also wanted to invite you to stay in my room with me once again," Lucious stated, wantonly staring at Eva, and added, "When you're not with a client, of course."

Eva gazed up at Lucious. She was afraid of him, yet something about him still pulled on her soul.

"Lucious, you said some very hurtful things to me…and you lied. You lied about our relationship and what it meant to you, among other things," Eva spoke hesitantly, looking down at the floor.

She knew that, at any moment, he could possibly react in a very hostile manner toward her. Instead, he carefully lifted her chin and gently caressed her face. Eva closed her eyes, his touch made her nervous. However, as she felt his fingers grazing her cheek, she began to calm down. There was something familiar and comforting about his hand touching her skin.

"I know that it will take some time for you to understand me, Eva, but I do want you to know that I care for you deeply. I may not be able to give you the love that you desire, but I can offer you my affection." Lucious leaned in, kissing Eva softly on the lips.

His kiss caused Eva to give in. She wrapped her arms around his body, welcoming his advances. After not being near him for two days, she missed him. Eva knew that Lucious could never really love her, but she decided that it was better to receive even one tiny morsel of his affection than to live and eat in the Hall alone, like Claudia. The Hall and Lucious were her life now and she needed to learn to make the best of it even though she was not truly loved.

* * *

The rooster outside the cottage began to crow, waking Georgie from his sleep. He smiled widely upon hearing the sound. It made him feel like he was back home again, on the farm in Oxfordshire. He had slept better the last few nights in the warm, comfortable bed. His mind had also rested well through the night, giving him a slight reprieve from relentlessly thinking about Eva. Georgie sat up in bed and tried bending his legs to see whether he could move them better. After two days of rest and Dr. Kenny providing him with various therapies, they were finally beginning to loosen up. Georgie let out a sigh of relief; he thought that, maybe, today he could make his way to town to gather some information about Liberation Hall.

He slowly moved his legs to the side of the bed and continued massaging them vigorously. Stretching his arms high into the air, he felt refreshed after two days of rest, which had given him a much needed second wind for the next part of his journey. Georgie slowly stood up since his legs were still somewhat stiff and painful. He made his way to the chair on which his clothes were and he dressed himself for the first time in days. The Kenny's had been so kind to him. Lillian had washed all of his clothing so that he didn't have to continue wearing dirty garments. He wasn't sure how he was ever going to repay the Kennys for everything they had done for him.

Looking out the small cottage window, he saw the horse barn not too far off and decided to check on the horses. He walked stiffly over to the barn and opened the door. Stepping inside, he began to take care of the horses just as he would have done for the magistrate's horses in Oxfordshire. Georgie wanted to do something for the Kennys in return for their hospitality. They had five horses, four of which were beautiful, amber-brown thoroughbreds, while the fifth one was a small Shetland pony, with a darker cream-colored coat and light blonde hair. Georgie worked as if he was completing his daily routine in Oxfordshire. He fed, watered, and cleaned the horses, then released them into the field to graze while he shoveled their stalls.

Dr. Kenny walked out to the cottage an hour later to help Georgie get dressed for the day. He knocked on the door.

"George!" he called, but there was no answer.

He finally decided to go inside the cottage, worried that there might be something wrong. Opening the door, he noticed that Georgie was missing, along with his clothing. He looked around the small cabin and thought that Georgie might have become desperate, deciding to go out and search for Eva. Dr. Kenny ran over to the barn, thinking that Georgie would most likely have taken a horse with him this time—if he were strong enough to mount one. The doctor came around the corner of the cottage, found the barn door wide open, and saw that the horses had been released to pasture. He walked over to the barn and saw Georgie shoveling horse dung out of the stalls.

"What on earth are you doing, George?" the doctor asked, eyes wide in shock, seeing him working away.

Georgie quickly glanced up at Dr. Kenny.

"Well, I was feeling a bit better, sir, and decided to come out here and help out with the horses this morning."

Dr. Kenny rushed over to Georgie, bent down, and checked the movements of his legs. "How's your pain level today?" the doctor inquired while bending Georgie's knees back and forth, checking to see how easily they moved.

"It's not bad at all, sir."

Dr. Kenny looked up at him, unsure if he was being honest.

"How about the stiffness?" the doctor stood up this time, looking Georgie straight in the eye.

"They're still a bit stiff—but once I'm up and moving, it's not that bad."

Dr. Kenny looked at him intensely.

"I still want you to continue doing the therapies and drinking plenty of water throughout the day. If they begin to worsen, then I insist that you rest them longer," said the good doctor, giving Georgie a tough and serious stare.

"I understand, sir," Georgie nodded his head in agreement.

Dr. Kenny wanted Georgie to find Eva as quickly as possible, but he also wished for him to be healthy when he does so. The Kennys felt guilty about what happened to Lila and wanted to do all they could to help Georgie rescue Eva from Liberation Hall.

Dr. Kenny began walking around, pacing the barn anxiously with his head down.

"George, I have some information for you, but I'm afraid you should sit down before I tell you what I know."

Georgie felt his nerves wrestle within him at the doctor's words. He hobbled over to a stool that sat next to one of the horse stalls, then looked up at Dr. Kenny in anticipation.

"Last evening, I spoke with an acquaintance of mine who is somewhat of a pillar in the community here in Shepperton." The doctor rolled his eyes. "I figured if anyone knew anything about Liberation Hall, it would be him. He was extremely apprehensive to talk about the Hall, as he called it, but, eventually, he released what information he had about the place." Dr. Kenny paused for a moment inhaling; then, he once again began pacing back and forth in the barn.

"I'm not sure how to tell you this...." the doctor's words trailed off.

Georgie looked up at him, anxiously shaking his head.

"Just tell me, sir, please!"

Dr. Kenny stopped pacing and stood, looking intently at Georgie.

"Liberation Hall is not merely Lucious Paddimir's home. It's a high-class brothel, known for having exclusive clientele—the wealthiest of men, including members of parliament and the royal hierarchy."

Georgie's face dropped and his heart began pounding in his chest at the horrific news. He felt great pain overtake his body. Breathing heavily, he leaned away from the stool and vomited onto the hay on the barn floor. Dr. Kenny knelt behind him, placing his hand on his back.

"It's alright, chap, it's alright," he said, consoling him.

Georgie covered his face with his hands and began weeping.

"Eva, my sweet Eva," he muttered. "How....why?" Then Georgie released a cry of agony. "Aaahhhhhh!" he cried out in anguish.

Dr. Kenny backed away. His heart was heavy for Georgie and how he must feel upon hearing such news. After all that he had been through searching for the girl. Georgie understood that Eva was probably addicted to the juice and that Lucious had apparently convinced her that he loved her, but he had no idea that this is what Lucious ultimately wanted with Eva.

Dr. Kenny rose. "I'm so very sorry, George." The doctor looked down at the ground with great remorse. "But it all makes sense now—why the other woman brought Lila to the house and left in such a hurry. She was probably risking her own life just bringing the girl here," Dr. Kenny said, shaking his head.

Georgie began wiping the tears from his eyes.

"I have to find her now, doc. I have to find Eva now and get her out of that place."

There was such intensity in Georgie's eyes. He was burning with anger toward Lucious and what he had done to Eva.

"I need you to listen to me, George."

Georgie gazed up at the doctor, his eyes inflamed with rage.

"There's more," the doctor paused and Georgie looked up at him in anticipation.

"I know where the Hall is located."

Georgie stood up at once. He stood so quickly that he almost fell, as his legs were not ready for the jolt.

"George!" Dr. Kenny caught him, setting him back down on the stool. "You have to calm down and take some deep breaths, son."

Georgie sat there for a moment, breathing deeply, as thoughts of Eva raced through his mind. He realized now that the nightmares he was having were a reflection of her being violated by vicious men who only desired one thing from her.

"Now, Liberation Hall is less than a mile away from here, which makes me sick to my stomach," Dr. Kenny humphed in disgust, thinking in how close a proximity his own daughter has been to a man like Lucious Paddimir. "But you may only enter the Hall by invitation. They won't allow you through the doors any other way."

Georgie looked up at the doctor. "I don't care. I don't care if I have to beat down the door. I will get her out of that house!" he spouted indignantly.

"I'm afraid, George, that your legs are still not able to go very far, and I don't see how you could possibly mount or dismount a horse at this time. Perhaps I should go instead of you?" the doctor asked.

"No," Georgie responded quickly. "It has to be me. Eva has to see me. She won't leave with a stranger," he explained. Dr. Kenny shook his head.

"I hate to break the news to you, George, but she already did when she left with Lucious Paddimir," Dr. Kenny spoke bluntly yet, at the same time, he was trying to be sensitive to Georgie's feelings.

"Yes, but this man..." Georgie said, clenching his teeth. "He bought her gifts and took her to a fancy restaurant. He treated her like a princess—he probably told her... he loved her." Georgie closed his eyes tightly, in agony, placing his elbows on his knees and laying his face in his hands. "He made her feel special. Eva needed to feel special and I should have been there for her. I should have been there, making her feel special. I should have been there to save her!" he yelled intensely as tears welled up in his eyes again.

Dr. Kenny walked over to Georgie, placing his hand on his shoulder.

"You will, George. You will save her—but, first, you have to help yourself."

Georgie looked down at his legs and began rubbing them. Dr. Kenny was right; he wouldn't be able to mount or dismount a horse and if he needed to pick Eva up and run, he wouldn't be able to do so. He didn't have the strength. Georgie knew that he had not been very wise—blowing full steam ahead, searching all over the country for Eva—but he also knew that he had to do something. He couldn't just leave her with Lucious Paddimir.

"Say, George, I have an idea," Dr. Kenny said, perking up, hope in his eyes. "It may take a couple of days to work out, which will give your legs extra time to heal and…might actually work, I think," he said with a pleasant grin on his face.

Georgie looked up at the doctor. He sure hoped that he was right because he couldn't bear to think of Eva staying in that house a moment longer.

Nineteen

E va placed the new sapphire ring on her finger and stared down at its illustrious beauty. Lucious had been very pleasant toward her over the last few days. She started staying in his room at night again and life was beginning to feel more normal. She glanced down at the ring once more, looking at how it rested upon her ring finger. Sadness suddenly overwhelmed her at the realization that she would most likely never marry and have a family of her own. She was ruined by Lucious on multiple levels and no good man would ever desire her to be his wife—nor would Lucious ever allow her to leave. Eva wrapped her arms tightly around her body as tears streamed uncontrollably down her face.

She began thinking about Georgie and how he would never want anything to do with her now. Her heart was so heavy from all the losses in her life—her father, Georgie, and her mother. Lucious told her that her mother most likely hated her for running off with him and that, if Eva ever did return home, she would turn her away in disgust. Eva felt isolation and disgrace flooding within her, and she feared that she would never truly live a normal life, ever again.

Suddenly, Eva doubled over, grabbing her waist. A wrenching feeling twisted her stomach and she hurried into the ensuite bath just in time to vomit into the toilet. After cleaning herself up, Eva took a few sips of the juice and headed downstairs to have her lessons with Claudia. Claudia was practicing her harp while she waited for Eva in the drawing room. When Eva walked into the room, Claudia could immediately tell that something was wrong with her.

"Are you alright?" she asked, concerned. Eva's face was extremely pale and drawn.

Eva shrugged. "I think I've caught an illness. I don't feel very well," she said drearily, looking as if she might faint.

"I think you need to go back upstairs to bed," Claudia insisted as she walked over to Eva and placed her hand on her forehead. "I don't think you have a fever. How long have you felt this way?" Claudia probed.

"I don't know? Last evening when I was in Lucious' bedroom, I started feeling nauseous, but then I drank some juice and was fine."

Claudia lowered her head, looking seriously into Eva's eyes. "Have you had your menses this month?"

Eva's eyes grew wide and she looked away, embarrassed by Claudia's question.

Claudia moved in front of Eva's face. "Eva, it's important that at you tell me," she insisted adamantly.

Eva tried hard to remember; it had been a while—perhaps even weeks—before she met Lucious. Eva shook her head no.

Claudia rolled her eyes, letting out a distressed sigh. "Go back upstairs and lie down. I'll bring you up some brandy and water to soothe your nausea."

Eva agreed and headed back upstairs to her room.

Claudia briskly walked down to the study where Lucious was working on his books. She burst through the study door.

"Lucious, we need to talk," she said, walking across the room and sitting on the desk while crossing her arms.

"Not now, Claudia, I'm very busy this morning, crunching numbers."

Claudia leaned over, closing the book that Lucious heavily focused his attention on. He looked up at her, annoyed.

"You better have a good reason for doing that," he spouted, glaring at Claudia.

"I do," she retorted.

"Well, what it is?" he asked impatiently.

Claudia had a very distressed look upon her face.

"I need you not to take this out on me," she said, looking at him intently.

"Oh God, now you've got me worried. Just tell me already," Lucious insisted, reclining back in his chair.

"I think Eva might be pregnant."

Lucious laughed uncomfortably while sitting back in his chair with his hands behind his head.

"I'm afraid that's not possible, Dia," he said calmly. "The juice has specific ingredients to take care of that sort of thing and, recently, I've even upped the dosage. It's always worked," Lucious continued shaking his head in dismay.

"Except with Lila," Claudia said, giving Lucious a hard stare.

Lucious hastily stood and leaned into Claudia's face.

"You know that we don't talk about Lila," Lucious said firmly and his eyes turned black, staring coldly at her.

"Well, we do need to talk about Eva," she said simply, changing the subject.

Lucious inhaled deeply, then exhaled, exasperated as he began pacing back and forth in his study.

"Are you sure it's not just an illness?" he asked Claudia, hoping for another explanation.

"No, I'm not sure, but have you not noticed that Eva hasn't had her menses since she's been with you? She says it's been six weeks, Lucious," Claudia replied nervously.

Lucious was staring at nothing, recollecting how he had probably impregnated Eva in London. He rolled his eyes and walked back over to Claudia, leaning once again into her face.

"Now, Claudia, I have better things to do than to worry when all the women in this house are on the rag! That's your job, remember! I pay you a lot of money to make sure things like this don't happen!" he yelled angrily.

Claudia braced herself, closing her eyes as Lucious yelled in her face. Lucious was fuming and had, once again, begun pacing back and forth in the study.

"You've been making sure she is using the contraceptive?" he asked and Claudia nodded.

"The only person Eva was intimate with while not using the contraceptive...is you."

Lucious turned around to find Claudia scowling at him.

"Oh, don't look at me like that; I know what you're implying. That...that thing is mine, if there's even a thing!" Lucious shouted, waving his hands around frantically. He continued thinking for a moment. "Alright, I'm going to go lace some of the juice with extra herbs and whatnot. Do not tell Eva that you believe she's...well, you know," Lucious demanded with a shrug. Then, he stormed off, slamming the study door behind him.

Claudia brought Eva a glass of brandy and water.

"Drink this, it should help ease your nausea," she said, sitting down next to Eva on the bed.

Eva sat up, taking the glass of brandy. She drank a few sips and made a distasteful face.

"I don't think it's helping. I feel like I might get sick again," she said holding onto her stomach.

Claudia helped Eva make her way to the ensuite bath and Eva leaned over and vomited into the toilet once again. Claudia grabbed a hand towel for Eva to wipe her face with.

"Claudia, what's wrong with me? I feel so strange," she asked.

"Here, let me help you back into bed," Claudia answered.

After Eva was tucked into her bed, Claudia went over and closed the door.

"Eva, there's something I need to talk to you about."

Eva looked at Claudia, doing her best to listen while her stomach continued twisting and turning. Claudia sat down next to Eva on the bed and placed her hand on Eva's. Inhaling a deep breath and looking at Eva's youth and frailty, Claudia decided it was best that she didn't know the truth.

"What is it, Claudia?" Eva inquired.

Claudia smiled, shaking her head. "I just want you to know that you'll be fine in a few days," Claudia said, hoping that Eva would, indeed, be fine—but she wasn't so sure after what she had encountered with Lila.

Eva rested in her bed most of the day and was feeling a bit stir-crazy by the mid-afternoon. The nausea had abated throughout the day and she was beginning to feel more like herself again. She sat up in bed, contemplating whether or not she should get on with her day, when Lucious knocked on the door and walked into her room.

"Lucious!" she exclaimed, thrilled at the sight of him.

"I came to check on you, love, and bring you a fresh batch of juice. I made it with some special herbs to help you feel better," he said, smiling while holding up the juice.

"Oh, how lovely of you," she said, grinning from ear to ear at his thoughtfulness. He poured a glass of the new juice concoction and brought it over to her, sitting down next to her on the bed.

"Now drink up, love. I need you to feel better as soon as possible," he said while gently caressing her hand.

Eva nodded, knowing that Lord Manchester was due to return the following day. Pushing that thought from of her mind, she decided to believe that Lucious was being sympathetic to her needs.

"How are you feeling now?" he asked.

"Much better, especially now that you're here," she responded, coyly gazing at him.

Eva leaned in toward Lucious, hoping to kiss him—but Lucious leaned back, turning his head away from her.

"Best not right now, Eva, in case you've caught something," he said, crinkling his nose and removing his hand from hers.

Eva felt rejected; giving a dismal nod, she lay back down on the bed.

"Well, I'll be back to check on you later, you get some rest now," Lucious said, patting her leg over the covers, then walking toward the door. He turned and smiled as he left the bedroom, closing the door behind him.

Eva turned onto her side and began holding herself. Lucious' rejection made her feel worthless but, having been sick all day, she knew that he was right. It was best for him to keep his distance in case she had caught something. She knew that she should just be happy that Lucious wasn't angry with her for being sick. Everything had been fine since they reconciled and she didn't want her illness to change things now.

* * *

Eva woke after sleeping on and off throughout the entire day. The room was pitch black and she began feeling around blindly, trying to find the matchbook on her nightstand.

"There you are," she said aloud, finding the matchbook and striking a match to light her lantern.

She held the lamp near the clock and peered closely to see what time it read. The clock said it was half-past two. Eva sighed in frustration; she was wide awake in the middle of the night. Leaning over, she grabbed a glass of the new juice that Lucious had brought her from the nightstand and took a generous drink while making a distasteful face. The new juice he had concocted was loaded with more herbs and spices, which did not improve its flavor. Eva sat up in her bed, realizing that she was feeling much better after resting all day and that she didn't want to stay in her room a minute longer.

Eva contemplated what she could do in the middle of the night. She wasn't hungry and there was probably no one downstairs at this time of night. Suddenly, she had an idea and popped out of bed excitedly. She decided to go over and surprise Lucious in his room. He had rejected her advances earlier in the day, but she thought that if she went over in the middle of the night, she could convince him to show her some affection.

Eva grabbed her lantern and walked into the ensuite bath to prepare herself for him. She washed her face, brushed her teeth, and let her hair down to cascade in long waves. Combing it, she then applied some perfume on her neck and wrists. Then, she changed from the nightgown into one of Lucious' favorite negligees and wrapped her robe around herself, placing her slippers on her feet.

She set the lantern down on top of the chest of drawers in her room, then quietly opened the door. Eva didn't want to draw any attention to herself, knowing there could possibly be gentlemen in the corridor at night who did not want to be seen. She looked down the hallway and saw no one in sight, so she tiptoed across the hall over to Lucious' bedroom door. Eva placed her hand on the doorknob and was about to enter when she heard a voice coming from his bedroom. Leaning her head closely to the door, she realized it was a woman's voice. She jolted back but then leaned in again, placing her ear right up against the door, trying to hear who was inside Lucious' bedroom. She heard Lucious and a woman making loud sounds of passion. Eva gasped, covering her mouth with her hand, her eyes wide in shock. Her heart sank as the sounds echoed louder and louder from Lucious' bedroom. She was rapidly shaking her head back and forth while still holding onto her mouth, trying not to make a sound. She slowly walked backward, away from the door, when she suddenly slammed against the other side of the corridor wall. Leaning against the wall, she let her body slowly sink onto the floor below as tears filled her eyes. How could he do this to her? But why should she expect anything different from him? Eva felt stupid for believing that Lucious had felt differently about her and would somehow be faithful to her—after all, she was sleeping with other men.

Claudia heard a loud bang against her bedroom wall. She opened her door to investigate the sound. Gazing around the dark corridor, she thought she saw Eva lying on the floor. Claudia hurried over, wondering whether she had fainted or something else was wrong. Claudia knelt down beside Eva and realized that the girl was crying.

"What's wrong, Eva?" she asked and rubbed her fingers through Eva's hair. "Are you alright?" Then, Claudia heard the sounds coming from Lucious' bedroom. She looked back over at Eva and inhaled a deep breath, realizing how Eva had planned to surprise Lucious in his bedroom when she probably heard how he was occupied. Looking down at Eva, she shook her head.

"Oh, Eva," she sighed sympathetically, then helped her up from the floor and led her back to her bedroom. "Come on, let's get you back to your room," Claudia said solemnly. She sat Eva down on the bed, grabbed Eva's glass of juice from the nightstand, and handed it to her, sitting down next to her.

Eva placed her face into her hands and sobbed uncontrollably. Claudia began rubbing Eva's back, trying to console her.

"I'm sorry that you heard…" Claudia's words trailed off and she swallowed hard. Eva looked up at Claudia, red-faced with swollen eyes.

"I thought we had something different. I thought it was something special," Eva continued crying as she spoke.

Claudia's heart went out to Eva as she remembered how she had felt the same way the first time she found Lucious with another woman in St. Lucia. They had only been together for two weeks—and that had been the first of many times that she would catch Lucious with someone else in his bed.

"I'm afraid Lucious has many demons, Eva. His addiction to his own juice is only one of them," Claudia said, patting Eva's back.

"But it felt so real and I thought that maybe I could get Lucious to—"

"To love you," Claudia interjected. "That you could teach him how to love and fall in love with you."

Eva looked up at Claudia pitifully.

"Eva, when you first arrived at Liberation Hall and I saw Lucious with you..." Claudia sighed. "I, too, thought that he might possibly be falling in love with you."

Eva looked up at Claudia, surprised.

"In fact, I hoped he was. It would have given me some sort of solace to think that maybe someone could help him change and make him experience love. But then I saw him, as always, pushing any real feelings deep down inside because of pride, greed, fear, and pain from his own past." Claudia looked Eva seriously in her eyes. "The truth is, Eva, if Lucious really loved you, he would have married you...and he certainly wouldn't be forcing you to sleep with other men."

Eva buried her face in her hands and began crying again. She knew that Claudia was right—if Lucious really loved her, he would have done the noble thing and would have married her at the start.

"I have seen this happen so many times." Claudia shook her head. "He scouts out young, beautiful girls, then watches them for months, studying and analyzing their every move in order to understand them and their needs."

Eva looked up at Claudia in astonishment. "What?" she asked.

"Oh yes, Eva, Lucious studied you for months before he ever approached you. He finds out everything he possibly can to make sure that the girl is a good candidate for Liberation Hall. Then he waits...and when they're most vulnerable, he strikes."

Eva was flabbergasted. She thought about that day in the market, when she had fallen, and how he had probably been watching her as well as on the day she had run into him at Bertram's flower shop.

"They always fall in love with him," Claudia said, shaking her head while staring into nothing. "Well, with his act really," she added. "Once they get to truly know Lucious, they soon realize he is nothing like the man they had fallen in love with... that man is only a persona," Claudia said, looking over at Eva and frowning.

"I've been such a fool!" Eva shouted, wringing her hands. "How can anyone be so cruel to do what he has done?" she lashed out furiously.

Claudia just looked down at the floor, without giving her an answer.

"I think I'm going to be sick again," Eva said as she stood up quickly from the bed and ran into the ensuite.

Claudia sat there, debating whether she should tell Eva that she is with child, but once again decided that it was best for her not to know everything at the moment.

Eva returned to the bedroom, sitting down next to Claudia on the bed.

"When we were in London, everything felt so genuine, and there was Mrs. Martindale. Does she know the truth?" Eva questioned, looking up at Claudia.

Claudia gave her a sorrowful look and nodded.

"Lucious hires Mrs. Martindale to play the 'mother' role in London, helping the girls acclimate to the process. While Lucious 'fathers' them, so to speak…giving them attention and buying them extravagant gifts."

Eva's eyes grew large and she shook her head; she was in utter shock and disappointment. Everything made sense now. It had all been a ploy to get her to come to Liberation Hall so Lucious could make money off of her. Lucious never cared about her, he only wanted to use her from the very beginning. Everything had been a lie.

"And the clothes and shoes?" Eva asked solemnly.

"I'm sorry. I have no idea what you're asking?" Claudia gently replied.

Eva gazed out across the room. "He knew my dress and shoe sizes," she said, looking over at Claudia, wanting an explanation.

"Ah, yes," Claudia said, shaking her head. "Did you ever leave your shoes outside on the porch in the evening? And when you washed your clothes, did you leave them outside on the clothesline to dry?"

Eva looked at Claudia with surprise.

"He'd been to my home at night. Going through my belongings?"

Eva started realizing that Lucious had followed her everywhere and knew everything about her life.

"I wonder if he knows about Georgie?" Eva pondered aloud.

"Who's Georgie?" Claudia asked inquisitively.

Eva looked up and quietly said, "No one, anymore." She gazed down at the ground and began crying again. Claudia continued rubbing her back to comfort and console her.

Suddenly, Eva cried out abruptly, grabbing her waist and clenching in pain.

"Eva, you should really lie down." Claudia was hoping that the new juice mixture that Lucious had given her was beginning to work. She did not know that Lila was pregnant for several months and, by the time she had finally realized it, Lila was far along already. Lucious had refused to allow Lila to have the baby and Claudia didn't want to see another girl go through the pain that Lila had had to endure, especially not Eva. She had already been damaged enough by Lucious.

Twenty

The following morning, Claudia walked into Lucious' study, holding an open letter in her hand.

"We've received a request from a doctor in town. A 'Dr. Edward Kenny'. It says here that he desires to purchase Eva for one evening."

Lucious' head shot up from his desk.

"Now that's interesting. Has he ever been to the Hall?" he asked, tilting his head and squinting.

"No, not that I'm aware of," Claudia shook her head.

"So how did he hear about Eva? It normally takes several months for word to spread around about the new stock and it's usually previous customers who purchase the girls first," Lucious questioned, looking up at Claudia, contemplating and waiting for an answer.

"Well, it says in the letter that he heard about the Hall from Lord Ambile. Perhaps Lord Manchester told him about Eva and he passed the information along?"

Lucious sat for a moment, rubbing his chin.

"I don't see Lord Manchester as a bloke who would bluster about his liaisons with Eva. But I am curious about this Dr. Kenny—so let's invite him to the Hall and check him out first. If Eva is going to be prepared for the evening, I want to make sure that this man is valid and is able to pay his dues," Lucious said, peering at Claudia.

Claudia nodded her head and started heading toward the door.

"Wait, Claudia!" Lucious called out.

She turned around.

"Is there any news about Eva's...," Lucious cleared his throat, "condition?"

Claudia rolled her eyes, looking up at the ceiling and sighed, "Well, she's still vomiting all morning long and still doesn't seem to know that she's pregnant. Oh, and she overheard you with Marissa last night."

Claudia gave him a cold glare.

Lucious stared back at her. "So, is the thing still in her, then?" he inquired.

Claudia rolled her eyes, disgusted by Lucious' lack of empathy.

"As far as I know, yes," she scowled at him.

"That will be all then," he said, annoyed, motioning for her to exit the room.

*   *   *

Eva had not been feeling well, on and off, for three days now. She sat on her bed, gazing out the window. A bluebird was chirping and fluttering around outside in the spring air.

She envied the bird—it was free to go anywhere it desired. Eva walked up to the window and shooed the bird away.

"Go on now, you don't want to stay here at this dreadful place. Go on…be free," she said to the bluebird.

When she turned back around, Lucious was standing in her doorway. Eva gasped and grabbed her chest upon seeing Lucious standing there, unannounced.

"I didn't mean to frighten you," he said quietly.

Eva turned back around and looked out the window.

"Claudia informed me that you overheard a delicate situation happening last evening in my bedroom?"

Eva stood silently and continued staring out the window, paying him no attention. Lucious walked up behind her and wrapped his hands around her waist, kissing the side of her head. Eva closed her eyes, she wanted to hate his touch, but she couldn't help that it comforted her. She was angry with herself for still loving him after everything that he had put her through and all the lying that he had done. She had promised herself that she would stay angry with him and never be intimate with him again.

"Eva, you have to understand. You were not available last evening and I have grown accustomed to enjoying the company of a woman."

Eva rolled her eyes. She could feel her blood boiling within as he tried to explain his behavior. Lucious turned Eva around, forcing her to look him in the face.

"You have to know that there is absolutely nothing more than a physical relationship between Marissa and I."

Eva glared up at him, scowling. She hadn't known who he was with last night.

"I care for you, Eva."

Lucious leaned down, trying to kiss Eva on the mouth, but she turned away. She wasn't falling for his "persona," as Claudia had called it last evening.

"I thought that you didn't want to kiss me in case I'd caught an illness?" she said disdainfully.

"I don't care if I catch whatever you have. I would rather be with you and have caught a cold than live my life without you, Eva."

Eva wanted to believe him, but she knew that this was how he acted—it was all a part of the role he played.

"I'm not falling for it!" she shouted.

"You're not falling for what?" he asked, calmly.

"I'm not falling for your lies, Lucious, and your persona! You pretend to be this charming, loving person," Eva shouted.

Lucious was surprised by Eva's comment.

"Persona?" Lucious let out a slight laugh. "Eva, what are you talking about, this is who I am."

Eva stared at Lucious angrily but didn't want to say anything about her conversation with Claudia, fearing that Lucious would be hostile toward her. She pressed her lips together, contemplating what she should do now. Lucious had caught on by now that, when Eva pressed her lips together, she was hiding something from him.

"What are you hiding from me?" Lucious asked.

Eva quickly turned around and, as she did, her hair hit Lucious in the face. He grabbed her arm, swinging her back around, forcing her to look at him.

"What are you hiding from me, Eva? Tell me now!" he demanded, holding onto her arms and shaking her.

Eva was scared. She didn't want to tell him but she also didn't want him to hurt her again.

"Claudia told me everything. How you find girls and follow them for months. Then, at the right time, you just happen to run into them, say...at a flower shop," Eva said snarkily, referring to her own situation.

Lucious sighed with a disgusted look on his face.

"Claudia hates me, Eva. She will tell you anything to pin you against me. I already told you that she's jealous of how I feel toward you. She knows that things are different between us and that I care for you more than I have ever cared for anyone... including her." Lucious placed his hands around Eva's waist, pulling her closer to himself. "Eva, you can only trust Claudia up to a certain point, but when it comes to me...well, I'm afraid she despises me and will do anything to keep us from being together," Lucious said, gazing at her amorously.

Eva looked up at him angrily, "That doesn't change the fact that you were with Marissa last evening and I can't get those sounds out of my mind, Lucious!" Eva yelled, grabbing at her head.

Lucious sucked in a deep breath while pressing his tongue against his front teeth.

"Well, I'm not sure what more I can say. You may ask Marissa, and she'll confirm that there's nothing between us. In fact, she went back to her room after we..." Lucious let his words trail off and he closed his eyes, realizing he was getting nowhere with her. "Please forgive me, Eva, I simply can't help myself." He leaned down, trying look into her eyes. "Please, I promise it will never happen again. I want you with me every evening."

Eva glanced up and noticed that Lucious had a tear in his eye. She couldn't figure him out, either what he was saying was true or his acting was incredibly convincing. Eva found herself feeling extremely concerned for him. Lucious seemed to dislike himself for being so lustful and she couldn't help but feel sorry for him. He continued staring intensely into her lush green eyes.

"I know Lord Manchester is coming here this evening, but I have decided to inform him that you are unwell and unable to entertain him for the evening. When you are ready, you may come stay in my room with me," Lucious offered.

"You'll do that for me?" she asked, surprised. "Even though I'm still not perfectly well?" Eva wondered if that would make him change his mind.

"I'll take care of you Eva and it will be alright," he said, caressing her face. Then, leaning down, he kissed her deeply. The way that Lucious was behaving made Eva wonder whether, perhaps, he was learning how to love, after all, by falling in love with her.

Lucious left Eva's room and immediately began searching the house for Claudia. He found her in the drawing room, talking to some of the other ladies at the house.

"Claudia!" Lucious roared while harshly motioning her toward the study.

Claudia looked up at Lucious and could tell that he was furious with her. She kept her eyes on him as she politely excused herself from the drawing room. Lucious hastily walked down the corridor to the study and Claudia quickly followed, fear beginning to rise in her, knowing that she was in terrible trouble. Lucious slammed the study door behind them and, immediately upon entering the room, he backhanded Claudia across the face. Claudia cried out in pain, grabbing her face.

"How dare you tell Eva my plans and betray me!"

Claudia was trembling as she held her face, tears flooding her eyes.

"You're supposed to be my confidant. If I can't trust you, then I will have to tighten your reigns!" he shouted. "Now, because of you, I have Eva staying in my room with me while she retches all over the place!" Lucious walked up to Claudia looking her harshly in the eyes. "If you do any such thing ever again, I promise you, Dia, I will kill you!"

Claudia knew that Lucious meant what he said and that he would kill her if she betrayed him.

"Do you understand?"

Claudia nodded while continuing to hold her face.

"Good! Now get out of here!" he demanded waving her away from the study.

Claudia slowly left the room, walking out into the corridor and closing the door behind her. She removed her hand from her cheek while standing in the hallway. Looking down, she noticed that her lip was bleeding. Claudia walked upstairs toward her bedroom to take care of her wound just as Eva entered the corridor.

Eva looked at Claudia and saw that she was covering her face.

"Are you alright?" Eva asked, concerned.

Claudia nodded her head, a loathsome expression on her face, and Eva realized that Lucious had hit Claudia.

"Oh, no, did Lucious do that to you?" she asked, feeling terrible. She worried that this was her fault.

Claudia said nothing as she turned around and continued walking down the corridor toward her bedroom. Eva ran up ahead of Claudia, blocking her from entering her room.

"This is all my fault, I'm so sorry Claudia!" Eva said with incredible care in her eyes as she went to touch Claudia's shoulder, but Claudia closed her eyes and moved away from Eva's reach. Eva pulled her hand back, realizing that Claudia didn't want her comfort.

"I knew I shouldn't have told him," Eva sighed, looking down at the ground.

"No, you shouldn't have," Claudia snapped back.

Eva looked up at her, feeling badly.

"He made it sound like you were making it all up and that none of it was true," Eva said, wanting Claudia to understand her predicament.

"Oh, I'm sure he did, Eva. Lucious is an incredibly good liar," she said, pushing Eva aside, entering her bedroom, and slamming the door behind her.

Eva felt absolutely horrible for what happened. Claudia had been so kind to her while she was sick. She wasn't sure how she was going to make things right. After a moment, she rushed over to Claudia's door, opening it. Claudia jumped at Eva's abrupt entrance and grabbed at her chest.

"I'm sorry for barging in on you, but I don't want us to be sore at one another. You are the closest thing I've ever had to a sister and I'm very sorry that I told Lucious. He knew that I wasn't telling him something and he was forcing me to be honest with him. I had no idea he would do this to you," Eva said, motioning toward Claudia's face.

Claudia was distressed for Eva. She knew how persuasive Lucious could be and how difficult it was to lie to him. He seemed to be able to get away with lying to everyone, but he could always tell when someone was lying to him. Claudia felt sorry for Eva—not just because she was so gullible for believing Lucious' lies but because she also played a role in this whole charade. She'd helped Lucious many times over the years, with his games, for money and because she feared him.

"I forgive you, Eva," Claudia stated without any emotion.

Eva ran up to Claudia, hugging her around the neck. Claudia closed her eyes but did not embrace Eva in return. Eva backed up, placing her hands on Claudia's shoulders.

"Thank you, Claudia. I will never, ever tell Lucious anything, ever again...I promise," Eva said solemnly while placing her hand over her heart, giving Claudia a pitiful look.

Claudia nodded sorrowfully, knowing that Eva meant what she said—but she didn't know if Eva would be able to keep her promise. Claudia decided it was best to keep her mouth shut and to no longer inform Eva of Lucious' intentions.

Eva closed Claudia's bedroom door, then made her way down the stairwell in search of some food. She was finally getting her appetite back, although there were still moments when she would feel a bit queasy. Standing in the foyer, she saw some of the ladies in the drawing room and decided to head in the opposite direction. Eva did not want to see Marissa after last night. She rounded the corner, almost running into Lucious.

"Oh, look at you, up and about," he chirped.

Eva was still hesitant with Lucious, especially after seeing Claudia's face.

Lucious could tell that Eva was still somewhat apprehensive toward him. "Come here," he beckoned for her to come closer.

Eva closed her eyes. She inhaled deeply as she allowed Lucious to wrap his arms around her.

"See, this isn't so bad," he said.

Eva continued breathing heavily, knowing that, at any moment, Lucious could possibly switch on her.

"Eva, I'm not going to hurt you," he said calmly and with affection toward her, like a father.

Eva looked up at him. "But you hurt Claudia?" she replied.

Lucious looked down at her. "That's because Claudia lied to you and she needed to be reproached," Lucious said firmly.

Eva wasn't sure what to think nor whether she could trust Lucious. She also wasn't sure that she wanted to stay in his room with him anymore. She knew that if he sent Lord Manchester away for the evening, then he would require her to stay with him in his bedroom. However, Eva also understood that if she wasn't in Lucious' room, then someone else would be with him.

Eva needed to decide before the end of the day whether she was going to love Lucious, despite his failings, or whether she would begin to try to pull her heart away from him—if that was even possible.

Lucious looked down at Eva lovingly. "Did you come down to the dining hall in search of some nourishment, love?" he asked compassionately.

Eva nodded her head.

"Let's find you some food then, you've been wasting away since you've been ill."

Eva walked with Lucious over to the kitchen. She waited outside, in the corridor, while Lucious asked the cook to prepare some food for her. She wandered down to the juice room, curious about what was in Lucious addicting elixir, exactly. Lucious returned from the kitchen to find Eva down the corridor standing in front of the juice room.

"Are you in need of some more juice, love?" he asked.

Eva shook her head no.

"I told the cook to send your lunch up to my room."

Eva stared at Lucious, wide-eyed, and he could tell that she still wasn't entirely convinced by him.

"Alright, I'll send your lunch to the dining hall, if that's what you prefer?" Lucious dipped his chin, giving her a pout. "The choice is yours, Eva."

Eva knew what Lucious was implying. She was either to choose him or be alone. She still felt torn about him but the words flowed from her mouth easily.

"No, lunch in your room sounds nice," she said with a polite smile.

Lucious' face twisted into a flirtatious grin. "That makes me very happy to hear, Eva, very happy indeed."

Twenty-One

In the mid-afternoon, Dr. Kenny and Georgie were sitting around the kitchen table and having a bite to eat, when Lilian burst through the front door. She hurried down the corridor toward the kitchen, yelling, "It's here, it's here!" Rounding the corner, they could see that she was holding up an envelope, waving it high into the air.

"It's a letter from Liberation Hall."

Georgie sat up straight up in his chair and Dr. Kenny stood up in haste. Lillian handed the doctor the envelope as he looked over at Georgie. The doctor opened it at once. He cleared his throat and read the contents of the letter aloud.

Dr. Edward Kenny,

I am pleased to inform you that we have received your request and wish to invite you to visit Liberation Hall tomorrow afternoon, at three o'clock sharp, for a pre-service interview.

Sincerely,

Lucious Paddimir

"Well, they're really quite thorough over there at the Hall, I say. A pre-service interview?" the doctor questioned, making an odd face.

Georgie spoke anxiously, "I have to go, I'm doing much better now. You know that, doc. I can go now." Georgie stood up quickly from the table. He wanted the doctor to see that his legs were healthy once again.

The doctor nodded his head in agreement.

"Yes, yes, of course, George, you should go. You're strong enough now," Dr. Kenny agreed. "But, if you want to look like a doctor, you're going to need a gentleman's attire," he added, glancing over at Lillian, who nodded in agreement.

Lillian sent Georgie into their bedroom to try on one of Dr. Kenny's ensembles. The clothing consisted of a pair of taupe-colored, wool trousers, accompanied by a black, high-buttoned coat, a smaller, brown waistcoat underneath, and a pair of fancy, black boots that were slightly small for his feet. Georgie put on the garments, then lastly placed a top hat on his head and black gloves on his hands. He walked over to the mirror, gazing at his reflection. Georgie had never seen himself in proper attire. Staring at himself in the mirror, he imagined Eva on his arm, dressed in a white gown as if it were their wedding day. Georgie wasn't sure whether they could afford a wedding comprising such formal attire, but it was pleasant to imagine. This wasn't the first time that he envisioned the moment but, for the first time in a long time, he did hope that it would become a reality one day soon.

Georgie walked out of the bedroom, holding out his arms and showing himself off.

"You look handsome as ever, George," Lillian said, grinning.

"Yes, I'm beginning to wonder whether I should be worried about having such a strapping, young lad in my house all day long with my wife," Dr. Kenny teased.

"Oh, stop it, Edward!" Lillian's cheeks were flushed with embarrassment.

"Where's your necktie, George?" Dr. Kenny inquired.

"Oh, that's right!" Georgie ran back into the bedroom and grabbed the blue necktie from the top of the dresser. He came out of the bedroom, holding it in his hand. "I'm afraid I don't know how to tie a necktie," he frowned.

"Oh, I'll do it for you," Lillian piped up and secured the tie around Georgie's neck. "There you go, you look splendid," she said looking pleased.

Little Suzie came out from around the corner.

"You look very handsome, Mr. George," she said, smiling, and they all laughed.

Georgie bent down, looking Suzie in the eye. "Well, thank you, Suzie," he replied, brightly smiling back at the little girl.

She gave him a shy grin then turned toward her mother, burying her head into Lillian's dress.

"Well, there is still a couple of things you need, George—a haircut and shave!" Dr. Kenny pointed out.

Georgie sat in one of the kitchen chairs, outside in the yard, while Lillian trimmed his hair and gave him a nice clean shave. When she finished, Dr. Kenny examined Georgie.

"Now you look like a doctor," he stated proudly.

Georgie was now officially prepared to show up at Liberation Hall as Dr. Edward Kenny.

* * *

The afternoon when Georgie would cross the threshold of Liberation Hall finally arrived. He waited anxiously, fully dressed and ready to go, counting down the minutes until it was time for him to proceed to the Hall. Pacing back and forth in the cottage, he tried his best to remain calm. He would, possibly, see Eva this afternoon for the first time in nearly five months—but he still didn't have an exact plan of how he was going to help her escape. He also knew that Eva may not even wish to leave Liberation Hall—and then there was also the juice to consider. If she was addicted to the juice, then things would be much more difficult for them. Georgie was thankful to have a doctor here in case he needed medical help or any other help for that matter.

Dr. Kenny opened the cottage door and said, "It's time George."

Georgie nodded and they both headed out to the barn. Georgie took one of the thoroughbreds out of the barn and mounted him.

"Now, I'm going to follow you over to the Hall and will wait for you out on the road, lagging behind a bit. I don't want anyone to notice that I'm there with you. Do you remember where the Hall is located—from here?"

Georgie nodded. The location of Liberation Hall was permanently seared into his brain. Dr. Kenny had taken Georgie past the Hall the day before so that he would know where to go for his "interview." They had driven the wagon and passed the Hall around dusk. He could barely see the mansion, sitting far away from the road at the end of a long lane. Georgie had desperately wanted to jump from the wagon and run up to the house but managed to refrain from doing so, knowing that he needed to stick to their plan.

"Alright, you head out first and I'll be five minutes behind you," the doctor said.

"Yes, sir," Georgie replied.

Then, with a whistle and slight nudge of his foot, the horse took off and headed out toward the road. Dr. Kenny waited patiently, glancing down at his watch every few minutes. When five minutes had passed, the doctor followed Georgie's path toward the Hall.

* * *

Claudia and Eva lounged in the drawing room, drinking the juice while they waited for the arrival of the mystery physician. Lucious told Eva last evening that a doctor had sent a letter, requesting her company. The man had never been to the Hall before, so Lucious had invited him to come by today in order to check him out first. He wanted to ensure that the doctor was "Liberation Hall material," as Lucious had put it.

"Are you curious about the doctor who's visiting today?" Claudia questioned Eva, then sipped juice from her glass.

"Yes, I would like to get a good look at him. I want to know what I'm getting into if he's allowed to come back this evening," Eva replied, rolling her eyes with a distasteful expression on her face.

Since arriving at the Hall, Eva had only spent time in the evenings with Lucious, Lord Manchester, and Reginald Wittaker. She was not looking forward to adding a fourth man to her resume. Lord Manchester had always behaved like a gentleman when he was with her and Eva was beginning to get used to being intimate with him. However, the time she'd been with Reginald Wittaker was extremely unpleasant. Eva was glad that it had only been one time and thankful that he did not live in England. She had thought that it was a bit odd for a doctor to request her based on her description alone. She only hoped that—if Lucious approved of him—he was a kind gentleman and at least somewhat attractive.

"How are you feeling today, Eva?" Claudia asked.

"Much better, I haven't been sick for over a day now. I think the flu has finally run its course," Eva replied, assuring Claudia.

Claudia knew that Eva's illness was far from over. Eva still hadn't had her menses, despite the polluted juice that Lucious has been forcing her to drink. She also wondered how much of it Eva was actually taking, now that she was feeling better.

The ladies continued to await the doctor's arrival anxiously. Claudia had met Dr. Kenny one time before today, although Lucious did not know that. One of Claudia's local clients had told her about Dr. Kenny and how he lived not far from the Hall in case she needed his services. When Lila had taken a turn for the worse, Claudia had convinced Archie to sneak her out of the Hall in the middle of the night and to go to this doctor for help. Thankfully, they found Dr. Kenny's house and left Lila in his care. Both Archie and Claudia were afraid that Lucious would find out where they really went, so the two of them conspired to tell Lucious that Lila had died from complications during the night. Archie told him that he sent Lila's body down the Thames. Lucious didn't seem to care much that the girl was gone but he did tell the entire household that no one was to mention Lila's name ever again. Claudia hoped that, if Dr. Kenny became a regular, she would have the opportunity to ask him about Lila.

The noise of a galloping horse was heard heading up the lane. Both ladies peeked out the picture window, trying to get a good look at the doctor, but he was still too far away. They both stood, fixing their dresses, then strolled toward the foyer while remaining within the threshold of the drawing room. Curtis hurried to fetch Lucious from the study when there was a knock at the door. Archie opened the door and the ladies could hear muttering but couldn't see the doctor's face yet. Lucious entered the foyer and summoned Eva to stand next to him. She sauntered over to him and he took her hand, making it clear that Eva was his possession.

Lucious peered at the front door, trying to see this Dr. Kenny.

"Let him in already, Archie," Lucious called out.

Archie cleared his throat. "Dr. Edward Kenny, sir," Archie announced with a nod.

Eva expectantly waited to catch a glimpse of this arcane doctor. He stepped through the front door of the Hall, but Eva still couldn't see him as he was removing his top hat. Finally, he lowered his hat, which allowed Eva to see him clearly. A jolt shot through her body, her eyes grew wide, and her heart began pounding. Much to Eva's surprise, the mysterious doctor was none other than her old friend, Georgie Thornber.

Twenty-Two

Eva was astounded and completely paralyzed by the sight of Georgie standing in front of her at Liberation Hall. She couldn't believe it was him and kept wondering whether he had really come all the way from Oxfordshire to find her here? She stood motionless, her eyes fixed upon him, without making a peep. Seeing Georgie again made Eva realize how much she still loved him. He looked so handsome in gentleman's attire, although Eva had no idea where he had obtained the clothing. The longer she stared at him, the more she realized that the love she had for Georgie had never changed—it had merely been masked by the enticements Lucious offered. She wanted, desperately, to run into his arms, kiss him all over his face, and beg for his forgiveness. She felt that she was in a daydream, which she had indulged in on numerous occasions over the past few weeks but never really believed would happen. Her emotions continued to stir within her as she remained standing, motionless, without an expression on her face. She didn't want Lucious to know that she knew the "doctor"—if he found out, Lucious would most certainly injure Georgie or worse.

Georgie's eyes lit up at the sight of Eva, his heart pounding in his chest as he looked upon his love. He had searched for her for so long and had been through so much in the past month—and now here she was, standing right before him. She was a vision; he had never seen her look so beautiful. Georgie's heart melted, his breath weakened, and he was entranced by her beauty. Georgie wanted to enclose her in his arms and to whisk her away, but he knew that he had to wait for the timing to be right.

Lucious peered back and forth between Georgie and Eva. The young lad's eyes were attentively fixed upon her. Eva also seemed quite taken with him, which caused a sting of jealousy to surge within Lucious. He cleared his throat, trying to gain Georgie's attention, a peevish expression on his face.

Finally, he spoke up, "Have you finished gawking yet?" Lucious raised his eyebrows indignantly.

Georgie looked over at Lucious and noticed that he was holding Eva's hand. He felt a surge of anger rising inside him at the site of this madman touching Eva, but he controlled his feelings and steadied his breathing. He wasn't going to let his emotions get the best of him nor allow himself to be intimidated by Lucious Paddimir.

Georgie walked confidently up to Lucious, offering his hand.

"Dr. Edward Kenny," he introduced himself, nodding.

Lucious was unmoved, giving him a cold hard stare. Georgie realized that Lucious was not going to shake his hand, so he clumsily lowered it, then ran it through his hair. He glanced over at Eva and saw how close in proximity he was to her now. He wanted to grab her hand from Lucious and run out the door with her. He realized, once again, that he was staring at Eva and quickly looked back over at Lucious.

Lucious knew immediately that this boy was not a stately doctor. The accent alone had given him away. What was this poor daft lad up to, Lucious wondered.

"Dr. Edward Kenny, is it? Where did you attend medical school?" Lucious asked with a diabolical smile on his face, thinking that the boy wouldn't have a response.

"Edinburgh," Georgie replied assuredly.

"And what year did you graduate, *doctor*?" Lucious asked jeeringly as he continued to glare at Georgie.

"Last year," Georgie answered smoothly.

Eva knew that Georgie didn't look old enough to be a doctor.

"Everyone is always saying how young I look for my age," continued Georgie, with a smile, looking around the Hall. Then, he locked eyes with Eva.

Looking at Georgie smile, Eva's heart leaped, and she saw light enter the room. She couldn't help but give him a slight smile in return. Lucious was not amused by Georgie's comment and stood there for a moment, saying nothing. Suddenly Lucious burst out laughing, hysterically, with deep rhythmic bellows. Everyone in the Hall was staring at him, most disturbed by his behavior. Eva had never heard Lucious laugh so loudly in all the time she had known him. Then, Lucious quieted and his demeanor shifted as he glared at Georgie.

"Don't insult my intelligence boy. You are no doctor," he said harshly, shaking his head as he leaned closer to Georgie's face and yelled, "Who... the hell...are...you?!"

Eva felt disheartened and she felt horrible for Georgie. Making people look foolish was one of Lucious' specialties. Georgie cleared his throat, standing a little straighter. He lifted his head high, appearing to be unfazed by Lucious' behavior.

"Are you quite finished, sir?" Georgie responded coolly.

Lucious peered at Georgie intensely.

"I want you out of my house—now!" he demanded contemptuously.

Georgie didn't take his eyes away from Lucious.

"I'm not leaving without Eva," Georgie demanded.

Eva's heart was beating faster with every passing second. She was frightened for Georgie and what Lucious might do to him. Lucious turned to Eva, looking at her severely, his eyes black as night. Her heart was beating so fast that she thought Lucious might be able to see it moving inside her chest.

"Eva love, do you know this boy?" Lucious asked, glaring at her.

Eva shrugged her shoulders, shaking her head.

"No, I have no idea who this person is, Lucious," she then glanced over at Georgie indignantly. She was doing her best to be convincing, but she wasn't sure how much longer she could hold her tongue as her nerves were coming undone. Georgie's heart ached at Eva's response—she could tell that he was hurt by her words from the look on his face.

"Do you wish to leave with this person?" Lucious asked, still staring at her.

"Lucious, why would I want to leave with someone I don't even know?" she asked, slightly laughing. She was doing her best to assure Lucious of her sincerity, hoping that he would let Georgie go free.

"Very well then," Lucious said, looking back over at Georgie. "Eva doesn't wish to leave with you...*doctor*. However, you are leaving now and you are not invited to return.

If you do decide to return, there will be severe consequences, I'm afraid," Lucious stated.

Georgie looked at Lucious for a moment longer, then switched his gaze over to Eva.

"Eva, do you really want to stay here? Be honest, I need to know," he asked her pleadingly. His only desire was to know the truth—if Eva wanted to stay with Lucious at Liberation Hall, Georgie knew he would have no choice but to leave her.

Lucious snapped his fingers, summoning Curtis and Archie over to remove Georgie from the Hall. Eva's eyes grew wide as she pressed her lips together. Georgie knew that that was a sign that Eva was withholding the truth and that she wasn't comfortable. He wasn't about to leave without her, unless he knew for certain that she wanted to stay.

"Eva, I love you. I've been looking for you all over the countryside!"

Lucious interrupted, "Oh, please!" His voice was laced with disgust. "I've heard enough, get him out of my presence!" Lucious was furious.

Emotions flooded Eva when she heard Georgie announce his love for her. She watched as the two guards started to drag him away from her. Georgie had a look of desperation on his face and something leapt inside her.

"Georgie!" she called out.

Removing her hand from Lucious', she ran over to Georgie. Eva embraced him, grabbing his waist, trying to hold on and use her weight to pull him away from the guards.

"Eva," Georgie said her name in a heartfelt manner, looking down at her but unable to touch her because of the guards that held back his arms. He fought vigorously against the guards, trying to get away when Lucious walked over quickly, pulled Eva off of him, and threw her down on the marble floor.

"Eva!" Georgie shouted.

"So you do know him, then?" Lucious asked, out of breath from the commotion. He motioned for the guards to wait, then leered back at Eva, her body sprawled out across the floor. She looked up at Lucious, breathing heavily with tears in her eyes.

"Let him go, Lucious, please! Please, let him go," she begged, trembling while trying to stand on her feet. She stumbled over to Lucious, placing her hands on his arm. "Please, if you care for me at all, you will let him go."

She looked up at Lucious, imploring him to release Georgie. Georgie's heart was breaking, he was doing his best to hold back tears while he watched Eva coddle Lucious. He was obviously violent and insolent toward her, which enraged Georgie. He now knew that he had no choice but to get her away from this man.

Lucious gazed down at Eva and gently grabbed her chin, bringing it up to his face. Lucious mouth was inches from Eva's.

"Oh, Eva, I do care for you, love."

Lucious pressed his lips against Eva's, kissing her as he ran his hands down her body and over her backside, pulling her into him. Georgie squeezed his eyes shut, tears streaming down his face as he watched this evil man kissing and caressing the woman he loved. Eva's eyes were wide open while tears rolled down her cheeks; her heart was in shambles. Lucious gently pulled away and Eva looked down at the ground. She couldn't bear to look back up at Georgie for fear of what he must think of her. Lucious let out a sigh of pleasure, gazing back over at Georgie.

"Now, what to do with Georgie-Porgy? Hmmm," Lucious questioned coolly.

He knew that he had the upper hand and decided to enjoy this little game. Lucious didn't want to just send Georgie away from Liberation Hall, he wanted to destroy him in the process.

"Say, I'll make a deal with you. If you bring me one hundred quid in exactly one week's time—and if Eva chooses to leave—then I will allow her to walk out that door."

Lucious pointed toward the front door of the Hall. Eva was astonished by his offer but, nevertheless, she also knew that Georgie didn't have that kind of money. One hundred quid was more than most Englishmen made in a year.

Georgie spoke up, "When you say 'walk out that door,' do you mean Eva's permitted to leave Liberation Hall and be free of you forever?"

Lucious slowly grinned. "Yes, Eva may leave Liberation Hall and be free of me, forever, if that is what she desires." Lucious looked down at Eva, grazing his hand along her hip and bum.

Georgie closed his eyes and turned his head, refusing to watch Lucious fondle Eva. She continued staring at the ground because she was ashamed of how Lucious was treating her in front of Georgie. She knew that Lucious was trying to aggravate him.

"Deal," Georgie said confidently, looking back over at Lucious and sounding sure of himself.

With his finger, Lucious motioned for the guards to release Georgie from their grasp.

"I'll be back in one week with the money to save you, Eva!" Georgie assured her.

Lucious shook his head, laughing. "Stupid boy," he scoffed.

Georgie took one more look at Eva as the guards pushed him out the door.

Eva's heart wrenched, watching him leave Liberation Hall without her.

The moment the door slammed shut behind Georgie, Lucious viciously grabbed Eva by the hair, forcing her toward the floor.

"Aahhhh," Eva cried out in pain.

Claudia placed her hand over her mouth in terror, refraining from making any noise.

Lucious pushed Eva to her knees, demanding her to bow to him. He leered down at her with angry black eyes.

"What a foolish ass to come here looking for you! You are mine and you will always be mine, Eva. Do not get any ideas that you will ever leave Liberation Hall!"

He pulled her up by her hair and she cried out in pain. Then, he threw her down on the floor once more and stormed off toward the study, leaving Eva on her knees, her hands covering her face as she continued to weep. Claudia waited for Lucious to leave the room, then she ran over and helped Eva stand up from the floor.

"Are you alright?" she asked.

Eva nodded her head while wiping the moisture from her face.

"Who is that boy, Eva?" Claudia inquired.

Eva said nothing because she wasn't sure she wanted to involve Claudia.

"Alright, you don't have to tell me but—just so know—I'm not your enemy, Eva," Claudia said, shaking her head, and walked down the corridor to the study.

Eva solemnly walked up the staircase to her bedroom. She was overwhelmed by everything that had just happened. Tears continued streaming down her face as she poured herself a glass of juice. Drinking the entire glass at once, she poured another one and gulped it down as well. The room began spinning as she stumbled over to the bed, crashing down on the mattress below. She could feel her heart beating in her chest and, every once in a while, she felt that it might stop. This would cause her to jolt, which, in turn, would restart her heart again.

Lying there on the bed, Eva's emotions and thoughts whirled around inside her. She wondered how long Georgie had searched for her and wondered how he found the Hall. Eva knew that Lucious' business was built upon secrecy and privacy, so why would he allow Georgie to come back for her? Lucious was playing some sort of sick game, but Eva didn't know what he had in mind. She was worried about Georgie, unsure of what Lucious might do. All she knew was that Lucious was capable of doing just about anything.

Twenty-Three

C laudia knocked on the study door soon after Lucious had sent Georgie away from the Hall.

"Go away!" Lucious yelled.

Claudia burst into the study anyway and marched across the room, releasing an angry sigh.

"What are you doing Lucious?" she asked, placing her hands on his desk. She leaned in toward him, trying to get his attention.

"Claudia, I'm really not in the mood!" he shouted, frustrated, as he continued to work.

"What do you think you are doing with that boy? You're not going to sell Eva for one hundred quid only!" Claudia protested harshly, unsure what Lucious was up to or why he would allow Georgie to return to the Hall in a week.

Lucious looked up at Claudia, his eyes black as midnight, glaring at her.

Claudia began backing away from the desk, slowly, seeing the darkness in his eyes. He stood up in haste and briskly walked around to the other side of the desk.

"Are you questioning my decisions, Dia!?" he shouted, firmly grabbing her by the throat, slamming her down on the desk, and choking her.

Claudia began making gasping sounds as she strained for air. Her eyes rolled in the back of her head. After several long seconds, Lucious loosened his grip while still keeping his hands tightly placed around her neck. He leaned in closely, staring down at her with an evil look in his eyes.

"I know what I'm doing. Don't ever question me again!" he yelled, giving her neck one last squeeze as he released her from his grasp.

Claudia grabbed her neck, sucking in gasps of air. Lucious walked back to the other side of the desk, gruffly sat down in his chair, and began working despite the fact that Claudia still lay across his desk. She slowly picked herself up and raised her hands to her neck, stumbling out of the room. Lucious leered at her hostilely as she walked out of the study.

Claudia had known immediately that the boy was not Dr. Kenny, but she did not expect to see the scene that took place in the foyer. She continued down the corridor, rubbing her throat while trying to inhale deeply, helping her windpipe expand. She walked up the stairs and knocked on Eva's door but there was no answer. Unable to call out as a result of the choking she had just received, she opened the door and went inside the bedroom. Eva was laying across the bed, her eyes glazed over.

"Oh, no!" Claudia squeaked out. "Eva, Eva!" Claudia was trying to speak loudly, but her voice was strained. "Eva!" Claudia shook her, trying to awaken her. Finally, Eva blinked her eyes and began to move, gasping for air.

"Oh, thank heavens!" Claudia squealed, laying herself across Eva's waist. Eva woke slowly, having almost overdosed on the juice, and her head was spinning. Claudia rose, sitting up on the bed.

"You need to be careful not to drink too much juice at one time. Are you alright?"

Eva leaned her head up to look at Claudia. She was still very groggy.

"Claudia, what happened to your voice," Eva mumbled.

Claudia gave her an unpleasant look while rubbing her neck. "Lucious," she softly replied rolling her eyes.

Eva could see the red finger outlines where Lucious' hands had been around Claudia's neck and let out a distressed sigh. "What's happened now?" she asked, concerned for Claudia but not surprised by Lucious' violence.

"He didn't like me questioning his decision about your friend," Claudia said, her voice still sounding rough.

Eva squinted, trying her best to focus on Claudia but she was still dizzy from drinking too much of the juice.

"What makes you question Lucious' decision?" she asked, desiring to know Claudia's opinion.

Claudia waited a moment, trying to clear her throat before responding. Eva put out her hand motioning for Claudia not to speak. Eva slowly got up from her bed, wobbling a bit, and made her way over to the mobile bar to retrieve Claudia a glass of juice.

Claudia nodded, grateful for Eva's kindness toward her. Claudia had always taken care of the girls in the house, but none of them had ever really cared about her in return.

"So, what made you question Lucious' decision?" Eva asked inquisitively, sitting back down on the bed.

"No one has ever shown up at the Hall looking for someone before and Georgie must have gone to great lengths to find you here." Claudia took another sip of the juice. "Lucious is furious and I'm terribly worried about your friend."

Eva felt a pang in her chest; she was also highly concerned for Georgie because she didn't know what Lucious intended. She walked over to the window, gazing out at the river.

"I never knew he loved me," she said and feelings of regret rose inside her. "He left for Oxfordshire to go work for a magistrate and I thought that he was moving on with his life— which is why I left with Lucious," Eva explained as she began crying and covered her face.

"Did you say a magistrate, Eva?" Claudia questioned. "Do you know which one?" she asked eagerly.

Eva turned around wiping her face. "Are you going to tell Lucious?" she asked, sucking in breaths of air.

"No," Claudia shook her head. "I'm just wondering because we have several magistrates who come to the Hall and he may have found out the location from one of them."

Eva thought for a moment. "I think his name is Magistrate Logan."

Claudia's eyes grew wide. "James Logan comes to see me," she said, still rubbing at her sore neck.

"How often does he come to the Hall?" Eva asked anxiously.

"Only twice...maybe three times a year. Which reminds me, I have to check the mail today as well as the schedule for tomorrow," Claudia sighed, laying her head in her hand. She wasn't in the mood to go downstairs to the study where Lucious was working.

"Also, I'm sorry to inform you, Eva, but Lord Manchester has requested to start coming to see you twice a week now. He'll be here tomorrow evening." Claudia gave her a glum look.

Eva sighed, "I suppose that's better than having someone new requesting me, although—had Georgie had been able to schedule—we might have been able to escape together." The words flew out of Eva's mouth before she had a chance to stop herself from saying them out loud.

Claudia gave her a troubled look. "Eva, you can't escape Lucious; he *will* find you. You are now both his investment and his asset. He's not going to allow you to leave the Hall," Claudia concluded, shaking her head.

Eva began weeping and fell to her knees.

Claudia walked over, kneeling down next to Eva, feeling extremely distressed for her. Eva had experienced a great deal in a very short amount of time and she was still unaware that she was carrying Lucious' unborn child.

"You know, I'm a bit jealous of you, Eva," Claudia said with her hands resting on her knees.

Eva looked up while wiping the tears away from her eyes. "Jealous of me?" Eva asked surprised.

"Yes, that boy Georgie, he must love you very much to show up here the way he did. If he found out the location of the Hall from Magistrate Logan and came all the way here from Oxfordshire pretending to be a doctor just to find you...he must really love you."

Eva stared sorrowfully at Claudia. "But he's not going to want to be with me now," Eva shook her head and covered her face. "Not after everything I've done and everyone I've been with!" Eva exclaimed as tears poured down her cheeks.

"I've ruined any chance of being with him, Dia. He won't want me now."

Claudia placed her hand on top of Eva's. "Eva, he was going to purchase an evening with you. He already knows what you've done and that you've slept with other men, yet he still came here to rescue you." She looked over at Eva smiling.

Eva inhaled a deep breath shaking her head. "I don't know. Maybe he just wanted to use me like everyone else," she said.

Claudia quickly piped up, "Oh, I don't think so." She shook her head. "There was much love and purity in his eyes for you, that much I do know." Claudia knew because no man had ever looked at her the way Georgie had stared at Eva.

He wasn't lusting after her—he was in love with her.

Eva knew that Georgie was a truly good man and that he wasn't out to use her. She was overwhelmed with gratitude that he came looking for her and, although she still loved him very much, a part of her felt that he deserved someone better than her.

"I need to be going," Claudia said, exhaling loudly. She picked herself up from the floor. "Please Eva, don't drink too much juice. You could die," Claudia warned and Eva sighed, nodding in agreement. Claudia walked over to the door. "Oh, and please let me know if your menses starts." Claudia worried more about Eva's pregnancy with each passing day.

"I will let you know I promise," Eva responded, then spoke up again with a question, "Dia, why have you been so worried about me?"

Claudia gave Eva a sorrowful look. "I just want to make sure you're alright," she replied, and Eva smiled, realizing that Claudia actually cared about her.

"Thank you, Dia, for taking care of me."

Claudia nodded, then left Eva's room, closing the door behind her.

* * *

That evening Eva requested for dinner to be brought up to her bedroom. She did not want to see Lucious, unsure of what his mood toward her would be after what happened that day. She also wasn't very hungry but knew she must eat or Lucious would grow even angrier than he already was with her. There was a knock and Eva cautiously opened her bedroom door. She peeked out and saw Nancy holding her dinner tray.

"Good evening, Miss," Nancy said curtsying.

"Good evening," Eva replied, opening the door to allow Nancy to come inside.

Nancy walked over, setting her tray down on the chest of drawers.

"Would you like me to draw you a bath, Miss?" she asked.

"Yes, please, that would be wonderful," Eva kindly replied.

Nancy prepared Eva's bath, then left the room so Eva could eat dinner. Eva picked at the food while the bath filled with water. After she finished eating, she rang the bell for Nancy to come and retrieve her tray. She went into the ensuite, turned off the water, and settled into the warm bath. She was hoping it would ease the aches and pains she accumulated that day.

Eva lay back in the tub when she heard someone enter her bedroom. Assuming it was Nancy coming to fetch her tray, she once again rested against the tub, closing her eyes. When Eva opened them again, Lucious was standing over her. She gasped at the sight of him. Closing her eyes for a moment, she swallowed hard.

"Lucious, you frightened me," she said, inhaling deeply several times.

Lucious said nothing as he glared down at her in the tub.

Eva's heart was racing as anxiety swelled within her, unsure of what he might do to her. Lucious' dark eyes fiercely looked at her while she continued to bathe. Eva felt intimidated by the way Lucious was acting and thought it would be best to remove herself from the tub.

"Would you please hand me my towel?" she asked, feeling exposed because he was glaring at her naked body.

Lucious didn't take his eyes off of her as he retrieved the bath towel. He slowly grabbed it and leaned over the bath, handing the towel to Eva.

"Thank you," she said graciously, still nervous because his eyes were glued on her.

Eva stood up in the bathtub and immediately wrapped the towel around her body. Water began running down her legs, hitting the tub below and making splashing sounds. She stepped out of the tub, not taking time to dry off, disturbed by Lucious' unrelenting gaze. She felt her nerves rising with each second that he stood there, saying nothing but only perusing her towel wrapped body. Eva started heading out of the ensuite to fetch her robe when Lucious grabbed her arm and forced her across the room. He threw her down on the bed and pulled the bath towel out from under her as Eva cried out in fear.

Nancy was on her way upstairs to collect Eva's dinner tray. She approached Eva's bedroom door but didn't knock, assuming that Eva was relaxing in the tub. She turned the doorknob and began opening the door when she caught sight of someone powerfully restraining Eva at the edge of the bed. Lucious was holding Eva's arms forcefully over her head with one of his hands while clasping her mouth shut with the other. Nancy could see the terror on Eva's face when, suddenly, Lucious' voice ferociously barked at her from behind the door.

"Get out!" he yelled viciously.

Nancy slammed the door, covering her mouth and shaking in horror at what she had witnessed. She could hear Lucious demanding on the other side of the door.

"Look at me! You look at me, you little bitch!!!" he shouted.

Nancy jolted back upon hearing Lucious roaring at Eva and her heart dropped as she realized what was happening inside the bedroom. After a few moments, she noticed that it had become very quiet and she quickly took off down the corridor, trying to get out of sight before Lucious exited the bedroom. Nancy waited in the distance, down the hallway, and peeked around the corner, seeing Lucious slam Eva's door closed. He stood there for a moment glancing around to see whether anyone noticed him leaving Eva's room. Not seeing anyone, Lucious quickly walked across the hall and entered his own bedroom.

Nancy hurried back down to Eva's room, knocking wildly on the door.

"Miss…Miss Eva, are you alright?" she called but Eva didn't respond.

Nancy hesitantly entered Eva's bedroom, unsure in what state she might find her. Eva had wrapped herself in the bed linens and was staring despondently out the bedroom window.

"Miss Eva?" Nancy quietly called. "Are you alright?"

Nancy walked around to the other side of the bed so Eva could see her—but Eva didn't respond or look up. She just continued staring out the window as tears streamed down her cheeks. Nancy wasn't sure what to do, so she hurried downstairs to find Claudia.

Claudia was finishing her daily tasks in the study when someone knocked on the door.

"Come in!" she called out, standing over the desk and trying to even out a stack of papers by hitting them against the top of the desk.

"I'm sorry to bother you, Miss, but something is wrong with Miss Eva," Nancy said, concerned.

Claudia immediately placed the papers down and ran out of the study and up the stairs to Eva's bedroom. Claudia thought that Eva had drunk too much juice and could possibly be overdosing in her room. As the ladies approached Eva's room, Lucious was exiting his bedroom with a very nasty look on his face. He glanced over at them both with his is dark, black eyes. Claudia became nervous looking at the expression he gave them but, thankfully, he walked past them and headed down the staircase. Claudia looked at Nancy before entering the bedroom.

"Thank you, Nancy, I will ring for you if I need anything," she said and Nancy nodded, then quickly bolted down the corridor to the servant's staircase. Claudia wasn't sure what she was getting into and didn't want Nancy there in case Eva had overdosed. She entered Eva's bedroom directly.

"Eva," she called out quietly, walking slowly over to the other side of the bed where Eva was lying. "Eva, are you alright?" she asked, leaning slightly over the bed to see whether Eva was alive.

When she bent over, she noticed that Eva was swaddled in her bedding. She was trembling and her face was red and swollen from crying. Claudia thought that Eva was beginning to miscarry her baby.

"It's alright dear, do you need me to bring you a sanitary belt?" Claudia asked while pulling back on the covers a bit to see if Eva was bleeding. She was taken back, realizing that Eva was naked and soaking wet. Eva jerked the blanket from Claudia, covering herself up to her chin.

"Are you bleeding?" Claudia inquired, concerned.

Eva didn't respond; she wouldn't even look up at Claudia. She just continued staring, motionless, out the bedroom window.

"Eva, what's going on? Please talk to me, what's happened?"

Eva didn't say a word, she didn't move or respond in any way.

Claudia inhaled a deep breath, remembering the look that Lucious had given her and Nancy in the corridor. Claudia gasped, realizing what had happened to Eva.

"Oh my, did he hurt you?" Claudia questioned in shock.

She knew that Lucious was capable of such things but never thought that he would do anything like that to Eva. Eva remained still as tears slowly trickled down her face.

"Eva, please tell me, did Lucious do something to you?"

Eva slowly nodded her head and Claudia released an angry sigh. "I'll be right back!" she spouted furiously.

Claudia was livid as she marched out of Eva's bedroom, down the stairs, and into the drawing room, where Lucious was smoking his pipe.

"Lucious, may I have a word with you?" Claudia asked harshly as Lucious released a puff of smoke high into the air.

He didn't turn around to look at her. "No, you may not," he stated assuredly.

Claudia walked over to where she could look at him in the face.

"Why? Why would you do such a horrible thing to Eva? No one deserves what you've done to her, ever, and Eva has done nothing to you!" she said, raising her voice, looking sternly at him while waiting for a response.

Lucious looked up at her, another puff of smoke seeping from his mouth.

"Eva needed to be reminded that she is mine and that I own her! She also needs to know that she will never leave Liberation Hall...especially not with that boy!" Lucious yelled, then gruffly placed the pipe back into his mouth.

"Oh, I see, you're jealous," she laughed, shaking her head as she began to rant. "You're jealous because you saw what love looked like when Georgie came for Eva and because you know that you are incapable of giving or receiving love yourself. So, you decided to take Eva by force, trying to steal their love away from them. Especially since you know that love is the only thing that Eva has ever really wanted—but that it's the one thing you'll never be able to give her." Claudia shook her head and smirked.

Lucious stood up from his chair and slowly walked over to Claudia. He stopped in front of her and gave her a long, hard stare. Claudia knew that Lucious was probably going to beat her senseless or that, perhaps, he might even kill her for what she said to him. She braced herself for whatever punishment he was about to unleash upon her, but Lucious did something even more terrifying—he simply gave her a devilish grin and walked away.

Twenty-Four

Georgie was quickly riding through the English countryside, making his way to London the day after his visit to Liberation Hall. The cool wind rushed past him as he rode one of Dr. Kenny's thoroughbred's, helping him reach his destination more efficiently. Georgie was on his way to obtain the money for Eva's release. He hoped that his plan would succeed and that he would receive the entire one hundred quid he needed to pay Lucious. The Kennys had been more than generous to Georgie. On top of everything else they had done for him, they also contributed twenty pounds of their own money toward saving Eva from Liberation Hall. Georgie was extremely grateful to them and didn't know how he was ever going to repay them for their generosity. He told the doctor that it was too much, but Dr. Kenny insisted on doing whatever he could to help them both.

Georgie made sure to take several breaks throughout his journey in order to properly care for himself and the horse. He knew that, if he was going to help Eva escape Lucious, he had to keep himself healthy. He also brought his own supply of food and water along in order to save financial resources since he had to pay Lucious by the end of the week. Georgie had twenty-five pounds that he had saved up himself over the last few years, which he had intended to use for starting his life together with Eva. The last thing he wanted to do was give his hard-earned money to Lucious but, without Eva, he knew that he had no life. He'd also been racked with guilt ever since he left the Hall without her. Georgie beat himself up for not trying harder to help Eva escape. He wasn't sure what she might possibly have to endure with Lucious and the other men until he returned. His heart ached all the more after seeing her and his only hope now was to somehow get all the money Lucious asked for to rescue Eva from the Hall.

Georgie arrived at the lodging house in London around half-past three. He dreaded having to tell Eva's mother that he'd had to leave her behind in Shepperton but hoped that Margie would understand his predicament. Georgie walked up to the lodging house and headed upstairs to Margie's lodging room right away. He knocked on the door removing his hat and prayed that she would answer this time. He didn't want to bear the burden of having to tell her about Eva's situation any longer.

"Miss Marg! You in there? It's George," he called as he pounded on the door. Margie opened the door, looking terrible. Her hair was a mess and she looked like she hadn't slept since Eva had gone missing.

"Oh, George!" Margie grabbed him, hugging his neck tightly as tears welled up in her eyes at the sight of him. "Alice and I have been so worried about you and Eva, it's been over a month!" She released Georgie's neck.

"I'm sure you have been," he replied solemnly.

"Did you find Eva?" she asked, looking anxiously down the corridor.

Georgie frowned as a terribly distressed look rested upon his face. The happiness on Margie's face turned into fear.

"What's wrong? What is it? What's happen to Eva?" she asked, frantically shaking her head.

"Eva's alright, Miss Marg, for the most part," Georgie said, tilting his head while his expression remained unchanged.

"Where is she, then?" Margie asked hastily.

"May I come in? I think we should sit down," Georgie suggested.

"Oh, of course, come in," she invited him to join her on the sofa.

Georgie looked around the house, which was in utter disarray. There were newspapers and empty bottles of alcohol lying all over the lodging room.

"Please tell me that you know something, George," Margie pleaded.

Georgie swallowed hard while glancing around at the mess in the lodging room, then finally fixed his eyes on Margie and took her hand. Tears ran down her cheeks.

"Well, out with it already!" she piped up as she wiped the tears from her face.

Georgie sighed, "Eva's still with Lucious Paddimir at his home, called Liberation Hall."

Margie glanced down at the floor as her heart dropped. "But you say she's alright?" she asked, looking back up at Georgie with hope.

"Yes, she appears to be fine—but there's more."

Margie listened intently.

"Lucious sells a juice that is actually a highly addictive drug of some sort."

Margie placed a hand over her mouth, tears continuing to stream down her face.

"I'd thought as much. You know gossip around town and such...but do you think that Eva's addicted to the juice?" Margie asked sadly.

"Yes, ma'am, I think she might be," Georgie replied, feeling Margie's ache for Eva.

"So, why isn't she with you, if you've seen her?"

Georgie bit his lip and began to feel nervous.

"Well, I went to the Hall to go bring her home but, when I got there, Lucious had two guards and, combined, they were stronger than me. There's an entire house full of people who live there, ma'am."

Margie was thinking hard about what Georgie was saying. "So, you weren't able to help her?" she asked, shaking her head as tears continued rolling down her cheeks.

Georgie felt remorseful and moisture began filling his eyes as well. Margie placed her other hand on top of Georgie's.

"I'm so sorry George, I wasn't trying to make you feel guilty. I'm just trying to understand, is all."

He wiped the tears away from his face with the back of his hand while shaking his head. "No, no, your right...I should have tried harder to get her out of there but I was worried that she might be harmed in the process." Georgie looked directly into Margie's eyes. "This Lucious Paddimir fellow is a very evil and cunning man. I think he's probably been abusive to Eva as well."

Margie gasped and more tears poured from her eyes, her lip beginning to quiver.

"Is there any way to help her? I mean, does Eva even want to leave?" Margie asked helplessly.

"I think so, I just don't think that she could say it directly because she fears him," Georgie replied.

Margie looked down at the floor, crying, the back of her hand covering her face.

"I hate to say it, but there's more ma'am."

Margie gazed up at him, anticipating what he was going to say next.

"Lucious runs more than just a juice operation from his home," Georgie explained. "He also runs a high-class prostitution ring from the same house."

Margie's eyes grew wide, as horror bellowed up within her. "You mean to tell me that Eva's…" Margie's words trailed off as she began breathing heavily and weeping uncontrollably. Georgie had tears in his eyes as he watched Margie's heart break over her daughter.

Once Margie gathered herself, she asked, "Is there anything we can do?" She looked up at Georgie, shaking her head in dismay.

"Well, Mr. Paddimir told me that if I bring him one hundred quid in a week, he'll let Eva walk out the front door," Georgie explained.

Margie's face dropped even lower in disappointment.

"One hundred quid? Where on earth are we going to get one hundred quid in a week!?" she asked indignantly.

"Well, I already have forty-five ma'am. I only need fifty-five more," Georgie stated.

Margie looked over at him, speechless. "You have forty-five quid saved up, George?" She was astonished.

"Yes ma'am, I've been saving up for years—but twenty of it came from a family in Shepperton who's been helping me find Eva," he explained.

"Well, I say, you're a very responsible lad to have saved up twenty-five quid over the years," Margie said with a sad smile while rigorously shaking Georgie's hand. "I hate to say it, but I feel like this whole thing is a trick," she continued, frowning. "What if he takes the money and doesn't let Eva go?" she asked, concerned.

"I know, I thought of that as well and, like I said, I have some help in Shepperton where the Hall is located. There are a doctor and his wife there who have been helping me and they assured me that if anything happens to me, they will get Eva out of there one way or another."

Margie's eyes grew wide again when she realized that she could lose Georgie along with Eva.

Georgie continued, "If Lucious Paddimir happens to be a man of his word, which, to be honest, I highly doubt, and if I get all the money, then there's a chance he'll let Eva go free."

Margie looked away, releasing a wearisome sigh.

"Well, let's see if we can somehow collect enough money then and try to get Eva home," she said, gazing up at Georgie, extremely unhopeful at the prospect of Eva ever returning home to her.

Georgie and Margie went downstairs to see Alice. They waited patiently for Alice to open the door.

"Georgie!" Alice grabbed him tightly.

"Grams!" he exclaimed, a great big grin on his face.

She stood back, looking at him and shaking her head with tears in her eyes.

"I was beginning to wonder if you'd ever return, it's been so long," she said, slapping her legs with her hands almost as if beckoning for him to come to her.

"I'm sorry Grams. It's been a long journey," he said his face suddenly showing his weariness.

"Well, have you brought Eva home?" she asked, looking at him optimistically.

He shook his head no and tears gathered in his eyes.

"Oh, dear," she grimaced. "Well, come on in and tell me what you've found out while I fix you some dinner." Alice motioned for Georgie and Margie to enter the lodging room.

Georgie explained everything to Alice, just as he had to Margie, while they were sitting at the dining table, having tea after dinner.

"So you're saying that this Paddimir fellow is asking for one hundred quid in one week—and then he'll let Eva go?" Alice asked as she poured some tea into Margie's cup.

"Yes, that's what George is saying, Alice," Margie confirmed.

"Well, there's got to be something Scotland Yard can do?" Alice said, holding out her hand and shrugging.

"Oh, don't get me started on them!" Margie spouted furiously.

"Well, what about the newspaper?" Alice inquired, sitting down at the table.

"They retracted the story I gave 'em and told me not to come back if I was just going to make up lies!" Margie sputtered, crossing her arms. "Then they told me that I wasn't allowed to return," she said, shaking her head. "Bloody fools, I say!" Margie glanced around, embarrassed when she realized she had cursed. "Oh, I'm sorry, I'm just so distraught," she apologized, an anxious look upon her face, her chin resting in her hand.

"The problem is, Grams, Lucious Paddimir has everyone who is someone in England coming to the Hall, including members of the Scotland Yard, and the people at the newspaper I'm sure. Which is most likely why they retracted your story, Miss Marg," Georgie explained.

They all sat there quietly for a moment and Alice sighed, "Well, I guess there's just one thing left to do then—get a hundred quid!" She huffed, eyes wide, then sipped her tea.

After several days of all of them working together, they managed to raise a little over ten pounds to help add to Eva's ransom. Margie's friend, Bert Darby, contributed five pounds from his savings and Alice sold some of her delicate porcelain, raising four pounds. Georgie didn't want his grandmother to feel pressured to contribute but Alice insisted—she said that she cared for Eva and wanted to see her come home. Alice knew how much Georgie loved Eva, and Alice loved Georgie. She also felt somewhat responsible for Eva going missing the day after their tiff at the lodging house. Alice hoped to see Eva again and make things right between them. The flower women had all pulled together to collect five shillings and Georgie was able to work for Mr. Gyles for a few days in London, making a few more shillings and obtaining a contribution from Mr. Gyles himself as well.

Georgie said his goodbyes to Margie and Alice early in the morning, three days after arriving in London. He began making his way toward Oxfordshire. The journey from London to Oxfordshire was nearly twice as long as the trip from Shepperton to London. He had to take his time to make sure he did not tire out the horse or himself, so he stayed overnight at an inn located halfway to his destination, in Wycombe. Finally, after a two-day long journey, he was almost in Oxfordshire when he began to feel weary. Regardless of how he felt, Georgie pressed on while thinking about Eva, which motivated him the rest of the way.

He knew that he needed to arrive in Oxfordshire before nightfall because he would only have one full day to see his family and talk to the magistrate before having to head back to Shepperton. Georgie was anxious—if anything didn't go as planned, he wouldn't make it back in time to meet Lucious' deadline. He was also extremely nervous about asking the magistrate for an advance in order to obtain the remainder of the ransom payment. Georgie wasn't even sure that he still had his position at the farm after being gone for more than a month and work was hard to come by these days. He prayed that Magistrate Logan would grace him with great leniency for being gone for so long as well as for asking for an advance. Georgie knew that it was a very tall order he expected from the magistrate, but it was his only option.

He arrived in Oxfordshire just before the sun began to set. Gazing out at the captivating landscape, he was pleased to be back at the farm but, once again grieved that Eva was not with him. He wanted to see his family, to inform them that he was all right, and to let them know about Eva's situation. Georgie headed out to the farmer's cottage, where his family lived. The magistrate had provided the Thornber family with a cottage away from the other servant quarters below the house. The cottage was a tight fit for the five of them, with only a small kitchen, living area, and one bedroom, but they managed to make it work.

Georgie saw his sisters, Marta and Mary, sitting on the front step and playing a game of dice called chicken-hazard. The game was one of Eva's favorite games and she would often beat Georgie at it. Georgie remembered several times when they had played for stakes and Eva had won, making Georgie her servant for the day. She would order him to bring her tea and pastries while she resided on the chaise lounge at Alice's, enjoying the delicacies. Eva would sit on the chaise, acting like a princess, while Georgie would read her stories. The thought of it made him smile. He had never minded the game; in fact, he had enjoyed taking care of Eva. Georgie looked down at the ground and let out a disheartened sigh, elicited by the memories of the happy times that he and Eva had spent together.

He looked back at the cottage, placing his hands around his mouth and calling out to his sisters, "Marta, Mary!"

The two girls looked up with excitement.

"Georgie!" they screamed, running over to him and grasping him tightly.

"Look at how you both have grown in only a month," Georgie said surprised to see that Marta, his sixteen-year old sister, was blossoming into a lovely young woman, and that Mary, who was thirteen, had already begun to change from a little girl into a young lady.

"Georgie, we have missed you so! And mother, well, she's been very worried about you."

Georgie nodded, understanding that his parents were probably wondering where he had been for the last month. He walked into the cottage with his sisters and his mother, Elizabeth Thornber, ran over to welcome him home with tears in her eyes. Georgie's father was still outside working.

"Alice had written to inform us that Eva has gone missing and that you were out looking for her. What's happened to Eva?" Elizabeth asked worriedly.

"Yes, Mum, that's right," Georgie answered, then glanced over at Marta and Mary. He didn't want to say much in front of his younger sisters. Elizabeth could tell that he wasn't going to share any information with the two girls present, so she asked them both to go and find their father.

After the girls left, Georgie's mother came over and sat next to him on the sofa, taking his hand, she asked, "Now, what's happened, George?"

Georgie couldn't help it, the tears started flowing from his eyes all on their own. How was he supposed to explain that the woman he loved and desired to marry was being kept at a brothel in Shepperton?

Elizabeth tipped her head down, looking Georgie in the eyes.

"It's alright son, you can tell me."

Georgie's heart raced and his hands trembled slightly. He inhaled a deep breath. "Alright, the truth is, Eva's in a lot of trouble."

Elizabeth continued intently staring at George and asked, "What sort of trouble is she in?"

Georgie swallowed hard before answering his mother.

"Eva went away with a man named Lucious Paddimir. Have you heard of him?" he asked and Elizabeth tilted her head contemplating whether she had heard that name before.

"Sounds familiar, but I can't place him. Should I know this fellow, Lucious Paddimir?" she asked.

Georgie shook his head, "I should hope not, he's an evil man."

Elizabeth squinted her eyes, slowly nodding as she was trying to make sense of everything Georgie was saying.

"This man, Mr. Paddimir, he sells a juice concoction. It's an addictive drug of sorts and I think that Eva might be…" Georgie's words trailed off as he became choked up thinking about Eva's predicament.

"There, there, George, I'm so sorry!" Elizabeth said wrapping her arms around her son, holding him tightly as he wept in his mother's arms. Georgie pulled away and wiped the tears from his face.

"Sorry, I just can't seem to control my emotions lately," he said, embarrassed by the fact that he was a grown man crying on his mother's shoulder.

"It's alright, son," she assured him once again, placing her hand on Georgie's. "I have found that most real men shed a tear or two from time to time. It sounds like you have been through a great ordeal—searching for Eva only to find that she's gone off with this man," Elizabeth said, looking up at him disheartened, knowing what Georgie's intentions toward Eva were.

"There's more, Mum," Georgie continued as he regained his composure. "It's not just that this man is with Eva. He's prostituting her to some of the wealthiest men in England."

Elizabeth leaned away, squinting in dismay, her mouth gaping open.

"Are you certain of this, George?" she questioned and Georgie nodded in reply. "Oh my." Elizabeth sat straight up on the sofa, glancing around the room and thinking about how this could have happened.

"Does Marg know?" she asked.

"Yes, ma'am," Georgie replied.

"Oh, dear, she must be in a state of shock." Elizabeth was concerned for Margie and how she must be feeling about what happened to her daughter.

"Yes, Miss Marg was deeply hurt, of course, but she'd heard of this man before and I think she already had her suspicions."

Elizabeth sat there with a most distraught look on her face.

"George, I'm afraid I don't know what to say. I know that you intended to marry Eva—" Elizabeth was still speaking when Georgie interrupted.

"And that hasn't changed!" he stated.

Elizabeth gave him a look of surprise. "I know you love her son, but Eva's…" she didn't want to finish what she was saying, knowing that it would hurt Georgie.

"You mean to say that she's ruined," he finished for her, looking up at his mother as discouragement filled his eyes.

Elizabeth stared at Georgie solemnly and, after a few moments, she spoke up.

"George, if you truly love Eva enough to want to marry her after all of this, then, you have my blessing," she said as she gazed out across the room, shaking her head. "I don't think

I've ever seen a man care this much about a woman in my entire life, to go to the extent you have gone to find her."

Georgie glanced up at his mother smiling. "Oh, thank you, Mum!" he said, relieved, wrapping his arms around her tightly.

Elizabeth smiled sorrowfully as Georgie embraced her, unsure how things would turn out for him and Eva. "Well, we're going to have to tell your father," she said pulling away and looking at him. Georgie sighed and nodded in agreement.

When Ruben Thornber arrived at the cottage, he shook Georgie's hand and gave him a pat on the back.

"Good to see you, son, it's been a while," he smiled.

"Yes, it has been," Georgie cordially replied.

Georgie didn't talk about the situation right away and Ruben didn't want to press the matter. He felt that, when Georgie was ready, he would share what information he had about Eva. The family sat around the kitchen table once again having dinner together. Ruben said a word of prayer as the family members held hands. He prayed for Eva's safety and that she would return home soon.

After the family had finished eating dinner, Georgie and his sisters cleared the table and washed the dishes, cleaning up the mess. When they finished, Marta and Mary returned to the bedroom to work on some of their studies, while Georgie sat with his parents in the living area, explaining Eva's situation to his father this time. He also told his parents about his legs growing weak and how the Kenny family had helped nurse him back to health. Georgie's dad was quiet about the whole matter and just sat there, listening intently as Georgie explained everything. Afterward, Ruben asked if he could speak with Georgie alone and the two men went outside to the front porch.

Georgie was standing on the porch, his hands tucked into his pockets as he inhaled the fresh evening air. Ruben looked over at him and waited a few moments before speaking.

"I know you love Eva, George, but there are a few things you have to understand. Eva, well, she could have an illness from being with different men or she might even be with child. Are you prepared to deal with those situations if they arise?"

Georgie looked down at the ground, thinking about what his father was saying.

"Yes, I am," he stated with certainty, nodding his head and gazing up earnestly into his father's eyes.

Ruben inhaled deeply. "You know, there are many nice, pretty, young ladies out there, many of whom would make a wonderful wife—"

Georgie shook his head and interjected.

"No, no, I love Eva. It's always been, Eva! I've always loved her—there's no one else for me," he said with conviction. He took a few long seconds to calm down. "I'm sorry, Pop, it's just..." Georgie shook his head trying to find his words. "I have spent the last two years of my life imagining being married to Eva. I decided a long time ago that I wanted to make her my wife and have planned, saved, and done everything I know how to do to make things the best they could possibly be for the two of us." Georgie paused for a moment, looking down. "But I hadn't planned for this," he said shaking his head.

Ruben stood there quietly, listening, and Georgie looked back at his father after a few moments.

"If I had to do it all over, I would have asked her to marry me sooner or, at least, I would have made my intentions known to her. And I most certainly would never have left her alone in London," Georgie said, gazing down at the porch floor.

Ruben rubbed his neck thinking about all that Georgie was saying.

"So, you feel responsible, then. You think this is your fault?" he asked.

Georgie looked up at him wide-eyed.

"Of course it is, I left her alone when she needed me most."

Georgie quickly looked back down, breathing heavily, and Ruben shook his head.

"No, George, this isn't your fault," he said with great assurance. "Eva chose to leave with that man. She's in this predicament because she made a wrong choice and not because of you."

Georgie kicked a beam on the porch, then gruffly grabbed the banister and began weeping.

"But if only I'd told her how I felt, then maybe she wouldn't have left with him! Just maybe, we'd be together right now!" Georgie shouted, tears streaming down his face.

Ruben walked over to Georgie and placed a hand on his shoulder.

"Yes, maybe in hindsight, things would have turned out differently, but they turned out this way. And, as your father, I need to make sure that you still desire to marry Eva for the right reasons—and not just out of guilt," he said shaking his head.

Georgie looked up at his father. "Yes, of course, I feel guilty," he said, nodding his head as he let go of the banister. Standing up straight, he looked his father in the eyes. "But, before I felt guilty about this situation, I spent two years of my life waiting to be with the woman I love. And I still love her, no matter what. There's no one else I will ever desire to be with, only Eva," Georgie claimed, leaning back once more and grabbing the banister.

Ruben nodded his head. "I understand, son, but do you know if Eva loves you?" he questioned.

"Yes, I believe she does, but I don't know for certain. I've never taken the opportunity to ask her. Still, regardless of how Eva feels about me..." Georgie closed his eyes for a moment, his heart dropping when he thought that Eva might not love him or not wish to marry him. "I'm still going to show up at Liberation Hall in three days to save her from that terrible man!" Georgie shouted and heatedly pointed out toward the field.

Georgie's father nodded. He understood that his son loved Eva and that his decision was final.

"Alright then, sounds like you've made up your mind," Ruben inhaled deeply, then turned around and started to head back inside the cottage.

"Wait, Pop!" Georgie called out, motioning him to stop.

Ruben turned back around, looking at Georgie.

"Do you think, if Eva does decide to marry me, that you and mum will be able to love her and look at her the same way you did before all this happened? To treat her respectably, as my wife?" Georgie asked most seriously.

Ruben looked Georgie earnestly in the eyes. "Absolutely," he stated without a doubt and nodded his head. Georgie nodded back, hoping that what his father said was true.

Ruben headed inside the cottage but Georgie stayed outside for a while longer, sitting on the porch step and thinking about everything they had discussed. Georgie did slightly fear that

Eva would reject his proposal. This was one of the reasons he didn't reveal his feelings for her that day on the stairs, but he did always believe that they had genuine love for one another and, based on her affectionate behavior toward him, he did believe she felt the same way. Georgie remembered how distraught she was when he left for Oxfordshire. She hadn't wanted him to leave—but that could have simply been because he was her best friend and nothing more. Eva's response at Liberation Hall had also given him hope that she loved him in return, but it could simply indicate that she just wanted to leave the Hall. Her reaction didn't necessarily have anything to do with wanting to be with him or with loving him. Georgie had to be realistic and to consider the possibility that Eva may not love him or may not want to marry him. He also knew that she may want to go back to the lodging house to live with her mother after being away for so long. Finally, there was also another grim possibility, one that Georgie didn't want to think about—that Eva loved Lucious and desired to stay with him at Liberation Hall.

Twenty-Five

C laudia slept on Eva's floor all night, making sure she didn't need anything after her traumatic encounter with Lucious. She also wanted to keep an eye on her because she worried that Eva might drink too much of the juice or that Lucious would come back to violate her again. The night had been mostly quiet, other than for the occasional sound of Eva sucking in gasps of air from crying so hard. Claudia was afraid that the ferocious attack last evening had utterly broken the young girl. She rose from the floor, rubbing her eyes, and slowly walked over to check on Eva. She slept soundly, looking very peaceful in her sleep. Claudia thought it was, perhaps, the most peaceful she had seen Eva look since she had first arrived at the Hall. She crept over to the door, exiting Eva's bedroom while trying not to wake her. She knew that the peace Eva was experiencing while sleeping would soon end upon waking.

Claudia walked down the corridor to her bedroom and began getting herself ready for the day, when she remembered that Lord Manchester was supposed to arrive that evening. Claudia rolled her eyes, shaking her head. What was she going to do? She thought to herself. Eva was in no state to be with Lord Manchester right after Lucious had violated her. Once Claudia finished getting herself ready, she entered the corridor at the same time as Lucious. She closed her eyes for a moment, inhaling deeply and trying to calm her nerves. She had not seen Lucious since last night when she had confronted him about his behavior toward Eva. Claudia feared that he may strike out at any time to repay her for her words.

"Good morning, Claudia," Lucious chirped, a big smile on his face, which made Claudia extremely nervous.

"Good morning Lucious," she replied cautiously.

Lucious lifted his eyebrows, then turned, heading down the stairwell. Claudia stood in the corridor, squinting and wondering what he was up to this morning. She followed him down into the dining hall to have some breakfast. She felt that Eva was safe as long as she was able to keep an eye on Lucious. Lucious ate his breakfast, flipping through the pages of the morning newspaper. He seemed to be in a rather pleasant mood.

Suddenly, he stood abruptly from the table and walked over toward Claudia. Standing behind her, he bent down and leaned his head next to her face. Claudia's eyes grew large and she clenched at his nearness.

Lucious leaned in even closer, whispering eerily into her ear, "I haven't forgotten what you said to me last night." He leaned in and gently kissed her neck.

Claudia cringed, closing her eyes, disgusted by the touch of Lucious lips against her skin. Lucious stood back up and walked out of the room. She inhaled deeply again after Lucious left the dining room and sat there for a moment, gathering herself as her heart raced wildly. Once Claudia's nerves had calmed down, she decided that she better go and check on Eva since she did not know where Lucious had gone to in the house.

Claudia knocked on Eva's door lightly, not expecting an answer. She assumed that Eva was still sleeping and, if so, she didn't want to wake her. Claudia waited a moment longer to see whether Eva would reply when the door flung wide open. Claudia was surprised to find Eva up, washed, and dressed for the day.

"Good morning, Claudia," Eva said with a smile as she sat down on the bed and placed her heels on her feet. Claudia was taken aback by Eva's high-spirits this morning, given her despondent behavior after what had taken place yesterday.

"Eva, are you alright?" Claudia asked worriedly.

"Yes, I'm fine. Why do you keep asking me that?" Eva replied. She didn't wait for Claudia to respond but continued talking, "Although, Nancy hasn't shown up this morning. I've been ringing for her for the last half hour." Eva looked confused, unsure why Nancy hadn't responded to her bell.

"Hmm, I will check on that; but, first, I want to know how you're feeling today?"

"Well, if by that you mean to ask whether I gotten my menses, the answer is still no," Eva said rudely.

"No, that isn't what I was referring to. I meant last evening… you were in a terrible state," Claudia said. She was trying to get Eva to talk about happened with Lucious.

"Dia, I really have no idea what you're talking about," Eva said, cheekily flipping her hair with her hand. "I'm going downstairs to get some breakfast. I'm starved." She walked over to the door from across the room. "Oh, if Nancy comes up, will you please tell her to change my bed linens. I'm expecting Lord Manchester this evening," Eva asked and Claudia peered at her, completely confused by her behavior.

"Eva, we need to talk," Claudia insisted, but Eva continued walking toward the bedroom door.

As Eva passed by her, Claudia gently touched her on the shoulder to keep her from leaving the room.

Eva turned around vigorously and shouted, "Don't touch me!"

Claudia flinched, surprised by Eva's reaction.

"I don't like it when people grab at me!" Eva said, trying to explain her response.

She had a dismal look upon her face with a trace of tears in her eyes.

Claudia stood there for a moment with her mouth gaping open.

"I'm sorry, Eva. I had no idea," Claudia apologized.

"I'm heading downstairs now," Eva said harshly, turning hastily as she left her bedroom.

Claudia stood there for a moment, contemplating Eva's behavior. The only thing she could figure was that Eva was pretending that the violation did not occur, but Claudia knew, based on Lucious' response, that something most definitely did occur. She realized that she was going to have to get Eva to open up somehow but decided it was best to give her some time right now.

Claudia inhaled deeply and walked down to the servant quarters to find out what happened to Nancy. A couple of the housemaids were in the cleaning wardrobe, changing supplies.

"Do either of you know where Nancy is at the moment?"

The maids turned around, surprised to see Claudia downstairs. Then, they glanced back and forth at one another.

"Nancy packed up her things and left, Miss."

Claudia peered at the maids, completely baffled.

"Did she say anything?" Claudia asked and one of the maids answered.

"No, Miss, she left in the middle of the night without a word."

Claudia assumed that Nancy must have seen something that frightened her but never said anything.

She released a frustrated sigh, "Alright then, thank you. And will you please change the bed linens in Eva's room?"

The maids curtsied as she headed back upstairs.

*　*　*

Claudia entered the study to find Lucious sitting at his desk.

"We need to get Eva more traction," he blurted out without even looking up at her.

"Lucious, did you dismiss Nancy?" Claudia asked and Lucious looked up, surprised by her question.

"No, why?"

"She packed up and left in the middle of the night," Claudia explained and Lucious humphed.

"Well, I suppose you'll have to hire a new lady's maid for Eva. Make sure you add that to your list of things to do," he said while fluttering his fingers at her. "So, back to what I was saying. I think I'm going to have another party in a few weeks to introduce Eva to some new clients. I need you to handle those arrangements as well."

Claudia let out another sigh and Lucious glared at her, irritated.

"Shouldn't you be writing this down?" he asked.

"I don't know if a party and more clients are what Eva needs right now. She is still pregnant with *your* baby."

Claudia quickly placed a hand over her mouth, regretting what she said.

Lucious rose from his desk and slowly walked over to Claudia.

"Then, perhaps, it's time to call Dr. Smithe to take care of the situation promptly," he said with ease, glaring at Claudia.

Claudia took a step back, away from him, and Lucious gave a slight laugh and a devilish grin.

"Are you afraid of me Claudia?"

Claudia didn't respond. She was breathing heavily, waiting to see what he would do next. Lucious popped out at Claudia, making her jump back, and began laughing again.

"I must admit, I do enjoy watching you squirm," he said, smiling at her wickedly.

He cleared his throat, "I want you to know that I've made a decision. I've decided to dock your pay." He walked back over to the front of his desk, then turned around to look at her.

"How much?" she asked calmly.

"Well...all of it," he said with certainty.

Claudia felt fury rising inside of her. "You can't do that! You've been paying me for years!" she spouted angrily back at him.

"Yes, but what good has it done me? You're saying things to Eva behind my back, you constantly undermine my authority, and you disrespect me in front of the girls!" Lucious yelled, walking briskly over to Claudia and leaning into her face. He paused for a moment, making sure she was looking at him. "I know what your problem is, Dia... Your problem is that you don't fear me enough!" he shouted.

Claudia backed away from him not saying anything.

"So, I'm going to have to change that, now, aren't I? Furthermore, if you ever want to receive payment again, then your attitude toward me better improve!" he yelled once again. "Now, go out there, find another lady's maid, send for Dr. Smithe, and plan me a bloody party!" he screamed, waving her away with his hand.

Claudia nodded, then turned around swiftly and left the study.

She entered the dining hall, where Eva was finishing breakfast.

"Eva, I need to inform you that Nancy has left the house."

Eva looked up at Claudia solemnly and nodded her head. Claudia noticed that Eva didn't seem surprised to hear that Nancy was gone.

"Dia, I wanted to let you know that I plan on going outside for a while, it looks like an absolutely breathtaking day," Eva stated excitedly.

Claudia stared at her for a moment. "Yes, I think that's a good idea," she agreed. "The sunshine might do you some good." Claudia smiled at her, trying to act normally along with Eva. "Would you like me to send anything out with you?" Claudia asked.

"Some juice would be nice," Eva said and Claudia nodded, leaving the room to fetch her a bottle of juice.

Eva sat outside, soaking up the sun, when Claudia joined her with a bottle of juice and two glasses. Claudia poured the juice and handed a glass to Eva.

"Tell me about Barbados, is it nice there?" Eva inquired and Claudia laughed briefly.

"Oh yes, Barbados is very beautiful and much warmer than England. When people come to visit, it feels like a holiday to them—but to me, it feels like home," Claudia answered, leaning her head back and pointing her face up toward the sun. She had a grand smile on her face thinking about home.

"Why did you leave?" Eva asked.

Claudia waited a moment, contemplating her decision. "Well, I met Lucious and he told me that he loved me. He had his own ship and crew at that time and he said that he was traveling the world in search of herbs to make an amazing juice that was going to help people."

Eva scoffed, shaking her head while facing the sun.

"My family were slaves and so was I—and I thought it was better to come to England with a dashing young man who owned his own ship than to stay working in the sugar fields day after day. So, one night, Lucious helped me escape. I thought he was my savior, coming to rescue me from the terrible white men who had me bound."

Claudia laughed slightly, shaking her head rapidly.

"I had no idea that I was going from one slave owner to another."

Eva turned and looked at Claudia but said nothing.

After a few moments, Eva spoke while staring out at the river.

"Have you ever thought of killing Lucious?" she asked and Claudia glanced over at her, surprised by her question.

Claudia paused, "Well, yes, actually...many times." Claudia tilted her head while looking back out over the Thames.

"Why haven't you?" Eva inquired.

Claudia looked back over and saw Eva staring at her most gravely. She inhaled deeply, "Well, I actually came close once, after Lucious took advantage of me."

Eva quickly turned her head, fixing her eyes back out across the landscape.

"But then I realized that if I killed Lucious...I would hang on the gallows and he would be considered my victim...and I refuse to die a criminal while Lucious Paddimir is remembered as my victim."

Eva gazed back at Claudia, thinking about everything she was saying.

They sat there silently for a while, watching the sunlight blossom over the river.

"Eva, what if Georgie returns for you, what will you do?" Claudia asked.

Eva didn't say anything for a moment, contemplating what she would do if Georgie returned for her.

"I hope he doesn't come back," she replied, continuing to stare out at the view.

Claudia looked over at her perplexed. "Why?" she asked, surprised.

Eva released a sigh and turned toward Claudia.

"Because if he returns and I see him look at me the way he did last time he was here, then I will love him more—but I know that I can never be with him. And when Lucious doesn't release me, my heart will break all over again and I will be left to deal with the consequences of my heart as well as the consequences that Lucious will devise," Eva said and tears flooded her eyes. She quickly wiped them away, forcing her pain deep down inside herself.

Eva wanted to forget that yesterday happened and that Georgie had ever come to Liberation Hall. She also wanted, desperately, to ignore the violent assault that Lucious had unleashed upon her. Eva believed that everything had been working out just fine before Georgie arrived at the Hall. She knew that her life was far from perfect but, if she was going to have to live at Liberation Hall, she wanted to try and do so in as much peace as possible.

Claudia looked over at Eva and, at that moment, decided that she was going to do whatever she could to help Eva be with Georgie. She'd been Lucious' pawn for far too long and she wanted to do something that would genuinely help Eva. Which, she realized, is something that she should have done a long time ago—and not just for Eva. It was time to stand up for what is right.

Twenty-Six

T wo more days remained until Georgie had to return to Liberation Hall with the ransom payment for Eva. He woke up early on his first morning in Oxfordshire and decided to go check on the magistrate's horses, as well as on Dr. Kenny's horse. Georgie worked all morning, taking care of the horses and exercising them, then headed to the servant quarters to take a bath. The family's cottage had an outhouse but, in order to clean up properly, the family had to go over to the main house and use the servants' communal washroom. After Georgie had cleaned up, he went into the kitchen in search of a snack. He saw a beautiful bowl of fruit sitting on the table in the dining hall. He picked out a ripe apple and was taking a large bite out of the juicy orb when he noticed a young girl, about the same age as Eva, sitting in the corner of the room next to the fireplace. She was sitting in a rocking chair, mending one of the magistrate's daughter's garments.

"Oh, hello there, I didn't see you. My name is George Thornber," he said as he strolled over, holding out his hand to introduce himself. The girl looked up at him shyly and smiled.

"My name is Alice," she said sweetly, extending her hand.

Alice was a natural beauty, with blonde hair, blue eyes, and bright, round, rosy cheeks.

"Aw, my Grams' name is Alice as well," Georgie said happily. "Do you mind if I join you?" he asked not wanting to be a bother to Alice while she was working.

"No, not at all. I welcome the company," she said smiling and looking deeply into Georgie's eyes.

Georgie swallowed hard and noticed that Alice was a beautiful young lady. He sat there for a moment gazing around the room, trying to avoid making eye contact. He took another large bite of the apple and its juice sprayed out in every direction. Alice laughed as she watched Georgie eat the apple.

"What's so funny?" he asked, smiling back at her.

"You work with the horses, right?" she inquired.

"Yes, I'm the stable master," he replied proudly.

"Perhaps you should try not eating like one," Alice said with a chuckle, grinning flirtatiously at Georgie.

Georgie's eyes connected with Alice and feelings rose inside him when he realized how much Alice reminded him of Eva.

"You know, my best friend Eva would have said the same thing," he said, smiling widely.

Reminiscing about Eva made Georgie's heart flutter and his stomach swell inside. Alice was pretty but he did not feel the same way about her as he did for Eva. The whole time he sat across from Alice, all he could think about was Eva. Georgie remained there for a few moments more, wondering whether he could possibly marry someone else if Eva didn't want to marry him. He continued gazing at Alice intently but knew that he could never love Alice or anyone else the way he loved Eva. He stood abruptly from the chair.

"Well, I need to be going, I have to go see the magistrate. It was nice meeting you, Alice," Georgie smiled and nodded. Alice smiled politely in return and Georgie went upstairs to wait until it was time to speak with Magistrate Logan.

He was waiting in the magistrate's foyer when Mr. Watkins, the butler, walked out from the study and announced, in a solemn tone, "Magistrate Logan will see you now."

He inhaled a deep breath as he strode into Magistrate Logan's office.

"Well, George, it's good to see you back on the farm," the magistrate extended his hand, smiling.

"It's good to be back here, sir," he replied.

The magistrate motioned for Georgie to sit down.

"So, have you found the friend you were out searching for George?"

Georgie swallowed hard, nodding his head.

"Yes, sir, I have."

The magistrate raised his eyebrows, surprised that Georgie had found the location of the Hall based on the information he had given him.

"Was she at Liberation Hall, then?" he inquired.

"Yes, sir, she was."

The magistrate grew nervous, wondering whether Georgie knew that he visited the Hall on occasion.

"Did Lucious allow you to come inside to see her?"

Georgie nodded his head while anxiously twisting his hat in his hands. "Yes, that's the reason I'm here, sir. Lucious Paddimir has offered me a deal in exchange for Eva."

The magistrate lowered his chin and squinted in suspicion as to what sort deal Lucious Paddimir would make with a young lad like George.

"He said that if I came back to the Hall with one hundred pounds in one week, he would allow Eva to leave."

Magistrate Logan sat for a moment, contemplating this deal. He knew that that price was almost the same price Lucious demanded for a single night with one of his girls and was surprised to hear that Lucious would be willing to sell one of his prized processions for release at such a low cost.

"And why is it that Lucious will not allow your friend to go if she no longer desires to stay with him?" the magistrate asked, trying not to let on that he knew much about the Hall or Lucious Paddimir.

"Well, sir, the truth is…Liberation Hall is actually…well, it's a place... of ill repute, if you know what I mean."

The magistrate cleared his throat. "Ah, I see, so Lucious is requiring payment for the girl?" he questioned.

Georgie looked down at his hat in hands. "Yes, it seems that way, sir."

The magistrate's heart went out to Georgie. He could tell that Georgie had deeper feelings than mere friendship for this girl.

"Did you ask him whether paying the ransom meant that she could officially leave the Hall and not return?" the magistrate questioned, wanting to make sure that Georgie wasn't going to be swindled by Lucious.

"Yes, sir, I did, and he said that if she so chooses...and I believe she will...that Eva is free to leave Liberation Hall."

The magistrate tilted his head, placing his chin in his hand while his elbow rested on his desk.

"Sir, I have fifty-five pounds, but I need forty-five more to meet his demand. I know this is a lot to ask of you...you have already been so generous to me...but I was wondering if I could have an advance on my salary. That is, of course, as long as I've still got my position here on the farm?"

The magistrate was keenly focused on Georgie but did not say anything, so Georgie continued to speak.

"I know I've been gone for over a month, sir, but it has taken me three weeks to find Liberation Hall. I walked the entire time I searched, until my legs finally gave out near Shepperton, where the Hall is located. A doctor there gave me a ride into town and helped me get better before I was able to visit the Hall," Georgie explained.

The magistrate stared at Georgie, guilt-stricken over the fact that he hadn't given Georgie the precise location of the Hall in the first place. The poor lad had searched on foot for three weeks.

"George, forty-five pounds is nearly a year's worth of wages...?" the magistrate questioned.

"I know, sir...I know it's a lot, asking you for a year's advance—but Eva's the love of my life. I know she's been in the Hall, but I still love her all the same. I want to marry her and bring her here to Oxfordshire," Georgie replied.

The magistrate cleared his throat, sitting straight up in the chair, surprised to hear that Georgie still planned on marrying this girl.

"You told me that it was alright," Georgie continued, "if I started fixing up that old shed next to the horse barn with my own money and—"

The magistrate cut him off, "You may have the advance, George."

Georgie was silent for a moment, his eyes growing large. He reached out and grabbed the magistrate's hand.

"Thank you, sir, thank you!" he exclaimed.

The magistrate nodded and Georgie released his grip.

"So, your plan is to still marry the girl even though she's..." the magistrate cleared his throat, allowing his words to trail off, but Georgie knew what he was implying.

He looked the magistrate straight in the eyes. "Yes, sir, I do," he replied solemnly, then swallowed hard. "Is it going to be a problem, if she comes to live here on your farm?"

The magistrate was surprised by Georgie's forward question. He cleared his throat again, "Well, I suppose it wouldn't be a problem if you manage to keep Eva's past to yourselves. I wouldn't want the servants of the house to gossip about her," the magistrate explained and Georgie nodded in agreement.

"I'm going to have to head back to Shepperton for a just little while longer. I hope that's alright? Mr. Hammond is going to continue filling in for me and pop will also help when needed. I promise to get back here as soon as possible," Georgie assured.

The magistrate peered at Georgie intently.

"Normally, I wouldn't be so lenient but, to be honest with you, George, I've never met a better stable master than you in all my days. You have a way with the horses and I like that. I've also never seen a man care so deeply for a woman before in my life. You truly make the lot of us look bad…Please, don't ever lose that," the magistrate said, sincerely nodding his head.

Georgie smiled in return, "Yes, sir."

Magistrate Logan knew it was hard to find honest and wholesome workers like Georgie these days. "Good, now, if you will please turn around, I will get you that advance out of my safe."

Georgie turned around and waited as the magistrate unlocked his safe. Magistrate Logan pulled out a strongbox, counted out forty-five pounds, and placed it in a money sack. He closed the box and shut the safe door, turning the lock.

"Alright, here it is…your forty-five pounds as an advance."

The magistrate handed the sack containing the money to Georgie. Georgie took a hard look at the bag of cash, thinking how that was one entire year's worth of his work.

"Thank you very much, sir," Georgie said, gratefully, as he once again shook Magistrate Logan's hand.

"Be careful George…I do hope that Lucious lives up to his side of the bargain," said the magistrate and Georgie nodded in agreement.

Georgie now had everything he needed—a total of one hundred pounds, a horse, and good physical health. He prayed that he wouldn't get robbed on the way to Shepperton and that his trip would go smoothly. The next morning he said his goodbyes. Hugging his mother tightly, he gave her a big kiss on the cheek.

"Now, the next time we see you, it better be for a wedding, with Eva on your arm," said Elizabeth.

"Yes, Mum, I agree," Georgie replied with a grin.

He hugged his sisters, Marta and Mary, who were both sad to see their brother leave but understood that he needed to help Eva.

"Pop," Georgie said, shaking his father's hand.

"Be careful son. We're praying for your safety...you and Eva both," Ruben assured.

Georgie nodded, "Thank you." He waved his last goodbye, then mounted the thoroughbred and rode off, heading down the long dirt lane.

*   *   *

Georgie stopped in Marlow for the night and, early the next day, he began making his way toward Shepperton. Today was the day he'd been waiting for—when he would return to Liberation Hall and deliver the funds to Lucious for Eva's release. He was pleased that everything had gone according to plan up to this point, but the heavy rain clouds in the distance made him nervous. Traveling in the rain posed a problem—not only would he be soaking wet but it would also create mud, which would slow down the horse. If the rains were extremely heavy, flash floods could occur, covering the roads. Georgie prayed that the bad weather would hold off until he had Eva in his arms and they could both arrive safely to the Kenny household for the night.

Twenty-Seven

E va waited anxiously, pacing back an forth in her bedroom all morning. Today was the day that Georgie was supposed to return to Liberation Hall with one hundred pounds in exchange for her life. She wondered if he was actually going to come back and try to save her. Eva believed that, even if he were unable to find the money, he would still return for her. Her emotions were running high as she contemplated the possibilities for what could occur if Georgie returned. The first thing that Eva was unsure of was Lucious' plan. She knew that he had conceived something sinister on the spot, but he had not shared his scheme with anyone. He'd been taunting her all week about whether Georgie-Porgy would come to her rescue. He made comments, saying that Georgie certainly no longer desired her, now anyway, knowing that she was a harlot. When Eva told Claudia that she didn't want Georgie to return for her, it was partly true because of fear. She feared that Lucious was right and that, even if Georgie had wanted to marry her before, perhaps his intentions toward her had changed since finding out that she was now a prostitute. She wouldn't blame him if he desired a chaste woman. Georgie deserved someone good and Eva wanted to see him happy.

She also feared what Lucious might do to her if Georgie returned but wasn't able to take her with him. She didn't know what could be worse than Lucious' sexual abuse toward her, but she cringed at the possibilities. Eva feared, most of all, for Georgie's life, knowing that—if it came down to it—Lucious would kill him. He had Scotland Yard and most of Parliament in his pocket, all of whom would willingly turn a blind eye to his indiscretions.

Yet, there was also another possibility—one that was highly improbable—that she and Georgie would somehow escape Liberation Hall together and be free of Lucious, forever. However, if Georgie didn't return, Eva knew that she would be eternally trapped at the Hall, with Lucious, for the rest of her life.

She decided, after worrying in her room all morning, that she should go downstairs to the drawing room to see whether Claudia was there. Claudia was planning to go to London the following day to pick up some dresses for a party that Lucious was hosting in a few weeks. Eva wanted to see her as much as possible before she left. Claudia was Eva's only real friend at the Hall and had become like a sister to her over the last few weeks. She recalled being jealous of Claudia and her relationship with Lucious when she first arrived. Now, everything had changed in barely a month and Eva enjoyed talking to Claudia far more than being in Lucious' company. She also wasn't sure how Lucious would behave toward her while Claudia was in London. Claudia had been helping her keep an eye out for Lucious in case he wanted to hurt Eva again. This all depended on whether or not Eva would still be at the Hall tomorrow. Lucious' plans for his party undoubtably included Eva.

Last night, Lucious asked Eva to stay in his room with him. This was the first time, since the attack, that he expressed a desire to be with her. Eva politely declined, but Lucious threatened that he would have no choice but to force her to be with him once again if she didn't agree. Eva consented, not wanting to be violated again, and stayed with him for the night. She had cried the entire time she was there and Lucious scolded her for it, saying that she was making his experience most terrible and that he hadn't gotten rough with her anyways. The intense love and emotions she had once felt for Lucious—and which had already been hanging by a thread—had entirely dissipated after he attacked her. Now, she couldn't stand being near him and it took everything she had to stop herself from killing him. Eva would think about what Claudia had said to her—if she killed Lucious, she would hang for his death. She, too, did not want to make Lucious her victim as he had made her his.

Eva entered the drawing room and found Lucious smoking his pipe. She was getting ready to turn around and leave when he saw her. She knew that if she left now, he might possibly be offended and do something harmful to her.

"Aw, Eva, what a pleasure it is to gaze upon you this morning. Oh, wait, I mean this afternoon," Lucious said sarcastically, placing his pipe in the corner of his mouth with a bloated grin.

"Good afternoon, Lucious," Eva said politely, sitting down across from him on the sofa.

Lucious blew out a puff of smoke and placed the pipe down next to his ashtray.

"You're so far away, come over here and sit on daddy's lap," Lucious said patting his legs and beckoning her to come and sit on his lap like a child.

332

Eva closed her eyes for a brief moment as a stabbing feeling flowed through her body at Lucious' words. She slowly stood up and walked over, sitting down on Lucious' lap.

"There that's better," he said as he caressed her face. Eva closed her eyes, repulsed by his touch. Oh, how she loathed the sight of him! She opened her eyes, smiling at him so he wouldn't realize how much she despised him.

"So, do you think that Georgie-Porgy will show up today and take my little Eva away?" he said patronizingly, with a pout.

Eva's smiled stalled and she pressed her lips together. Lucious let out a laugh and his false, kind demeanor changed into a sinister grin. Eva backed away slightly, fearing what he might do. Lucious brought his face closer to hers, his eyes black as sin, and stared at her hauntingly.

"Just so you know, if he does return...I will most certainly kill him," Lucious said and gave her an emphatic frown while nodding his head.

Eva was breathing heavily and gazing down, no longer wishing to look him in the eyes. Lucious grabbed Eva's jaw tightly forcing her head up with his hand.

"Don't you turn your face from me, ever again!" he shouted.

She could feel his breath and saliva spraying out all over her face as he chastised her. She clinched, closing her eyes, then quickly opened them so Lucious wouldn't grow even angrier with her. Tears began welling up as she looked upon his face, realizing that this was going to be her life from now on.

"That is one of the things I enjoy about you Eva, you have an impressive learning curve. You're always trying to please me and I do appreciate that so." Lucious lifted her hand and he kissed it while continuing to pierce her with his eyes.

She thought that she might retch just looking at him.

Eva inhaled deeply. "Lucious, may I get off your lap now?" she asked politely. "I have to go to my ensuite," she added, making an excuse to leave the room.

He continued staring at her intensely. "If you must," he responded with displeasure.

Eva removed herself from Lucious' lap, rolling her eyes as she walked away. She headed directly up to her ensuite bath, quickly washing her face and scrubbing the kiss from her hand while tears filled her eyes. She was rubbing her hand so hard without even realizing that she was hurting herself. Quickly, Eva dried her hands and walked across the bedroom to pick up a glass of juice from her nightstand. She drank the entire glass, then went over to the drawer chest to retrieve a fresh bottle.

Eva had noticed that, for the past week, the juice was beginning to lose its calming effect. She now had to drink more of the juice or to mix it with alcohol to obtain soothing sensations. Eva lay down on her bed, her face against the mattress, and began to sob. She had cried far too much over the last few months, especially since she had met Lucious. She wasn't sure what else she could do so she decided to pray. She had seen Georgie and Alice pray many times, but Eva wasn't brought up that way. She wasn't even sure that there was a God but, if there was, she prayed that he would send Georgie and that they would both be able to leave Liberation Hall safely.

Curtis fetched Claudia for Lucious. He summoned her to his study to discuss business matters. Claudia marched hastily through the study door; she had much to do before leaving for London and didn't want to be bothered by Lucious.

"Yes, Lucious, what is it you need?" Claudia asked, annoyed.

Lucious was lounging back in his chair behind his desk.

"I wanted to know how the planning was going for the party. Have you sent out the invites?"

Claudia walked over toward his desk, nodding her head. "Yes, I sent out thirty invitations to our highest paying clients."

Lucious smiled deviously. "Good, and you are heading to London tomorrow morning to pick up the dresses? I hope that you picked out something exceptional for Eva. She will need to look her best for the occasion."

Claudia sighed, "Yes, everything has been arranged and I have an extra special dress planned for Eva."

Lucious leaned back, placing his hands behind his head.

"Excellent. I was wondering whether you had heard back from Dr. Smithe or, perhaps, things have begun to run their natural course?" Lucious asked, hoping that Eva had begun miscarrying on her own.

"No, Eva is still pregnant," Claudia retorted outright and sighed, "and yes, I received a letter this morning from Dr. Smithe's secretary, informing me that he is on holiday until late next week. When he returns to the office, his own patients have first priority. She said it could be three weeks before he would be able to come and visit the Hall." Claudia had a distasteful look on her face and Lucious glared at her, unhappy about the news.

"Well, perhaps we can do it ourselves?" he suggested looking vexed.

Claudia raised her eyebrows. "That is very dangerous Lucious, we can't do that to Eva!" She was appalled that he would even propose such a thing.

"Are you defying me, Claudia?" Lucious' eyes glared angrily as he stood up from his desk and began leaning closer to her. "And we've been getting along so well lately. I wouldn't want to have to take more away from you, so don't force me to do so!" he shouted, frustrated.

"No, I am not trying to defy you, Lucious—but what is wrong with waiting three weeks? Perhaps, by then, Eva would miscarry naturally, on her own." She was trying to convince Lucious to wait for Eva's sake. Claudia knew that the process was extremely dangerous, especially if they didn't know what they were doing.

Lucious rolled his eyes, releasing an impatient sigh. "Alright, but while you are in London, go visit Dr. Smithe's secretary in person and inform her that we will make it worth his while if he makes us a priority."

Claudia wasn't sure what Lucious meant by that comment, but she wasn't about to ask him. "Is that all?" she inquired, trying to sound cordial.

"Have you found a new lady's maid for Eva?" he questioned, a dull look upon his face. Lucious had assumed that it was Nancy who had walked in on him while he was forcing himself on Eva. He had people out searching for her but, so far, they'd had no luck finding her.

"I am interviewing someone this afternoon," Claudia replied.

"Well, I hope she's attractive, at least," he said while rubbing his chin.

Claudia briefly closed her eyes, disgusted by Lucious' comment. She decided that she was going to choose what he would consider to be the most unattractive woman in order to ensure that Lucious left her alone.

"That will be all," he said, motioning for her to leave his study.

Claudia left the study hoping that Georgie would show up sometime today. She didn't want to see Eva go through a termination or endure the continual abuse of Lucious. The terminations themselves were extremely painful and dangerous, and the process left emotional scars that never truly healed.

*   *   *

The evening was approaching and it looked like a storm was gathering in the distance. Georgie had not yet shown up at the Hall and Eva was beginning to lose hope with each passing hour. She didn't know where Georgie might be coming from and nightfall was setting in, along with dark storm clouds. Eva was relentlessly pacing back and forth in the foyer, hoping that Georgie would show up soon. Thankfully, she had not seen Lucious much today and he didn't appear to be downstairs. Suddenly, Claudia came strolling down the staircase.

"Eva, why don't we have a drink in the drawing room?"

Eva looked up at her with concern. "No, thank you," she solemnly replied.

"You can't spend the whole evening out here, pacing back and forth in the foyer. Why don't we play a card game to get your mind off things?" Claudia suggested.

Eva shrugged, releasing a sigh, then slowly roamed over to the drawing room. Eva sat down at the table while Claudia grabbed a deck of cards from the behind the bar.

"What shall we play?" she asked.

Eva thought for a moment about what game would be best to get her mind off of Georgie. "How about, Euchre?" she recommended.

"Alright," Claudia agreed, shuffling the deck and dealing out the cards.

A little while later, Lucious entered the drawing room and both women released a disheartening sigh, glancing at one another across the table.

"What do we have here, a game of cards?" Lucious questioned, surprised to see them playing. "Who's winning?" he inquired, walking over to the bar and pouring himself a tumbler of brandy.

"Eva," Claudia replied.

"Really? I'm astounded. I didn't know you played cards, Eva?" Lucious exclaimed, coming up behind Eva's chair and placing his hand on her shoulders.

She glanced up at Claudia as her heart began racing in fear of his touch.

Claudia could tell that Eva was uncomfortable.

"Yes, Lucious, Eva is an excellent card player," she said while refraining from looking up at him.

"Really? Oh, this is very smart!" Lucious said excitedly. "A woman playing cards is extremely attractive, especially if she is a decent player."

Eva closed her eyes for a moment and breathed deeply, irritated by his words.

Claudia glanced up at him with her eyes but kept her head down toward her cards.

"Yes, I think I will set you up at the party, Eva, with some of the blokes who fancy cards. That way they will be able to see all your qualities and not just your exquisite beauty," Lucious stated happily.

Eva pressed her lips together tightly, furious with Lucious. She wondered if he was always going to use everything she enjoyed in life for his benefit.

"Well, Eva, it is half-past eight. I'm not sure if your knight in shining armor is going to show?" Lucious said jeeringly.

Claudia and Eva didn't respond to Lucious crude comment, although Eva was beginning to wonder the same thing. She worriedly peered out the drawing-room window, watching the fierce lighting and the rain that had begun pouring down in troves. She swallowed hard, holding back desperate tears. She didn't want to cry because it would upset Lucious and give him fuel to badger her further.

*   *   *

The grandfather clock struck eleven as Eva sat on the staircase, with her elbows resting on her knees, holding her face in her hands. Claudia came downstairs in her nightgown and robe. Sitting down next to Eva, she let out a disheartening sigh.

"He's not coming, is he?" Eva questioned without looking up at her.

Claudia didn't know what to say.

"He has either given up on me or he didn't get all the money and felt too ashamed to show up to the Hall," Eva continued.

Claudia carefully placed her hand on Eva's shoulder, knowing that she had been somewhat jumpy since her attack.

"He may be on his way here, but the storm is making it difficult for him to reach the Hall?"

Eva looked up at Claudia, worried. "Yes, I thought of that and it makes me nervous. He could be injured somewhere out in the country." Eva pushed back tears—something that she'd learned to do lately and was getting better at each day.

"There's still time, Eva," Claudia said, looking up at Eva hopefully.

They sat there quietly for a few minutes when Eva asked, "Claudia, you said that one of the reasons Lucious couldn't love is because of pain from his past. What did you mean by that?"

Claudia glanced up quickly, gazing around the foyer, worried that someone might overhear Eva's question. She leaned her head close to Eva's and looked her seriously in the eyes.

"I can't talk about that Eva, especially not here. Someone might hear us," she whispered, continuing to peer around the foyer.

"Don't worry Claudia. Lucious is upstairs in his room with one of the maids," Eva said expressionlessly.

Claudia rolled her eyes and shook her head. She sucked in a deep breath and began speaking very softly.

"Lucious and I are were on an island in the Caribbean, called Jamaica. He'd been trying different drugs and herbs on all the islands we visited to see what substances would be perfect for his juice. One evening, he came back to the ship in a most terrible state. Whatever substance he consumed that evening had caused him to have a breakdown. I found him in his room, curled up in a ball, sobbing on the floor."

Eva leaned back, surprised to hear that Lucious had acted that way.

"He was spouting all sorts of things, some of which weren't making any sense. So, of course, I went over to him to comfort him and he began opening up to me about his childhood."

Eva continued listening intently. Claudia inhaled another deep breath and exhaled, distressed. "He told me how he was born in a brothel in France."

Eva's eyes grew wide.

"He saw things that no child should ever see and, apparently, the madam of the house took him in as her own. From what I gathered from his ramblings, she may have used Lucious for unspeakable things—having him service her client's desires— until he eventually became her protégé."

Eva's abdomen began turning in knots and she felt nauseous. She shook her head wildly and did not want to hear any more details of their relationship.

"Apparently, this madam raised him to take over her brothel and taught him everything she knew about her business. When Lucious was older, he left one night, stealing all her money. Then, he purchased a ship and crew and went out in search of the ingredients to create his juice."

Eva sat there, somberly thinking about everything Claudia had just told her about Lucious.

"You must never tell anyone Eva or use it against him. I'm not even sure he remembers saying anything to me," Claudia explained and Eva slowly nodded her head.

She was surprised that she could still feel sympathy for Lucious.

"See, Eva, Lucious doesn't know how to be normal. He doesn't understand how to be a kind and decent human being because all he has ever known is pain. I have to believe that that night happened so that I would have mercy toward him when he became unbearable toward me," Claudia said, reminding herself.

Eva felt a ping of sorrow in her heart for Lucious and understood now that he didn't know how to be any other way.

Claudia's heart dropped, thinking about Eva's baby and how—if Georgie didn't show up tonight—she was going to have to tell Eva that she was pregnant with Lucious' child. She sat there with Eva, fervently wishing that Georgie would show up before midnight to help Eva and her baby escape.

Twenty-Eight

The wind began bloing furiously as Georgie did his best to make it to Shepperton on time. He'd made it all the way out of Windsor before the rain began pouring down from the sky. He looked down at his pocket watch and realized that it was already half-past eight and was getting very dark outside. The horse had begun wearing down from the extensive travels he had to endure over the last week. Georgie was starting to worry that he might not make it to Liberation Hall by the appointed time. He had expected it to take him two more hours without the rain but now he knew that it was going to take longer. He didn't want to drive Mr. Kenny's thoroughbred too hard, but Georgie hoped that if he galloped quickly, they could possibly exit and outrun the storm.

The horse galloped for nearly a mile, but the rain was only coming down harder. Georgie was having trouble seeing in the dark and lightning began, making the horse feel anxious. He stopped off the road, consoling the horse.

"It's alright, boy, we don't have much further to go. Please don't quit on me now," he begged the beautiful animal.

The horse moved his head around wildly as the storm raged around them. Georgie decided to try and wait it out but, after a half-hour had passed without reprieve, he couldn't afford to waste any more time. He mounted the horse and continued trotting down the dark, muddy road.

Georgie was upset with himself for not leaving Oxfordshire sooner. He shouldn't have planned to travel on the appointed day of his arrival to Liberation Hall. He was so close yet still so far away. He couldn't imagine what Eva must be feeling right now, thinking that he may not show up at the Hall to save her. Georgie was so deep in thought that he didn't realize quickly enough that the horse was again galloping through the thick, dark mud. The horse speedily traveled down the road, blindly, without the moonlight to guide their way. Suddenly, a flash of lightning struck and thunder pounded at the same time, in close proximity to Georgie and the horse. The horse jumped backward, throwing Georgie off. He slammed hard onto the ground.

Georgie had taught himself how to land when being thrown from a horse but, unable to see in the dark, he crash-landed into a large tree that had fallen down next to the road. Georgie heard a snap in his arm and cried out in pain. He lay there for a moment, knowing that his arm was probably either fractured or broken. He started to feel light-headed and, leaning over, he vomited into the mud.

"Please, Lord, help me, please!" he pleaded as he tried to raise himself from the ground, letting out groans because any pressure at all caused his arm to ache. He soon realized that he couldn't see the horse in the dark. A flash of lightning hit and Georgie looked around, trying to spot him. He waited a moment longer, for another flash of lightning to hit, and spotted the horse on the other side of the road.

"Come here, boy!" he hollered and whistled, tromping through the mud toward the horse. "Come here, boy!" he called out again and the horse came over toward him.

Georgie trembled slightly, in pain, but he still comforted the horse, knowing how frightened the animal must be by the storm. He inhaled deeply, not knowing how bad his arm was but determined to mount the horse one-handed. He finally pulled himself up with one arm, then, lying down on the horse, he slowly placed one leg over the other side of the horse. Georgie raised himself up, trying not to lean or put any pressure on his bad arm.

Once he had mounted the horse again, he slowly made his way to Shepperton, hoping he was heading in the right direction. He also hoped that he hadn't gotten turned around by the accident. Georgie had no idea where he was, precisely, so he just continued going straight, hoping to find a town or house to stop at soon in order to find out whether he was heading in the correct direction. He finally spotted a house that appeared to have some light coming from the inside.

"Oh, thank heavens," he said out loud.

He trotted the horse up in front of the house and knocked on the front door. An older man, wearing a nightgown and nightcap, came to the door looking at him suspiciously.

"Hello, sir, my name is George Thornber and I'm trying to get to Shepperton, but I'm afraid that I have lost my way in the storm and dark. Would you be so kind as to tell me where we are located?" Georgie asked loudly, trying to speak over the storm.

The man stared at him oddly for a moment and motioned for him to come inside the house. Once they stepped inside the house, the old man asked, "What was it you needed?" He had been unable to hear him with the storm bellowing outside.

"Where are we located, sir? I need to get to Shepperton by midnight."

The man continued giving him a strange look while scratching his head as Georgie stood in his home, muddy and dripping wet.

"Shepperton? Well, that's not too far from here. I'd say in this weather you probably have another hour of travel if you keep heading south that a way," the man answered, pointing in the direction Georgie was already heading in.

"Thank you, sir," Georgie replied, relieved and rubbing the top of his hurt shoulder. "I have to be going now. Thank you again, sir!" he said, leaving the house at once and closing the door behind him.

He pulled himself on top of the horse once more and continued heading down the road in the same direction he had come from, forging ahead to Shepperton. He was extremely thankful that he had somehow navigated his way toward the Hall in the dark. The rain had finally begun slowing down and the moon was starting to shine, helping light his way.

Georgie saw Dr. Kenny waiting for him at the end of Liberation Hall's lane, riding on one of his other thoroughbreds.

"George!" he called out in a whisper. "I was wondering whether you were ever going to show," he whispered.

"I'm sorry, the storm made travel hard," Georgie replied wearily.

"I'm sure," Dr. Kenny replied. "Did you get all the money?" he inquired.

"Yes, sir, all one hundred pounds," Georgie said with a nod.

"I say! That's good news—but I'm afraid you have only minutes to get down to the Hall on time. Now, just as last time, I'll wait out here on the road for you," Dr. Kenny said and Georgie nodded, heading down the lane toward Liberation Hall.

When he arrived, he tied the horse to a tree using his good arm and his teeth, then he hurried up to the house, banging on the door. There appeared to be no lanterns lit inside the house, as if no one was home. Georgie continued hitting the door as hard as he could with his good arm, but no one came to open it.

"Come on! Open the door!" he shouted.

Georgie started wondering whether Lucious had tricked him and had taken Eva back to London. He didn't care if he had to break down the door and wait inside the Hall until they returned. One way or another he was going to save Eva.

Twenty-Nine

E va had just settled into bed. A sinking feeling swirled in her gut as she gave up on Georgie returning for her. She began to feel tired and decided to come upstairs twenty minutes before midnight. She lay in bed, realizing her destiny had been decided for her. She was going to remain at Liberation Hall forever and would never see Georgie again.

Eva felt the tears rising within her once again when she thought she heard a pounding sound and rose from her bed. Listening intently for a moment, she realized there was definitely a thumping noise resonating from downstairs. She hurriedly grabbed her robe and entered the corridor, noticing that the sound was coming from the front door. She gasped and sped down the stairwell in the dark. Running over to the door, she opened it at once—there stood Georgie, wet and muddy. Eva had never seen such a glorious sight.

"Georgie!" she cried out, wrapping her arms around him and hugging him tightly as the rainwater soaked her robe and nightgown.

"Eva. Oh my, Eva," Georgie sighed, relieved as he held her close.

He closed his eyes, placing his one, good arm firmly around her back and pressing his cheek against the top of her head. Eva felt solace and peace enter her being as Georgie held her in his arms—something she hadn't felt in a long time.

"Georgie, I didn't think you were coming. I thought you had given up on me," she whispered, gazing up at him with tears in her eyes.

"How I could ever give up on you, Eva? You're my chuckaboo," Georgie replied.

He desired to kiss her but avoided doing so, knowing that this wasn't the time. He needed to get her out of the Hall while there was no one in sight.

"Let's go, Eva," he spoke in a loud whisper, eagerly taking her by the hand, when an unexpected voice came from the foyer.

"Not so fast!" the voice called loudly, only a few feet away from where Eva and Georgie were standing.

Eva quickly turned around at the sound of Lucious' voice echoing through the darkness. She thought that he was in his room with the maid, but he must have come out, unnoticed, to carry out his plan against Georgie.

Lucious lit a lantern and, in the shadows, Curtis and another large man—whom Eva had never seen at the Hall before—appeared. Archie came up from behind Georgie and Eva, standing outside the front door. He pushed them both forward, closing the door behind them, then went around lighting a few of the gas lanterns that graced the walls of the foyer.

Lucious looked down at Eva hatefully. "Oh Eva, I'm very disappointed in you. Did you really think Georgie-Porgy wouldn't make it back in time to save you from the big bad wolf?" he said, condescendingly. "I think I may have had more faith in him than you did," he continued, glaring at Georgie. "So, do you have my money?" Lucious asked arrogantly.

"Here," Georgie said pulling the money bag from the inside of his jacket.

He threw the bag at Lucious, then once again quickly grabbed hold of Eva's hand with his good arm. Lucious opened the bag and began looking through the money.

"You managed to gather the entire one hundred quid?" Lucious questioned, surprised, and Georgie nodded his head. "I have to say I'm quite impressed," he continued with a sly grin on his face.

Georgie said nothing but kept his eyes on everyone in the room.

"Count it," Lucious commanded, throwing the bag over to Archie.

"So, what did you have to do to get all that money?" Lucious asked jeeringly, wanting to know the suffering that Georgie had endured over the last week. "Did you have to break the law?" he asked.

Georgie remained silent; he didn't feel the need to answer Lucious. Georgie was contemplating possibly making a run for it with Eva, but he knew that with his hurt arm he wouldn't be able to mount his horse swiftly and get away in time.

"Answer me!" Lucious yelled.

"No, I didn't have to break the law," Georgie replied solemnly.

Lucious peered at Georgie, trying to figure him out.

"So, how did a poor lad like you come up with one hundred quid in a week's time?" Lucious asked, annoyed.

350

"It's all here, sir," Archie piped up.

Georgie looked up at Lucious, his eyes wide. "That means you'll let Eva go free from the Hall and from you!" he stated with a hopeful expression on his face.

"Oh, yes, Eva is free to go—but I can't promise that she'll stay away," Lucious said shaking his head, believing Eva would return to him.

Suddenly, Curtis and the other large man came over, grabbing Georgie by the arms while Archie pulled Eva away from Georgie's grasp.

Eva cried out, "Georgie!" as he cried out in pain.

Curtis had yanked his bad arm upward, intertwining it with his own.

Lucious walked over to Georgie. "But I'm afraid that you are going to have to stay," he continued cunningly, a wicked smile stretched across his face.

"No!" Eva cried out. "Let him go! Keep me, keep me here! I don't want to leave!" she shouted, begging Lucious.

"Eva, it's alright," Georgie said, gritting his teeth because of his aching arm.

"Oh, now I see that we have a little problem," Lucious said sardonically. "It seems that Eva doesn't want to leave the Hall after all. So, what am I to do?" he asked sarcastically, tapping his finger against his chin while roaming around the foyer. "How about I make Georgie another offer. I will allow him to choose who stays and who leaves the Hall. But I want you to know, George..." Lucious walked over, carefully leaning into Georgie's face. "If you choose to stay—I will kill you," he stated with a devilish grin. "So, what will it be? Eva goes free out the front door while you stay here and die. Or, you go free, and Eva remains at Liberation Hall as my harlot for the rest of her days?" Lucious asked, raising his hands into a prayer stance while tapping his fingers against one another.

Lucious wanted to see just how much this boy truly loved Eva and whether he would go as far as willingly exchanging his own life for hers.

Georgie didn't hesitate. He looked over at Eva and said, "Let Eva go."

Lucious was taken aback by the lad's love for her.

"No! No!" Eva cried out as she bent over, weeping uncontrollably.

All the tears she'd been holding back for days now, began to flow out of her. Georgie's heart ached upon seeing how much Eva cared for him. His heart was grieved, knowing that they would never be together, but just to get a glimpse of how much she loved him gave him more than enough reason to sacrifice his life for hers.

Lucious let out a short laugh. "You're willing to die for a meaningless, common whore?" Lucious cackled loudly.

Georgie was outraged by Lucious' description of Eva. He leaped at Lucious, punching him with his good arm across the face and knocking him to the floor. Curtis and the other large man grabbed Georgie's arms once again as he kneeled over Lucious.

Lucious wiped the blood from his mouth, then spat at Georgie, spraying blood across his face. Lucious began laughing again while the two men picked Georgie up from the floor.

Eva couldn't bear to watch as they started beating him. She was huddled in a fetal position on the floor, covering her ears, not wanting to hear the sounds coming from Georgie as he cried out in pain. Eva looked up briefly, just as Lucious kneed him in the face. She quickly put her head down again and covered her ears, unable to watch.

Lucious stopped for a moment and called out to Archie, "You know where to take her."

Archie grabbed Eva, pulling her outside toward the carriage.

"See, Georgie-Porgy. I'm a man of my word."

Then Lucious punched him in the face. Georgie's head hung as the men continued beating him. Eva sobbed while Archie pulled her away from the Hall, softly saying in-between her breaths, "Georgie no...no..." Sobs and tears wept out of her as Archie threw her into the carriage and trotted quickly down the lane.

Dr. Kenny noticed a carriage coming down the lane and hurriedly moved his horse behind some trees, trying not to be seen. He waited quietly as the transport went by, then turned to the right and headed down the main road. Dr. Kenny listened carefully and thought he heard a woman crying inside the carriage. He considered following the carriage, but Georgie had not yet come out of the house. He decided that he should go closer to the Hall to make sure that Georgie was all right. He gingerly moved forward on the horse and was about fifty feet away when he saw two men dragging a body out of the house. He realized that the men were going behind the Hall to dump the body into the river, which was raging from the heavy rainfall. Dr. Kenny expediently rode his horse through the front yard of the Hall, heading around to the other side of the house. He slowed down to avoid being seen as he rounded the corner of the house further down from the river. He watched as the men threw Georgie's body into the Thames and it began rapidly flowing down the rushing river.

Dr. Kenny jumped down from the horse, trying to see Georgie in the river with only the moon to light the way. He looked closely and thought he spotted him. Dr. Kenny knew that his timing had to be perfect in order to grab ahold of him. He waited for the ideal moment, then jumped in the river and grasped one of Georgie's legs. Dr. Kenny cried out from the sharp coldness of the water as they both quickly traveled downstream. He tried to swim to the edge, but his body was stunned and the current of the river forcibly moved them forward. He did his best to keep Georgie's head above the water when he noticed that they were heading toward something substantial, located further downstream. Peering down the river, the doctor realized that it was a tree that had fallen and that they were about to slam right into it. He turned himself around, floating backward while holding Georgie's head above the water and coddling it near his body to protect it from the upcoming jolt. He saw that they were getting closer to the tree trunk as he continued looking backward and he braced himself as his back smashed into the tree. The doctor cried out in pain from the impact but, moving swiftly, he used his one arm to scoot them along the trunk of the tree. He lifted Georgie up, placing his body on the riverbank, then lifted himself out and dragged Georgie's body away from the river.

"George!" the doctor called out as he knelt down and placed his ear against Georgie's chest to see whether he was breathing.

Georgie was unresponsive and his heart was no longer beating. Dr. Kenny began pressing on Georgie's chest, trying to resuscitate him. He placed his mouth against Georgie's, trying to fill his lungs with air, then again started rhythmically pressing against Georgie's rib cage, trying to get his heart going.

"Come on George!" Dr. Kenny said as he continued trying, again and again, to bring Georgie back to life.

Georgie's body was fading away and he saw himself drifting further and further away from Eva with each passing second. He could see Eva's face fading in the distance of his mind. She was reaching out for him, calling out his name. Georgie's soul was being pulled toward a white light when, suddenly, he cried out, "Noooooooo!" and coughed out the cold water that had settled in his lungs.

"George!" Dr. Kenny cried out, laughing with relief. "How in the world?!" the doctor exclaimed in shock, as Georgie's heart began beating again and he started breathing on his own.

"Eva," Georgie murmured in pain as he tried to move his body.

"George, you stay right here and don't move while I go fetch the horse," the doctor commanded, then ran back toward Liberation Hall whistling for his thoroughbred.

A few minutes later he returned with the horse and, with a rush of adrenaline, he slung Georgie's body over the horse. Georgie bellowed in pain, then the doctor mounted the horse and quickly rode back to his home.

They arrived at the Kenny household and the doctor jumped down from the horse. Rushing inside, he called out to Lilian. He grabbed the reigns and ran the horse over to the cottage, carefully pulling Georgie down onto his shoulder. He carried Georgie inside the cottage and placed him down on the bed, lighting a lantern to illuminate the room.

"Alright, I'm going to have to assess the damage, George."

Georgie mumbled, barely coherent.

Dr. Kenny ripped Georgie's shirt and noticed several injured ribs. Lillian came running into the cottage.

"Oh my!" she exclaimed placing her hands on her face.

"I'm afraid George had been beaten badly and had almost drowned. I'm going to need my kit, along with some bandages and antiseptic."

Lillian nodded her head and hurried out of the cottage to fetch the doctor's things.

Dr. Kenny touched Georgie's arm and Georgie shrieked out in pain.

"Oh my, your arm is badly fractured, George. I'm going to have to set the bone and cast it."

Georgie was trying to get up from the bed. "Eva, I have to find Eva," he muttered.

"I'm afraid that you are in absolutely no condition to find Eva right now. I'm going to have to give you a sedative and set your arm to save it," Dr. Kenny explained.

"I don't care about my arm! I only care about Eva!" Georgie yelled back, making a distasteful face from all the pain.

Lillian returned with Dr. Kenny's bag and the doctor turned to her quietly, saying, "Lillian, I need the chloroform. Just pray that his heart can handle it."

Lillian reached over, pulling out the chloroform and dousing it on a cloth. She closed her eyes, extremely worried for Georgie.

"George, I need you to breathe this in. It will relax you while I set your bone."

The doctor placed the cloth over Georgie's face and he inhaled the chloroform, which knocked him out cold.

Dr. Kenny continued to monitor Georgie's heart while he set the bone and bandaged it. By the time Georgie finally came to, the doctor had already wrapped his ribs and his arm was in a cast. Georgie's nose was also bound and there were several stitches in his eyebrow and chin. He was groggy and still in a lot of pain.

"George," Dr. Kenny said softly.

Georgie coughed when he tried to breathe deeply.

"Yes, your ribs have been badly bruised, that is probably creating some pressure on your lungs but, at least, they're not broken and should heal quickly with proper rest."

Georgie realized that he was only able to see out of one eye. He swallowed hard; his mouth was parched.

"Oh, do you need some water?" Dr. Kenny walked over to the water basin and poured him a glass.

Georgie grimaced as he tried leaning up to take a sip of the water as Dr. Kenny held the glass for him.

"Eva, do you know where Eva has gone?" Georgie's voice was rough as he spoke.

"No, I am afraid I don't know where they took her. I saw the carriage pull away with her in it, but I came after you. I wasn't sure whether she was in the carriage, but now I'm certain it was her."

Dr. Kenny felt awful for letting Georgie down.

"I'm so sorry, George. I'm so very, very sorry," Dr. Kenny apologized, greatly grieved that they'd been unable to help Eva.

"It's not your fault. You had no way of knowing that I wouldn't walk out of the Hall with Eva." Georgie had assumed that if Eva walked out the front door, he was going to be holding her hand.

"We'll find her, George. We'll find her," Dr. Kenny assured him, hoping that if they did find Eva, she would still be alive.

Thirty

Claudia heard all the commotion downstairs when Georgie arrived at the Hall. Walking cautiously out of her room, she quietly stepped out on the balcony and remained there, hiding in the shadows. Claudia watched as Lucious' entire devious plan played out. She shook her head, thinking how she should have known that he would plan on taking Eva to the abandoned house on the hill. She had nearly forgotten about the old house. It had been many years since any of the girls had been sent there—but she couldn't think of any other place that he would have instructed Archie to take her.

Lucious' plan had been to make Georgie suffer by having him work hard all week to obtain the funds that would secure Eva's life. Claudia realized that the amount chosen by Lucious was a somewhat-obtainable amount for someone of Georgie's class but, possibly, only through sinister means. Lucious wanted Georgie to return to the Hall so that he could take the money, kill Georgie, and release Eva to the house on the hill, where she would begin detoxing from the juice. After a certain amount of time, when Eva would start feeling repentant because of her addiction to the juice, he would bring her back to the Hall and continue using her for profit. Claudia shook her head in amazement at how quickly Lucious had come up with this evil scheme. He may have had that plan but Claudia also had a plot of her own.

After the two guards dragged Georgie's body out the front door, Claudia quietly dashed down the corridor toward the servant staircase in order to not be seen by Lucious. She hurried into the servant quarters and headed to the back door, where she had strategically placed a pair of her boots earlier. She quickly put the boots on her feet, then discreetly exited through the side door as the two guards dragged Georgie's body toward the Thames. Lowering her head in dismay, Claudia's heart felt heavy for Eva as she watched the guards carry Georgie's limp body away. She peered around for a moment, making sure she wouldn't be noticed, then ran quickly to the front of the house, untying Georgie's horse from the tree trunk. She mounted the horse and headed behind the tree line, riding along the edge of the lane, all the while continuing to be very careful not to be seen.

The house was about a mile away from the Hall and sat high up on a hill so that everyone could see it, settled in the distance while remaining on the road. No one had lived in the house for years and it sat there, barren and worn down after years of abandonment. Lucious would use it to retain unruly girls, until they were in such dire need of the juice and food that they would beg him to come back to the Hall. Usually, after their experience at the house on the hill, they would never give Lucious any trouble again. He would only send girls there under extremely trying circumstances. The only reason Claudia knew about the house was because one of the girls, whom Lucious had held there, told her where it was located. One time, when Claudia was going to London, she recognized the home based on the girl's description. She wasn't entirely positive that it was the right house, but she had to try and see whether Eva was in there.

As she made her way toward the house, she heard a carriage coming down the road and veered off to the side, hiding behind some trees until it had passed. Claudia could tell that it was Archie on his way back to the Hall. Once Archie passed by, Claudia began galloping the rest of the way, until she saw the dark, gruesome house perched up on the side of the hill.

Dismounting from the horse, she slowly walked toward the eerie, broken-down building.

"Eva, are you in there?" she called but there was no answer. "Eva!" Claudia shouted, until she finally heard something pounding from inside the house. Claudia ran through the broken front door and followed the sound through the old house.

"Eva!" Claudia yelled as she hurried over to where Eva was, barely able to see her sitting on the ground in the back of the house, banging her foot against the old hardwood floor. Eva's arms had been tied and her mouth bound with a cloth, so she wouldn't be able to scream for help. Claudia carefully untied Eva's mouth.

"Dia, how did you find me? How did you get here?" Eva asked anxiously.

"I took Georgie's horse."

Eva felt disheartened; her heart dropped as she quickly glanced down, thinking about Georgie.

"I'm going to take you to Dr. Kenny's house," Claudia said as she tried to loosen the ropes around Eva's hands. Eva looked at Claudia, confused.

"There *is* a Dr. Kenny?" she questioned.

Claudia continued untying her hands.

"Yes, and I think that your friend Georgie knew him," she said, finally getting the ropes untied. Then, the two of them scurried speedily out of the spooky house.

They both mounted the thoroughbred and Eva held onto Claudia as they rode down to Dr. Kenny's house. Once they arrived, they tied the horse to the tree out front and both ladies rushed to the front door, beginning to knock rapidly. Mrs. Kenny answered, surprised to see two young ladies standing on her doorstep.

"Mrs. Kenny, we are friends of Georgie, do you know him?" Claudia asked in a rushed tone. Mrs. Kenny's eyes lit up as she looked over at Eva.

"Are you Eva?" Lillian asked, surprised, and Eva was taken back that the woman knew her name.

"Yes, I am," she replied and Mrs. Kenny screamed with joy, grabbing Eva and hugging her tightly.

Eva had no idea what was going on and Claudia looked equally surprised by Mrs. Kenny's welcome. Lillian released Eva from her grasp and invited them both inside the house.

"Come in ladies. You wait here and I'm going to get Edward."

Lilian rushed out the back door toward the cottage.

Claudia turned to Eva. "I have to go back to the Hall," she said, placing her hands on Eva's shoulder.

Eva shook her head wildly. "No, Dia, don't go back there. You don't have to go back to the Hall—you can also be free," Eva begged excitedly.

Claudia inhaled deeply and sighed. "Yes I do, Eva. My goal was to help you, not myself. I could have left the Hall years ago, but I didn't. Anyway, I'll be back tomorrow to bring some of your things," Claudia said as she hugged Eva goodbye.

"Dia, don't leave me here alone!" Eva exclaimed.

"Eva, you are safe now. Dr. Kenny is a good man and if Georgie trusted him, so can you," Claudia spoke sharply, then turned and briskly headed toward the front door.

Eva watched sadly as Claudia left the house when, suddenly, Claudia turned back around.

"Eva," she looked at her most seriously, "your body is going to start having serious symptoms without the juice and I'm afraid it's not going to be pleasant."

Claudia had a distasteful expression on her face, then she briskly bolted out the front door. Eva's heart raced as she stood there, alone, in the modest foyer. She began anxiously pacing back and forth as she waited.

A few moments later, Mrs. Kenny bustled down the corridor, dragging a man along with her.

"This is Eva, Georgie's girl!" Lillian said to Dr. Kenny.

"Oh, Eva, it is thrilling to finally meet you!" the doctor said enthusiastically, grabbing Eva by the hand and shaking it rapidly with great hope in his eyes.

"Where did your friend go, Eva?" Lillian questioned, gazing around her house.

"Claudia had to go back to the Hall," Eva said sadly.

The Kennys looked at one another, concerned, and then Mr. Kenny glanced at Eva.

"I have something to show you. Will you come with me, please?" Eva was perplexed, wondering what Dr. Kenny possibly had to show her, especially since she had just met them, unexpectedly, a few minutes ago.

Dr. and Mrs. Kenny walked Eva out to the cottage where Georgie was resting. The doctor slowly opened the door and spoke quietly, "George." He smiled tenderly.

Georgie slowly opened his one eye and glanced over at Dr. Kenny, when Eva appeared in the doorway.

"Georgie!" she exclaimed, placing her hands over her mouth as tears filled her eyes at the sight of him. She ran over to him and kneeled down next to his bed.

"Eva," Georgie whispered softly, relieved at the sight of her. She grazed his forehead with her finger. She couldn't believe he was alive.

"But I thought..." Eva's words trailed off as she was utterly shocked by the sight of him. Shaking her head, she was astonished to see Georgie laying there before her—when she had expected to never see him again.

"Eva," Georgie said, choking up as he looked at her. A tear rolled down his cheek.

"I'm so sorry. I am so sorry for what I have done to you," Eva apologized as tears continued flowing down her face.

The Kennys stood there for a moment, watching the young couple, when the doctor cleared his voice and spoke up, "We're going to give you two some time alone. I'll check on you in a bit." He and Lillian excused themselves from the cottage to give Georgie and Eva some time alone.

"How did you get here, Eva? How did you know where to come?" Georgie muttered ruggedly.

"It was Dia, she knew Dr. Kenny and, when you came to the Hall saying you were him—well, she must have figured out that you knew him and brought me here," Eva said, smiling widely at him. Her heart was warm just having him near her.

Georgie reached over to take her hand with his good arm.

"Eva, there's so much I want to say to you," Georgie said, wanting to make his intentions known to her.

Suddenly, Eva began breathing heavily. The color of her skin started fading and she had a strange look on her face. Georgie noticed her hands were trembling feverishly.

"Eva, are you alright?" Georgie asked concerned.

Eva's eyes rolled to the back of her head and she collapsed on the floor.

"Dr. Kenny! Doctor!" Georgie cried out.

The doctor rushed into the cottage and saw Eva lying on the floor. He hastened over to her, checking her pulse, and noticed it was extremely slow.

"I'm going to lie her down next to you, George."

Georgie gave a slight nod as he was concerned for Eva. The doctor picked up Eva and placed her next to Georgie. Georgie reached over, taking Eva's limp hand. He held on to it, tightly, as his heart raced.

"Is she alright, doctor?" Georgie asked anxiously.

"I'm not sure? I think her body is beginning to withdraw from the juice and it's causing her heartbeat to become very irregular," he said, looking up at Georgie, extremely worried for Eva.

"Detoxing from a substance like this is very drastic on a person's body. I need you to know George..." Dr. Kenny looked at him most intently, "that Eva could die while detoxing from the juice."

Georgie began shaking his head. "No, no, she's not going to die!" he said stonily and his heart was heavy for Eva.

"I will do everything I can to help her get through this, but it could take some time. I will have to monitor her very closely." The doctor was doing his best to reassure Georgie.

Georgie nodded and continued holding Eva's hand as she lay next to him in bed. He was staring over at Eva, relieved that she was safe and free of Lucious, but he worried about her health and the effects of the juice on her small body. Georgie wasn't sure how things were going to turn out for either one of them, but he was extremely grateful that they were at least together now.

*   *   *

Eva woke up at the break of dawn, sitting straight up in bed, soaking wet from perspiration and gasping for air. Georgie stirred, feeling Eva move around in the bed while he still held onto her hand. She grabbed at her chest, breathing heavily. Georgie looked over at her; she was shivering and extremely pale. Eva started to reach out to him.

"I need some of the juice, Georgie. I need the juice! We have to get some juice."

Georgie looked at her, distressed; he didn't know what to do.

"Dr. Kenny!" Georgie called out.

The doctor had fallen asleep in a chair across from the bed. His head was hanging down but he slightly shook his head at the sound of Georgie's voice. Inhaling deeply, he opened his eyes.

"Doctor, it's Eva!" Georgie called out; his voice a bit stronger now.

"Oh my!" the doctor rushed over to Eva checking her pulse, which was now beating rapidly.

"Is she alright?" Georgie asked the doctor while rubbing Eva's hand, trying to comfort her.

"I need the juice doctor, please give me something. Please, go get me some juice!" she begged letting go of Georgie's hand and grabbed ahold of Dr. Kenny's hands.

"I'll do anything! I'll do anything for the juice, doctor. You can have me, you can sleep with me, just please give some juice!" she cried out desperately, as she brought Dr. Kenny's hand to her breast and began pulling at her dress, trying to remove it from her body.

"Just please bring me something, doctor. I need something to take this pain away!" she cried out.

The doctor pulled his hand away from Eva, then looked over at Georgie and frowned. Georgie's heart was breaking as he watched Eva's behavior and how desperate she was for Lucious' juice. He knew that Eva obviously didn't know what she was doing because she was in terrible anguish and pain. She continued pleading for the addictive substance over and over. All of a sudden, she stopped and started swallowing hard. She kept gulping over and over again. When Dr. Kenny realized what was happening, he hurried across the room. He grabbed a bucket and charged over to Eva just in time for her to vomit in the bucket.

"I'm afraid it's begun—I think I should move Eva into the house."

Georgie looked up at the doctor wide-eyed.

"No, she's staying here with me," he said, trying to sit up in the bed.

"Lie down, George!" the doctor demanded. "This could get very violent," Dr. Kenny warned, looking at him grimly.

"I don't care, I will remain by her side through it all," he said unrelentingly. Dr. Kenny closed his eyes for a moment and slowly nodded his head as Eva continued to dry heave into the bucket.

Georgie held onto Eva's hair making sure it didn't get any retch in it and began rubbing her back, trying to console her. When she had finished, Dr. Kenny handed her a wet cloth to wipe her face. Eva looked back over at Georgie sorrowfully, as she had calmed down a bit after getting sick.

"I'm so sorry, Georgie. I'm so sorry that I want the juice." Eva was remorseful, feeling guilty for her addiction. "I'm sorry that I got sick in your bed. I'll try harder next time to stop myself." She looked over at him embarrassed and ashamed.

"Eva, it's alright, I'm here. You be as sick as you need, but I'm right here. I'm not going anywhere," Georgie replied lovingly.

Eva looked at him with a sorrowful smile, then cuddled up next to him, holding onto his arm. Georgie sucked a quick breath as waves went through his body at having Eva lying so close to him. He breathed in deeply, calming down and wrapping his arm around her. Eva felt safe resting next to Georgie.

"Are you alright, George? Are you sure you don't want me to move Eva into the house?" the doctor asked, bending down his chin to look Georgie in the eyes.

Georgie thought about it for a moment but then shook his head no. He didn't want Eva going through this alone without him.

* * *

Eva would doze off for a while, then abruptly wake up while trembling and sweating. Lillian sat next to her with a cold cloth, dabbing her forehead while she rested. After some time passed, Eva leaned forward, groaning in pain. Her body was aching dreadfully and she began sobbing uncontrollably.

"I want the juice! I can't do this! I have to have the juice!" she exclaimed, looking helplessly at Lillian and pleading with her. "My body is throbbing, please give me the juice or give me something!" she demanded, grabbing Lillian.

Lillian gave her a dismal look and slowly shook her head no.

"Ah!" Eva yelled as she turned to Georgie. "I need the juice, Georgie, if you love me, then you'll get me the juice, please!" she begged, looking hopelessly at him with tears streaming down her face.

Georgie wanted to do anything he could to help her. He gazed over at Lillian raising his eyebrows in question. He was almost considering trying to get Eva some juice, for it was far too difficult to watch her be in so much pain. Lillian looked back at him, firmly shaking her head no.

"Soon you will be better, Eva," Lillian said trying to comfort her.

Eva began shaking her head crazily as she started to climb out of bed.

"No, I have to go find some of the juice. I'm going back to the Hall!" she threatened, trying to remove herself from the bed.

Georgie was holding on to her hand and refused to let go.

"Eva, you can do this. You can beat this; I believe in you!" he said trying to encourage her.

She looked back at him shaking her head, "I can't, I can't do it." She hopelessly plummeted herself back down on the bed, turning over. She buried her face into the linens.

Georgie glanced back up at Lillian.

"Isn't there something more we can do for her?" he pleaded on Eva's behalf.

"I'm sorry, George, she's just going to have to wait it out," Lillian replied with a grievous expression.

Eva's erratic behavior continued all night and into the morning. Everyone was exhausted and doing everything they could to keep Eva from running back to the Hall in search of the juice. Georgie decided to ask Eva if he could hold her in his arms and she had agreed, leaning back against him.

"She's not hurting your ribs?" Lillian asked, worried about Georgie.

He looked at Lillian and shook his head no. Georgie then caressed Eva's forehead as she closed her eyes and her breathing finally began to calm. She fell asleep eventually while leaning against him. He laid her down carefully on her side with Lillian's help and he watched her as she slept.

Doctor Kenny came in while Eva was sleeping and changed Georgie's bandages.

"Doctor, how long is this going to last?" Georgie asked, hoping it would be over soon.

The doctor gave him a sympathetic look while shaking his head.

"This could last from a few days to a few weeks."

Georgie's eyes grew wide and his heart dropped.

"George, I would like to talk about you for a moment."

Georgie looked up at the doctor, worried about what he might say.

"You are actually mending quite well, considering everything you encountered. Your recovery is rather quick and I'm pleased with your progress. I'd say it's pretty much a miracle," Dr. Kenny stated proudly, smiling at Georgie. "I think that, perhaps, if you feel up to it, you should try to walk around a bit while Eva is resting."

Georgie nodded his head in agreement and Dr. Kenny helped him rise from the bed. Georgie walked around while continuing to look down at Eva as she slept. She looked so peaceful, but he knew that she would awaken soon and would be begging him for more of the juice. Georgie decided to walk outside the cottage to get some fresh air. He breathed in deeply and the doctor was right—considering what had happened to him the previous night, he was breathing reasonably well now. His face and arm were still on the mend but, overall, he was stable. Georgie stood there, looking out at the countryside and thinking about everything he had endured over the last month and a half. This had been the most difficult time in his life but it was all worth it to help Eva, especially since they were now together. Georgie hoped that Eva's detoxing would end soon and that her body would begin recovering quickly, just as his had done.

Georgie continued striding slowly, working his legs, when he heard a shrill shriek coming from inside the cottage. He turned quickly and painfully hobbled back into the house as fast as he could while Eva's scream continued to pierce his ears.

Thirty-One

Georgie expediently rushed his battered body back toward the cottage, wide-eyed upon hearing Eva scream relentlessly inside. When he entered, he was astonished to find that the bed linens surrounding Eva were saturated in blood.

"What's happening, doctor?" Georgie asked, panicked and horrified at seeing Eva's nightgown soaked in blood as well. The doctor looked up at Georgie, bewildered.

"I have no idea," he replied in wonder.

Georgie's heart began racing as Eva wrapped her arms around herself. She was leaning forward writhing in pain.

"Uuhhhh!" Eva groaned, bending over and holding onto her waist.

Georgie briskly walked over to the bed, carefully sitting down next to her. Eva was rocking back and forth as blood continued pouring from her body. Georgie was stunned at the amount of blood she was losing. Lilian was doing her best to wipe it up as fast as possible, but it continued pouring. Georgie's breathing was labored and he was starting to feel dizzy as he watched Eva bleeding to death.

"George," the doctor called out, but Georgie continued staring down, watching as the blood flowed from Eva's body.

"George!" the doctor yelled louder.

His head shot up, "Huh?" He looked up at the doctor, stunned and overwhelmed by the scene.

"May I have a word with you?"

Georgie nodded and Dr. Kenny helped him up from the bed once again.

Georgie followed the doctor outside, where he explained the situation.

"I think Eva is miscarrying," he said flat out. "I'm sorry George. I know this is the last thing Eva needs right now but, unless something has ruptured internally, it's the only thing that makes sense."

Georgie looked at the doctor confused. "I'm sorry, doc, but what does that mean?"

The doctor stared at Georgie solemnly, leaning in a little closer; then, he placed his hand on Georgie's shoulder.

"That means that she was with child George but is not any longer." The doctor frowned.

Georgie stood motionless for a moment and tears filled his eyes. Emotions began swelling inside him as he faced the reality that Eva had lost her child. Georgie stared down at the ground, wiping his tears with the back of his hand.

"I know I've said this several times in the past few weeks, but I truly am sorry. It must be challenging knowing that the woman you love was carrying someone else's child," the doctor said, sympathizing with Georgie.

Georgie shook his head, "That's not why I'm crying doc."

The doctor glanced up at him, surprised.

"I'm crying because Eva has lost her baby," Georgie explained and Dr. Kenny's eyes grew wide.

He couldn't believe Georgie's heart for Eva and her child.

"George, I'm at a loss for words." The doctor had never seen anyone love someone the way Georgie loved Eva. He shook his head, baffled by his response. Inhaling deeply, he gently patted Georgie's shoulder. "You're a very good man, George."

Georgie looked over at the doctor without saying anything in return. He was thinking how he was going to deliver the news to Eva that she had lost her baby.

Later on in the day, the doctor confirmed that Eva had fully miscarried. Lillian had taken Eva into the house to help her bathe and dress in a new nightgown. She also cleaned up the cottage, laying down fresh bed linens on the bed. Despite Eva's bleeding, Georgie still didn't want her moved to the house. He felt that Eva needed to be with him now more than ever, given all that she had been through. Lillian helped Eva return to the cottage because she was shaking uncontrollably, looking very frail. A few hours later, Georgie tried feeding her some broth. Eva was doing her best to take a few sips but the tremors were so strong that she had trouble getting the soup into her mouth. She was also sweating profusely while having cold chills at the same time. Eva finally shook her head, letting Georgie know that she didn't want to try eating any longer.

The night was falling and Eva only seemed to be getting worse. She would lie in the bed, turned away from Georgie, writhing as she continued to groan and hold her stomach in agony. She would occasionally lean over the side of the bed and throw up whatever little bit of liquid there was in her body. Georgie felt so helpless; he would rub her back or pull her hair away from her face but, other than that, there wasn't much that he could do for her. He was glad that the first day was over and was hoping that Eva's health would improve overnight.

*   *   *

Claudia and Archie were heading home from their day trip to London. Claudia told Archie that she needed to stop in the small town of Shepperton on their way to the Hall to pick up a few more items for the party. She knew that Archie liked to visit the local pub in town whenever he had the opportunity, which was only on rare occasions because Lucious required him to stay nearby most of the time.

Archie parked the carriage near the town pub just as the sun was starting to set. Claudia pretended to be looking for something in the array of bags that were nestled inside the carriage.

"Archie, why don't you head inside the pub? I'll join you after I run my errand," she said, urging him to go inside the tavern without her.

Claudia watched Archie, making sure that he was in the pub before pulling out a large garment bag and gift box from the carriage. She cautiously walked a few blocks with the luggage to the Kenny house and began knocking rapidly on their front door. Dr. Kenny answered, assuming it was someone in need of his services.

"Hello, Dr. Kenny?" Claudia inquired, making sure it was him.

The doctor tilted his head, giving Claudia a sideways glare.

"Yes...how may I help you?" he questioned, thinking how the woman looked somewhat familiar to him. "I'm a friend of

Eva's. I came by to bring her some of her belongings," Claudia said, handing Dr. Kenny the large garment bag she was holding.

"Oh, thank you, that was very kind of you," he replied, retrieving the bag while realizing that Claudia was the woman who had brought Lila to his house several years ago.

"Also, this is a new dress that I ordered for Eva," Claudia explained handing the doctor the large gift box. Dr. Kenny nodded, taking the box from Claudia's grasp. She was about to turn around and walk away, but then she stopped and looked at him.

"Doctor, I was wondering...about a girl I brought here a few years ago. Her name was Lila," Claudia asked nervously.

The doctor's eyes grew wide and he swallowed hard.

"I was wondering how she was doing?" Claudia inquired, somewhat hopefully.

The doctor looked down, sighing, then he gazed back at her after a moment.

"I'm sorry to inform you that Lila passed away, I'm afraid, not long after she was brought here," the doctor replied sadly.

Claudia gasped and her mouth hung open, not knowing what to say. She lowered her head and began scanning the porch, lost in thought. The doctor could tell that Claudia was deeply distressed by the news.

"I want to thank you for bringing Eva to us," he said kindly.

Claudia glanced up at him and sighed. "Oh, well, it was the least I could do," she said, slightly nodding. "How is Eva?" she asked solemnly, knowing that Eva was probably detoxing from the juice by now.

The doctor bit his bottom lip and tilted his head.

"Eva is recovering from her addiction. So far, it's been very traumatic, but I believe she'll make it through alright," he explained. Suddenly his expression changed and he became greatly worried. "You didn't place any juice in her bag?" he asked with concern.

Claudia stared at him wide-eyed.

"Oh, no. I wouldn't do that to her," she said, lowering her head and thinking of her own addiction.

Dr. Kenny realized that Claudia was probably addicted to the juice as well and didn't want to talk about it any longer. He thought about asking Claudia if she would like to see Eva but realized that it would probably not be a good idea since she was at a critical time in the detoxing process. Seeing Claudia could trigger Eva, sending her back into a downward spiral.

"Well, thank you again for bringing Eva's belongings to her and please know that you are welcome to come here anytime if you are in need of help," the doctor informed her, smiling.

Claudia nodded in return, "Thank you again, doctor." She lowered her head and swiftly jaunted down the porch stairs.

Dr. Kenny placed Eva's things on a long table in the foyer, then walked back out to the cottage to see how things were going with Eva and Georgie. When he arrived at the cottage, Eva was still clinging to the side of the bed and trembling, as sweat dripped from her brow. Lillian looked up at Dr. Kenny, desiring some reprieve.

"You go and head in for the evening, dear. I will keep watch over Eva and George through the night," said Dr. Kenny sympathetically to his wife.

Georgie knew that the Kenny's were beginning to grow very weary from taking care of both him and Eva.

"Why don't you both go in for the night and I'll watch over Eva. You have done so much for us. You should be in the house with your little ones," Georgie insisted.

"No, George," the doctor replied, shaking his head. "This isn't even the worst of what is to come. One of us must be here with you and Eva through the night."

Georgie's eyes grew wide and he looked over at Eva nervously, not knowing whether she could handle any more of the withdrawal. She was already so frail and weak, what with the blood loss, tremors, and vomiting. Georgie couldn't imagine things getting worse than they already were and didn't know how much more of Eva's detoxing any of them could take.

Thirty-Two

The carriage pulled up to the Hallwell after dark. As Claudia stepped out of it, Lucious came flying through the front door of the Hall.

"Where in hell have the two of you been?!" he yelled as he marched toward Claudia.

"We've just arrived from London. Where do you think we have been?" Claudia asked annoyed.

"Eva could be dead!" Lucious shouted at Archie.

Claudia closed her eyes at the sound of Lucious' screaming.

"What do you mean, Eva could be dead? She was perfectly fine last night when I saw her," Claudia inquired.

Lucious ignored her, pushing past her to enter the carriage.

"Let's go, Archie," he commanded and Archie slapped the reigns against the horses' backs to get them moving.

Claudia watched as the carriage pulled away and headed down the lane. She turned around to face the Hall and smiled deviously, knowing she had done the right thing for Eva.

Lucious and Archie stopped in front of the house on the hill. The black night surrounded them. Lucious slowly stepped from the carriage and began looking around the eerie exterior of the home. There were nighttime noises and creepy sounds encircling them in the dark. Lucious dipped his chin, glaring around in an attempt to see his surroundings.

"Where did you put her?" he inquired.

"In the back of the house, sir. I tied her up and bound her mouth just like you asked," Archie explained.

"Well, go get her then!" Lucious barked loudly while motioning toward the house with his hand.

Lucious waited outside, pacing with his hands in his pockets. He was nervously glancing to and fro in the dark when Archie anxiously came running out of the house.

"Sir, she's gone!" he cried out.

Lucious looked up, confused. "What do you mean she's gone?" he questioned Archie indignantly.

"She's disappeared. She's not in there," Archie said shaking his head in bewilderment.

Lucious heatedly followed Archie into the black, abandoned house.

"She was right here, sir. See, here are the ropes. Someone's untied them?"

Lucious looked down at the ropes, then gazed lividly around the house, thinking about where Eva could have gone.

"Well, she didn't just untie the bloody ropes herself now, did she!? Where the hell is she!?" Lucious questioned furiously.

Archie didn't know how to respond; he had no idea where Eva could have gone.

Lucious began pacing back and forth in the house, thinking about who could have helped Eva.

"And her mouth was bound?" Lucious huffed.

"Yes, sir, tightly bound," Archie replied.

Lucious continued pacing deliriously, realizing that his prized possession had disappeared without a trace.

"Damn!" he shouted and kicked over an old, broken chair that stood in the middle of the deserted house. "Let's go! I need to get back to the Hall!" he demanded, indicating for Archie to exit the house.

They returned to the Hall and Lucious hastily entered through the front door, slamming it behind him.

"Dia!" he barked ferociously.

Claudia heard him yelling for her while she was getting ready for bed. She closed her eyes and breathed deeply, trying to prepare herself for her performance.

"Dia!" he shouted again.

Claudia quickly took a drink of the juice that was sitting on her nightstand and hurried out into the corridor. She calmly sauntered out to the top of the balcony and, before Lucious had a chance to speak, she immediately questioned him.

"Where's Eva?" she asked firmly.

Lucious paused and peered up at her, livid.

"I don't in the bloody hell know!" he shouted back at her with all his might while doubling over in exasperation. His face was inflamed in anger and he spewed saliva as he shouted.

Seeing Lucious so distraught made Claudia feel giddy inside; however, she inhaled deeply to refrain from breaking out of character.

"What do you mean you don't know? You are the one who did something with her! Have you forgotten where you placed her?" Claudia shouted back furiously.

Lucious marched up the stairs toward Claudia, a heinous expression on his face.

Claudia's eyes grew huge and she quickly ran into her room, locking the door behind her. Lucious vigorously banged on her door. She knew that if she opened it he might kill her.

"Open the door! Open the damn door, Dia, or I will break it down and leave it off its hinges so that when you are with one of your clients, the entire house will watch you!"

Claudia's eyebrows raised and she breathed heavily, frightened of Lucious. She had never seen him this vexed before. Usually, he would flip like a switch without cause—but now he was acting all-out murderous.

"I'm not opening the door until you calm down," she demanded through the door. She didn't hear anything for a few moments; then, suddenly, he began banging harder. Claudia hurried into her ensuite, locking that door behind her and huddling against the back of the tub. After a while, the hammering diminished and she rose and hesitantly walked toward her bedroom door. She waited several more minutes, until she finally heard Lucious' bedroom door slam shut. She cautiously opened her door, gazing around the corridor, surprised to find that Lucious was gone. She went back inside her room, locking the door behind her and hoping that Lucious would not remove it in the middle of the night.

The next day, Claudia spent all morning preparing herself for the possible types of abuse that Lucious could unleash on her. She gingerly walked down to the dining hall and found Lucious sitting at the dining table, reading the newspaper while eating his poached eggs, as usual. Claudia decided it was best to eat their breakfast in peace without bringing up Eva. She looked over, noticing that Lucious wasn't reading the London paper but the local Surrey newspaper. He lowered the paper to see who sat next to him at the dining table. Rolling his eyes, he saw that it was Claudia, then loudly wafted the paper open and continued to flip through it rapidly.

"Looking for something in the local newspaper this morning?" Claudia asked, assuming that Lucious was trying to see whether a man's body had turned up in the Thames last night.

Lucious shifted the paper over to look at Claudia.

"Yes...as a matter of fact, I am looking for something," he said, standing up abruptly from his chair and throwing the paper down on the table. Walking behind Claudia, he bent down next to her face and inquired, "You wouldn't know by chance where it...is?" He emphasized the last two words, leaning closer to Claudia's face.

Claudia turned her head, unafraid, and looked him directly in the eyes.

"No, I don't know where 'it is.' In fact, I didn't even know 'it' was missing until last evening," she said, staring unyieldingly at Lucious.

Lucious glared at her for a moment, assessing whether she was lying to him. He stood back up and marched out of the room, heading into the foyer. Claudia inhaled a deep breath, then slowly took a sip of tea. She placed the cup back on top of a saucer while a satisfied smile covered her face.

Later on in the day, Claudia strode into the study as she was going through her daily duties.

"The mail is here," she called out as she filed through several letters while strolling toward Lucious' desk.

Lucious stood up promptly and gazed at her coldly.

"You don't have any idea where Eva has gone, do you, Claudia?" he asked firmly.

Claudia looked back at Lucious, expressionless.

"I have told you, Lucious, I didn't even know that she was missing in the first place. If you have misplaced her somewhere and now she has gone missing, then I don't know how I'm supposed to help you," she replied, raising her voice at him with a shrug.

Lucious remained silent for a moment while staring at her with his wide, dark eyes. Claudia began feeling nervous but tried hard not to show it when, all of a sudden, Lucious let out a loud cry, "Aaaahhhhhhh!"

He rashly wiped his hand across his desk and angrily pushed everything sitting on top of it onto the floor.

Claudia stepped back as he rushed over in front of the desk and grabbed her by the clavicle. She gripped her eyes shut, flinching back, and braced herself for Lucious' abuse. He forced her across the room, throwing her down on the sofa and violently holding her neck in his hands.

"Do you know anything!?" he demanded, yelling at her and shaking her head violently. "Tell me, Dia. Do you know where Eva is!?"

Claudia had tears welling up as she slowly shook her head no.

Lucious dark, coal eyes were hauntingly staring back at her as he breathed heavily. After a few more breaths, he jerked away and furiously vacated the study.

Claudia lay there for a moment without moving, knowing that she had definitely made the right decision to help Eva leave Liberation Hall. Eva was a fragile girl who wouldn't have been able to handle Lucious' torments as she herself had endured them over the years. Claudia somewhat envied Eva for getting away but, at the same time, she knew that she could leave the Hall anytime she desired. Lucious would no longer come looking for her as he would have a long time ago. The truth was that this is the only life Claudia knew and she didn't know whether she would be able to survive if she needed to find real work. She figured that, if she left the Hall, she would probably end up at a lower-class whore house in London. At Liberation Hall, she at least had a beautiful home, good food, and, usually, a small income if Lucious felt gracious. Claudia knew she would never get married or have a family of her own. She was too old for all that now. She had chosen to stay and, over the years, she had fully accepted that this was her life.

Thirty-Three

D r. Kenny was right. Eva only got worse over the past few days. She was beginning to get violent and started throwing things around the cottage, demanding that they give her the juice.

"You all hate me!" she shouted.

Georgie grabbed ahold of her arms, trying to keep her from hurting herself or someone else.

"Don't grab at me!" she yelled, glaring at him venomously. Her eyes were dark gray in color, instead of their usual light green.

"Eva, I'm only trying to keep you from hurting yourself," Georgie stated calmly.

Eva looked up at the ceiling and screamed, "Aaaaaahhhhh!"

Lillian jolted from the shrill sound of her voice. Eva buried her face into the bed, covering her head with her hands.

"Make it stop! Make it stop!" she cried, the sound somewhat muffled by the blankets.

Georgie looked at Lillian hopelessly and she gave him the same look in return. He wanted to take away Eva's pain away so badly and wished that he could somehow transfer her pain onto himself. If only he could go through the withdrawal for her, he thought. Eva suddenly leaped back up, sitting on her knees in the bed as she leaned into Georgie's face, pointing at him vigorously.

"You did this! You did this to me! This is all your fault! You should have just left me at the Hall!" Eva shouted in his face. "Why did you come for me? Why?" she cried as she began weakening. Then, she began to cry while covering her face with her hands. "I miss Lucious, he really loved me. He would have given me more juice!"

Georgie felt like he was stabbed in the heart by Eva's words. He swallowed hard as tears began to fill his eyes as well. Lillian looked over at him, heartbroken. The poor lad had been through so much already and now he also had to go through all this with Eva. Georgie rose from the bed and began leaving the cottage when Lilian grabbed his arm.

"George, she doesn't mean it, it's the drug talking," she said, gazing up at him sadly.

Georgie nodded his head and continued out of the cottage.

He was somberly walking around outside when he began sobbing. He wasn't sure how much more of Eva's detoxing he could take. This was day five and it seemed as if was only getting worse with each passing day.

"Please, God, please help Eva and help me be strong for her. Please help me not take the things she says personally," Georgie prayed and sighed, wiping the tears away from his face.

As Georgie stood outside the cottage, Dr. Kenny walked toward him. He noticed that Georgie was upset and approached him cautiously.

"You alright, George?" the doctor inquired with concern.

Georgie didn't look up at him, he just nodded his head.

"I know it's a terrible ordeal. I have probably done this a dozen times and it's always the same," the doctor said, shaking his head, "but I have good news." His tone was more upbeat and Georgie looked up at him with hope.

"Eva has made it through the most difficult stages and, by this evening, she should begin to calm down and will, possibly, even sleep—perhaps even through the night. Just a few more days and she'll be pretty much back to normal," the doctor said cheerfully.

Georgie closed his eyes, released a sigh of relief, and began thanking God.

A few more days passed and Eva began improving, just as the doctor had said. She slept for almost two days straight, making up for lost time. She would only wake up to use the outhouse and Lillian would try feeding her some broth; then, she would fall back asleep for several more hours. Georgie realized that he and Eva had been at the Kenny cottage for over a week now. Yesterday, Georgie decided to write several letters informing all their loved ones, as well as Magistrate Logan, that they would be arriving to London soon, hopefully. The Kennys had been with Georgie and Eva for the entire week and Georgie could tell that they were both grateful that Eva was doing well. However, he also knew that they probably desired to get back to their own lives.

"Doctor, now that Eva is feeling better, perhaps you and Lillian would both like go in for the night? I'll keep watch over her," Georgie offered, looking at Eva as she slept.

Dr. Kenny rubbed his chin, contemplating Georgie's offer.

"George, I know that you are doing better, but I really do feel that someone who has some medical experience should still be out here to keep watch over her," he explained and Georgie sighed.

"You have both done so much more for us than I ever expected—how will I ever be able to repay you? Please, go in for the night and have a good rest," Georgie pleaded with them. "If I need anything, I'll come get you," he promised.

Dr. Kenny looked over at Lilian, unsure that this was the best decision; but he also knew that they were both exhausted and could use a good night's sleep themselves.

"Well, first, Lilian will help Eva into the house to take a bath and get a change of clothes. I would also like to check and redress your bandages. Then, I suppose, we could head in for the night—but I will most certainly be out here bright and early in the morning to check on you both," the doctor insisted and Georgie nodded in agreement.

After Eva woke up, Lillian took her into the house to help her get washed up and dressed for bed. Eva's bleeding had ended a few days ago, but Lillian was still supplying her padding, just in case. Eva brushed her teeth and then placed a fresh nightgown on herself; her strength was increasing each day now. She was feeling much better, especially after getting proper rest. She also noticed that the aches and pains were beginning to dissipate. She walked into the guest room, where Lillian had placed the bag with her belongings that Claudia had brought for her, and began rummaging through them to find her robe. The silky satin material caused memories to stir and swirl through Eva's mind. She swung the robe around herself, tying it at the waist, and began remembering her experiences at the Hall. Eva stared out into oblivion, deep in thought, when Lillian came over and began winding her wet hair up into a bun.

"Are you alright, Eva?" Lillian asked.

Eva slowly nodded, saying nothing in return. Her mind was beginning to clear after what felt like years of living in a fog but, as her mind was clearing, her emotions were also starting to bubble up inside as well. Eva immediately pushed them deep down into her core, swallowing hard. She turned around looking at Lillian.

"I'm fine, Mrs. Kenny. Thank you for everything. I'm so very sorry for acting violently toward you," Eva said apologetically, giving Lillian a sorrowful smile. Lillian's eyes filled with hope because Eva was speaking regularly again, instead of producing rambling, fast-paced speech and constantly asking for the juice. Eva had also noticed that she was speaking with more ease and that the unbearable anxiety she had felt all week was ceasing.

Georgie had changed the bed linens for them so that they would be clean for the night, while Lillian helped Eva walk back out to the cottage because she was still shaking a bit. When Eva entered the cottage, Georgie looked up as he was pulling the top blanket over the bed. His eyes lit up at the sight of Eva, seeing that the color had returned to her face and that her emerald green eyes were now again illuminated and shining brightly. Eva smiled at him and he smiled happily at her, pleased that she was looking so much healthier.

Eva could see the light beaming out of Georgie as he smiled at her, which was incredibly refreshing in comparison to the darkness that she had lived with at the Hall. She thought about how Georgie had been so good to her for the past week and how she had treated him terribly. Eva slowly walked over to the bed and sat down, still shaking a little and fixing her eyes upon him. Then, she gently placed her hand on his.

"I am so sorry for the hurtful things I said to you. Will you ever forgive me?" she asked regretfully, feeling horrible about her behavior toward him.

Georgie leaned in toward her.

"Of course I forgive you, Eva. I know you—and that was not you," Georgie said tenderly with love in his eyes.

She tearfully nodded her head in agreement, although she still felt awful for the way she had behaved.

Dr. Kenny looked over at Lillian and whispered, "Perhaps we shouldn't leave them alone together for the night?"

Lillian looked up at him wide-eyed, knowing what he was implying.

"I think they'll be alright. They're both still on the mend, dear," Lillian replied.

Dr. Kenny spoke loudly enough for them to hear him, "George, are you certain that the two of you should stay here, alone, for the night?"

Georgie looked over at Eva, understanding the temptations involved with them sleeping in the same bed, unmarried. Eva shook her head, gazing at Georgie.

"Please don't leave me, Georgie," she pleaded with him.

He didn't want to leave her alone after all she had experienced during the past week, but he understood what the doctor was saying. He thought for a moment before answering.

"We'll be alright," Georgie finally said, nodding assuredly.

They were both still recuperating and he assumed that—after miscarrying and everything else Eva had endured over the last week—such intimacy would be the furthest thing from her mind. He also didn't know what sort of abuse she had experienced at the Hall and had already considered that she may not be ready for intimacy even after they were married. That is, if she even desired to marry him.

"Alright then, I'll be checking in on you first thing in the morning," Dr. Kenny said.

"I think you have everything you need," Lillian stated, gazing around the room one more time.

"We'll see you in the morning then," Dr. Kenny said again, wondering whether he was making the right decision by allowing them to stay at the cottage alone. The Kennys wished them goodnight, then headed to the house.

Once the door closed, Georgie gazed over at Eva, who sat across from him on the bed. Things were much different now that they were both feeling better and Georgie hadn't expected to feel this way as he stared into Eva's eyes. He swallowed hard, inhaling a deep breath, trying to manage the sensations rising up inside him.

He cleared his throat and asked Eva, "How are you feeling now?"

Eva looked down at the bed.

"Well, I feel strange. I still want the juice, but I can control myself now. I no longer feel like I absolutely need it to survive," she explained, glancing at Georgie. "I'm also still trembling a bit," she added, lifting her hand into the air, showing Georgie how it shook.

Georgie took hold of her raised hand and looked her seriously in the eyes. He fervently wanted to tell Eva how much he loved her, but he also knew that it was incredibly dangerous to do so—what with them being alone in the cottage for the night and all. He decided to change the subject and get his mind off of his love for Eva.

"Would you like to talk about something? Perhaps all that you have gone through in the last month?" he questioned.

Eva was taken back at Georgie's question. She was hoping that he would profess his love for her. She thought for a moment, breathing deeply.

"Well, there's so much that happened," she said slowly, shaking her head. "I don't even know where to begin."

Georgie understood that she'd been through a lot and wanted to give her all the time she needed. He also knew that she may never desire to talk about her experiences at the Hall and didn't want to pressure her.

"Well, if you do ever want to talk about anything, I want you to know that I'm here for you, Eva," he told her tenderly and Eva smiled.

"I've always been able to talk to you, Georgie," she replied softly, gazing at him intensely. "I do have a question for you,"— she said suddenly, and Georgie perked up, intrigued and ready to answer her—"where on earth did you find one hundred quid, Georgie Thornber?"

Georgie laughed out loud, making Eva's heart flutter.

"Well, most of it came from Magistrate Logan. I had to ask for a year's advance," he said, glancing down and then back up her again, his cheeks flushed. "Some of it came from the Kenny's, Bert Darby, Grams, and the flower women. The rest was the money I had saved over the last few years," Georgie said, gazing at Eva with great care in his eyes.

She quickly put her head down, embarrassed, covering her forehead. She couldn't believe that everyone had given money to save her and that Georgie had spent his life's savings, plus a year's advance.

"Everyone did that me?" she inquired, looking up at him with tears in her eyes. "Georgie, you spent all the money you saved and a year's advance on me?" she asked, shaking her head in distress.

"Of course, Eva. I would do anything for you," he said, lightly caressing her hand, flashing her with one of his beautiful smiles that caused Eva's stomach to swell.

She was extremely flattered that Georgie had cared so much for her and finally believed that he obviously loved her more than just a friend. She gazed deeply into Georgie's eyes, looking at him wantonly. She pressed her lips together and began licking them as she glanced down at Georgie's lips— she wanted to kiss him very much. Georgie noticed how Eva was staring at him, which caused feelings to swirl within him. He tried to change the subject quickly, before he gave in and kissed her. He inhaled deeply.

"Eva, may I ask you a question now?"

Eva blinked rapidly, refocusing her mind. "Yes, of course," she replied nodding.

"Why did you leave London with Lucious?"

Eva leaned back, extremely surprised by Georgie's forward question. She waited a few moments before speaking. She didn't want to lie to Georgie, but she was also afraid to tell him the entire truth without knowing whether he cared for her the same way. Georgie had said he loved her at the Hall, but he hadn't said anything similar since. She wasn't sure if he was just saying that to get her to leave with him and save her from Lucious. Eva swallowed and sighed.

"Well...everyone was moving on with their lives. Mum was courting Bert Darby," Eva said, rolling her eyes while shaking her head in disgust, "and you...went off to Oxfordshire...and I was left alone," she explained sadly.

Georgie closed his eyes, inhaling deeply as he realized that he had been right—Eva left with Lucious because he moved away to Oxfordshire, leaving her behind.

"I'm so sorry Eva..." he said, shaking his head.

"No—let me finish," she insisted, placing her hand in the air.

Georgie leaned on his elbow and listened to Eva intently.

"Lucious, well, he..." Eva closed her eyes and swallowed hard. "He has a way about him that draws you to him. He's debonair, charming, and enticing," Eva said, casting her head down in shame as she spoke, "but that is only a facade and not who he truly is." She gazed out across the room. "He brought me to his house in London, and he—" Eva bit her lip hard, closing her eyes for a moment, "and he told me that he loved me."

Georgie felt a stab in his heart. He knew that that's what Eva had wanted to hear and he never told her how he felt about her.

She continued, "Lucious then slipped a ring on my finger and promised me that—if I chose to be with him that night—everything that was his would become mine. Including his houses and his money. He said that I would be treated like nobility. The only catch was—he could never marry me. He claimed it was so because of his businesses and reputation," she huffed in a haughty tone. "He also said that, if I chose him, I would have to leave my old life behind. I couldn't go back to mum or anyone from my past because we were beginning a new life together." Eva's head dropped even lower in shame.

Georgie was heartbroken; he didn't know how to respond. This man had offered Eva everything she could want in a matter of minutes. She was so young, kind-hearted, and trusting that she had believed him. Eva looked up at Georgie harshly.

"I was so foolish!" she exclaimed angrily, tears running down her face.

Georgie jerked back, surprised by Eva's anger.

Once Eva began sharing her feelings with Georgie, the words simply flowed out of her mouth. She told Georgie how Lucious had lied to her, saying that he owed Lord Manchester money, in order to make her sleep with another man. She had found out only much later that she was actually put on display and that the Baron had actually purchased the evening with her for an exceedingly high price. Eva continued, telling him about Reginald Whittaker and how he had been abrasive with her in the bedroom. Georgie's heart sank lower and lower with each horrific experience she recounted. She explained how Lucious finally told her the truth about who he really was and why she was at the Hall. She also explained how Lucious had threatened her life, as well as the lives of everyone she loved, if she tried to leave. Georgie said nothing as he continued listening to Eva uncover and place before him all her repressed guilt and shame.

"After you showed up at the Hall the first time, I had so much hope. I thought that, maybe, we would escape together. I thought that, perhaps, I would be free of Lucious—but I knew how impossible that was going to be; he's such a vicious man!" she shouted, covering her face with her hands. "I knew he was violent—he was always terrible to Dia—but I had no idea just how horrible he truly was until that night you came to the Hall," Eva stopped talking and began crying so hard that her mouth was no longer uttering sounds.

Georgie's heart was heavy, he had worried that Lucious might harm her after he showed up at the Hall that day. Eva started calming down while sucking in gasps of air and wiping the tears from her eyes. Georgie didn't want to ask her what Lucious had done—if she wasn't ready to talk about it—when she continued to speak voluntarily.

"I was in the bath that evening when he came into my ensuite."

Georgie felt a tightening in his stomach.

"He just kept staring at me in the bathtub," she said looking down at the bed, recalling the event. "Just staring, trying to intimidate me. His eyes were so black. They would get that way when he was angry," she recalled, gazing up at Georgie but then quickly looked down again. "When I stepped out of the bath, I swiftly covered myself so that he was no longer staring at my exposed body," she said, annoyed.

Georgie closed his eyes while his stomach continued to churn.

"As I walked passed him, he grabbed my arm, forcing me across the room and down onto the bed." Eva began sobbing uncontrollably.

Georgie closed his eyes because his heart was racing. He sucked in a deep breath and tightened his fist, while anger welled up inside him. He knew what had happened, he didn't need Eva to tell him anything else—but then Eva lifted her head, looking him directly in the face.

"He raped me! Lucious lied to me, took away everything I loved, and then raped me, Georgie!" she yelled again, weeping uncontrollably.

Georgie also began sobbing. His heart broke for Eva and everything she had suffered. He swiftly rose from the bed and Eva quickly looked down, mortified. She thought that he must be quite disgusted with her since he could no longer even sit next to her on the bed. Covering her face, tears streaming, Eva began rocking back and forth trying to comfort herself. Georgie carefully walked around to Eva's side of the bed. He sat down behind her and wrapped his arms around her warmly, embracing her while placing his head against her back. Georgie held Eva tightly in his arms, comforting and consoling her while she wept—and Georgie cried right along with her, together with her in all her guilt, pain, and shame. They stayed that way for a while without saying a word.

Eventually, Georgie noticed that Eva had cried herself to sleep. He gently kissed the top of her head and then gracefully laid her down across the bed. Walking back over to his side, he lay awake thinking about everything Eva had told him. He was furious with Lucious—he wanted to go over to the Hall and rip off his head for what he had done to Eva. However, Georgie knew that going after Lucious would do no good. The time had come for both him and Eva to move on so that they would be free to start a new life together.

* * *

Eva awoke the next morning and rubbed her eyes, looking across the bed and seeing Georgie sleeping next to her. She smiled while gazing at her love, who looked so handsome as he slept. She crawled closer to him, thinking how wonderful it would be to wake up next to him every morning. Eva would be amazed if Georgie told her that he loved her after everything she told him last night. She'd never experienced such attentiveness from anyone and she wanted to thank him for listening to her. She also wanted to show him how much she loved him in return. Eva unwrapped her hair, allowing her blonde waves to settle around her shoulders and back. She sat up on her knees, leaning over Georgie, and began unbuttoning his shirt. Staring down at his bare chest, she started kissing him while working her way down his body.

Georgie was awakened by what he thought was an insect or rodent dancing on top of his chest. When he looked down, he noticed that Eva was trying to unbutton his trousers. He sat up in shock.

"Eva, what are you doing?" he asked gruffly.

Eva's head shot up and her eyes widened as she sat up on the bed.

"I was just going to thank you," she said, giving a slight, sultry smirk.

Georgie shook his head rapidly. "No Eva! No," he stated.

Eva's heart dropped. She felt like she was in trouble and was humiliated by his response. She assumed that Georgie was repulsed by her and didn't want to be intimate with her after everything she had shared with him. He obviously didn't love her, at least not romantically, the way she loved him.

Eva felt rejected. Covering her face with her hands, she turned her head away from him and began to cry. Georgie sat up in bed releasing a sigh. "Eva, I'm sorry if I hurt your feelings, but—"

Eva interjected, "But you don't love me the way I love you! You love me like one of your sisters!" Eva once again covered her face and turned away.

Georgie felt horrible. He should have told Eva how he felt about her by now, but he was trying to prevent a situation like this one from happening.

"Eva," Georgie said while gently touching her shoulder. "I do love you. I have always loved you!" he spoke tenderly, pausing for a moment. "The way that a man loves his wife... definitely not a sister," Georgie said, shaking his head with a slight laugh.

Eva looked up at him confused. "Then why would you reject me?" she asked with a shake of her head.

Georgie took Eva's hands and inhaled deeply.

"Eva, I want to do things the right way. I don't want to do what those other men have done to you. I want us to be married and when we're together..." Georgie cleared throat and swallowed hard, his face turning slightly red, "in that way... then I want us to wake up the next morning in one another's arms and to know that we will be together for the rest of our lives—that neither one of us is going anywhere. I love you, Eva," Georgie finally said it all, heartfelt and sincere.

"Oh, Georgie! I love you so much!" she cried excitedly, wrapping her arms around him tightly.

Georgie smiled and his heart warmed upon hearing Eva say the words in return.

Eva gently pulled away, looking deeply into Georgie's eyes. She gently grabbed his face in her hands. She began leaning in to kiss him but stopped, not wanting to come across as too forward. Instead, she quietly asked, "I would like very much to kiss you now, Georgie Thornber, if I may?"

She was looking at him wantonly when he shook his head and said, "No."

Eva was taken aback and began moving away from him when he grabbed her hand and said, "But I would like very much to kiss you, Eva, if I may?"

Eva smiled and bit her lip in exhilaration as Georgie carefully leaned in, closing his eyes. He gently tilted his head as Eva remained very still, then locked his lips with hers. She felt light shoot through her entire body. She had never experienced anything like Georgie's kiss in her entire life. She could feel his love for her radiating into her whole being and her feet were tingling.

Georgie felt sensations coursing through his body and he trembled from the touch of Eva's lips pressed against his own. He was thrilled that he had waited for the perfect moment, instead of rushing into his first kiss with her. After a few seconds, he gently pulled his mouth away from Eva's. She stared at him affectionately, while her heart raced and her breathing was labored. Georgie was also breathing heavily and his heart pounded in his chest.

"Eva, I think I'm going to go outside for some fresh air, if that's alright?" he said.

Eva laughed gently and smiled, nodding in agreement.

Georgie stood up from the bed, released Eva's hand, and walked outside into the fresh morning air. He inhaled it deeply. He had never felt so alive in his entire life. Georgie was looking around, thinking how it was about time for him and Eva to plan on going back to London—when he realized that he had forgotten to ask her to marry him.

Eva lay back down on the bed, jubilantly grinning from ear to ear. She was thankful for Georgie and for the fact that he did love her the same way that she loved him. She was honored that he was a respectable and good man who wanted to do the right thing and treat her like a lady. Suddenly, Georgie burst through the cottage door and briskly walked over to Eva, interrupting her reverie. She sat up quickly, startled by his entrance, and worried about why he rushed back into the cottage so quickly. Georgie knelt down beside her, taking both of her hands into his and gazing up at her most intently.

"Eva, I don't have much to offer you. I don't have a fancy house or an ensuite bath—not even a ring," Georgie stated, looked away.

Eva waited patiently for him to continue.

He looked back up into her eyes, "However, I do love you with everything that I am and will go to the ends of the Earth for you, Eva Alderson. I want to have children with you, to grow old with you, and to spend the rest of my life with you. So, Eva, would you do me the honor of becoming my wife?" Georgie asked, looking at her nervously.

Eva was breathing heavily and tears of happiness settled in her eyes.

"Yes! Yes, of course!" she answered ecstatically, nodding her head wildly.

Georgie embraced her tightly.

"Oh, Eva, you've made me the happiest man in the world!" he exclaimed, overjoyed, and kissed her cheek.

While Georgie and Eva were wrapped in one another's arms, Dr. Kenny walked into the cottage.

"Oh, I'm sorry," he apologized, embarrassed at walking in on Georgie and Eva embracing. He quickly turned around to leave.

"Oh no, please come in, doctor," Georgie called out.

"I've just asked Eva to marry me—and she accepted," Georgie said, looking happily at the doctor.

Dr. Kenny's expression changed from a worried frown into a broad smile.

"I say, congratulations to you both!" he said as he walked over to shake Georgie's hand. "Congratulations, Eva," he repeated, smiling as he looked down at her.

"Thank you, doctor, for everything that you have done for us both," Eva said, most appreciatively.

Georgie glanced over at Eva, then back at the doctor. "Ummm, doctor…I think that now would be a great time to move Eva into the house."

Eva's face turned red as she blushed and Dr. Kenny let out a laugh. "Yes, I think that's an excellent idea," he agreed, raising his eyebrows.

Thirty-Four

L illian helped Eva move into the upstairs spare bedroom in the Kenny house. Eva wished that she could have stayed in the cottage with Georgie but knew that he was right—they should stay in separate rooms until they were married. She was filtering through the belongings that Claudia had brought for her when Lillian came walking into the bedroom.

"I had forgotten that your friend also dropped this box off for you, Eva, together with your luggage. It's been sitting downstairs in the foyer this whole time," Lillian said, handing a large extravagant gift box to Eva.

As soon as Eva saw the box, she knew that it contained the party dress that Claudia had purchased for her in London. Eva untied the bow and lifted the lid, removing the tissue paper from inside the box. Pulling out the gorgeous white garment, she held it out, puzzled, and studied it from a distance.

"Oh, my goodness!" Lillian exclaimed. "What a beautiful wedding dress Eva!" She looked over at Eva, overjoyed, clasping her hands together.

Eva was expressionless as she held the beautiful white gown near her body.

"A wedding dress? But why would Claudia have ordered me a wedding dress for the party?" Eva looked up at Lillian, perplexed.

"She didn't, silly, she wanted you to have a new and proper dress for your wedding," Lillian explained.

Eva pressed her lips together and began to cry.

"What is it, dear?" Lillian asked, worried, placing her hand on Eva's shoulder.

"I just miss her, that's all. Claudia was like a sister to me," Eva said solemnly and Lillian embraced her warmly.

"There, there…good friends are hard to come by and you've been blessed to have made several in such a short amount of time," Lillian said wisely, releasing Eva from her grasp while looking up at her smiling.

"You and Dr. Kenny are more than friends…everything you've done for us—you're family, Lillian." Eva's words were most heartfelt and Lillian grinned coyly.

"Now, don't let George see this dress until you walk down the aisle. Let it be a surprise," Lillian suggested and Eva nodded in agreement.

Dr. Kenny called from downstairs, "Eva, you have some company!" Eva glanced at Lillian curiously and Lillian raised her eyebrows excitedly. Walking down the stairs, Eva stopped halfway down the stairwell. There stood Georgie, freshly washed and dressed in gentleman's attire. Dr. Kenny had removed the last of his stitches from his face and his hair had been trimmed. The sight of him took Eva's breath away. She thought that she had experienced love at first sight with Lucious—but that could never compare to how she felt about

Georgie. Eva stood motionless for a moment, her mouth gaping open while she stared at him.

"You look very handsome," she finally said, slightly breathless.

Georgie had a satisfied look on his face. He was quite pleased with Eva's comment. She smiled at him, taking in all of him with her eyes as she slowly sauntered up to him.

"It's a nice evening, perhaps we could go for a walk before sunset?" Georgie inquired, reaching for Eva's hand.

She placed her hand in his and they walked outside into the cool, early evening.

Georgie and Eva strolled behind the house toward the countryside.

"Dr. Kenny said that he will give us a ride back to London on his wagon tomorrow morning," Georgie told Eva.

She turned around, looking back at the house. "I'm going to miss them," she grinned sadly.

Georgie looked back as well. "Yes, I couldn't have done anything without them," he said solemnly, shaking his head as he took a deep breath. Releasing it slowly, he turned back toward Eva and gazed deeply into her eyes. "So, are you ready to be Mrs. George Thornber?" he asked, smiling at her lovingly.

She grinned widely at him. "Hmmm…how about…six months ago?" she teased.

"Oh, Eva, I'm so sorry for leaving you without making my intentions known," he apologized, releasing her hand, pulling her close to himself, and embracing her tightly in his arms.

Eva stared up at Georgie. "If you can forgive me for running off with a loony nutter—and for everything else I've done—

then I can certainly forgive you for not telling me you loved me before leaving for Oxfordshire," Eva replied as she gently grazed the place where his stitches had been with her finger.

Eva turned around, taking hold of Georgie's hand, and they continued walking through the grass. As they strolled hand in hand, Georgie stopped and turned toward her.

"There are a few things I need to tell you," he said soberly.

Eva turned, somewhat concerned, and waited intently for what he was about to say.

"I'm afraid that this will be hard for you to hear," he said, looking her seriously in the eyes.

Eva's heart began racing and she grew nervous, unsure of what Georgie was about to say. He waited another moment, swallowing hard.

"Eva, did you know that you were with child?" Georgie asked her as tenderly as possible.

Eva gasped slightly, completely taken aback by Georgie's question. She shook her head no, looking down at the ground.

"I'm so sorry, Eva," he said with regret.

She continued to stare down at the ground.

"The baby would have been Lucious'," she murmured as she turned and continued walking again, holding Georgie's hand.

Georgie closed his eyes briefly as a pang hit his gut. "And how do you know that the baby was his?" he inquired.

Eva swallowed as she continued walking forward. "Well, because I was required to wear something to ensure that I didn't get a disease from or become pregnant by any of my clients," she explained and Georgie nodded his head.

"Oh," he said quietly, disheartened.

Eva turned toward him and said, "I had no idea." She shook her head. "But Claudia must have known. She was terribly worried about me and I should have put it all together but, well… mum…didn't explain much about these sorts of things. I think she figured she had more time." Eva looked back down at the ground, wanting to grieve the loss of her baby, but this was hard to do since she didn't even know she was pregnant in the first place. She looked back up at Georgie and saw that he had a tear in his eye. "Georgie, I'm so sorry," she said, feeling bad that she had gotten pregnant by Lucious.

Georgie shook his head. "I would have cared for you both, you know. I'm so sorry for your loss, Eva," he said, sincerely.

Eva gazed up at him in shock. He had such a loving and caring heart, grieving for her and Lucious' child. "Oh, Georgie," she said, reaching up and around his neck, hugging him closely.

They stood there silently for a few moments, holding one another in their arms, when Georgie spoke, "There's something else."

Eva released his neck and looked up at him, somewhat worried after what he had just told her.

"When we get to Oxfordshire, I'm afraid we don't have a very proper place in which to live." He glanced down sadly, then back up at Eva. "The money I paid Lucious wasn't just for me…it was for us. I had been putting money away for years, trying to save enough for us to start a life together. I was also planning on fixing up a small shed for us to live in so we would have privacy, but I never had the chance to finish it. Now…I have run out of funds and will have to start saving again." He looked down at Eva, worried about what she might think.

409

"A shed?" Eva questioned with a light laugh.

Georgie looked back down, ashamed. How could he expect her to live in a shed with him after she had lived in a mansion with Lucious? Eva gently lifted Georgie's chin with her finger, forcing him to look her in the eyes.

"Georgie Thornber, I would live in the middle of a field if it meant that I could be with you," she stated, giving him a sweet grin. "And I really cannot believe that you spent every pence of your savings to rescue me from Lucious." She shook her head in disbelief.

"How could I not Eva? You are my life—without you I have nothing," Georgie said, looking deeply into Eva's eyes.

He leaned down and kissed her gently on the lips, both of their bodies quickening at the intimacy. Eva passionately returned Georgie's kiss, grabbing ahold of his arms and pulling him even closer. Georgie broke away, breathing heavily. He looked at her while catching his breath.

"We really do need to get married," he said, smiling at her with raised eyebrows.

Eva chuckled and nodded in agreement. Then, he grabbed her hand and they walked back to the Kenny house just as the sun was setting.

"I hate to pull you away, George, but I have to rewrap your arm before bed. Which, thankfully, is the only injury that has not healed yet," said Dr. Kenny brightly.

Georgie nodded. Eva didn't want to let him go. They waited until the last moment to pull away from one another and continued locking eyes until Georgie vanished through the front door. Eva somberly climbed the stairwell to get ready for bed. The Kenny children were running through the corridor, making a lot of noise at the top of the stairs.

"Quiet down, Miss Eva's in the guest room for the night," Lillian reprimanded them gently.

Eva didn't mind hearing the children's laughter in the corridor. She looked down at her abdomen and gently glided her hand across her stomach, feeling for what would have been her baby. She wished that Claudia had told her she was pregnant, but she understood why she hadn't since she probably would not have been allowed to keep the baby at the Hall. Eva wondered if Lucious had known and then remembered that he must have since he was giving her that special horrid-tasting juice to drink. He was probably trying to cause her to miscarry on her own, but the baby had held on inside her womb.

Eva began crying, realizing she had lost her first child. The reality of the depth of such a loss began to sink in. She sat down on her bed, weeping for several minutes, when little Suzie stopped at the threshold of her door. Eva looked up, seeing the beautiful brown-haired girl standing there in the doorway.

"Are you alright, Miss Eva?" Suzie asked kindly, then walked over and placed her hand on Eva's, just as Lillian would have done.

Eva began crying harder from the touch of the little girl's soft hand. Suzie's kittenish, brown eyes sadly stared up at her.

"Please don't cry, Miss Eva," the girl pleaded, shaking her head.

"I'm sorry Suzie, I'll do my best," Eva replied, wiping the tears away from her eyes.

Lillian was walking through the corridor when she noticed Suzie standing in Eva's bedroom.

"Suzie, are you bothering Miss Eva?" she questioned, tilting her head.

The little girl looked up at her mother, wide-eyed, worried she was in trouble.

"Oh no, Suzie was only trying to comfort me," Eva said, looking up at Lillian.

"Alright, then," Lillian said, smiling. She looked down at the little girl. "That is very sweet of you, Suzie, but you need to be heading off to bed now," Lillian instructed and little Suzie nodded.

"Goodnight, Miss Eva," she said, waving her hand.

"Goodnight," Eva replied sadly.

Lillian sat down next to Eva on the bed. "Are you missing Georgie?" she asked.

Eva nodded her head. "Well, yes, but..." she stopped speaking for a moment and began crying again, placing her head in her hands. "I never knew I was pregnant." She said between taking gasps of air. Eva looked up. "Georgie told me this evening on our walk," she explained.

Lillian looked at Eva, a bit surprised she hadn't known.

"Oh, dear, I'm so sorry, Eva," she said sadly, placing her hand on Eva's just as Suzie had done. "We thought you knew dear."

Eva wiped her eyes and didn't say anything.

Lillian sighed, empathizing with Eva.

"Just give it some time, it will get better; right now, you go ahead and grieve. Soon enough, the time will come when you and George will have babes of your own," Lillian said, patting Eva's hand.

Eva looked up at her and smiled, nodding her head. Lillian was right, Eva would finally have the opportunity to have a family with Georgie. Something that would never have been possible with Lucious.

"Alright now, I'm off to bed—and so should you be as well. You have a big day tomorrow, traveling back to London, seeing your mother, and planning a wedding," Lillian said happily, rising from the bed.

Eva was very excited to see her mum again. She wished that her mother could have been there when she was detoxing, although it was probably better for her not to have seen her that way.

"Goodnight," Lillian said, smiling.

"Goodnight," Eva replied.

Eva couldn't wait to tell her mother that she was marrying Georgie but, just as the thought entered her mind, she also realized that she wouldn't live at the lodging house with her mother ever again. Eva was going to have to leave and go live in Oxfordshire with Georgie, right after returning home. Feelings of sadness billowed up inside her. She started crying again at the thought of not being close to her mother, although she knew that Georgie would allow her to see her mum whenever she desired, unlike Lucious. She also knew that she had grown up a great deal in the last couple of months and that things would be different between them now.

Eva lay down and reached across the bed. She wanted to feel Georgie lying next to her. She tossed for a while, missing his warmth next to her. Closing her eyes, she pretended that he was lying there—just as she had done at Liberation Hall on the picnic blanket outside. This time, she was thinking how, in a matter of days, she would become Mrs. George Thornber.

The thought made her smile and she began to relax, falling fast asleep.

Georgie couldn't sleep all night, he continued shifting from side to side, trying not to lie on his arm, which was making it very uncomfortable. He was also worried about Eva being in the house alone. Georgie didn't like having her so far away from him after what they had been through for the past month and a half. He thought about going into the house and lying outside her door, just to make sure that she was safe, but he knew the Kennys were upstairs with her. He closed his eyes, thankful that they would be married soon and that Eva would always be near him. He also wanted to get back to Oxfordshire and be on the farm, safely away from Lucious. Georgie knew that Lucious could be in London searching for Eva and he didn't like taking the risk of being there with her, especially without being married. Lucious may be able to coerce young girls into his harem, but Eva wasn't just going to willingly go back with him. If he did try to take her after they were married, then he would be kidnapping Georgie's wife, which was a crime.

The next morning, Georgie woke up, bright and early, after not sleeping well all night. No one would have been able to tell that he had a restless night by his demeanor—he had boundless energy and was ready to make his way back to London with Eva. Georgie took care of the horses, then prepared the wagon for their journey. Eva strolled out of the house just as the doctor finished loading the wagon for their journey.

"Well, we're all packed up now; it's time to say our goodbyes," Dr. Kenny announced.

Lillian had tears in her eyes looking at Georgie and Eva. They walked up to the porch and gave her grand hugs.

"I don't know how I would have been able to get Eva back without you both. I truly appreciate everything you've done for us, Lillian. How can we ever thank you enough for your kindness and generosity?" Georgie asked, wondering how he would ever repay the Kennys for their care and hospitality toward them.

"Well, this is what the doctor and I do. We help people, it's who we are. I'm just happy that things have turned out the way you had hoped George. I wish you both the best of luck and a long, happy life together," Lillian said, smiling proudly. "Oh, and don't let her out of your sight," She added, with raised brows, pointing over at Eva.

"That I can most certainly promise," Georgie agreed, smiling as he glanced toward Eva and taking her hand.

Suddenly, Suzie burst out the front door and ran up to Georgie and Eva, tearing their hands apart.

"I'm going to marry Mr. George!" she spouted angrily, looking up at Eva.

Everyone's eyes grew wide, surprised by the little girl's remark.

"Georgie, I had no idea?" Eva teased with a surprised grin.

Georgie's face turned ruby-red at Suzie's comment. He knelt down, looked the little girl in the eyes and took her tiny hand.

"I am honored, Suzie, but I'm afraid I'm too old for you," he said gently with a slight pout.

Suzie looked down at the porch floor with a very sad expression. Eva bit her lip, smiling but trying to not laugh. Lillian had a slight grin on her face as well, rolling her eyes and shaking her head at her daughter's comment.

"I think you have many more years ahead of you before you should think about marrying, Suzie," Dr. Kenny said, glancing over at Lillian. Everyone was trying their best to refrain from laughter because they did not want to hurt the little girl's feelings.

Eva and Georgie said their last goodbyes and Eva sat up at the front of the wagon with Dr. Kenny, while Georgie sat in the back with the luggage. The wagon was getting ready to pull away when Lillian called out, "And please write!" She waved her hand wildly.

"We will!" both Georgie and Eva yelled back, waving in return. The wagon rolled down the lane and onto the country road, heading toward London.

Eva was sitting in the wagon, feeling both anxious and excited at the same time. She was hoping that she would be hugging her mother at the lodging house in London in an hour. They had only been riding in the wagon for about eight minutes, when Georgie reached forward and grabbed Eva's hand. He had a concerned look on his face and Eva gazed back at him, perplexed. She looked up, realizing that they were passing by Liberation Hall. Everyone sat very quietly as the wagon rolled by the mansion. She didn't want to look, but she couldn't help thinking of Claudia in that dreadful place. Glancing over toward the Hall, she didn't see the carriage out front, which caused her heart to race as she wondered whether Lucious might possibly be on the road to London or in the city itself. She hoped that, after missing for nine days, he would be over the fact that she was gone—but she couldn't count on it, remembering how he had threatened her. She also heard Claudia's words running through her mind about how she was Lucious' asset and that he wouldn't let her go easily. Eva inhaled deeply and sighed, choosing to leave that place behind her as they passed it, heading toward London. She only wanted to focus on beginning a new life together with Georgie and she wasn't going to allow Lucious to get in the way.

Thirty-Five

Lucious had been in a foul mood ever since Eva went missing eight days ago. Claudia did her best to stay away from him as much as possible since he was very volatile toward everyone, especially her. She was on her way into the study when she heard Lucious yelling at someone from the other side of the door. Standing in the corridor, she leaned her ear close to the door to hear what Lucious was saying.

"When you say you looked everywhere in London, what do you mean, exactly?" Lucious questioned loudly.

"It's like I said, sir, me and the boys we searched the lodging house and there's was no sign of her. Then's we's went over to Covent Gard'n and she wasn' there neither. We searched anywhere and everywhere that you said Eva might be, including your terraced flat, and she's nowhere to be found," the man explained.

Claudia listened carefully but couldn't recognize the voice of the man that echoed from the study. Everything was silent for a moment and Claudia pressed her ear even closer against the door when, suddenly, a loud crash hit the study door. Claudia jumped back, clasping her mouth with her hands, trying not to make a sound.

"That's not good enough!" Lucious shouted. "She has to be somewhere and I want you to find her!" he demanded.

The study door burst open and Claudia stepped away as a scrawny bald man came walking out, scratching his slick head. The man looked to be of questionable character, which was typical of the men Lucious would hire. He turned, walking down the corridor with a perplexed look on his face, and Claudia approached the threshold of the study. She gazed down at the floor, seeing the broken vessel sprayed across the entrance, then casually stepped over the mess.

"Don't harass me, Claudia, I'm warning you!" Lucious cautioned harshly as she entered the study.

"I just need my scheduling book," she said as she sauntered across the room, grabbing the book from the top of Lucious' desk. Claudia opened the book and began glancing through the schedule for the day. She realized that Lord Manchester was due to arrive this evening for Eva.

Claudia released a loud distressing sigh.

"What is it, Dia?" Lucious asked indignantly.

"Oh, it's nothing to bother you with, I'll take care of it," she said, trying to reassure Lucious, but he was unconvinced.

"Let me see it!" he demanded, motioning harshly with his finger toward the book.

He opened it, looked inside, and rolled his eyes. Pacing, he began to rant.

"This looks very bad. Very, very bad. The fact that I can't seem to keep track of my own whores!" he yelled.

"Perhaps you should go to London and scout out a new girl. I think it's time to accept that Eva is gone," Claudia suggested, although she didn't truly desire for Lucious to find a new, innocent victim. Nevertheless, she knew it was just a matter of time.

Lucious peered at her and heatedly approached her.

"Do you realize that I spent six months studying Eva. She was my diamond in the rough, Dia. I'm not going to just find another girl who is poor, clean, and beautiful! All that is hard to come by in London these days! The place smells like death!" Lucious huffed in disgust. "The perfect vessels don't just grow on trees. It takes time and precision to find the right girl, not to mention that the party is less than two weeks away!" he spouted, waving his hand angrily.

Claudia closed her eyes for a brief second, inhaling, trying to calm her nerves from Lucious' yelling. "Well, then, you better get a move on it," she stated, then headed toward the study door and quickly vanished into the corridor, before Lucious had a chance to be violent toward her.

Lucious slammed his fists against the desk, outraged that Eva had still not been found. What bothered him most was how she seemed to have disappeared into thin air. He had never had any problems in the past when sending the girls to the abandoned house. They would always come back willing to do anything and everything that he required of them, without any complaints. Lucious didn't think Archie was lying to him. They had been partners in crime for over twenty years and Archie had never betrayed Lucious in all that time. The only thing he could figure is that Eva somehow managed to unbind her mouth, then screamed for help until someone heard and rescued her. There was also a possibility that Georgie had lived and found her, which was highly unlikely since he had no idea where Eva had been taken. Still, a body never did turn up in the

Thames in the vicinity of either Surry or Shepperton. Lucious couldn't actually confirm that Georgie had died since the goal was to keep him alive, albeit barely, when he was thrown into the river—that way, it would look like an accident.

Lucious hated to admit it, but Claudia might be right. The chances of him finding Eva were beginning to look bleaker with each passing day. Even if she were alive, she would be detoxed from the juice by now and it would be much more difficult to convince her to return to the Hall with him. He decided that there was no other choice than for him to go to London tomorrow and start looking for another girl. He was going to have to move expediently to coerce the new candidate to come with him to the Hall in time for the party. If he did, by any chance, find Eva while he was in London, then he would have to do what was necessary to bring her back with him.

*   *   *

The wagon pulled up to the lodging house and Eva couldn't exit fast enough. She jumped down from the buggy while it was still moving.

"Eva, be careful; you don't want to hurt yourself," Georgie called out worried.

"Come on Georgie!" she hollered at him, smiling brightly. "I want to walk in with you," Eva said motioning him to hurry along.

"We need to say goodbye to Dr. Kenny first," Georgie said as he unloaded the luggage.

Eva ran back over to the wagon, out of breath. "Yes, of course, I'm so sorry. I just got so excited," she said apologetically to the doctor.

"It's alright, I perfectly understand," he replied, smiling back at her.

Eva climbed back onto the wagon, giving the doctor a big warm hug.

"Thank you so much, Dr. Kenny, for saving our lives," she said with sincere gratitude.

Dr. Kenny gave a shy grin and nodded, "You're very welcome, of course."

Georgie came around the side of the wagon and the doctor hopped down to stretch his legs.

"George, I wish you both the best of luck. Now, be sure to take care of yourself and Eva." The doctor smiled while shaking Georgie's hand.

"Yes, of course, doc," Georgie replied, smiling and giving the doctor a pat on the back. "There really aren't any words that would express how thankful I am for everything you have done for us. You and Lillian are truly a one of a kind pair, that's for sure," Georgie said, smiling and shaking his head.

"Your most welcome, George. I also have solace in knowing that we helped Eva escape that wretched place and get the medical help she needed," Dr. Kenny said assuredly.

The two men stood there, silent for a moment, when Eva spoke up, "Georgie, I'm sorry to hurry things along, but I'm terribly anxious to see my mum." She held her luggage in both arms.

The men looked up at her, smiling.

"Well, I need to be on my way anyhow, I have to pick up a few items while I'm here in London," Dr. Kenny said while climbing back up on the wagon. He settled into his seat, then slapped the reigns on the horse's backs, jolting the wagon forward.

"Goodbye doctor!" they both called out, waving, and Dr. Kenny smiled proudly as the wagon rolled down the road.

Eva looked up at Georgie, still breathing heavily from the excitement at and anticipation of seeing her mother.

"Let's bring the luggage in first and then we'll head straight up to see your mum," Georgie promised.

They managed to get all the luggage inside the lodging house, then Eva looked up at him with an expectant, kittenish grin.

"Alright, yes, let's go," he said, nodding.

They quickly stomped up the lodging stairs, holding hands. Eva was hoping her mother had not left yet for the market since it was still pretty early in the morning.

Georgie knocked on the door while Eva hid against the wall so as not to be seen right away. She was grinning from ear to ear as Georgie knocked several times in a row. They could hear Margie on the other side of the door, spouting off as she neared the door.

"Alright now, hold your horses, for goodness' sake," she said as the door flew open. Margie saw Georgie standing there in front of her and paused for a moment.

"George!" she exclaimed in great relief, hugging him tightly.

While Margie was embracing Georgie, Eva stepped out and appeared in front of her, smiling widely. Margie opened her eyes wide at seeing her daughter and spoke breathily, "Eva."

Margie sounded as if this was the first time that she had exhaled since Eva had gone missing. She quickly released Georgie from her grasp and wrapped her arms tightly around

Eva. They were holding one another for several moments, tears rolling down their cheeks, neither of them saying a word. Georgie smiled joyfully, watching them reunite with one another and giving them all the time they needed. Eva pulled away from her mother's arms and Margie grabbed Eva's hands, continuing to stare at her daughter in shock. She stood there, taking in the sight of Eva, all the while shaking her head as if she couldn't believe that Eva was really standing there in front of her after all this time.

"I am so sorry, mother," Eva said sadly and tears rolled down Margie's cheeks even faster.

"It's alright, I have you back now—and that's all that matters," she muttered, once again embracing Eva firmly.

After a few more moments of hugging, they entered the lodging room. Walking through the threshold of the doorway, Eva immediately noticed the condition of her mother's home. Her jaw dropped as she scanned the room. The lodging room was in utter chaos—dishes piled up high on the countertops, newspapers covering the entire table, and liquor bottles scattered across the house. Eva looked around and her mouth gaped open at seeing the filthy state of her mother's home.

Margie noticed Eva's expression as she looked around at the mess and began cleaning up as she spoke, "I'm sorry that the house isn't in order, Eva." Margie began hurriedly picking up glasses and mugs from the side tables. "I've just been so distraught over you missing, I haven't—"

Eva interrupted, placing her hand in the air. "It's alright, Mum, I'll help you clean it up today," she reassured her mother with a smile.

Margie nodded and stopped cleaning. She slowly set down the drinkware and welcomed Eva and Georgie to sit down on the sofa while she sat down in the chair.

"Well, tell me all about..." Margie said, then stopped talking, trying to find the rest of her words as she shook her head. She wasn't sure what to say to Eva after all this time.

Georgie gently picked up Eva's hand, entwining his fingers with hers. Margie looked down at their hands, a bit surprised by this show of affection. Georgie swallowed hard.

"Actually, Miss Marg, Eva and I have some news."

Eva's eyes grew wide as she glanced over at Georgie. She wasn't sure she wanted to tell her mother about their engagement so soon after reconnecting with her.

"Oh, you do?" Margie asked while she continued to nervously stare at Georgie and Eva's hands.

Georgie looked over at Eva. She sat there, still unsure of what to say.

"I was actually wondering, Miss Marg, if I could ask you for your permission to ask for Eva's hand in marriage?"

Margie fidgeted and sat up straight in her chair. "Oh well, I suppose I knew this was coming. I just didn't realize it was going to be so soon," she replied, looking concerned and anxious. "When do you plan to marry?"

"Well, Mum, we were planning to go to court early tomorrow morning and get married there," Eva explained.

Margie raised her eyebrows, astonished. "Oh, I see, so very soon then?" she said pressing her lips together and covering her mouth with her hand as she began to cry.

Georgie looked over at Eva, perplexed by Margie's response.

"I'm so sorry. I'm really very happy for you both, truly I am," Margie said looking back up at them, tears in her eyes. "I couldn't have picked a better man for Eva than you George, but...I've only just gotten her back," she mumbled, feeling terrible for breaking down after hearing their happy news.

Eva hadn't thought about her mother being alone in the lodging house, once again without her. She looked over at Georgie, releasing his hand and rising from the couch. Georgie was growing nervous that Eva might change her mind about marrying him so soon. Eva walked over and knelt down beside her mother, taking hold of her hand.

"I know, I feel the same way, Mum," Eva said and Georgie's heart dropped. "But, a lot has changed in a very short amount of time and I'm not a little girl anymore," Eva continued, shaking her head as tears welled up in her eyes. "I have loved Georgie for years."

Margie nodded her head, sniffing. "Yes, I know you have, even though you never said it."

Georgie took out his handkerchief from his pocket and handed it to Margie.

"Thank you, George," she said gratefully, wiping the tears from her eyes.

"I do feel that Georgie and I should be married right away. Not only are we in love and want to be together...but Lucious can't harm me if I'm married," Eva stated calmly, trying to console her mother while explaining her heart.

Margie paused staring at Eva. She saw the maturity and sincerity of love in her eyes. This wasn't a rash decision, but something that both Georgie and Eva truly desired.

"Of course, this is what's best for both of you. You should be married, especially after everything you have gone through together. I'm sorry, I'm so sorry for being selfish." Margie was now embarrassed of her breakdown. She looked down and touched Eva's ring finger.

"Well, if you're going to do things properly, you will need a proper ring," she said and started pulling off her wedding band from her finger.

Eva rapidly shook her head. "No, that's the ring father gave you. I can't take your ring, Mum," she said, frowning, not wanting to see her mother give up her wedding band.

Georgie was about to speak up when Margie motioned for him to stop.

"No, it served its purpose for your father and me and now it's your turn," Margie insisted, dipping her chin and looking into Eva's eyes.

Tears began flowing down Eva's face as she embraced her mother tightly. Margie closed her eyes, holding her daughter in her arms.

"Thank you, Mum, thank you," Eva said, releasing her mother from her grasp.

Margie stood and walked over to Georgie. Grabbing his hand, she placed the ring in his palm and closed his fingers around the golden circle. Margie held firmly to Georgie's hand while gazing at him.

"You most certainly have my blessing George and thank you for bringing Eva home safely," Margie stated sincerely, most grateful for everything Georgie had done for Eva.

He stood up from the sofa and said, "Thank you very much, Miss Marg. I promise to love Eva and take care of her for the rest of her days." He hugged Margie, grateful for her blessing.

Margie pulled away slightly while still holding onto his arms. "George, please just call me Marg," she said with a smile and Georgie smiled back, nodding.

Margie inhaled deeply, releasing Georgie's arms.

"Well, does your grandmother know the good news?" Margie asked, wiping the tears away from her face.

Georgie shook his head no and they all decided to go downstairs to give Alice the happy news.

Georgie pounded on the door of Alice's lodging room and, after several long moments, the door bounded open.

"George!" Alice exclaimed brightly. "Oh my, George, you're finally home!" she exclaimed, grabbing and embracing him securely. "Is Eva with you?" she asked anxiously, with a hopeful look in her eyes.

Eva stepped out from behind Georgie, giving Alice an apologetic grin.

"Oh, Eva, come here," Alice said, grabbing ahold of her and wrapping her arms around her. Eva could smell Alice's rosewater perfume and she felt like she was home. "Oh, I have missed you both so much! Been on my knees most days and nights, praying. Well, come on in," Alice ushered them in with a wave of her hand as she began hobbling away from the door.

Everyone started following Alice inside the lodging house when she abruptly turned around and glanced back at Eva.

"Dear girl, we need to get some food in ya. You're wastin' away! Haven't you been feeding her George?" Alice spouted, questionably turning back around as she headed toward the kitchen.

Eva looked over at Georgie and gave a slight laugh.

"Good ol' Grams," he said, shaking his head and running his hand through his hair.

They all sat down around the table, while Alice began preparing food in the kitchen.

"Let me help you grams," Georgie rose from the table.

"You go ahead and sit down, boy. You've been through quite enough already, now let your grandmother fix you some grub," Alice insisted as she continued hobbling around the tiny kitchen.

"Will you at least allow me to help you, Alice?" Margie inquired.

"Alright, if you insist, Marg," Alice replied and Margie stood up from the table, retrieving the tableware from the cupboard. Alice looked over at Georgie and Eva, sitting quietly at the table.

"Well, is someone going talk to me, for goodness' sake? Tell me what's been happening!" Alice spouted.

"We would like to talk to you while you are sitting down, Grams," Georgie explained and Alice gave him an inquisitive side look.

"Oh, I see, well, Marg, if you will just heat up that stew on the stove there," Alice commanded and Margie nodded her head.

Alice wobbled over, taking a seat at the table. Georgie reached across the tabletop, taking Eva's hand in his. A sly smirk appeared on Alice's face.

"Grams, I've asked Eva to marry me and she's accepted," Georgie said, smiling brightly at Eva and his grandmother. Alice gazed back and forth between the two of them with a hearty grin on her face.

"Well, it's about time!" she said with a clap of her hands. She quickly rose from the table and hobbled up behind Georgie's chair giving him a congratulatory hug, then she hobbled over to Eva to do the same.

"Congratulations to you both! I also want to say that I'm sorry, Eva, for our conversation on the day you left. It was not my place to say anything," Alice apologized, looking down at Eva.

"I'm sorry, too, Alice. I shouldn't have spoken to you that way. When you'd said that Georgie had made plans, I thought that he'd met someone in Oxfordshire and was planning to get married," Eva explained.

Georgie perked up, unaware of what had transpired between his grandmother and Eva.

"Oh, dear," Alice sighed, "I can see how you would have thought that now." She nodded her head and inhaled deeply. "But I can assure you, Eva, George has only ever had eyes for you. There has never been another." Alice shook her head with great certainty.

Eva gazed over at Georgie, who was looking at her affectionately while nodding his head in agreement. Tears started forming in Eva's eyes and her heart filled with joy upon realizing that Georgie had always loved her. She seemed to be the only one who hadn't known his feelings for her.

"Well, I wanted to inform you both that I already figured as much, and booked the church on Saturday," Alice stated as she headed back into the kitchen without looking at either one of them.

Georgie and Eva glanced up at her surprised. "Grams, we were just going to get married in court tomorrow," Georgie explained.

Alice looked over him indignantly. "No grandson of my mine is getting married in court!" she huffed. "Did you hear them, Marg? No... you must have a proper wedding," Alice insisted, nodding her head while her cheeks shook rapidly.

Georgie glanced at Eva wide-eyed and shrugged. "What do you think Eva?" he asked her seriously.

"Saturday is three days away?" Eva questioned. She had hoped that they would be married and out of London by that time.

"That will give your parents enough time to attend the wedding, George," Alice stated.

Then Margie piped up, "And that would also give Eva and me a few more days together before she becomes your wife." She was hopeful, smiling at Eva.

Georgie nodded his head. "Well, I have always wanted a church wedding and Dr. Kenny gave me an outfit to wear for the occasion."

He glanced back over at Eva, unsure of what she would wear. She did have several fancy dresses from the Hall, but he didn't really want her to wear one of those for their wedding. Also, he had always pictured Eva in a white wedding gown, walking down the aisle. Georgie wished that he had his savings to supply Eva with everything she needed for their special day.

"I don't know what Eva will wear?" Georgie questioned.

"Oh, I'll figure something out," she stated quickly with a wave of her hand.

"Well, it's settled then?" Alice inquired and they both nodded their heads. "Good, because I wrote to your parents days ago and told them you would be getting married on Saturday at the church. They'll be there!" Alice said, grinning from ear to ear.

Eva looked over at Georgie in astonishment and couldn't help but burst out laughing. Everyone joined in her laughter at Alice's presumptuous comment.

Once they had eaten lunch, Georgie and Eva cleared the table and washed all the dishes. Afterward, Georgie asked if he could speak with Eva, alone, out in the lodging hall and the two of them excused themselves from the room. They walked out, hand in hand, into the lodging house foyer and sat down on the steps—just like the last time they were in London together. Georgie inhaled deeply, releasing a distressed sigh.

"Well, it looks like our plans have changed," he said solemnly.

Eva smiled at him.

"But isn't it nice that your family will be here for the wedding now?"

Georgie nodded his head in agreement.

"Yes, I wanted them here, but I didn't think it would be possible. They will probably come down on Friday evening, then head back to Oxfordshire right after the wedding and we should probably go back with them," he said, dipping his chin down, looking Eva seriously in the eyes.

She nodded her head sadly, not wanting to leave her mother so soon.

"I know you don't want to leave Marg, but I can't stay away any longer. The magistrate's already been very gracious to me and I need to get back to work," Georgie explained eagerly. He wasn't entirely sure what they were going to do without any income for an entire year and knew that he was probably going to have to take extra work so that they would have enough money.

"I understand," Eva softly replied.

"You're not changing your mind?" he asked, worried.

"No, not all," she replied. "I want to be your wife more than anything," Eva said emphatically, gazing deeply into his eyes.

Georgie's heart was pounding as Eva's bright, green eyes pierced his own. He leaned in, kissing her lips softly.

"I should have done that the last time we were here on these steps," he said, thinking about the day when Eva was devastated by the news that he was moving to Oxfordshire.

Eva was remembering the same moment when, suddenly, she grabbed Georgie's face in haste and kissed him passionately. Georgie felt his entire body begin to lose control from Eva's intense kisses and he passionately returned them while grabbing her waist and pulling her closer to himself. Eva grabbed Georgie's back, bringing him deeply against her as she lay down on the stairs while Georgie leaned on top of her.

Eva and Georgie were kissing fervently when, all of a sudden, someone cleared their throat loudly. The sound echoed throughout the entire foyer. Eva and Georgie glanced up quickly, seeing Mr. Roberts glaring over at them from the front door of the lodging house.

"Should you two be doing that?" he asked stoically, while walking toward them with his dark wooden cane in hand.

Georgie and Eva looked up at him wide-eyed, feeling as if they had been caught sneaking rats into his lodging room. Georgie cleared his throat, sitting upon the stairs. Eva followed.

"Probably not, sir," Georgie replied, embarrassed by their behavior.

"Well, if you'll excuse me, I need to be heading up to my room now," he stated with no expression upon his face as he waited for Georgie to move out of the way.

Georgie stood up, allowing Mr. Roberts to pass by so he could make his way to his lodging room. Georgie and Eva watched the old man climb the staircase until he rounded the corner, then Eva covered her mouth, silently laughing, while looking up at Georgie. Georgie's face was red and he was shaking his head as he sat back down next to Eva on the staircase. He took her hand and gazed seriously into her eyes.

"I absolutely love kissing you and I can't wait to do it every day for the rest of our lives...but I think we should wait for our wedding day to kiss again—to make things easier on ourselves," he suggested, worried that Eva might feel rejected.

Eva released a sigh of disappointment, then nodded in agreement. She knew it was beginning to become too difficult to restrain herself from being with Georgie.

"Alright," she said.

Georgie kissed her forehead and Eva closed her eyes, relishing his lips against her skin.

"Well, it looks like we have a small wedding to plan now," he said, thinking about how they had no money and were going to have a wedding.

"Don't worry, mum and Alice are probably already in there, planning it all out for us," Eva said laughing.

"Probably," Georgie agreed tilting his head, "and we should probably head back inside to help them," he suggested, assisting Eva up from the step and leading her back to Alice's lodging room to make a plan for their wedding day.

After they had plotted out the special occasion, Georgie carried Eva's garment bag upstairs to the lodging room, while Eva held tightly on to the box that contained her wedding dress. She placed the box inside, on top of her mother's kitchen table.

"So, what's in the box?" he asked inquisitively.

"It's a surprise," she replied, smiling at him mysteriously.

Georgie took her hand and gave her a side glare, trying to figure out what was inside the box as they walked back out to the corridor.

"I don't want you to go," she murmured sadly, swinging his hand side to side.

"I know, I really don't want to leave you," he replied, looking down at her sorrowfully. "But I have to go, and you need to spend some time with your mum," he reasoned, and she nodded in agreement.

Eva embraced him one last time and Georgie remembered one of the reasons why he didn't tell Eva of his intentions before leaving for Oxfordshire. He knew it would have been even more difficult for them to stay apart from one another.

"Alright, time to go," he said gently, pulling away from her and gazing down affectionately. "I love you, Eva, and I'm only downstairs if you need anything."

She nodded her head. "I love you too," she replied, looking up at him with a pout and asking, "When will I see you again?"

"I'll check in on you later this evening."

Eva stayed in the corridor until Georgie disappeared down the staircase.

She sighed as she entered the lodging room. Margie had already started cleaning up without her and Eva immediately joined in, picking up all the old newspapers and empty liquor bottles and throwing them into a large basket to trade for money. Margie walked over to the dress box sitting on the table.

"What's in the box, Eva?" she asked.

Eva opened it, revealing the stunning white wedding gown.

"Eva!" Margie gasped, placing her hands on her cheeks as her jaw dropped. "Where on earth did you get such a lovely dress?" she asked, taken aback by its beauty.

"A friend from the Hall purchased it for me, believing that Georgie and I would somehow manage to escape and be married," Eva sighed, gazing down sadly at the dress.

"Why are you so sad? You don't like the dress?" Margie inquired, surprised by Eva's reaction.

"I love it, it's the most beautiful gown I have ever seen… but I miss my friend Claudia—the one who purchased it for me. I wanted her to leave the Hall with me, but she said she couldn't go. She's is the one who saved my life," Eva said, looking back up at her mother with tears in her eyes.

Margie looked at Eva with compassion. "I would like to hear more about your friend if you're willing to tell me," Margie said dipping her chin, hoping that Eva would share some of her experiences from the last month with her.

Eva nodded and they both sat down on the sofa, while Eva told her mother some of what had happened to her with Lucious and at Liberation Hall. Margie did her best to hold back her tears through Eva's tragic tales. She hugged Eva closely to her side on the sofa, gently rubbing her daughter's hair and trying to comfort her from all the pain she had endured. Margie felt so helpless as she listened to the terrible things Lucious had done to Eva—but hearing Eva explain everything also helped Margie understand why she left with him in the first place. Margie had always assumed that Eva hadn't come back home because she was angry with her. Now she knew the truth—that Eva had been manipulated and coerced by that scoundrel and his juice. Margie didn't want to see Eva move away but, after hearing her stories of Lucious, she realized that it was best for her to marry Georgie as soon as possible.

After Eva shared with her mother, they finished cleaning the lodging room. Eva walked over, opening her bag of exquisite garments. She and Margie started going through all her extravagant dresses from the Hall.

"Eva, these are very expensive dresses dear."

Margie looked through the bag, wide-eyed when Eva held up one of the dresses against her body. She gazed down at the beautiful dress and frowned.

"I don't want them anymore," she said shaking her head.

Margie looked at her surprised. "Why not?"

Eva placed the dress back inside the bag. "Well, because of what they represent. I want to get rid of everything that reminds me of Lucious and the Hall, except for the wedding dress, which is brand new and a gift from Claudia."

Margie nodded her head, understanding why Eva felt that way.

"Well, you could sell them and make some money for you and George," Margie suggested and Eva perked up.

"That's a great idea, Mum," she stated excitedly, then thought about it for a moment and shook her head no.

"Except, I don't want Lucious to find me. If he is out there searching for me, he will be sure to look for me at Covent Garden," she said, pressing her lips together. "And he would also search here, at the lodging house, for that matter," Eva said, realizing that Lucious could be lurking around any corner, trying to find her. Eva started breathing heavily and her heart raced, thinking of how Lucious could break into the lodging house at any moment if he so desired.

Margie had a concerned look on her face, thinking seriously about something while placing her index finger and thumb on her chin.

"You know," she said, "a few days ago, a couple dodgy-looking fellows showed up here, at the house. They said they were checking the pipes and that they needed to go into every room in the lodging house. Mr. Lyons was with them, so I didn't think anything of it but, come to think of it now, they just sort of looked around—it was very strange."

Eva's heart was beating frantically. She was feeling faint, thinking about how Lucious might find her.

"Mum, I know this isn't exactly appropriate but—what if I stayed in your room with you and Georgie slept out here, on the cot, just in case someone comes back to the house looking for me?" Eva suggested.

Margie thought about it for a moment and let out a sigh, nodding her head.

"Well, I suppose you're right; it's best to have a man here if anything should happen," her mother agreed and Eva was relieved.

She felt better already, knowing that Georgie would be there in the room at night to keep watch over them.

Georgie agreed to stay on the cot in the lodging room until he and Eva were married. He thought it was best to be as close to her as possible until they were safely in Oxfordshire. He lay there at night on the cot, with his hands behind his head, thinking about everything. He assumed that Lucious would be furious when he found out that Eva went missing, mostly because he was the type of man who didn't like losing control. Even if Lucious wanted nothing more to do with Eva, Georgie wondered whether he would look for her to kill her just to get revenge. The more Georgie thought about it, the more he wished that he and Eva were going to court tomorrow to be married. He didn't want to fear Lucious or to allow him to agitate them for the rest of their lives. However, with it only being a week and a half since Eva left the Hall, Georgie felt it was necessary to be cautious.

He was also thinking about the letter that had arrived that day from Magistrate Logan. The magistrate was in London for the week and had requested to see Georgie and Eva in his office on Friday morning. Georgie was nervous that the magistrate would release him from his job even though he still owed him a year's worth of wages. He figured he should go see his old boss, Mr. Gyles, the following afternoon about working for a few days while he was in London, just so he and Eva would have a little bit of money in their pockets. This was the very thing Georgie had tried to avoid—being penniless and married. He didn't want to start his marriage off this way, scrapping for any bit of money he could possibly earn. He knew that he was going to have to work very hard to secure enough money for both him and Eva to have respectable lives.

Georgie rolled over on the cot, hoping to get some sleep. He switched his thoughts to Eva and felt a calm come over him. He was picturing her walking down the church aisle toward him dressed in a white wedding gown and the vision made his heart swell. Georgie knew what the two most important things right now were—Eva's safety and getting married. Placing his focus on their wedding day made Georgie feel at peace, allowing him to fall fast asleep.

Thirty-Six

Georgie and Eva strolled through the city, hand in hand, tending to the final preparations for their wedding tomorrow morning. They were on their way across town to see Magistrate Logan at his request and had already visited the church to discuss the wedding with the clergymen and the priest.

The city streets were very busy on Friday and Eva held tightly onto Georgie as they made their way through the crowd. They were making their way through town when Eva spotted someone she recognized.

"Oh my!" she gasped.

"What is it?" Georgie looked down at her concerned.

"I think that's Nancy, across the way?" Eva murmured the question to herself, standing on her tippy-toes and peering through the mass of people. She quickly pulled Georgie along and bolted across the busy dirt road.

"Nancy!" Eva shouted and the small, blonde-haired girl turned around, gazing at her in wide-eyed shock upon seeing Eva standing there.

"Miss Eva?" she questioned, gazing around the street. "What are you doing in London? Are you here with Master Lucious?" Nancy asked, a fearful look on her face as she continued glancing around hastily.

Eva looked up at Georgie, then back over to Nancy.

"No, Nancy, Lucious released me from the Hall," she explained, not wanting to go into further detail.

Nancy tilted her head wondering why Lucious would ever allow Eva to leave.

"This is Georgie, my fiancé," Eva introduced.

Georgie cordially nodded and politely said, "It's nice to meet you, Nancy."

Nancy gave a slight curtsy with no expression on her face. "How do you do," she muttered nervously.

Eva looked at Nancy, wondering, "Nancy, why did you just disappear from the Hall that night? You didn't even say goodbye." She sounded a bit wounded.

Nancy continued anxiously gazing around the street, then glanced back at Eva.

"I'm sorry, Miss. I just couldn't stay there any longer," she said, hurriedly shaking her head.

Eva realized that it must have been Nancy who had walked into her room while Lucious was violating her. Realizing that Nancy was uncomfortable, Eva decided to change the subject.

"Where are you working now?"

Nancy hesitated, "Well...I'm the lady's maid for an opera singer. In fact, I need to be going—we are taking the afternoon train to Italy."

Eva perked up. "Oh, that sounds lovely. Well, it was good seeing you again."

Nancy gave her a sorrowful smile.

"It was nice seeing you too, Miss. Goodbye," she said, then swiftly took off down the street.

Eva stood there for a moment, thinking after Nancy had walked away.

Georgie noticed that Eva was deep in thought "What's wrong Eva?" he asked.

She looked up at him troubled. "Nancy saw what happened to me. She walked in on Lucious while he was…" Eva pressed her lips together allowing her words trail off and Georgie knew that she was referring to the rape. "She was my lady's maid at the Hall and the next day she just disappeared, without a trace. I even think Lucious may have had people searching for her, so it's probably best that she's leaving London." Eva was looking at Georgie, clearly bothered that Nancy had seen what happened to her.

Georgie began rubbing Eva's arms, trying to console her. "I'm so sorry."

Eva gave a sad nod. She sucked in a deep breath, then abruptly turned around and pulled Georgie's hand, making their way down the street to the magistrate's office.

When they arrived at Magistrate Logan's office, Georgie informed the secretary that Magistrate Logan had requested to see them that morning.

"Please wait one moment," she said and they sat on a bench in the corridor outside his office.

The secretary knocked on the magistrate's office door and peeked in, letting him know that they had arrived. A few minutes later, Magistrate Logan stepped out into the corridor.

"Hello, it's good to see you, George," he said happily.

Georgie removed his hat and stood from the bench on which he and Eva were sitting.

"Magistrate Logan, sir," Georgie replied, putting out his hand.

Gladly taking Georgie's hand in his own, Magistrate Logan shook it firmly.

"And this must be Eva?" he inquired, gazing over at Eva as she nervously rubbed her hands together.

"How do you do, sir," she said with a shy nod.

Magistrate Logan recognized Eva from the party months back at Liberation Hall, but he wasn't sure whether she recognized him.

"It's very nice to meet you. Well, come to my office. I would like to speak with both of you," he said cordially. They both looked at one another, then followed Magistrate Logan into his office.

Georgie had been extremely anxious, worrying that he was going to be released from his position at the farm. He had already informed Eva of the possibility so she would be prepared for the bad news.

"Have a seat." The magistrate motioned for them to sit down in the chairs adjacent to his desk. "Well, it's been a long few months, hasn't it George?" he asked.

"Yes, sir, it most certainly has," Georgie replied, looking over at Eva.

She was sitting very still, staring solemnly at the magistrate. Eva remembered Claudia mentioning that Magistrate Logan would come visit her from time to time at the Hall, although Eva didn't remember seeing him there.

"You're probably both wondering why I asked you to come meet with me today." The magistrate folded his hands on his desk as he spoke, then fixed his gaze on Eva. "Eva, I asked you to join George here today to offer you a position on the farm," he stated.

Eva's eyes grew wide and she moved around restlessly in the chair, glancing over at Georgie.

"I was thinking about the fact that my daughter, Cora, is coming of age and has been inquiring about getting a lady's maid of her own. I thought, perhaps, that that might be an adequate position for you?"

Eva perked up once again, surprised, and looked over at Georgie, who was grinning from ear to ear, extremely pleased that the magistrate would offer Eva such a high position at the farm. She would be making almost as much money as him if she accepted the position.

"Uh...yes, sir, I think I could do that job very well," Eva said, considering what her responsibilities would be as she nodded her head.

Eva had seen how Nancy took care of her each day at the Hall and believed that she would be a good lady's maid. She knew that many girls would be honored to have such a high position, especially without any experience.

"Thank you kindly, sir, for considering me," she replied, greatly appreciating that the magistrate would have the confidence to offer the position to her.

The magistrate smiled and nodded at Eva. "Well, it's settled then—starting Tuesday morning, I will have Alice, who is my eldest daughter's lady's maid, train you around the house."

Eva nodded in agreement and Georgie thought about how he had met Alice the last time he was at the farm. He believed that she would make a good friend for Eva.

The magistrate continued, "Eva, if you don't mind, I would now like to speak to George privately?" he asked kindly.

Eva looked over at Georgie timidly, then back at Magistrate Logan. "Oh no, sir, of course not," she replied graciously and exited his office.

Once Eva left the room, the magistrate fixed his gaze on Georgie.

"How are you doing, George?" he asked, concerned, knowing the great ordeal that Georgie and Eva had endured.

"Well, sir...I'm doing quite well now that Eva and I are together again. Also, knowing that she is safe and away from Lucious and his toxic juice," Georgie replied seriously.

The magistrate gave him a dismayed look and nod. "And what about your arm?" he asked, worried that Georgie wouldn't be able to get back to work when he returned home.

Georgie looked down at his arm in the sling.

"Well, it's on the mend and getting better each day. I won't let it interfere with my work," he promised convincingly, nodding his head.

The magistrate looked at him oddly. "Did Lucious do that to you?" he inquired.

Georgie bit his lip and began apprehensively gazing around the room, then brought his eyes back to the magistrate.

446

"No, sir, I fell off my horse during a storm as I was trying to make my way back to Liberation Hall in time to pay Lucious the money."

The magistrate closed his eyes; he felt bad for Georgie.

"Well, I feel that you should probably still have some help for a while until it's completely healed," the magistrate recommended and Georgie agreed.

Then, Magistrate Logan cleared his throat, "Your father informed me that you and Eva will be getting married tomorrow morning and I was wondering what your plans were for your honeymoon?"

Georgie replied quickly, "Well, sir, I had planned to head back to Oxfordshire straight away after the wedding so I could get back to work early on Sunday morning." Georgie was enthusiastic, wanting to reassure the magistrate that he would return to work promptly, having been away for so long.

"Oh, I see. Well, I was thinking…I have a friend who owns a hotel here in town and I was wondering…perhaps, whether you and Eva would like to stay there until Monday? Then you could head back to Oxfordshire on the Monday afternoon train," the magistrate proposed happily.

Georgie was taken aback by Magistrate Logan's kind offer and remained speechless at his generosity toward them.

Magistrate Logan realized that Georgie had no words and continued speaking, "I believe every couple should have a honeymoon, George. I think it would be good for you and Eva to have some time together after the wedding." He dipped his chin, looking at him seriously. "Especially, after everything that you have been through in the past couple of months."

Georgie looked at the magistrate in awe. "Yes, sir, that would be quite nice," he said, shaking his head in disbelief while smiling brightly.

"Good, I will have my secretary make the arrangements for you and everything will be paid for, including meals." The magistrate leaned forward. "I suggest ordering room service," he said with a smirk, then pulled out a piece of paper from his desk and wrote down the location of the hotel on a piece of paper, handing it to Georgie. "Finally, I was wondering about your plans for your living arrangements upon returning to the farm?"

Georgie suddenly felt his demeanor shift and he swallowed hard. "To be honest with you, sir, I'm not entirely sure what we're going to do. The shed I was working on isn't finished. I suppose that we'll make do until I can fix it up so that it's suitable to live in," he replied, embarrassed that Eva didn't have a proper place to live in once they were married.

The magistrate stared at him for a moment, pensively, and sighed. "Well…we'll figure something out for the two of you," he stated. "I wish you both the best on your special day George." Magistrate Logan sounded most sincere.

"Thank you sir," Georgie replied.

Georgie started to stand up from his chair when he hesitated and sat back down.

"I was wondering, sir, if I could ask you about a legal matter?" he inquired.

The magistrate cleared his throat, wondering what Georgie had in mind.

"Yes, what is your question, George?" he asked, once again folding his hands upon his desk, listening to Georgie intently.

"I know that neither prostitution nor the juice that Lucious sells are illegal. However, I was wondering about…" Georgie bit the side of his cheek and waited a moment, "I was wondering about rape?"

The magistrate raised his eyebrows, giving Georgie a very distressed look. He inhaled deeply and sighed.

"Well, sexual violations are against the law…but, unfortunately, they're difficult to prove."

Georgie nodded his head. "I understand what you are saying…but…what if there was a witness?" Georgie questioned.

The magistrate squinted his eyes, feeling very disheartened for Eva and Georgie.

"Well, you may not know this George, but I'm a barrister of the law as well as a magistrate and if you have a witness that is willing to testify in court, then, yes, that could be extremely damning evidence, indeed. I could proceed with the charges against the individual," Magistrate Logan stated, then leaned forward and looked Georgie most seriously in the eyes. "Did something happen to Eva?"

Georgie inhaled and looked back at the door through which Eva had walked out, then gazed back over at the magistrate.

"Lucious raped Eva at the Hall," he whispered and the magistrate's eyes grew wide. "And there was a witness, a young lady's maid." Georgie swallowed hard, trying to control his emotions.

The magistrate closed his eyes, briefly appalled by Lucious' behavior. "Do you think she will testify?" he asked, hoping to put Lucious in prison.

Georgie glanced around the room, thinking for a moment and began shaking his head. "No… probably not."

He glowered, discouraged by the realization that Nancy would probably never testify against Lucious in court. Also, he didn't want to put Eva through a trial. The magistrate sighed giving him a sympathetic expression.

"I am very sorry for you and Eva. You've both been through quite an ordeal because of Lucious Paddimir," Magistrate Logan said and Georgie nodded, lowering his head and looking down at the floor.

The magistrate had not known or thought about what he was condoning by participating in Lucious' festivities at Liberation Hall. Now that he was fully aware, it made his stomach turn. Georgie looked up at Magistrate Logan.

"Well, that's all I wanted to know, sir," he said, heartsore.

Magistrate Logan put his hand out. "I truly hope that you and Eva will be able to make a fresh start together out on the farm," he commented, a hopeful look on his face.

Georgie shook his hand. "Yes, I do believe we will, sir." He stood up from this chair. "Do you think you might be able to make it to the wedding tomorrow?" Georgie inquired. "I would be honored to have you attend."

The magistrate sat up in his chair. "Well, I don't see why not," he accepted the invitation, smiling at Georgie.

"Nine o'clock at St. James Church on Piccadilly," Georgie replied.

"See you tomorrow, George."

"Thank you again, sir...for everything." Georgie nodded, then headed out into the corridor, where Eva was waiting for him.

As Georgie exited the magistrate's office, Eva immediately rose from the bench.

"What did Magistrate Logan say?" she asked anxiously.

Georgie took her by the hand, gazing into her eyes.

"He asked what our plans were for our honeymoon."

Eva blushed and pressed her lips together, grinning.

"Why would he ask about that?" she inquired, peering at Georgie.

"He said that he has a friend who owns a hotel." Georgie pulled out the paper from his trouser pocket and handed it to Eva. "And he asked if we would like to stay at that hotel for a couple of nights—for our honeymoon—before heading back to Oxfordshire."

Eva looked up at Georgie excitedly. "That's brilliant, Georgie!" she exclaimed.

Georgie beamed down at Eva. "I'll admit, I'm thankful that our first night together won't be on the floor in a shed," he said, laughing, and Eva smiled, nodding in agreement.

* * *

When they returned to the lodging house, Georgie's family had just arrived from Oxfordshire. He and Eva welcomed his family. The Thornbers were thrilled to see them both. Georgie's mother hugged Eva tightly.

"We are so happy that you're safe, Eva, and that you're finally going to be a part of our family. We've been anticipating this day for a long time," Elizabeth said, glancing over at Georgie and smiling proudly.

"Thank you, Elizabeth," Eva replied and her face shone like the sun. Eva glanced over and saw Georgie's sisters.

"Marta and Mary!" she exclaimed, wrapping her arms around them both.

"Oh, Eva! We're so thankful that you're alright and that you're finally going to be our sister," Marta said.

Eva had also been close with Georgie's sisters before they moved to Oxfordshire, but, growing up, it was Georgie, in particular, with whom she'd had a special bond. Suddenly Margie came quickly out of the lodging house to welcome the Thornber family.

"Oh, Elizabeth, it's been too long," Margie stated while reaching out for a hug.

"It certainly has," Elizabeth agreed.

After settling in at the logging house, everyone chipped in to help Alice prepare the food for the wedding day picnic. The families were enjoying each other's company, chatting and laughing as they worked together to prepare the event. As evening approached, Eva and Georgie both begin to feel tired. It was a long and busy day. They decided to head up to Margie and Eva's lodging room for the night. Margie followed closely behind. Entering through the door of the lodging room, she found them sitting together on Georgie's cot, talking.

"Alright, you two, five more minutes. Then, Eva, you need to come to bed and get your beauty sleep," Margie insisted.

Eva nodded her head, then looked back, fixing her gaze on Georgie.

"Next time I see you, you'll be walking down the aisle," he said as his heart fluttered thinking about their wedding day tomorrow.

Eva smiled brilliantly. "I'm so excited. I don't know how I'll be able to sleep a wink tonight," she gushed, staring into his eyes.

Georgie closed his eyes for a brief moment, taking a deep breath to stop himself from fulfilling his desire to kiss Eva. Instead, he embraced her tightly with his good arm and brushed his fingers through her hair. Eva closed her eyes, cherishing the moment; she felt extremely safe with Georgie holding her. He gently released her from his embrace.

"We should be getting to sleep now," he suggested and Eva nodded in agreement, standing up from the cot on the floor.

"Oh—Georgie, don't forget that you have to leave first thing in the morning," she commanded. "You're not allowed to see me before the wedding."

Georgie smiled and nodded. He wanted to savor watching Eva walk down the aisle and he was definitely going to be gone before she would wake. "Goodnight, Eva. I love you," he said.

"I love you, too," she replied and walked back toward the bedroom without taking her eyes off of Georgie. Smiling coyly, she blew him a kiss, then vanished behind the bedroom door.

Thirty-Seven

The day when Georgie and Eva would exchange their wedding vows and become husband and wife had finally arrived. Eva was right, she'd barely slept a wink all night. She was too busy lying awake pondering things—how the wedding would go, what would happen if she tripped down the aisle with everyone staring at her, and whether she would make a good wife.

When Eva opened her eyes groggily, she saw that her mother was already dressed and curling her hair. Margie looked down at Eva as she wrapped her hair around the iron.

"You tossed and turned all night, did you get any sleep?" Margie questioned.

Eva let out a sigh, sitting up slowly in the bed. "Not much, I'm afraid." Eva yawned. "Is Georgie still out in the sitting room?"

Margie looked over at her. "No, he left an hour ago," she replied.

Eva decided to try and pull herself from the bed as she released another yawn. She was setting her feet on the floor when it began to sink in that today was her wedding day.

Suddenly, Eva bounced out of bed and scurried across the room, kissing her mother on the cheek and smiling at her wondrously.

"Aw, was what's that for?" Margie asked, surprised, looking happily at Eva.

"Thank you for allowing me to marry Georgie so soon," Eva said to her mother with a twinkle in her eye.

Margie looked back at her, trying not to allow tears to well up.

"I love you so much and I know you're going to be very happy with him; I also know that he loves you very, very much, too," Margie said, embracing Eva. They hugged for a few long seconds, then Margie pulled away. "Well, you'd better get ready for your wedding," she suggested eagerly and Eva squealed loudly in excitement and began gathering her bath toiletries together.

Eva took a warm bath, then dried off and started getting ready for the day. She walked back into the lodging room and pulled out her wedding dress from the wardrobe, placing it on the bed. Margie helped Eva tighten her corset, then Eva carefully slipped the white gown over her body. She stared at herself in the dressing mirror, while Margie buttoned up the back of the dress for her.

"Eva, my goodness, you look absolutely stunning!" Margie exclaimed, looking at her reflection.

Eva took a deep breath, then exhaled it slowly as she smiled brilliantly, looking in the mirror at herself. Eva never thought that she would have an actual white gown for her wedding day. She was thankful that Claudia had taken the chance and purchased the gown for her. The gown was made of silky, ivory-colored taffeta and had a tight bodice around the waist, which rounded out into a small bustle. The top of the dress hung around Eva's shoulders and was trimmed with lace and short, tight sleeves. The skirt flared into an a-frame shape, while flowing taffeta tiers and a lace train adorned the bottom of the gown. Every tier had intricately placed soft pink roses that wrapped around the backside of the gown, tumbling toward the train.

Margie helped Eva curl her hair, then Eva pulled it back, her golden tresses smoothly covering her ears. She gathered it low, near the nape of her neck, and bound it loosely to one side, wrapping it into an elegant, loose spiral. The very ends of her hair draped down, allowing curly tendrils to softly hang about her neck and shoulders. She pinned it in place, allowing wavy pieces to fall naturally, caressing and framing her face. Eva had learned how to do several different hairstyles from Nancy but she had come up with this one on her own. Finally, she placed the butterfly pin that her mother had given her to secure her hair tightly in place. The flower women made Eva a flower wreath to wear as a crown on her head. It was made out of an assortment of spring flowers and baby's breath. They also created a small, matching bouquet for her to hold as she walked down the aisle.

Eva gazed upon her own reflection in the mirror, tears filling her eyes as she looked at her own natural beauty. She wasn't covered in rouge or dolled up; instead, she looked pure and elegant. Her heart swelled on the inside and she truly never felt more beautiful or satisfied in her entire life.

Margie walked into the bedroom and gasped upon seeing Eva.

"Eva, you're the most beautiful bride I have ever seen!"

Eva glistened and beamed at her mother. Margie walked over, giving her daughter another hug.

"Oh, how I wish Henry were here to see you," her mother said with tears flowing down her face.

Eva pulled away looking her in the eyes. "Pop is here with us. I know that he is smiling down on me today," she said softly.

Margie smiled, wiping the tears from her eyes and they headed downstairs together.

When Eva and Margie arrived downstairs, Mr. Gyles— Georgie's old boss—awaited their arrival. Georgie had asked Mr. Gyles if he would supply Eva with a carriage ride to the church on the morning of the wedding, so that she wouldn't have to walk through the mud and muck of the city streets. He held out his hand, helping the ladies onto the carriage.

"Oh my, that George is a lucky bloke, I say!" Mr. Gyles exclaimed, bright-eyed.

Eva looked down and blushed. "Thank you, Mr. Gyles," she responded coyly.

After Eva and Margie were settled into the carriage, Mr. Gyles yelled out, "St. James Church!" stating where they were headed as he climbed to the front of the carriage.

Margie sat across from Eva in the carriage and noticed that Eva played with her fingers while tightly pressing her lips together.

"Are you alright Eva?" Margie asked, slightly worried that Eva might get sick.

"I'm extremely nervous for some reason. Excited—but extremely nervous," Eva replied.

Margie smiled, placing her hand over Eva's to console her. "You'll be just fine, my dear," she reassured.

The carriage took off and, as they traveled down the road, several little children were waving at her as if she were Queen Victoria. One little girl exclaimed, "Mommy, look at the princess!" as she pointed at Eva. Eva chuckled and waved back.

The carriage pulled up at the back of St. James' Church and Eva's heart began pounding. She sucked in a deep breath, trying to maintain her composure and calm her nerves. Mr. Gyles helped her out of the carriage and she quickly walked into the church. Georgie's mother and sisters were waiting at the back door for their arrival.

"Oh, Eva, you look absolutely breathtaking," Elizabeth exclaimed, hugging her tightly.

"Your dress, Eva, is exquisite," Marta gushed.

"I just love the pink roses," exclaimed Mary, as she delicately touched one of the silky blooms.

"Georgie doesn't know about the wedding dress—it's a surprise," Eva whispered to Marta and Mary, smiling happily.

"George is going to drop his jaw when he sees you, Eva," Marta cried.

Georgie was waiting patiently, feeling more and more excited as he stood at the front of the church while the guests arrived. Everyone they loved was present and they were all together, celebrating his and Eva's unity. Georgie was hoping that he wouldn't sweat through the heavy gentleman's attire that Dr. Kenny had given him to wear for the occasion. He breathed in deeply and his heart heavily pounded in his chest. Georgie had been waiting for this moment for two years. He had pictured it, longed for it, and, recently, had thought it might never actually happen—but here it was. The day that he and Eva would become husband and wife.

The wedding was about to begin. The priest asked the ladies to move inside the church and take their seats. They all scurried into the chapel, sitting in the pews. Eva could barely breathe as she waited for the ceremony to start. She stood there, thinking about how she was going to walk down the aisle alone with everyone's eyes upon her. She continued inhaling slowly, making sure that she didn't faint. Eva wanted to be sure she made it to the other end of the aisle, where Georgie was waiting for her. The music began to play and she knew that that was her cue. She waited until she heard the guests stand up in the pews, then slowly stepped over the threshold, waiting just a moment before entering the aisle.

As Eva stepped into the aisle, all eyes were on her. Georgie's breath was stolen from him at the sight of Eva in a white wedding gown. He gasped, trying not to lose his balance, completely taken aback and in awe of her beauty. Eva was wearing the most elegant white wedding dress that he had ever seen. He had never seen her look as beautiful as she did at that very moment. Eva smiled radiantly and strolled up the aisle toward Georgie gingerly. He beamed as he looked upon her while she came closer him with each step. Georgie had imagined this moment over a hundred times—but none of his visions did it justice. Eva looked more exquisite, elegant, and graceful than he could have ever imagined.

Eva saw Georgie looking proud and debonair as he stood at the end of the aisle waiting for her. She was doing her best to hold back tears. Her dreams were nearer to coming true with each graceful step she took. Eva couldn't help but smile at Georgie; he was glowing. The light beamed from his eyes, which were fixated upon her. Finally, she reached the end of the long, daunting aisle and stood face to face with her love.

Georgie whispered, with tears in eyes, "You look absolutely beautiful."

Eva gave a bashful grin and gazed at him lovingly.

The priest started officiating the wedding and Eva did her best to listen, but all she could think about was Georgie. They were staring so intently at one another that, when the priest asked for the ring, Georgie didn't respond—he was too infatuated with Eva.

Eva dipped her head. "Georgie, the ring," she whispered quietly after hearing the priest.

"Oh!"

He reached into his pocket and his face turned bright red. Everyone chuckled lightly and the wedding continued. Georgie and Eva partook in communion and then the priest recited some scriptures and prayers. The ceremony ended with Georgie and Eva signing their names in the register and—once they had finished signing—Georgie looked over at Eva, grinning from ear to ear. He took her hand as they proceeded down the aisle together, as husband and wife.

All their friends and family were smiling, looking happily upon them. When they reached the corridor, they hurried around the corner and Georgie picked Eva up, kissing her passionately, while Eva held his face and returned the kisses. They continued kissing as all guests made their way outside. After a few moments, realizing that their guests were waiting, they gently pulled away from one another.

"Are you ready, Mrs. Thornber?" Georgie asked happily.

Eva smirked and nodded, then they strolled out of the church together, as husband and wife, while their guests threw bird seeds at them to commence the celebration.

The wedding breakfast was held down the road, at St. James Park, where the family was already setting up a large picnic with all the splendid food they had prepared the day before. Eva was thankful that it was a warm, sunny day. The atmosphere in the park was breathtaking. The flowers bloomed and the shrubbery was a rich, green color. All guests enjoyed delicious sweetmeats and cheeses, along with some refreshments. Alice had made a heavenly, three-tiered, white wedding cake and had decorated it with frosting and white marzipan dots. She'd placed light pink roses on the cake tiers, matching the roses on Eva's wedding dress. Eva glanced around at her friends and family and her heart ached a bit—wishing that Claudia and the Kennys could also have been there. There weren't many guests invited to the wedding. There was only Georgie's family, including Alice, Eva's mother, Bert Darby, the flower women, Mr. Gyles, and Magistrate Logan.

Magistrate Logan walked merrily up to Georgie.

"Congratulations, George! You and Eva make a fine couple," he said as he shook Georgie's hand.

"Thank you, sir," Georgie replied proudly, looking over at Eva.

He could barely keep his eyes off of her. Eva noticed him staring at her and she gave him a flirtatious grin that sent tingles down his body.

"I wanted you to know that everything is in order at the hotel today," the magistrate said, grinning.

Georgie looked up at him. "Thank you again, sir."

The magistrate gave him a smile and a nod, then turned around to take a good look at the park. As Magistrate Logan scanned the landscape, he thought he saw—out of the corner of his eye—a man with a golden cane slipping behind a row of trees. The magistrate nonchalantly made his way nearer the group of trees, looking intently to see who was there. As he looked around, he hoped that it wasn't Lucious who was lurking in the shadows. Magistrate Logan stepped inside the tree line, glancing through to the other side, but it seemed that the man had disappeared into thin air.

Thirty-Eight

L ucious had been in London, following a young girl, for the past several days. He was almost ready to make his move but wanted to be completely sure of himself before doing so. There was strategy involved when choosing his prey. He needed just a little more time before he approached the debutante, waiting until her most vulnerable moment.

The girl was pretty, naïve, and very young. Lucious thought that she was, perhaps, only fourteen or fifteen years old. The young lady was extremely poor and would wander aimlessly around the city, which made her schedule rather unpredictable. She was also quite dirty—not being properly cared for—and Lucious thought he was going to have to somehow get her into a bath before executing his plans for her.

Early on Saturday morning, the girl was heading toward Westminster and Lucious was casually lagging behind while keeping a close eye on her. She headed through St. James Park and Lucious cautiously followed behind, doing his best to remain unseen. Glancing around the park, he noticed a wedding breakfast taking place. Lucious rolled his eyes at the happy occasion. He gazed over, setting his sight on the beautiful, young, blonde bride. Lucious' eyes grew larger because he thought that the bride looked quite familiar. He wanted to get a better look at the happy couple and so he crept closer, trying his best to stay behind some blooming trees. He fixed his gaze on the lovely bride and was astonished to see that it was Eva, wearing an elegant, white, wedding gown. Georgie was gazing at her amorously and she looked at him affectionately in return. Georgie walked over to Eva, placed his hand in hers, and then gently kissed her on the cheek. Eva closed her eyes, obviously cherishing her husband's touch.

The scene caused a wave of fury to rise inside Lucious, who realized that they had both managed to outdo him and escape his plans for them. He observed them for a while, contemplating what he should do, while his blood boiled all the more with every second that he spent watching them. They were surrounded by friends and family, at the moment, which meant that now was clearly not the time to approach them. There was also something very different about Eva; she seemed to be glowing. A light surrounded her, almost like there was a protective covering enveloping her, which made Lucious feel nervous. He remained at a distance, observing Eva with Georgie and knowing that he could no longer have her as his own. She was another man's wife now and, if he tried to take her back to Liberation Hall, he could go to prison. The thought of this caused the rage inside him to increase as he could sense the intense love and protection that Georgie lavished upon his bride. Lucious burned, hostile from watching the young lad look so joyous to have Eva as his wife. He felt jealousy and the need for revenge building within his inner core, as Eva gazed at Georgie lovingly—the way she used to look at him. Lucious could not allow them to get away with what they had done and he was going to make them pay.

Lucious scoured the other guests and was surprised to see Magistrate James Logan at the festivities. The magistrate walked over to Georgie, shaking his hand and smiling, obviously congratulating him on the big day. Lucious spied on them as they conversed for a while when, suddenly, Magistrate Logan glanced over to where he was standing. Lucious smoothly sauntered between a row of trees, then quickly headed down a path and exited onto the street. After making sure he was out of sight, Lucious looked around anxiously for the girl he had been following. He slammed his cane against a brick walk, furious that he had lost track of the girl and would now have to hunt her down again. Lucious inhaled several deep breaths, trying to calm himself. He decided to wait around the park and follow the newly married couple instead. He was interested to see where they were headed after their celebratory wedding breakfast. Lucious stood down on the side of the road, scrutinizing Georgie and Eva's every move. He was very careful, making sure to not lose sight of them.

*   *   *

After a few hours of celebrating, the guests helped gather the remains of the picnic and started heading back to the lodging house.

"George, I have to be going...There is something I need to do," Magistrate Logan said. "It was a lovely wedding," he added, shaking Georgie's hand.

"Thank you, sir, are you planning on going back to Oxfordshire this evening?" Georgie asked.

The magistrate gazed over to where he had seen Lucious lurking in the trees.

"No, I think I'll stick around for the next few days. I have some more business to attend to here at the moment," he replied.

Georgie nodded, then waved Eva over to come say goodbye to the magistrate.

The flower women had plans in town as well and were saying their goodbyes while still in the park. Gladys held tightly onto Eva.

"I just still can't believe you've gone off and gotten married so soon after returning home. We will miss seeing you around the market," she muttered with tears in her eyes.

"I will come and visit Gladys, I promise," Eva stated sadly because she was going to miss all the women. They had been a special part of life over the past two years.

"Well, this is it then, I'm going to be the old maid out of the bunch. I just know it!" spouted Ruby.

"Oh Ruby, I'm sure you will find someone one day who doesn't mind being mistreated by you," Gladys teased and they all snickered, while Ruby peered at Gladys indignantly.

"Well, I know I won't be an old maid," Clara stated, her nose high in the air. "I have several gentlemen callers and it's only a matter of days before I receive a proposal."

Ruby positioned herself closer to Clara's face. "Just remember Clara, men don't put a ring on what you're willing to give out for free, dear," Ruby jeered, glaring at Clara.

Clara's jaw dropped and her eyes widened at Ruby's comment.

"Alright, ladies, that's enough," Margie spoke up. "It's Eva's wedding day and we're not going to ruin it with bantering."

"Well, I have to be going anyhow. I have an engagement this evening," Clara said haughtily. "Eva, you looked very handsome today, almost as handsome as that husband of yours," Clara added, while staring at Georgie.

"I suppose I should take that as a compliment," Eva mumbled, pressing her lips together and rolling her eyes.

"Well, best wishes to you both," Clara said with a slight wave of her hand, then sauntered toward town.

"The nerve of that one," Ruby said, shaking her head while inhaling deeply. "Well, Eva, I'm very happy for you and George and I wish you all the best, really," Ruby said with a grin.

"And we're all glad that you're safe," Gladys piped up. "Now, give me one more hug." Gladys reached out, embracing Eva once more.

Margie gave Ruby and Gladys one last squeeze, thanking them for attending the wedding, and then the two ladies made their way into the city.

The rest of the wedding guests were grabbing baskets of food and were already heading back to the lodging house. Georgie held Eva's hand tightly as they made their way down the road.

"I can't wait to kiss you all night long, Mrs. Thornber," he whispered in Eva's ear.

Eva briefly closed her eyes, relishing her husband's words, then glanced up at him.

"Georgie Thornber!" she exclaimed teasingly, as she pretended to backhand him gently in the gut.

Georgie smiled widely, looking down at Eva, and she felt entirely grateful that she was going to be able to see that smile every day for the rest of her life.

When they entered the lodging-house, Eva hurried upstairs to change out of her wedding dress and into a more suitable dress for walking through town. She quickly dashed back down the stairs, carrying her weekend travel bag and placing it next to Georgie's by the lodging house's door. The family were all saying their goodbyes to Georgie and Eva before they headed off to the hotel for their honeymoon.

"Now, we'll see you in Oxfordshire in a few days," Elizabeth stated joyously as she hugged Georgie, kissing him on the cheek. "I'm so proud of you, son," she gushed with tears in her eyes. Georgie grinned at his mother's words, knowing he had done the right thing by marrying Eva.

Eva hugged Margie. "Now, Mum, I was going to come back and say goodbye before we leave for Oxfordshire on Monday."

Margie nodded, tears streaming down her face. Then, the bride and groom each went over and embraced the other's family members, saying their last goodbyes before heading to the hotel for the next few days. Ruben Thornber grabbed the small bags they had prepared for the weekend and carried them out to Georgie.

"Congratulations son. I'm very proud that you followed your heart," Ruben said, patting Georgie on the back.

Georgie nodded, satisfied that his father understood how much he loved Eva.

"Thank you, Pop."

Georgie slung his bag around his shoulder, then picked up Eva's suitcase with his good arm.

"You can't carry all that by yourself," Eva exclaimed. "Here, I'll take my bag," she insisted.

"Nonsense, you're not lifting a finger. I'll be fine," he assured her and Eva pouted but was thankful that Georgie was such a gentleman to carry her bag for her. She hooked her arm through Georgie's and they started walking toward the hotel. Eva turned around one last time and waved a final goodbye.

Georgie and Eva arrived at the hotel and stood outside for a moment, gazing up at the large, brick building. They entered inside the lobby, glancing around at the extravagant and charming ambiance. The decor was lovely, with wood trim features, crystal chandeliers, and fashionable furniture. Georgie's eyebrows shot up as he admired the grand hotel foyer. He walked up to the clerk's desk.

"We have a reservation under the name of James Logan," he stated.

"Oh, yes sir, I have your reservation right here. Your room is on the second floor," the man said looking up at Georgie and Eva.

"Thank you," Georgie kindly replied.

"Would you like any assistance today, sir?" the hotel clerk asked.

"Uh, I think we'll be fine, thank you," Georgie replied, peering around the spacious lobby. Eva continued looking around the hotel while Georgie received their room number and key, then the clerk pointed them in the direction of the stairwell.

They, thankfully, only had one story to climb, then continued walking down the corridor in search of their room.

"Here it is," Georgie said, looking over at Eva. He set down the luggage and opened the door.

Eva tried to enter the room immediately, but Georgie stopped her.

"Hold on, I have to carry you over the threshold," he insisted.

"You can't carry me with one good arm," Eva retorted, surprised that he would even suggest such a thing.

"I most certainly can and will. Eva, you're lighter than a feather," he joked.

Eva rolled her eyes at him. "Well, if you insist," she sighed.

In one scoop, Georgie picked her up easily. She held onto him, tightly hold his neck to help ease some of the strain. He smiled at her as they entered the room, then placed her feet carefully on the ground.

"See that wasn't so terrible," he said as she looked at him with a smirk.

Georgie walked back into the corridor to retrieve their bags, closing the door behind him. They both glanced around the hotel room, captivated by the very English decor. The room was overlaid with strong masculine colors, wood features, and pictures of horses. Eva pointed to one of the horse pictures.

"You should feel right at home," she teased.

"I say, this is rather nice," Georgie said, placing the bags down on the floor.

Eva stood across the room, staring at Georgie while her nerves quickened within her. She couldn't understand why she was so nervous as she fixed her eyes upon her husband. Georgie removed his jacket, necktie, and shoes, placing them on a chair adjacent to the bed. Eva slipped her heels off to get more comfortable and stood in the middle of the room, trembling. Georgie walked across the room toward Eva, staring at her fervently. He wrapped his arm around her, looking deeply into her eyes.

"Words cannot describe how beautiful you look today, Eva. When I saw you at the other end of the aisle, I thought…no…" he shook his head, "I *knew* that I was the luckiest man in all of England, to have you as my wife."

Eva was filled with flutters bouncing around inside her. She wanted to be intimate with Georgie very much, but there was something extremely awakening about the moment. Eva suddenly realized that she had never been with anyone physically without drinking the juice first. This was the first time that she would truly feel and experience the reality of it, without being entangled in a fog generated by the toxic substance. Georgie and Eva stood there, continuing to stare at one another wantonly until, finally, Georgie leaned in and kissed Eva softly on the lips. His gentle kisses became more intense but, after a few moments, he noticed that Eva trembled and seemed a little apprehensive. Georgie pulled away, troubled that something was wrong.

"Are you alright?" he asked, sounding as if he worried that she remembered her violent encounter with Lucious or that her body wasn't completely healed from the miscarriage. "If you're not ready for this, I completely understand. You have been through a lot in the last few weeks alone and I'm more than willing to give you whatever time you need," Georgie continued, concerned about Eva.

"Oh, Georgie, you are such a sweet man, but that's not it at all," Eva said shaking her head. "I want nothing more than to be with you intimately, but I just realized that I'm quite nervous. I've never done this before without the juice. I can actually think about what I'm doing for the first time."

Georgie sighed, closed his eyes, and leaned his forehead against Eva's. He breathed in deeply and spoke softly to her.

"Well, this time Eva, it will be real and pure. This time it will be for true love," he said softly.

Eva looked up at him, gazing deeply into his eyes. Then, she ever so slightly tilted her head and firmly pressed her lips against Georgie's.

They continued kissing one another devotedly, while Georgie gracefully unbuttoned Eva's dress. She moved her arms, allowing the garment to slowly slip onto the floor, and he began untying her corset as they continued to kiss passionately. He pulled his mouth away from hers to carefully remove the corset over Eva's head, while she unhinged her undergarments, allowing them to leisurely fall from her body. Eva stood there before her husband completely unafraid and unashamed in her nakedness. Georgie's heart pounded in his chest and his breathing was labored. He pulled away from his wife's lips to look down upon her beauty. He picked Eva up and carried her across the room, placing her delicately down on the bed as they continued kissing one another fervidly.

Georgie and Eva made love for the first time that afternoon, on their wedding day. Eva had never experienced anything more authentic and unadulterated in her entire life. After being with Georgie, she couldn't remember any other times that she had been intimate with a man—because making love to her husband had completely cleansed her of any other time before that day. She finally knew what love was. It wasn't just being intimate with Georgie—it was everything that they had together and that they shared. Their relationship was not based on lust or greed, but on trust, friendship, and unconditional love.

Eva lay against Georgie, resting her head upon his arm. She felt completely safe, knowing that he would never leave her or forsake her. She didn't have to fear that she would wake up the next morning and he wouldn't be there. Eva knew that Georgie was hers and she was his forever and that no one, not even Lucious Paddimir, could take that kind of love away from them.

Thirty-Nine

Georgie and Eva remained in their hotel room for nearly two days straight, talking and laughing together, just like old times. They shared stories of "remember when" and reminisced about the nostalgia of their history together.

"I remember the exact moment that I decided I wanted to marry you," Georgie said with a smirk.

Eva was curious. Sitting up in bed, she waited anxiously for what Georgie was about to say.

"When you picked that fat rat up by the tail and threw it into Mr. Roberts's lodging room. I knew right then and there that you were the girl for me!" Georgie teased.

"Georgie Thornber!" Eva said, slapping him flirtatiously on the chest.

He grabbed her, pulling her down on top of himself and kissing her intensely. A few moments later, he slowly pulled away.

"I decided that, every time you call me Georgie Thornber, I'm going to grab you and kiss you," he said, smiling widely.

"Then, I'll have to do it more often," Eva replied with a coquettish grin.

Eva sat up on the bed, brushing her hair away from her face.

"Really, when was the moment you realized you wanted to marry me?" she asked, shyly lowering her chin while still gazing into his eyes.

Georgie sat up, leaning on his elbow as he lay across the bed thinking.

"Well, I suppose it was the time when our family came over to Grams' for Sunday dinner. I hadn't seen you for several months. I was heading upstairs to fetch you while, at the same time, you were heading downstairs. When I looked up and saw you," Georgie swallowed hard, "you took my breath away. I mean...I've always loved you and was excited to see you, but it was different this time. I felt something richer and I realized that I didn't just love you—but that I was in love with you," he related sincerely.

"Oh, Georgie," Eva said breathily, gently placing her hand on his face. She reached up kissing him softly.

"When your father passed away, I saw how devastated you were and I knew that it was time to start saving money so that I could be the man in your life, taking care of you," he said from the heart.

Eva was speechless for a moment, shaking her head.

"I've always loved you...and I'd always hoped that one day we would marry—but I was never quite sure whether you saw me as more than just a friend. As we got older, well, I think I would have been incredibly crushed had you married someone else. Just the thought of it caused me to behave irrationally," Eva said, looking down at the bed and then glancing back up at him. "I feel absolutely blessed that you chose me...and that you came all the way to the Hall searching for me. I see what we have together and I think of how I almost lost it because of my selfishness and pride," she said as tears filled her eyes.

Georgie sighed and wiped away her tears, taking her hand.

"I can't help it, Eva. I love you and I would do all over again just to be with you," he said lovingly.

Eva didn't know what to think. She had never known a love like this and she felt honored to have been gifted it with a man like Georgie.

"But, I certainly hope that I never have to do anything like that again," he said, eyes wide.

Eva looked up at him seriously. "No, you will never have to again, I promise."

Georgie wrapped his arm around Eva, kissing her passionately and pulling her back down onto the bed. They made love one last time before leaving for Oxfordshire.

* * *

Eva gazed out the hotel room window while sitting up in bed and eating her breakfast. They were going to have to get ready and leave soon if she was going to say goodbye to her mother before catching the train. Georgie sat down next to her.

"Enjoy the room and the ensuite bath because when we get to Oxfordshire, well..." Georgie looked around the room, "it's not going to be anything like this." He raised his eyebrows.

Eva smiled and nodded, then went into the ensuite and prepared a bath. She pinned her hair up again and got dressed in her old clothes. The days of ensuite baths and fancy dresses were over for Eva but she didn't care. None of those things mattered in comparison to being married to Georgie.

They packed their belongings and went down to the clerk's desk in the hotel lobby.

"I wanted to let you know that we're heading out," Georgie said to the clerk, giving him the room number.

"Everything has been taken care of, sir, by Mr. Logan. He paid for the bill this morning."

Georgie was pleased and relieved; he knew he would never have been able to afford to pay the bill. "Thank you," he warmly replied. Georgie was getting ready to pick up the bags when the hotel clerk stopped him.

"Oh, sir, James Logan asked me to give you this."

The desk clerk handed Georgie a white envelope. He began opening it, wondering what could possibly be inside.

"What is it?" Eva inquired.

"I'm not exactly sure," Georgie answered, puzzled. "It looks like a key and map of the farm. It seems "x" marks the spot?" Georgie questioned, confused, trying to think what this could mean. "I suppose we'll have to find out when we get to Oxfordshire," he said shrugging. Folding the white envelope, he placed in his trouser pocket.

Georgie and Eva strolled out the front door of the hotel, then Eva turned around for one last glance at the chic building in which they had spent their first few days together as a married couple.

"Aw," she sighed breathily, "now we have another memory to share when we return to London and see this beautiful building." She gazed up at the tall structure.

Georgie kept his eyes on Eva as she soaked up the last little bit of their honeymoon holiday. "And we will make plenty more memories together, Eva," he reassured her of their future together.

Eva looked at him with a blooming smile and they made their way back to the lodging house to see Eva's mother and Alice one last time before heading home to Oxfordshire.

When they reached the lodging house, Margie was already waiting outside for them. Georgie and Eva both looked very refreshed and Eva had put on a tiny bit of weight—which was good, Margie thought, it meant she was happy.

"Mum!" Eva called out, releasing Georgie's hand as she ran up to her mother.

"Eva!" Margie called, standing with her arms open, waiting to receive her daughter's hug. Margie pulled back, dipping her chin and looking at Eva seriously. "How was your honeymoon?" she asked in a subtle tone, not wanting Georgie to hear her.

Eva looked back at Georgie and her face turned slightly pink.

"It was incredible, Mum, everything was amazing! The hotel was extravagant and elegant—we really have so much to be thankful for with everyone supporting us," Eva gushed and Margie listened with a smile.

"I am so happy for you; but I am going to miss you something terrible," her mother said with a distressed look on her face.

Eva frowned. "I know, I will miss you too, but I will be able to come back and see you very soon hopefully," Eva replied, trying to comfort her mother.

Georgie stayed back, giving Eva and Margie a chance to speak alone.

"Come on George!" Margie called out, waving for Georgie to join them. Margie grabbed ahold of Georgie, hugging him tightly. "You take care of her now," she said, looking up at him.

"I promise ma'am. I will do everything in my power to be a wonderful husband and provider for Eva," Georgie assured her and Margie nodded, trying to hold back tears.

"I know you will, George."

Margie held onto both of them for a moment longer, then released them.

"I'm going to head in and say goodbye to Grams," Georgie said with a nod.

He walked up to his grandmother's door, knocking several times, until Alice finally answered.

"Georgie!" she exclaimed. "How was your honeymoon?" she inquired immediately.

Georgie swallowed hard and his face turned apple red.

"It was nice Grams, thanks for asking," he replied quickly, wanting to switch the subject. "Eva and I have to get back to the farm. I wanted to say thank you for helping us have such a beautiful wedding."

Alice grinned. "You're welcome. I know it wasn't easy to wait a few more days, but I hope you both felt it was worth it in the end."

Georgie nodded his head. "Yes, we certainly do." He gave his grandmother a good squeeze and a kiss on the cheek.

"Thank you for keeping your promise, Georgie, to love Eva no matter what. You're a good man," Alice said with tears in her eyes.

Georgie nodded, smiling brightly at his grandmother.

"Alright, you tell Eva that I'll be missing her and that I expect you to come visit me," Alice commanded and Georgie nodded in return.

"Goodbye, Grams," he said with a slight wave.

"Goodbye, George—take care of yourselves!" Alice said, smiling happily as she watched Georgie walk through the corridor and head back outside to the front of the lodging house.

Margie and Eva chatted away.

"I hate to be the bearer of bad news, but we really have to get going, Eva," Georgie stated.

Margie sighed and gave a sorrowful smile. "Alright, just one last hug," she said, enveloping them both in her arms thoroughly. She finally released them and Georgie looked at her sincerely.

"Now, when Eva and I get a place of our own, we would like you to come live with us. If that sounds like something you would like to do," Georgie offered.

Margie's eyes grew wide and her mouth fell open. "Oh... well, that's very sweet of you and we'll see when it gets to that point, but right now you two need to make a life together without old mum in the way," Margie said, nodding her head.

Eva looked over at Georgie in agreement. They needed their privacy and time to allow their marriage to grow. Georgie took Eva's hand.

"Are you ready?" he asked.

Eva looked at her mother; Margie had tears rapidly flowing down her cheeks. She pressed her lips together tightly and nodded her head at Georgie. Eva turned away from her mother, only glancing back once more, then they made their way down the road—beginning their journey as husband and wife.

*   *   *

Lucious had been keeping his eye on Georgie and Eva since they entered the hotel. When he wasn't watching them, he had someone else waiting outside, on the lookout, just in case they exited the building. Lucious was becoming bored of waiting, as they hadn't left the hotel for two days. He couldn't understand how they could stay cooped up in such a small hotel room together for so long. He was about to summon one of his minions to keep watch over them, when he glanced up and saw Georgie and Eva walking out of the hotel. Leering at them, he saw how happy they looked together. Their deep love and affection for one another ate away at Lucious. How he loathed the sight of them. He hated the way Georgie would stare at Eva, always gawking at her as if she was his prized possession—it sickened him.

Lucious followed Georgie and Eva to the lodging house, where Eva's mother lived. He waited in the distance, standing behind some carriages and watching them carefully. Lucious thought that, from the looks of it, Eva and Georgie were saying their goodbyes.

"Where are you two going?" he whispered to himself.

Finally, Eva and Georgie began making their way back through town and Lucious cautiously walked behind them while fluidly making his way through the crowded streets.

They strode into the train station and purchased a pair of tickets. Lucious still wasn't sure what their destination was, so he continued tracing their steps, following them inside the waiting area. Georgie and Eva stood off to the side, doing their best to be alone and away from other travelers. Lucious knew of a short cut through some tunnels, leading over to the other side of the waiting area in which Georgie and Eva were standing. He carefully made his way through the tunnel that leads to a second tunnel, exiting in the exact spot where he had seen them standing. Lucious was acting cautiously in order not to be seen. He carefully gazed down the second tunnel before entering inside, making sure that no one was coming from the opposite direction. When he glanced into the tunnel, he saw Georgie with Eva at the other end, hiding in order not be seen by the other waiting passengers. Georgie had Eva pressed up against the tunnel wall and was kissing her intensely. Arousal of anger inflamed Lucious as he slowly strolled closer toward them. They were paying him no attention, which infuriated him all the more. Lucious slammed his cane harshly against the tunnel wall creating a loud echoing sound. They both jumped and Eva let out a short scream, covering her mouth, as they looked up, wide-eyed, to see Lucious standing before them.

Eva's heart raced and fear gripped her at the sight of Lucious sneaking up on them.

"What are you doing here!?" she shouted angrily.

"Oh, I just wanted to congratulate the happy, newlywed couple," Lucious stated in a snarky tone.

"What do you want, Lucious?" Georgie responded indignantly, blocking off Eva between himself and the wall while she clutched his arm tightly.

Lucious gave a slight laugh, "I think you know what I want."

Georgie stared at Lucious hostilely for a moment. "Yes, and you can't have her. She is my wife!" he spouted back.

"Yes, that does pose a problem, I suppose. Unless, of course, Eva desires to come home with me," Lucious said, gazing at her enticingly.

Georgie felt fury rising inside him. He was doing his best to suppress his anger but, with every second that Lucious was standing there, it was becoming more difficult for him to do so.

Lucious leisurely opened his jacket pocket, retrieving a flask of the juice. He turned the top of the flask slowly while gazing teasingly at Eva with raised eyebrows. Placing the juice flask high into the air, he nodded, then brought the flask to his mouth, taking a tantalizing, slow drink while closing his eyes, savoring every drop. He removed the flask and casually wiped his mouth.

"Aw, that's better...isn't it Eva?" he questioned, coaxing her with the juice.

Eva's breathing became heavy as she stared at the shiny flask. She remembered the ecstasy and tranquility that the liquid substance caused her to feel.

"So, Eva, would you like a drink?" Lucious asked, dipping his head down and offering her the juice while holding out the flask. He nodded his head, motioning for Eva to come near him and take the flask from his hand. "Come here, love, you may have all the juice you desire with me," he said tauntingly, looking over at Georgie. Lucious could tell that Eva desired the juice desperately.

Georgie looked over at Eva, whose eyes were fixated upon the flask. He knew she was contemplating going over to Lucious to retrieve the flask from his hand.

"Eva, please don't!" Georgie pleaded with her anxiously, trying to get her to look at him.

Eva's eyes remained on the juice, captivated, as she pressed her lips together and inhaled small, rapid breaths of air.

"Eva, I love you, please don't," Georgie said, disappointedly shaking his head, begging her to not take the juice.

Eva swallowed and blinked several times, then pulled her eyes away from the flask to look over at Georgie. She continued looking at him while inhaling deeply.

"Oh, my goodness," she said breathily, shaking her head and coming to her senses. Then she looked back at Lucious. "No. No! I don't want your juice and I certainly don't want you!" she yelled angrily.

Georgie closed his eyes briefly, relieved that Eva didn't go over to Lucious. He knew that seeing the flask of juice before her eyes was almost too much for her to handle.

"I've seen what your juice does to people, Lucious—it should be illegal!" Georgie shouted at him.

Lucious retorted, "Aw, but, somehow, it isn't." He pouted tilting his head and giving a heartless shrug. "Well, I suppose I'm just going to have to move on—and here I thought we had something special Eva," Lucious said, dipping his chin and looking deeply into her eyes, trying to entice her.

She peered at him for a moment.

"Good!" she replied with certainty. "I stopped loving you months ago," she said hostilely. "I love Georgie more than I ever loved you," she concluded, glancing lovingly over at Georgie.

Lucious was seething—he wanted to go over and grab Eva by the hair, drag her to her knees, and force her to submit to him. Lucious inhaled deeply and raised his chin high into the air.

"Oh well. You already made me my investment back anyway," Lucious stated haughtily, then looked over at Georgie. "Say, George, I enjoy getting feedback from my customers. Have I taught Eva well?" he asked with a devilish grin.

Georgie swallowed, tightening his fist, and Eva started rubbing his hand trying to help him calm down.

"You see, Eva, whores like you are rubbish. Disposable," Lucious scoffed, waving his hand, trying to hurt Eva and provoke Georgie.

Georgie was about to step forward but stopped, knowing that Lucious wanted him to lose control so he would have reason to hit him with his cane.

"How dare you speak to my wife that way!" Georgie shouted.

Lucious began laughing when, suddenly, the train pulled up into the railway station.

"It's time for us to go," Georgie said harshly.

Georgie didn't want to turn his back on Lucious, so he grabbed the luggage while continuing to keep his eyes on him. Eva's was trembling as she held her hands tightly secured around Georgie's arm and they began walking away.

"George!" Lucious called out and Georgie turned around, looking up at him. "I wonder—is Eva as good for you as she was for me?" Lucious inquired, giving one last jeer while peering at him with a sly smirk.

Georgie stepped forward; he wanted to beat Lucious to a pulp for how he was speaking about Eva.

"Please, Georgie," Eva said calmly, placing her hand on Georgie's chest to stop him from attacking Lucious. "He's not worth it, we have to catch our train," she said as Georgie continued glaring at him; then, they slowly turned around while he guarded Eva in front of himself. Entering the crowd, they disappeared in a herd of people.

"I will hunt you down and kill you both!" Lucious yelled, threatening them, but Georgie and Eva were already gone. Lucious lost them in the crowd of people and let out a humph. Sharply turning around—he found himself face to face with Magistrate Logan, who stood there, leering at him. Lucious jerked back, not expecting to see the magistrate standing behind him.

The magistrate had paid the bill at the hotel and then waited around to see whether Lucious would make an appearance. After briefly seeing him at the wedding breakfast, he assumed that Lucious would be waiting for Georgie and Eva to come out of the hotel.

"Not much fun being snuck up on, is it, Lucious?" the magistrate asked condescendingly.

"Magistrate Logan. What an unpleasant surprise," Lucious sneered.

"I've been following you as you followed them," he said simply. "You're a very persistent little fowler," Magistrate Logan observed.

"Well, I do my best," Lucious said with a smirk, peering at the magistrate.

Lucious slowly strolled toward Magistrate Logan, swinging his cane.

"And I have to ask myself, why would a magistrate give a damn about a poor lad like George and his whore of a wife?" Lucious sneered, tilting his head.

The magistrate leered at Lucious, provoked by his words.

"Perhaps because I am tired of watching them be robbed, beaten, and raped by you!" he shouted back and Lucious let out a slight laugh.

"What are you talking about?" Lucious inquired, curious about how the magistrate knew everything, especially the rape.

"An eye witness has come forward. They saw you rape Eva and—as I'm sure you know, Lucious—an eyewitness to a rape means that the perpetrator is imprisoned for life."

Lucious' eyes turned black, piercing the magistrate. He released a distressed sigh.

"What do you want, Logan?" he asked, glowering at him.

The magistrate came closer to Lucious. "I want my one hundred quid back," he stated firmly and Lucious' eyes grew large.

"Aaah, so that's where the little bugger got the money... from you?" Lucious questioned.

The magistrate ignored him. "And I want you to leave Georgie, Eva, and their families alone. Fix your attention elsewhere, Lucious," he demanded.

Lucious stared at Magistrate Logan hostilely.

"And what if I don't?" he asked haughtily.

"Then I will have to take Eva's case to Crown Court... And, as a barrister of the law, I will most certainly send you to prison," the magistrate promised. "But if you pay me back and leave them alone—with them never reporting seeing you again—then you will be free to go and continue running your house, as usual."

Lucious inhaled deeply and sighed. "And what happens when everyone finds out that you have attended the Hall... *magistrate*?" Lucious questioned, mockingly nodding his head. "Because I will certainly make that known. I have my own eyewitnesses, you know" Lucious threatened.

Magistrate Logan stared at Lucious. "Yes, I thought of that and I know my reputation would be ruined. I would most likely lose my position as magistrate," he concurred. "But I am still a barrister of law and that would not change!" the magistrate yelled, shaking his head as he strode quickly toward Lucious to stand face to face with him. "You might be powerful and influential, Lucious Paddimir—but so am I!" He looked Lucious harshly in the eyes. "If you take my offer, then I expect to have one hundred quid on my desk by tomorrow afternoon. If I don't have the money by then, I will proceed with charges," the magistrate threatened, giving Lucious one, last, hard stare.

Magistrate Logan turned abruptly, walking back through the passageway. Lucious started laughing hysterically for a few moments; then, gritting his teeth, his demeanor quickly changed into anger. Lucious threw his cane and released a loud roar that resounded through the tunnels.

*   *   *

Georgie and Eva stepped onto the train and shuffled on their way, finding a couple of seats toward the back. Georgie glanced around, making sure that Lucious wasn't still following them. He didn't see him anywhere—but that didn't mean that he wasn't on the train. They both sat there quietly for a while, when Eva finally spoke up, "I'm so sorry. I would never want to be with Lucious again, never...but the juice."

She closed her eyes while tears ran down her cheeks. "It's just so hard and, when I saw him drinking it, I remembered how it felt," Eva said lowering her head in embarrassment. Raising her head again, she gazed sadly into Georgie's eyes.

"Then I looked at you and I realized that I don't need the juice anymore. I have you now," she said, wiping the tears from her face.

Georgie turned to her. "I understand. It's a drug, Eva, and Lucious knows that, which is why he enticed you with it in the first place. He also despises the fact that now you are my wife and you are happy with me," Georgie explained, trying to let Eva know that he understood why she behaved that way.

Eva felt repentant for the way she acted and lowered her head in shame. Georgie could tell that she was feeling guilty for desiring the juice.

"Eva, it's alright to be enticed. It's just not alright to give in to it—because it's not what's best for you," he said, shaking his head, and Eva looked up at him.

"So, you're not angry with me?" she asked, surprised.

Georgie turned toward her, looking at her sympathetically. "No, Eva, not at all. I feel bad for you. I wish I could take your pain and experience it myself instead, so that I would feel the power of addiction and not you." Georgie shook his head, trying to reassure her of how much he cared for her.

Eva gazed deeply into his eyes. She couldn't believe that this man could love her so much that he wanted to take her pain upon himself.

"Oh, Georgie," she said with a sigh, "I love you so much." She looked at him again.

Georgie smiled softly, caressing Eva's cheek with the back of his finger.

"I love you, I think, perhaps even more than you realize," he replied tenderly.

Eva knew that Georgie was right and that, with each passing day, she was beginning to understand just how much he loved her—so much more than she ever even knew was possible. Eva wrapped her arms around Georgie's arm, placing her head on his shoulder. They both gazed out of the train window in silence, making their way to Oxfordshire.

Forty

The train pulled up to the station at half-past five and Georgie's father Ruben was there to pick them up in the farm wagon.

"Let me give you a hand with your luggage, son," Ruben said, retrieving the bags from their hands and loading them onto the wagon.

The Thornbers had already taken the rest of Eva's belongings with them to Oxfordshire when they traveled back from London on the day of the wedding. Eva climbed into the back of the wagon with Georgie and they cuddled together all the way to the farm.

"So, how was your holiday?" Mr. Thornber asked as he held the reigns.

They both looked at one another, but neither one of them said anything for a moment. Finally, Eva blurted, "It was brilliant!" saying it loud enough so that Ruben could hear her over the trotting horses. Georgie looked at her, surprised, giving her a smirk and raising his eyebrows as he cleared his throat.

"Yes, it was very nice," he added.

Mr. Thornber grinned. "That's good to hear," he replied, tapping the reigns to move the horse along.

The farm was only a couple miles away from the train station. Eva leaned against Georgie while she inhaled the fresh country air.

"I see why you love it out here, it's beautiful," she said, looking up at him with a twinkle in her eyes.

Georgie smiled brightly. He had longed for Eva to be with him in Oxfordshire for so long and it warmed his heart to hear that she was already enjoying the landscape.

The wagon turned a corner and headed down a long lane with trees in full bloom lining the entrance of the property. The magistrate's farm sat high up, on a large hill overlooking the town and countryside. The wagon stopped in front of the horse barn, which was across the lane from the Thornber cottage. Georgie held Eva's hand as she jumped down from the wagon and Ruben helped Georgie grab the bags.

"Elizabeth and the girls have prepared a special dinner to welcome you home," Ruben said.

"Oh, that's very kind of them," Eva replied happily, appreciating their hospitality.

She had not eaten since breakfast and her stomach was rumbling.

"Actually, Pop, we'll meet you inside; I need to show Eva something," Georgie said, sounding a bit nervous.

"Alright, I'll let your mother know," Ruben replied and continued into the cottage.

Georgie was beginning to feel anxious about showing Eva the shed in which they would have to live before he could get it fixed up properly. He had tried to not think about it until it was time to reveal their new home to her. He led her over to the horse shed and her eyes grew wide, realizing that this was their new home. The white paint on the shed was wearing off and it looked like any other ordinary old shed.

"Now, I know this isn't at all what you're used to, but I'm afraid that—until we save enough money to either fix it up or buy a place of our own—it will have to do," Georgie said with a distressed look on his face.

Eva was beginning to feel very anxious, staring at the outside of the shed. Georgie opened the door and Eva peered inside but couldn't see very well because there was no light. There was no light at all, except through the cracks and crevices of the shed walls and the open door. When Eva's eyes had finally adjusted, she looked around at the very small, damp, cold quarters. The only things in the shed were Eva's belongings, sitting in the back corner, and a wood-paneled floor that had been laid. There were no windows, furniture, washbasins, nor a fireplace to keep them warm. Eva sucked in a deep breath and did her best to refrain from pressing her lips together. She gazed around, knowing that it was her fault that the shed wasn't finished in the first place. Georgie had been trying to get it done before he asked her to marry him, but she had muddled up his plans.

"Well, if I'm here alone with you, then it's perfect," she said, quite content.

"Really?" Georgie asked, extremely surprised.

Eva walked over to him, taking his hand and placing her arm around his waist.

"What I said is still true—we could put a blanket out in the middle of the field and I would be happy. We only need a place in which we can be alone and where we can spend time together. What more do we need?" Eva asked, showing Georgie that their love was enough for her.

Georgie stared at Eva in awe. "Just when I thought I couldn't love you more, I find myself doing so," he said, looking at her affectionately. He turned, glancing around the shed. "Well, I'll have to build a fireplace first and then I'll add some windows."

Eva smiled and Georgie walked over to her, dipping his head down and kissing her fervidly. After he pulled away, Eva glanced around the empty shed once more.

"And some blankets would be nice," she suggested, giving him a clenched smile.

"I think I can handle that," he replied affirmatively.

Georgie placed his arm around Eva and they walked over to his family's cottage. Elizabeth, Marta, and Mary welcomed the newlyweds. Then, they all sat around the table to have a nice meal together.

"So, where are you two planning to live?" Elizabeth inquired while spooning out some vegetables onto her plate.

Georgie inhaled deeply. "Well, I suppose we'll stay in the shed," he answered with a grimace on his face.

Elizabeth looked over at Ruben, concerned.

"I thought the magistrate said he was going to work something out for the two of you?" she asked while Ruben scratched his head.

Georgie didn't answer her right away.

"I don't mind," Eva spoke up.

He felt horrible for not having a proper place for them to live. He thought, once again, how this was not how he had wanted to start his marriage.

Georgie suddenly remembered the map and key that he received at the hotel from Magistrate Logan. He had forgotten all about it with the commotion at the train station.

"I just remembered," he said, pulling the map and key from his trouser pocket. "Magistrate Logan left this for me at the hotel clerk's desk this morning." Georgie handed it to Ruben, who took a good look at the hand-drawn map.

"I know where this is," Ruben said, "it's on the property next door that the magistrate bought last year."

"Have you ever seen what's over there?" Georgie questioned.

"Well, I've farmed over there many times, but this seems to be somewhere back in the woods. Why don't I walk you two out there and we'll go take a look before it gets dark," Rueben suggested, and they agreed.

Georgie hoped that it was better living quarters than the shed by the barn, but he wasn't entirely sure and didn't want to get his hopes up.

* * *

After dinner, Georgie and Eva walked outside together with Elizabeth and Ruben, while Georgie's sisters washed the dishes. Elizabeth and Ruben were standing on the cottage porch while Eva and Georgie walked down toward the horse barn.

"You notice how he can't keep his eyes off of her," Elizabeth mentioned smiling. "Or his hands for that matter," she added, looking over at Ruben with a smirk.

"Yes, I noticed," he replied, nodding as he watched Georgie and Eva holding one another and looking out across the rolling hills. "I wasn't sure if he was doing the right thing by marrying her," Ruben admitted.

Elizabeth looked up at him in surprise. "Did you say anything to him?" she asked.

Ruben pursed his lips and looked down at the cottage porch. "I may have said something along those lines. I was just trying to make sure that he really loved her and wasn't pursuing her out of guilt," Ruben explained, glancing back up.

Elizabeth sighed and closed her eyes. "Well, he obviously truly loves Eva," she said without a doubt and Ruben nodded, then they continued watching the young couple from a distance.

"Hey George, we should probably head out before the sun starts setting!" Ruben called out.

"Sounds good!" Georgie yelled back, then looked over at Eva expectantly.

"Would you like to take one of the horses?" Georgie asked excitedly.

Eva was tickled by how enthusiastic he sounded about taking her on a horse ride.

"Yes, that would be rather nice," she replied, smiling up at him.

Georgie called out to his father, "I'm going to grab a couple stallions from the barn to ride over to the property!"

Ruben nodded, then came down to help Georgie prepare the horses.

Eva walked up to the porch to chat with Elizabeth.

"That was a lovely dinner you prepared for us. Thank you," Eva said cordially.

"You're very welcome," Elizabeth warmly replied. "I want you to know, Eva, that we are very blessed to have you as a part of our family." Her voice was most sincere.

Eva looked over at her, surprised by her kind words.

"Thank you, that means a great deal to me. I love your son very much," Eva said simply and seriously.

Elizabeth smiled back brightly. "I know, and George, well…" Elizabeth sighed. "It's been very obvious, for a long time now—that he was in love with you. I'm not sure whether he has ever looked at another woman," Elizabeth spoke honestly.

Eva blushed and her heart felt full, hearing Georgie's mother talk about his affections toward her.

"I mean, any man who travels by foot for three weeks until his legs completely give out in search of the woman he loves—well, it sounds like a fairytale, doesn't it?" Elizabeth said letting out a slight laugh while crossing her arms.

Eva looked up at her stunned. "He did what for me?" Eva asked and Elizabeth could tell that Eva had no idea what she was referring to.

"He never told you what he went through to find you?" Elizabeth questioned.

Eva looked down, embarrassed, shaking her head.

"Oh, I'm sorry Eva. I just assumed you knew."

Elizabeth felt bad for saying anything.

Eva inhaled deeply, looking out at the fields and wondering why Georgie had never told her all that he had endured while searching for her.

*   *   *

Georgie realized how difficult it was to work with the horses with only one arm. He thought he could manage pretty well on his own but, after trying to attach the saddle with one hand, he knew he wouldn't be able to properly take care of them without extra help. Ruben helped Georgie fix up the horses and, soon, they were exiting the barn on the trotting stallions.

"Come on Eva!" Georgie called, motioning her over and grinning proudly.

Eva jaunted over to the horses, looking up at Georgie.

"Climb on up," he said while patting the saddle in front of him.

When Eva had ridden with Claudia, she had sat behind her on the saddle so that she could hold on to Claudia.

"Like this?" Eva questioned, referring to sitting in front of him.

"Yes, I've got you," Georgie assured her as he helped pull her up onto the horse using his good arm.

Eva slung her leg over the side of the horse, sitting on the saddle in front of Georgie. He pulled Eva's body closer to his own, scooting her back so she could lean right up against him.

"There you are," he said, leaning forward to kiss her on the cheek.

Eva blushed and her heart pounded. There was something about riding the horse with Georgie that made Eva feel regal. And it was very romantic, she thought.

"Alright, Pop, where are we headed?" Georgie asked and Ruben pulled out the map from his pocket.

"You still have the key?" he asked Georgie.

"Yes, sir, I do," Georgie replied.

Ruben nodded his head, then made a clicking noise with his tongue to get the horse trotting and Georgie followed his lead. They rode past the farm's machinery barns, the main house, and out into the farming fields, until Ruben stopped.

"This is where the original property line ends," he said pointing. "Now, over there is where the farmland continues onto the new property. You remember working out there last fall?" Georgie nodded his head. "But right here, in front of us, where the woods start is where I think we need to go," Ruben stated and Georgie agreed, following him into the woods.

There wasn't a clear path from the magistrate's farm through the woods, so they had to make their way slowly through the thickets and leaves. Suddenly, Ruben spotted something through the forest in the distance.

"Hey, George, I think I see something up ahead," Ruben called out while peering through the clutter of trees.

Eva was peeking around Ruben, trying to see what was in front of them. Georgie moved the horse over and they both set their eyes on a small cabin in the middle of the woods. Georgie closed his eyes for a moment, thanking God, and hoping that it was a home for him and Eva to live in. Eva's eyes lit up at the sight of the small quaint cabin sitting back in the woods. The cabin was at least five times the size of the shed and looked to be in pretty good condition. Georgie helped Eva down from the horse and no one said a word as they walked up to the cabin. It had a small porch with a rocking chair near a window. They all climbed the rickety stairs leading up to the front door. The steps creaked as they walked up them. Georgie took the key out of his pocket and placed it in the lock. He turned the key and they heard a clicking sound. Georgie looked up at Eva eagerly and she smiled at him, expectantly raising her brows.

The cabin had one, large, open space—with a large, brick, two-sided cooking fireplace, that sat in the middle of the room as a separation. There were a set of cupboards, a water basin, and a small kitchen table with chairs on one side of the room. A bed, a bathtub, and a woven rug were on the other side of it. There was no wardrobe, no sofa, sitting chairs, or a chest of drawers. Eva opened the cupboard and found only a few pots and pans inside, along with some mugs. The kitchen table had one lantern sitting on top. Everyone was looking around the cabin in awe.

Eva finally spoke up. "Well, I say, if this is ours…then, Georgie, we are very blessed indeed." Eva thought that this was much better than living in the tiny shed. She noticed that there was a letter on the kitchen counter. Clasping the letter in her hand, she carried it over to Georgie.

He opened the letter and began reading it silently to himself. Georgie's eyes grew wide and his jaw dropped as he read the letter.

"Well, Georgie, what does it say?" Eva asked anxiously.

Georgie glanced up at her and smiled. "This was the old owners hunting cabin and Magistrate Logan says that he welcomes us to live here," Georgie said with hope in his eyes.

"He also says that he has no use for it," Georgie continued and Eva walked over, sitting down on the bed.

She ran her hand over the quilted blanket, feeling its soft pillow-like form.

"He says that he knows it needs some work but hopes that I will help fix it up while we live here," Georgie stated enthusiastically.

Eva smiled brightly as she glanced over at Georgie when, suddenly, his face dropped.

"Oh," he said solemnly.

"What's wrong?" Eva asked, concerned, standing up in haste and walking over to place her hand on Georgie's arm.

"There's no outhouse, so I'll have to build one right away— but that shouldn't take too long," he said looking over at her.

Ruben spoke up, "I'll help you this week and we'll get it done for the two of you."

Georgie looked over at him smiling.

"Oh, Georgie!" Eva said excitedly. "I can't believe that we have our own home!" she exclaimed, wrapping her arms around his neck and kissing him firmly on the mouth.

Georgie was in shock, thinking that somehow he was going to have to get the shed fixed up in a hurry. Now they actually had this suitable home—which was much nicer than the shed would ever have been even if he had fixed it up in the first place.

They took one last glance around the cabin, then made their way back to the Thornber cottage on the other side of the farm.

"It's a long way over there, George. You might want to ask the magistrate if you can take a horse along with you at night."

Georgie nodded. He thought that he would like to purchase a few horses of his own, eventually, and build a small barn next to the cabin.

"The wagon is still hooked up to the mares, so I'll take you and Eva out to the cabin tonight along with your belongings. But, before you head out there, you should probably take Eva into the main house and show her where she needs to be tomorrow morning for duty," Ruben suggested.

"Oh yes, that's right, thanks, Pop!" Georgie replied cheerfully, greatly appreciating his father's help.

Georgie and Eva strolled up to the main house just before the sun started setting. He led Eva downstairs to the servant quarters and began introducing everyone to his new wife. Alice, the young maid, was hurrying around the house when she popped out from behind a corner and ran directly into Georgie and Eva.

"Oh, George!" she exclaimed, surprised to see him and smiling widely.

Eva noticed that Alice's eyes lit up at the sight of Georgie and she felt a pang hit her in the pit of her gut.

"Alice!" Georgie replied, pleased to see her as well.

"You are just the gal we're trying to find," he stated confidently.

"I am?" she asked, pleased to hear it as she stared up at Georgie all wide-eyed. She had not even noticed that Eva was standing there nor the fact that Georgie was holding someone's hand.

"Yes, I want to introduce you to my wife, Mrs. Eva Thornber."

Alice's face dropped and her mouth slightly gaped open as she looked over at Eva and then back over at Georgie. "Oh, I had no idea you were married," Alice said sounding surprised.

"Oh, well, I told you about Eva when we met. We were only married this past Saturday," Georgie explained and Alice squinted, trying to understand.

She looked over at Eva again, smiling as she wiped her hand on her apron. "Well, how do you do..." she greeted, extending her hand toward Eva.

Eva didn't budge, caught up in thinking about how Georgie and Alice obviously had affection for one another.

"Eva?" Georgie questioned, slightly nudging her arm.

"Oh, I'm sorry, I was deep in thought...How do you do," she replied, shaking Alice's hand and trying to give her best fake smile.

Georgie cleared his throat. "Eva is going to be Miss Cora's new lady's maid and she starts tomorrow. I thought it was best to introduce you to one another this evening," he said, proudly.

Alice was gazing up at him affectionately and Eva could tell that, even though he was married, Alice still had an interest in him. Eva began pressing her lips tightly together as anger welled up inside of her.

"Oh yes, that's right, Mrs. Woodward, the housekeeper, said that you would be starting tomorrow morning," Alice said pointing her finger in the air, reminding herself. "Well, let me go fetch you a uniform." She turned at once and quickly went to retrieve it. Several moments later, she returned, holding a lady's maid uniform and handing it to Eva.

"Thank you," Eva replied stoically.

"What time should Eva be here in the morning?" Georgie asked.

"Well, you really should be here by half-past five in case Miss Cora should need anything upon waking," she stared up at Georgie while he gave her one of his glistening smiles. Alice's face beamed in return, as her eyes tightly fixed upon his.

Eva wanted to bolt out of the servants' quarters and never return. She felt completely ignored as they both focused on one another, speaking about her as if she were a child.

"Well, that works out, I have to be at the horse barn by then so we can walk out for work together," Georgie stated, glancing over at Eva.

Eva began breathing heavily and continued staring at Alice, thinking how Alice was very pretty. She finally looked up at Georgie.

"Yes, that will work out perfectly," she said, flashing another false grin at Georgie and then at Alice pretending to be alright.

"Well, it was nice seeing you again Alice," Georgie said with a cordial smile.

Alice was gazing at George fixing her eyes intently upon him. "It was very nice seeing you again, George," she said, giving him a coquettish grin, then she quickly turned and rounded the corner.

Georgie held Eva's hand as he led her out of the servants' quarters, making their way back over to the wagon. He sighed.

"It is going to be a long walk from the cabin to the horse barn every morning..." Georgie said, rubbing his hand through his hair and looking at the distance between the two locations. "…seems it may even be a mile away if not further?" he asked.

Eva wasn't listening, her head was spinning. She thought that Georgie hadn't even looked at another girl, but there was obviously a connection between him and Alice.

Georgie noticed that Eva wasn't responding to him. "Are you alright?" he asked, looking down at her in concern. When Eva glanced up at him, there were tears in her eyes. Georgie stopped and wrapped his arm around her.

"What is it? What's wrong?" he wondered.

Eva didn't want to say anything, but she finally pulled herself away from him and spoke. "Alice...she's a very pretty girl."

Georgie pulled back, looking down at her in confusion—not saying anything for a moment.

"Do you think she is a pretty girl?" Eva asked, looking up at him intently.

Georgie was silent for a moment with a bewildered look on his face.

"Well...yes, I suppose, but why are you crying?" he asked, leaning in closer and wiping the tears from her cheeks with his fingers.

"She's fond of you, Georgie!" Eva spouted distressed.

Georgie leaned back, surprised by Eva's comment.

"Eva...we are married...and you know that I love you," he said, astonished she would even think of such a thing.

"So, what does that matter! I watched married men come back week after week to the Hall. Some of them even spoke about their wives and how they loved their companionship but needed to find pleasure elsewhere," Eva spouted, moving her hands wildly.

Georgie stared down at Eva heartbroken. He realized that there were things she had seen and experienced at the Hall that had skewed her interpretation of love and marriage. It never crossed his mind that Eva would be concerned that he would have an affair.

"Eva, that is not love," he said, seriously shaking his head, looking her steadily in the eyes.

Eva thought about bringing up how Magistrate Logan was one of those men, but she knew it would do no good. Tears continued rolling down her face.

"I saw it, there was a connection between the two of you!" Eva swallowed hard. "Be honest with me, was there ever a moment when you considered marrying Alice?"

Georgie's eyes grew large and his breathing became rapid. He had wondered if he could marry Alice, but it was only when he wasn't sure if Eva loved him and would marry him. Georgie said nothing for a few seconds, then gazed down at the ground.

"So it's true then!" she shouted at him.

"Eva, you don't understand," he said as she turned, marching away from him. Georgie didn't know what to think. His heart was pounding and he was grieved that Eva was so upset. He rushed toward her.

"Eva, please...wait and listen to me!" he pleaded.

Eva continued furiously marching back toward the wagon.

He didn't want to grab her, knowing what Lucious had done, so he started talking while they walked quickly together. "Eva, my father asked me what I would do if you didn't want to marry me and I wasn't sure," he said with great fervor.

Eva stopped and turned waiting for his explanation. Georgie closed his eyes and inhaled a few deep breaths, then continued explaining himself.

"I had come to the farm to ask the magistrate for the advance. While I was here, my pop pulled me aside and asked me some difficult questions. One of those questions was—what I would do if you didn't love me and wanted to stay with Lucious at the Hall," Georgie squeezed his eyes closed for a moment at the terrible thought of her desiring to be with Lucious. "I had pretty much assumed that you loved me and that we would marry, but I couldn't be positive that you felt the same way," he explained, frowning.

Eva stood there staring at him wide-eyed, her heart hurting for him as she listened to his story.

"So, the next day, I went to the servant quarters to take a bath. When I finished bathing and dressed myself, I decided to grab a snack. I was meeting with the magistrate to ask him for the advance and I didn't want to leave the house. There was a bowl of fruit on the table. I picked up an apple and noticed Alice sitting alone doing some needlework. So, I went over to introduce myself, never seeing her before at the farm. We spoke to one another for only a few minutes," Georgie said, adamantly shaking his head. "During that time, I did wonder whether I could possibly marry someone other than you. Also, at that same moment, I decided that I could not," he said solemnly, opening his heart fully to her.

Eva placed her hands over her face and began crying. Georgie didn't know what to do, so he brought her to his chest and allowed her to weep. Eva sobbed, wondering why she had never asked Georgie whether he had been intimate with someone other than her. She had never thought about it before because he seemed so set on the two of them remaining chaste before the wedding.

After a few moments, Eva lifted her head, wiping away her tears. "I should have asked this a long time ago—but have you ever been intimate with another woman? Georgie, please just tell me the truth," she asked firmly, looking up at him sadly.

Georgie glanced down at her astonished. "Eva, my first kiss was with you in the cottage the day before I asked you to marry me," he said, gazing down at her most sincerely and Eva felt relieved.

"I'm sorry, but I just don't trust men, Georgie," she said, squeezing her eyes closed while shaking her head. "Lucious slept with other women behind my back when I thought he was only with me. I even overheard him with one of the prostitutes in his bedroom late one evening."

Georgie's eyes grew large and he swallowed hard.

"Oh my," he sighed, disheartened for Eva.

Georgie thought that he had heard everything that had happened at the Hall but, apparently, he had not. The entire thing made his stomach turn and his heart broke for her all the more. He leaned in closer to Eva, staring seriously into her eyes.

"Eva, I want you to know that I would never, ever do that to you. When I said my marriage vows, I meant them. I don't know how other men separate love and intimacy, but I cannot. I wondered, for only a brief moment, whether I could marry someone else..." Georgie swallowed hard, "...and then I thought about you—and I knew that I could not marry another woman. Eva, you are my love and the only one I can ever love," he stated honestly as Eva began crying again.

"I'm sorry. I'm so, so sorry," she said as she embraced him tightly.

Georgie held Eva for a while, comforting her. He gently pulled away so he could look into her eyes once more.

"And I don't care if Alice is fond of me or whatever the case may be—I love you," he stated firmly.

Eva reached up and softly kissed him on the lips. She had felt silly for thinking that Georgie wouldn't be faithful to her. He had only ever given her unconditional love, but Lucious had confused her about what love truly represented.

"Will you please do me a favor?" Eva asked, looking up at him wide-eyed. "Will you keep your distance from Alice?" she asked.

Georgie looked down at her lovingly. "Of course," he replied. Georgie had already planned to stay away from Alice even if she didn't have feelings toward him. He didn't want to be around her at all after what happened this evening.

"Thank you," Eva said, relieved as she leaned her head against Georgie's.

After hearing all of this, he was not surprised that Eva didn't trust men. Georgie took Eva's hand and they finally made their way back to the wagon.

"Where have you two been? It's going to be dark by the time we get back out there, so I brought a couple lanterns with us." Ruben sounded concerned.

"Sorry, Pop, we had a delay," Georgie explained as briefly as possible.

"Alright, well, we need to be going. I also pumped you some water from the well and put it in a barrel," he said pointing to the large wooden tub. "You'll have to see if there's a well located near the cabin," Ruben suggested.

"Thanks, we really appreciate it," Georgie replied. He just wanted to be in the cabin with Eva and didn't want his father knowing that she had been upset. Everyone sat quietly as they made their way through the dark, back to the cabin.

Ruben stopped the wagon in front of the woods. It was pitch black outside, with the moon hiding behind some clouds. Eva thought that it was somewhat spooky out in the woods at night. Ruben lit the lanterns and handed one to Eva.

"Here you are, Eva," he said kindly. "George, help me move this barrel off the wagon," Ruben commanded. Georgie ran over and helped his father move the tremendous cask filled with water onto the ground. "Eva, will you light the way so that George and I can carry the barrel up near the cabin?"

"Yes, sir," she answered.

Ruben and Georgie carried the barrel to the cabin, being careful not trip over the foliage that lay on the ground. The water in the barrel kept sloshing out as they made their way up to the porch. Eva couldn't believe that Georgie could pick up his portion of the heavy vessel with only one arm. The men set the barrel down next to the front door on porch, then Ruben made several trips back to the wagon while Georgie held a lantern for him to light the way. Ruben didn't want Georgie injuring his left arm while compensating for his right one. Eva remained in the cabin, putting away their belongings and some fruits and veggies that Elizabeth had given them. Then, she filled up the water basin with the fresh water from the barrel.

"We're gonna have to clear some of these woods so you two can get back here more easily," Ruben said to Georgie as they were making their way back and forth.

Georgie didn't respond, but he had thought the same thing. Ruben and Georgie entered the cabin and Georgie immediately started a fire in the fireplace. Once the fire was lit, Ruben asked to speak with Georgie outside alone. The men walked down from the porch, listening to the nighttime sounds of the woods that surrounded them.

"Everything alright?" Ruben asked.

"Yes, I suppose," Georgie said with a shrug, then he closed his eyes tightly. "No, not really," he sighed, shaking his head. "This day hasn't gone exactly the way I thought it would," Georgie explained, inhaling deeply. "Lucious Paddimir appeared at the train station today. He snuck up on Eva and me, saying some terrible things," Georgie continued.

Ruben didn't know what to say; he sat there quietly for a moment thinking. "So you think this fellow's always going to hound the two of you?" he asked, slightly worried.

Georgie ran his hand through his hair and looked up to the sky. "I don't know? I certainly hope not, but I can't be certain. He had obviously been following us and, somehow, he knew we were married," Georgie explained and Ruben let out a humph, shaking his head.

"Is that why Eva was so upset this evening after visiting the house?" Ruben inquired.

"No," Georgie replied, closing his eyes again and shaking his head.

Ruben didn't say anything, he waited to see whether Georgie wanted to talk about what was happening.

Georgie glared down at the ground and started pacing back and forth in front of the cabin. "There's a new girl, a lady's maid named Alice," Georgie said and Ruben nodded his head.

"Yes, I know, Alice. She reminds me a little of Eva," Ruben said and Georgie scoffed.

"Eva thinks that Alice is fond of me for some reason," Georgie explained, shaking his head. He was embarrassed to even say it aloud since he thought it was a ridiculous notion.

Ruben pursed his lips together and peered at Georgie. "Eva knows she has nothing to worry about with you, right?" he questioned.

Georgie spoke up quickly. "She knows I love her, but seeing the married men come to the Hall to sleep with all the prosti…" Georgie allowed his words to trail off. He swallowed hard, looking back up to the sky. "Well, to put it simply, Eva has a difficult time trusting," he explained, looking at Ruben.

Ruben placed his hands in his pockets. "I see," he said. They were both silent for a while, until Ruben finally spoke up again, "It might take Eva some time to understand what love really means. She's been through a lot, but you keep loving her the way you do, being an example of what love really means, and she'll come along."

Georgie inhaled another deep breath and nodded in agreement. "Thank you, Pop," he replied.

Ruben sighed loudly. "Alright, I need to be heading back to the cottage for the night. Goodnight, son." Ruben gave slight wave as he started heading back through the woods, his lantern held low so he could see where he was stepping.

"Goodnight and thank you!" Georgie called out.

When Georgie entered the cabin, Eva had already changed into her nightgown, let her hair down and climbed into bed for the night. Georgie removed his clothing and slipped under the covers. He moved close to Eva.

"Eva, are you awake?" he asked whispering.

When Eva turned around, there were tears rolling down her face. "I'm sorry, today wasn't what I'd expected," she said, looking up at Georgie.

His face was softly lit by the glow of the fireplace from across the room.

"I agree, it was strange," he said quietly.

Eva smiled. "But I am thankful we're not sleeping in a shed tonight," she added, slightly laughing, and Georgie joined her.

"Eva, it hurts my heart to think that you don't trust me, but I do understand. I know that it may take time and that's okay," Georgie said gazing down at her as he caressed her face.

Eva was lying down on the bed gazing up at him. "Thank you—thank you, for being a man of your word and for being so understanding with me. I know this whole situation has been as difficult for you as it has for me, just in different ways," she said softly and Georgie didn't say anything. He just gazed at her lovingly, rubbing his fingers through her hair.

"Georgie, I have to ask you something," Eva said, sitting up in bed. She moved her hair away from her face and wrapped it around one of her shoulders. "Why didn't you tell me about your legs giving out on you while searching for me?" she asked, squinting. Eva was somewhat hurt that Georgie had never mentioned it to her.

He sat there for a moment, thinking how he had never told her about everything that he had gone through to find her.

"I had forgotten all about it," he said, shaking his head. "I guess I was so concerned about you that I didn't even think to tell you about my legs—or anything else I went through to find you. But that's the truth, Eva. I wasn't trying to keep it from you on purpose," he explained.

"I believe you," she said softly, "would you mind telling me what happened while you were out searching for me?" she asked, wondering about all that Georgie had experienced for her sake.

Georgie told her everything, from the nightmares he had to walking for weeks on end. He explained how he had met the pub owner, William Bartley, who had helped him when he had almost given up. Eva silently cried and her tears flowed down her cheeks as she listened to everything that Georgie had endured on her behalf. He mentioned how he met Dr. Kenny and about Lila, which caused a twinge in Eva's heart—confirming that Lucious had probably planned to terminate her baby as well. He told her how, on the night he returned back to the Hall, such a great storm befell him that he fell off the horse that the Kennys had lent him, breaking his arm. Eva had assumed his arm was injured in the beating that Lucious and his men gave him. Finally, he explained to her how he had no heartbeat for several minutes after being thrown into the river by Lucious' men and how Dr. Kenny had resuscitated him, bringing him back to life. He mentioned how, during that time, as he lay there with no heartbeat, all he could see was Eva—and he knew that he couldn't die and leave her alone.

Eva covered her face and sobbed, while Georgie held her, much like on the night during which she had revealed everything that she had encountered at the Hall. Eva couldn't believe all the things Georgie had suffered for her sake—nor that he did it all without even knowing whether she loved him in return. He cared for her so greatly that he was willing to go through such ordeals just to save her life. He even told her that, if she had truly desired to be with Lucious, he would have left her at Liberation Hall.

Eva had no words to utter. The depth of Georgie's love for her surpassed anything and everything that she had ever thought was possible. She looked at him with great, heartfelt, affection and placed his hand over her heart.

"I love you so much and, yet, somehow, those words don't seem to be enough to describe the way that you love me," Eva said.

Georgie's eyes were filled with tears as he continued gazing at Eva and thinking of the providence that had occurred for the two of them to be together. He knew that without Magistrate Logan, William Bartley, the Kennys, and Claudia, they would not be together—and Eva would have been stuck with Lucious at Liberation Hall forever. They had so much to be thankful for and so much love to share.

Eva leaned into Georgie, kissing him tenderly while his hand still rested upon her heart. She wrapped her arms around him, laying him down on their bed. The love they shared was far greater than any hardship that they had had to endure over the last few months. Eva never worried about Georgie having an affair again. She knew that he was not like the men who attended the Hall and certainly nothing like Lucious. Georgie had immeasurable values, noble character, and integrity that far surpassed anything that Eva had ever encountered. She was beyond blessed to have had Georgie pursue her in such a relentless, passionate, and downright reckless manner—all because of the depth of love he had for her.

Forty-One

Eva stretched her ars and rubbed her eyes upon waking. She turned over in the bed, fixing her gaze upon Georgie, who was still fast asleep. She smiled, watching him breathe deeply. She scooted closer to him, trying to get a glimpse of the time on his watch. Eva wanted to snuggle up next to him but refrained from doing so, trying not to wake him. Glancing down at the time, she was thankful that she had woken an hour before she was supposed to be at the magistrate's house. Eva's nerves were running high as she thought about starting her new position as a lady's maid. She had wondered whether the magistrate had offered her the position to keep his secret about attending the Hall, but she didn't want to say anything to Georgie since he had been so kind to them. She had also felt bad about how she treated Alice last evening and decided that it was best to apologize for her rude behavior first thing in the morning.

Eva gently rose from the bed and quietly tiptoed over to the fireplace, rekindling its embers. She then grabbed a large pot from the cupboard and went outside, filling it with water from the barrel on the front porch. The crisp, woodsy morning air smelled fresh as Eva inhaled deeply, clearing her lungs for a new day. She stood outside, gazing at the beautiful forest surrounding her, just as the light was beginning to appear. Eva couldn't believe that she was living the life she had always desired. She was married to the man she loved, living in their own home, out in the middle of the beautiful, serene woods. When Eva had finished taking in the atmosphere, she carried the large pot of water back into the house, being careful not to spill, then heated it up on the fireplace. Eva looked through the drawers, finding a couple of potholders and using them to help her carry the extremely hot water over to the bath. She poured the water carefully into the tub, trying to be very quiet; but, when she looked up, she noticed that Georgie was staring at her with a grin on his face.

"Oh, I'm sorry. I was trying not to wake you," she apologized.

Eva set the pot down on the floor and walked over to Georgie, sitting down next to him on the bed. He gazed up at her with so much love in his eyes.

"Eva, I woke up as soon as your feet touched the floor, you're heavy-footed, you know?" Georgie said letting out a soft laugh.

"Well, good morning to you, too," she replied grinning down at him. Eva dipped her head down, locking her lips with Georgie's. "Aw, I don't want to be away from you today," she said with a pout as she ran her fingers through his hair.

"I know, but we have to start doing life and work is a part of it," he said softly.

Eva thought about what a hard worker Georgie was and she hoped that she would be as well.

After they got ready for the day, they headed out toward the magistrate's house. They were holding hands as the sun cast a parade of colors across the sky. Georgie looked over at Eva, remembering the day he returned to London to check on her after his numerous nightmares. He had watched the sunrise that morning, dreaming of the day that he and Eva would be married, holding hands, walking across the countryside. He realized, at this moment, that his dream had finally come true. Georgie stopped abruptly and pulled Eva to him, wrapping his arm around her. Eva let out a slight laugh.

"That was unexpected," she said, surprised by his sudden affection.

"Thank you, Eva," Georgie said sincerely, gazing deeply into her sea-green eyes.

Eva smiled at him. "Thank you—for what?"

"Thank you for making my dreams come true," he replied, then lightly kissed her, embracing her firmly as the sun shined brilliantly over them.

Georgie and Eva finally made their way to the magistrate's house a few minutes before half-past five.

"Now, I'll come to check on you around lunchtime. Please don't worry, you're going to do just fine," Georgie reassured her.

Eva sighed, "I hope you're right," she said with a frown.

He leaned in, kissing her once more, then Eva turned around and slowly walked toward the magistrate's home. She looked back to glance at Georgie one last time before entering the house, but he was already eagerly making his way over to the horse barn.

Eva slowly strolled through the back door of the servant's hall. There was a lot of hustle and bustle going on downstairs for so early in the morning.

"Eva!" Alice called out. Eva quickly turned around looking at Alice. "Would you like to go upstairs with me so I can show you Miss Cora's room?" Alice commanded more than asked.

Eva nodded her head and they hastily made their way up the servants' staircase. Eva thought that this would be a good time to apologize to Alice for her rude behavior yesterday.

"Alice, I'm afraid that we may have gotten off on the wrong foot yesterday. I wanted to say I'm sorry if I was acting a bit odd," Eva apologized as they climbed the steps together.

"Oh, it's fine. I didn't even notice," she shrugged, waving her hand.

They arrived at the top of the second floor and, immediately, Alice began rambling.

"This is Miss Adeline's room and across here is Miss Cora's. The magistrate and the missus are in the other wing and those four rooms are guest rooms. Now, Miss Cora hasn't rung for the day yet, but, while you are here in the mornings before she wakes, there is ample time to remove stains from her clothes, do her needlework, iron her garments, and starch her bed linens. Once she rings for the day, the real work begins."

Eva wanted to take a breath for Alice, who continued her long-winded talking, without stopping for a moment.

"First, you prepare her bath, then do her hair, pick out her outfit for the day, and you help her get her dressed. Once Miss Cora goes downstairs for breakfast, you must open all the windows, allowing the room to air out while making her bed. Wipe down her belongings, clean her combs, brushes, and, last, bring the chamber pot down if it has been used," Alice continued as Eva's head started spinning wildly.

Finally, Eva couldn't take anymore. "Alice!" Eva interjected, getting her attention.

Alice abruptly stopped and looked over at Eva without an expression.

"You are speaking too quickly and I can't remember everything you're saying," Eva informed her.

Alice peered at Eva sternly. "Well, it's not my fault that you're a ninny! Really, I don't know what he sees in you," Alice said harshly, turning around as she marched down the servants' stairwell.

Eva was standing alone in the middle of the upstairs corridor. Her heart sank and she wanted to cry, but she restrained herself. Breathing deeply, she started thinking about the juice and how it would have made her feel better in this situation. Eva remembered feeling the pain melt away as the juice hit her insides, calming and soothing her. She looked down and noticed that her hands were trembling and her breathing was labored.

"No," she said firmly to herself out loud while closing her eyes and shaking her head. "No, you don't want the juice," she affirmed, frustrated by the fact that she would even consider the juice as an option for relief. Eva inhaled deeply, calming her nerves. She then climbed down the stairs to the servants' quarters and sat at the dining hall table. She put her head down on her arms doing her best to get the juice out of her mind. This was the first time she had wanted it since seeing Lucious with the flask at the train station.

Eva was sitting at the table for a while, wondering whether Georgie would be disappointed with her if she wasn't able to do her job as a lady's maid, when suddenly she heard a bell ring. Eva glanced up at the wall where the bells were installed and, next to the ringing bell, it said, "Cora."

Eva popped up out of her seat and scurried up two flights of stairs, arriving at Miss Cora's bedroom. She knocked at the door before she had a chance to think about what she was doing.

"Come in!" Cora called.

Eva stepped inside and a young, thirteen-year-old girl that was still in her bed looked up at her. Miss Cora seemed to be shorter and slightly heavy-set, with long, thick, black, wavy hair. She had large, brown, doe eyes and a small, button nose. Cora was a cute girl on the verge of womanhood, Eva thought.

Eva walked over to the edge of the bed. "Good morning, Miss." She curtsied.

"Where's Alice?" the young girl asked directly, sitting up in bed.

Eva inhaled deeply. "My name is Eva and I am your personal lady's maid. Is there anything I can do for you this morning, Miss?" Eva inquired, doing her best to play the part of Nancy.

Cora sat up in bed, placing a pillow on her lap. "Oh, that's right, father told me you were starting today. I had forgotten." A devilish grin grew on Cora's face. "You married the flutter-bum stable master, right?" Cora asked as her eyes grew large with excitement.

Eva swallowed, shocked by the young girl's comment. She waited a moment, thinking how she should answer her. Eva inhaled a deep breath.

"Yes, actually, we were just married this past Saturday," she politely replied.

"And how do you like being married?" Cora asked excitedly. "Is it absolutely brilliant?!" she inquired energetically, while tossing her head back.

Eva's mouth slightly gaped open. "Well, yes, Miss, actually…it is absolutely brilliant," Eva replied honestly with furrowed brows, trying to figure out the young girl.

"Oh, I can't wait to be married!" Cora declared proudly. "I already have my honeymoon all planned out," she said as she stretched her hands out through the air. "We're going to go to Paris!" she exclaimed dramatically, then slowly fell back onto the bed pretending to faint.

Eva raised her eyebrows at the young girl's performance and thought that Cora was doing a better job acting than herself.

Cora quickly sat back up in the bed. "Did you go on a honeymoon?" she asked, eagerly smiling and leaning back on her hands.

Eva's faced turned pink with embarrassment. "Yes, we did, Miss," Eva replied expressionlessly.

Cora gasped. "Oh, where did you go?" she asked, anxiously awaiting a response with great expectation.

"We just stayed in London, Miss," Eva answered politely.

"Oh," Cora pursed her lips and frowned, crinkling her nose. She then glanced down at her nails. "Do you do nails?" she questioned, squinting at Eva.

"Yes, I suppose I could, Miss," Eva replied with a nod.

"Good, my nail kit is in the second drawer of my vanity, on the right side," Cora instructed while pointing.

Eva walked over to the large elegant wooden vanity and found the nail kit where Cora had pointed.

"Come, sit," Cora directed happily, patting the bed, summoning Eva to come to sit next to her. Eva sat down on the bed, opened the nail kit, and pulled out a file.

"May I, Miss?" she asked and Cora stuck her head in the air while gracefully hanging her hand in front of Eva.

Eva smiled, taking the young girl's hand and began filing her nails. Eva had learned how to file and paint nails at the Hall when the ladies were having a slow day.

She painted Cora's fingernails as the inquisitive and highly talkative young girl flooded Eva with more questions. Eva didn't mind. Cora was young and lively, which was refreshing. She was also very kind, never being demanding, and very helpful, offering information without any judgment if Eva didn't know how to do something correctly. Eva liked working for Cora and they seemed to be getting along very well on her first day.

"Eva!" Cora exclaimed. "My hair looks absolutely stunning!" she gushed, turning her head from side to side as she gazed in the mirror patting her hair.

"Yes, you look very pretty, Miss," Eva said, encouraging the young girl.

Cora turned around in her chair, looking directly at Eva. "You're so much friendlier than Alice. She can be somewhat of a snob," Cora said rolling her eyes. "You know she actually told me to shut up once," Cora huffed shaking her head in disgust.

Eva wasn't surprised, Miss Cora talked a lot and Alice had not been very kind to her at all so far. Cora grabbed Eva's hand looking up at her wide-eyed.

"I'm so glad that you're my new lady's maid, Eva. I think this is going to work out splendidly!" she exclaimed dramatically while grinning happily.

Eva smiled politely in return.

523

*   *   *

Georgie had been working hard all morning in the horse barn, making up for the lost time. He thought it felt good being back on the farm and caring for all the horses. He knew it was getting close to lunchtime; glancing down at his watch he realized it was half-past one.

"Yikes!" he said aloud.

He told Eva that he would stop by to check in on her. Georgie put the shovel away and washed his hands over at the cottage. Then, he made his way over toward the magistrate's house, heading through the back door to the servants' hall. Georgie asked around to see whether anyone had seen Eva, when suddenly she came rushing down the back staircase.

Eva looked over and saw Georgie standing in the middle of the dining hall. His eyes lit up upon seeing her looking so happy.

"Georgie!" she cheered excitedly, hurrying over and wrapping her arms tightly around him. Georgie closed his eyes relishing Eva's embrace.

"I thought I had missed you," he said, shaking his head in relief.

"How has your day been?" he asked hopefully.

"Well, it sort of started off rough—but I really like Miss Cora and I think we'll get along just fine," Eva said, smiling.

Georgie smiled brightly and started leaning in to kiss her when she placed her hands on his chest to stop him from coming any closer.

"Not here, Georgie," Eva said, glancing around as several people were making their way through the dining hall.

He stood there for a moment with his eyes closed and mouth slightly hanging open. "Oh, alright," he sighed, disappointed.

"Why don't we go for a walk? It's a lovely day," Eva suggested.

"You're not hungry?" Georgie inquired, giving her a sideways look.

"Oh, you're probably starved after working hard with the horses all morning. I'll go fix you a plate," she insisted.

"Thank you, Eva," he said appreciatively as he took a seat at the dining hall table while Eva went into the kitchen to fetch him some food.

Alice was walking down the corridor toward the dining hall when she saw Georgie sitting alone. He had his arms crossed and his eyes closed with his hat covering his face as if he were taking a nap in the chair. Alice smiled and glanced around to see whether Eva was anywhere in sight. She didn't see her in the vicinity, so she walked over and quietly sat down next to Georgie at the table. Alice was grinning as she reached over, picking up an apple from the fruit bowl. She clasped the apple in her palm, holding it up at eye level.

"Would you like an apple?" she asked Georgie enticingly.

Georgie pulled his hat off of his face as his eyes popped open in shock. He was surprised to see Alice sitting next to him at the table and staring at him flirtatiously. Georgie cleared his throat and promptly sat up straight in his chair.

"Umm, no, thank you," he said, standing in haste.

Alice grabbed his arm while gazing up at him seductively.

Georgie looked down, feeling extremely uncomfortable from how Alice was looking up at him.

"What, George, you don't like apples anymore?" she asked, continuing to look at him wantonly.

Georgie was frozen solid; he couldn't believe Alice was acting this way. She stood up and pressed her body up against Georgie's.

"Here, take a bite," she insisted, holding the apple in front of his mouth and giving him an inviting smirk.

Georgie stepped back nervously and his breathing became labored.

"No, thank you," he said, shaking his spinning head, extremely put off by Alice's forward behavior toward him.

Alice leaned in even closer and traced her index finger from the top of Georgie's chest and down his torso, continuing to look at him seductively. He now knew, most certainly, that Alice was coming on to him and he needed to confront her before things got out of hand.

"Alice, I am a married man and you are acting extremely inappropriately," he spouted while still trying to sound somewhat kind to her.

Eva cheerfully walked into the dining hall, holding Georgie's plate of food, when she saw Alice leaning into Georgie. She stopped suddenly as her heart dropped at the sight of them.

"Oh, George, what Eva doesn't know won't hurt her," Alice stated as she closed her eyes and leaned up to kiss him.

Georgie stepped back and peered down at Alice very harshly.

"I am in love with Eva, my wife, and I'm not interested, Alice!" Georgie spoke with conviction. "In fact, it would hurt everyone very much to do such a thing!" he added firmly.

Alice's flirtatious smirk turned into a scowl and she covered her face and ran down the corridor. Georgie closed his eyes inhaling deeply. He sighed loudly, shaking his head in dismay. When he opened his eyes, he saw Eva standing there, holding his plate of food in her hand. She didn't move at first but continued standing, still staring at him. He thought she was going be scolding mad and very hurt by what she had seen.

Eva strolled over and sat down at the table. She set his lunch plate down next to her, then looked up at him. "Well, aren't you going to come to eat?" she questioned calmly.

Georgie tilted his head in surprise and slowly sat down in his chair, looking over at Eva. "I owe you a great apology," he said regretfully.

She looked over at him with raised brows, pressing her lips together, anticipating what he was going to say next.

"I admit I thought you were overreacting a bit when you said that Alice was fond of me, but, obviously…" Georgie swallowed, "you were right," he said sorrowfully. "I am so sorry," he apologized with a pitiful look on his face.

Eva placed her hand on top of Georgie's. "I'm very proud of you, Georgie, and I want you to know that I trust you," she said with a grin.

"Really?" Georgie asked amazed. He thought that, after the situation with Alice, it would take Eva even longer to trust him. Georgie leaned his forehead against Eva's.

"I love you, Eva Thornber," he said, gazing into her eyes affectionally.

"And I love you, Georgie Thornber," she replied softly.

Georgie quickly grabbed her and pulled her close, kissing her passionately for several long moments. He didn't care who could see them. He wanted to kiss his wife and wasn't ashamed to do so.

Suddenly, a voice came out of nowhere.

"No public affection in the servants' hall," Mr. Watkins, the butler, called out in a serious, low tone.

Georgie pulled away from Eva, looking up at him. "I'm sorry, sir, we'll try to behave ourselves," Georgie spoke with slight sarcasm while smiling and Eva dipped her head shyly with a grin on her face.

Mr. Watkins didn't look amused as he cleared his throat. "George, the coachmen are picking up the magistrate on the evening train and he'll be needing the carriage to be ready to go by five o'clock," Mr. Watkins informed Georgie.

"Yes, sir, I'll have it ready for him," Georgie replied with a nod and Mr. Watkins walked away.

Georgie looked back over at Eva. "Alright, I need to eat and head back to the barn but, first, I want to hear all about your morning," he said as he dug into the plate of roast beef and potatoes.

Eva told Georgie all about Cora and how well they were getting along. She also informed him that Cora had referred to him as the flutter-bum stable master.

"What?" Georgie retorted. "I don't think I've ever even seen Miss Cora?" Georgie questioned.

"Well, she's seen you from her bedroom window. She has a nice view of the horse barn," Eva said with raised eyebrows and a smirk.

Georgie's face turned beet red and he continued eating his food.

"I didn't know when I married you that I would have to be swatting away the women," she teased. "Did you have this problem before we were married?" she inquired.

"Actually, no, I didn't," Georgie said, wide-eyed, shaking his head.

The day passed by quickly and Georgie finished his daily duties. He bathed, changed his clothes, and ate some dinner, then waited for Eva at the dining table in the servants' quarters. He kept looking down at his watch, wondering when she would be released from her duties. Miss Cora finally relieved Eva around half-past seven and she walked tiredly down to the servant quarters. Eva noticed that Georgie sat at the dining table, glancing down at his watch. He looked like he had been waiting for her in the dining hall for a while.

Georgie sat with his back to her. His elbow was on the table while his chin was resting on his fist. Eva strolled up quietly behind him, placing her hands on his shoulders and Georgie jumped up immediately from his chair, turning around in haste. Eva shot back in shock.

"Oh, thank heavens, it's you, Eva," he said with a huge sigh of relief.

Eva started laughing heartily, covering her mouth. "Did you have another run-in with Alice?" she asked while still laughing.

"I'm pleased to say that no, I have not, and I hope it stays that way," he stated. "Are you ready to go home?" he asked, clasping her hand.

"I'm not sure that I'm allowed?" Eva said looking around the servants' hall.

"Nancy had always helped me dress for bed in the evenings," Eva spoke while tapping her finger against her chin. "Except, of course, when I was expecting Lord Manchester, then Dia…" Eva caught herself and allowed her words to trail off.

Georgie looked down at the ground inhaling deeply. "Well, maybe you should ask Miss Woodward?" he suggested looking up at Eva.

"Yes, that's a grand idea," she agreed.

Eva jaunted over to the housekeeper's, Miss Woodward's, room, and lightly tapped on her open door.

"Yes, come in," she called.

"Hello, Miss Woodward?" Eva questioned.

The older woman was sitting at her desk, writing something down in her books for the day. She turned around in her chair looking up at Eva.

"I was wondering what exactly my hours are?" Eva inquired and Miss Woodward raised her eyebrows, surprised.

"You mean Alice didn't tell you?"

Eva shook her head no. She hadn't seen Alice since her run-in with Georgie at the dining hall.

Miss Woodward squinted. "You may leave when George is done with his work for the day. Typically, a lady's maid lives at the house because they are here from morning until night but, since Miss Cora is only thirteen, Alice can handle her evening routine," Miss Woodward explained.

Eva nodded her head, delighted that she was allowed to leave with Georgie.

"Thank you, Miss Woodward, goodnight," she replied happily.

Miss Woodward turned back around facing her desk. "Goodnight," she said as she continued to write in her books.

Eva returned to the servant's dining hall and found Georgie pacing back forth, ready to go home for the evening.

"I'm allowed to leave when you are done with your work for the day," she said happily.

Georgie clapped with excitement. "Let's go home then!" he cheered. "If we leave now, we will get there before dark." He was excited.

Eva and Georgie were about to walk out of the servant quarters when Mr. Watkins, the butler, called out, "George!"

Georgie and Eva turned around expediently. "Magistrate Logan would like to see you in his office," the butler said expressionlessly, with raised brows. Georgie looked over at Eva, disappointed.

"Sorry," he said and Eva sighed.

"It's alright, I'll make some dinner for myself and I'll be down here waiting for you," she replied.

Georgie gave her a sad smile and nodded his head.

Georgie was not dressed in the proper attire to be upstairs, but Mr. Watkins said it was all right since Magistrate Logan asked to meet with him. He walked up to the magistrate's study and the door was already open. While peeking his head in the door, Georgie knocked gently.

"George," the magistrate said, looking happy to see him. "Please come in and shut the door." He motioned to Georgie to come inside the study. "Have a seat," he invited.

Georgie removed his hat and looked up at the magistrate expectantly.

"So, how is the cabin working out for you and Eva?" he inquired, dipping his chin.

"It's working out very nicely, sir. Thank you very much for allowing us to live there," Georgie said, most appreciative.

"Yes, well...you and Eva need your own privacy and I'm not big on hunting—so it all worked out. I also wanted to let you know that you're welcome to take a horse out there with you. That way, you and Eva don't have to walk all that way in the dark and cold. I know it is quite a distance from the cabin to the house."

Georgie's eyes lit up. "Thank you, sir. Yes, that would be very helpful," he replied gratefully.

The magistrate inhaled a deep breath, "Well, I wanted to let you know that Cora absolutely adores Eva. So, I do hope that Eva had a decent first day here, at the house?" the magistrate asked, tilting his head, unsure of how Eva felt about Cora.

Georgie nodded his head. "Yes, she said that Miss Cora is delightful," Georgie replied and the magistrate smiled, folding his hands across his desk.

"Oh, good," he said, sounding relieved. "Cora's not the easiest personality for everyone to be around—she's quite dramatic. I am very pleased to hear that Eva is all right with her," he explained with raised eyebrows.

Georgie nodded, wondering if that was all the magistrate wanted with him, but he had a feeling there was more.

Magistrate Logan looked at Georgie intently and sighed. "Well, now that's all out of the way, let's talk about the real reason I asked you to come and see me."

Georgie sat up straighter in his chair and cleared his throat. He was beginning to feel a little anxious about how the magistrate was acting. Magistrate Logan opened his desk drawer and pulled out of sack, placing it down on the desk in front of Georgie. Georgie's eyes grew wide as he stared intently at the sack in disbelief.

"That's the sack of money I gave to Lucious," Georgie said, perplexed, pointing and not taking his eyes off the money bag.

"Yes," the magistrate stated.

"But, how did you ever get it back?" Georgie inquired eagerly, looking up at Magistrate Logan.

"Let's just say that I gave Lucious an ultimatum—and he chose to return your money instead of going to prison," the magistrate said with raised brows.

Georgie was still in shock that the magistrate had gotten his money back.

"I don't know what to say," he shook his head and again looked at the money bag that contained his life savings. Georgie gazed up at the magistrate. "Why? Why would you do all of this for us?" Georgie wondered. The magistrate had given them so much already, Georgie thought.

Magistrate Logan lifted his chin in the air, clearing his throat. He realized that Georgie apparently didn't know that he had participated in the Hall.

"Well, it was my money as well, George. I have already taken back your advance, so you'll now be receiving a salary throughout the year," the magistrate said, motioning Georgie to pick up the sack.

Georgie gently grabbed the bag and opened it, looking inside, and there were fifty-five quid in total.

"I also told Lucious that, as part of the deal, he was to leave you and Eva alone permanently—as well as your family members."

Georgie looked up in awe of the situation once again, shaking his head. "I just don't know—"

The magistrate interjected, "It's alright, George, I know you appreciate everything I have done for you and Eva." He gave a slight smile and nod.

"You're a good man, sir," Georgie stated seriously.

The magistrate swallowed hard and looked down at his desk, still feeling guilt-ridden, knowing that he had contributed to the lifestyle of the Hall as well as to the hardships that Georgie had to endure as he searched for Eva. He glanced back up at Georgie.

"I grew really tired of watching Lucious torture you and Eva. You both deserve a fresh start together," he explained.

Georgie nodded and grinned.

"Well, you best be getting back to your wife now," the magistrate suggested.

Georgie held out his hand and the magistrate reciprocated, firmly shaking Georgie's hand in return. "Thank you again, sir," Georgie said most sincerely and the magistrate smiled and nodded.

Georgie quickly walked down to the servant's hall and found Eva sitting there alone at the table, finishing up her dinner. She looked up at him and noticed the blank expression on his face.

"What's wrong?" she asked, concerned. "You look like you've seen a ghost." She stood from the table.

Georgie just kept staring at her while he continued walking toward the table.

Eva grew extremely nervous observing his strange behavior. Once he stood in front of her, he picked up her hand, placed the bag of money in it, and gazed up at her with tears in his eyes.

"What's this George?" she inquired while lightly touching his arm.

"Magistrate Logan gave Lucious an ultimatum."

Eva's heart started racing, not knowing what Georgie was about to say.

"He told Lucious that he could either give us back the one hundred quid and leave us alone or go to prison," Georgie explained, nodding his head.

Eva's expression changed from worried to surprised.

"Lucious chose to give back the money. I suppose he didn't want to spend the rest of his life in prison," Georgie continued and Eva inhaled deeply while her mouth gaped open.

"How was he going to send Lucious to prison?" she asked in astonishment.

Georgie shook his head. "I don't exactly know and, to be honest, I really don't care. I'm just happy we have our lives back." He smiled and looked deeply into her eyes, wrapping his arm around her waist and pulling her closer toward himself.

Eva sighed in relief. She felt like a weight had been lifted off of her.

"Oh, Georgie!" she cried out, embracing him tightly and thinking about how she was finally free of Lucious. Eva pulled away gazing up at him.

"And the money?" she inquired, holding out the bag.

"There's fifty-five quid in there," Georgie said smiling.

"I'll have to return everyone's money to them," he said as his head was slightly spinning from all the excitement.

"And the advance?" she questioned.

"There is no advance; it's been cleared. I'll be getting a salary for the year," Georgie said, gazing at Eva and smiling proudly. He started laughing as he picked Eva up in his arm, swinging her around with joy. After a few spins, he set her back down on the ground, looking at her affectionately.

"Eva, everything that was being stolen from us has been restored," he said with tears in his eyes.

"I know, it's all so surreal," she said, shaking her head and thinking of where they were just a few weeks ago in comparison to where they were today.

"I think the strangest part is that everything has actually worked out better than I had originally planned," said Georgie. "I would have used up all my savings fixing up that shed. But now, we have a much nicer home…a private one, in the woods…out there all alone—"

"And beautiful," Eva interjected.

Georgie leaned and lightly kissed her lips. After a few moments, Eva pulled away.

"And doesn't smell like the horse barn," she added, snickering.

He smiled widely at her, shaking his head in complete awe of how everything had worked out for them.

Eva walked with Georgie over to the horse barn and they rode one of the horses back to the cabin. Entering it, Eva yawned.

"I'm so tired, but I do want to take a warm bath," she said groggily.

"Then I'll make one for you," Georgie offered.

"No, please don't worry about it. I will wait until morning," she said, motioning with her hands toward the bed and changing into her nightgown.

Georgie lit the fireplace and crawled into bed next to Eva, cuddling up against her.

"Well, I'll have to write to the Kennys and let them know that we have their money," he said. "And we'll have to go back to London to pay everyone their amounts back as well," he continued and Eva nodded in agreement.

"Are you nervous about going back to London?" Eva asked Georgie.

He was quiet for a moment, thinking.

"No," he said firmly, shaking his head. "I finally feel like it's over and that we are truly free of him," Georgie replied.

"Yes, I feel it too, like he has no hold on us any longer."

Georgie and Eva had officially begun their new life together, without the fear and turmoil that Lucious could be lurking around every corner. They were now fully liberated from Lucious, his juice, and the false liberation he peddled at his Liberation Hall.

Forty-Two

The train paced down the track, heading through the green meadows. Eva gazed up at the tall hills as the train floated by. Two months had passed since Magistrate Logan had given Georgie the money and Georgie and Eva were now on their way to London to return everyone's financial contributions. Georgie had written to the Kennys, informing them of what had happened and how he desired to return their portion. The doctor wrote back, however, saying that Georgie and Eva should keep the money for themselves, but that he definitely wanted them to come and visit them in a couple of months. Georgie felt bad for keeping their money but knew that the doctor would never accept it back from him.

They had just stepped off the train, when Eva's mind flashed back, remembering how Lucious had surprised them at the train station. She closed her eyes for a moment, breathing deeply and reminding herself that Lucious could no longer harm them—if he did, he would certainly go to prison. Georgie held her hand tightly as he looked at her.

"Are you alright?" he questioned.

Eva nodded her head. "Yes, I'm fine." She smiled at him.

Georgie nodded and they made their way to the lodging house.

They walked up to Margie's room, rapidly knocking on the door and she answered excitedly.

"Eva!' She grabbed her daughter and embraced her tightly in her arms.

Eva closed her eyes, smiling and fully receiving her mother's hug.

"Oh, I have missed you so much!" she exclaimed.

"I have missed you too, Mum," Eva replied.

Margie finally released Eva and glanced over at Georgie. "George, it's so good to see you," she said, smiling proudly up at him.

"It's nice to see you as well," he said, nodding with a kind smile.

"Well, come on in," Margie said, welcoming them into the lodging room.

Eva entered and saw that most of her mother's belongings were missing or packed away in boxes.

"Mum?" Eva questioned, sounding concerned as she glanced around the lodging room. "Are you leaving?" she asked as confusion covered her face at the sight of the room.

"Why don't you have a seat," Margie suggested, motioning them toward the sofa.

Eva was staring at her mother, wondering what on earth was happening.

Margie had a nervous expression upon her face, then blurted out, "Bert and I have married!"

Eva leaned back and gasped wide-eyed. She didn't know what to say; the words were stuck in her throat.

"We married just last weekend and I'm packing to move in with him. There's no sense of keeping the lodging room any longer," Margie explained.

Eva's heart was heavy as she pressed her lips together firmly. Georgie reached over, taking her hand to console her.

"Well," Margie swallowed hard. "I'll still be here in London. I'm not going very far," she said, trying to reassure her daughter.

Eva inhaled deeply, then slightly shook her head and raised her brows.

"Congratulations, I suppose," she muttered, with furrowed brows, trying to sound happy for her mother.

Margie's demeanor lightened and she let out a sigh of relief.

"I wanted to write to you, but when I received your letter that you were coming to town for a visit, I decided to wait and tell you in person," Margie explained.

Georgie piped up, "Congratulations, to you and Bert." He was grinning happily.

Eva looked over at Georgie, troubled. He knew she wasn't very thrilled about the news.

"Mum, may I be bold?" Eva asked.

Margie stared at Eva, wide-eyed and wondering what she was going to say.

"Are you really happy with Bert?" she questioned, peering at her mother.

Margie laughed slightly and nodded her head. "Yes, Eva, I am very happy," she answered with a sincere grin on her face. "And oh, I forgot to tell you, Bert's stopped drinking," Margie said joyfully.

"Oh well, that is good news," Georgie said and looked over at Eva.

"Yes, I told him that I wouldn't marry him if he was going to be a lush—so he quit, just like that," Margie said as she snapped her fingers. She looked over at Eva tenderly. "It's because he loves me, dear." Tears began forming in Margie's eyes.

"Oh, Mum," Eva sighed, standing. She walked over to her mother and leaned down to embrace her once more. "If you are happy, then I am happy for you," Eva spoke honestly.

For the rest of the morning, they talked and laughed, catching up with one another in the old lodging room. Eva told her mother all about Miss Cora and the astonishing questions that the young girl would ask her. She also explained how Alice had tried to seduce Georgie and, after he turned her down cold, she resigned from her position the next day. Eva was left having to pick up the slack and take care of both Cora and Adeline but, thankfully, Miss Woodward had hired a new lady's maid for Adeline a few weeks back.

Margie explained to Eva that, since Bert had quit drinking, he received a new position at the bank. Now Margie no longer had to sell goods at the Covent Garden market to make ends meet, although she still visited with the flower women from time to time. Bert was also teaching Margie numbers, hoping to help her find a clerk's position somewhere to keep her busy. Eva was very pleased with her mother's happiness with Bert and how Margie truly seemed to be in love with him.

Alice had invited the three of them to have lunch with her and Georgie's stomach was beginning to rumble after an hour.

"We should probably head down to Grams' for luncheon, soon," he stated, standing as he stretched his arms.

Eva insisted that Georgie head downstairs without them so that he and his grandmother could spend some time together. Georgie nodded in agreement, although he thought it was a bit odd for Eva to make such a request. He figured that she wanted to spend some time alone with her mother.

"Alright, I'll see you downstairs in a little while, then?" he questioned.

"Yes, we'll be down soon," Eva reassured him.

After Georgie left the lodging room, Eva asked her mother to come to sit next to her on the sofa. Margie knew she was going to tell her something important from the way that she was behaving. Eva dipped her chin, looking very seriously into her mother's eyes. A large smile covered her face.

"Mum, I'm pregnant!" Eva cried excitedly.

"Oh my goodness, darling!" Margie covered her mouth, grinning widely. "Eva! I'm so happy for you and George!" she exclaimed, embracing Eva with her eyes closed tightly. Margie released her and picked up both of her hands.

"Does George know?" Margie asked.

Eva shook her head. "No, I haven't told him yet, but his birthday's next week and I want to surprise him then," Eva explained.

"Oh, Eva, I'm so very happy for you!" Margie said with tears in her eyes and Eva smiled.

They went downstairs and knocked on Alice's door. Georgie opened it and his eyes lit up at the sight of Eva, which warmed Margie's heart.

"Grams, you have some visitors," he called out teasingly.

Alice looked up. "Oh, Eva, it's so good to see you, dear," she said as she hobbled over from the kitchen.

"Alice, we have missed you," Eva said, embracing the soft, old woman.

"Well, sit down...lunch is ready and George has already set up the table," she said as she hobbled back over toward the kitchen.

They were all sitting around the table, finishing up their lunch when Margie spoke up, "Everything was delicious as usual, Alice." She patted her mouth with her napkin.

"Yes, Grams, your pies are still the best," Georgie happily agreed.

Alice looked over at Eva's plate, noticing that she had hardly eaten a bite. Eva had a distressed expression on her face as she gazed at the center of the table, breathing deeply.

"Eva, did you not like the food?" Alice asked slightly offended.

"Oh no, Alice, the pies are absolutely wonderful," Eva said, nodding trying to reassure her. "I'm just not feeling very well, I'm afraid," she explained.

"Eva, you haven't felt well on and off for two months now," Georgie said, concerned. Standing hastily from the table, he walked over and placed his hand on Eva's forehead.

Eva pressed her lips together and her eyes grew wide—she didn't want Alice to figure out that she was pregnant and give it away. Eva laughed and removed Georgie's hand from her forehead. She held his hands in her own, patting them gently.

"You worry too much about me, I'm fine," she said, looking up at him and smiling, then she glanced over at the rest of the table.

Alice was rubbing her chin and squinting at Eva. "Eva, would you please help me prepare the desserts," she asked while removing herself from the table.

"Grams, Eva doesn't feel well, I think it's best that she should be resting for now," Georgie insisted.

"Really, I'm fine Georgie," Eva reassured him, patting his hand.

Georgie gazed down at her for a moment, then pulled out her chair so she could stand. Eva walked over to the kitchen with Alice to prepare the deserts when Alice cornered her in the kitchen.

"Congratulations," the old lady whispered to Eva, smiling while patting her stomach. "George doesn't know yet, does he?" Alice grinned. Eva shook her head no and smiled proudly. "It'll be our little secret," Alice said softly and Eva nodded in return.

Eva brought over the cakes and jelly while Alice carried the pot of tea and began pouring it into everyone's cups. Eva took a large scoop of the strawberry jelly, gobbling it up quickly, then helped herself to another serving of the dessert. Georgie glanced over at her strangely.

"It's funny how certain foods lately have made your stomach turn, but you can't seem to get enough of the sweets."

All the ladies looked at him for a moment, saying nothing as he continued eating his cake.

"I don't know what it is...but there's something about the sour-sweetness of the jelly that helps my tum feel better," Eva said with a shake of her head.

Margie and Alice looked over at one another and slightly chuckled.

After everyone had eaten, Georgie cleaned up the mess and told Eva to sit down, not allowing her to help. He wanted her to rest since she had not been feeling well.

"What time are you heading back to Oxfordshire?" Alice asked as she lay back in her chair.

"We're taking the evening train. Georgie has to stop by the bank on the way to the train station. Which reminds me, George, we need to give them their share of the money," Eva said, calling out across the room.

"Oh, yes, it's in my pocket," he said, drying off his hands with a dishtowel.

"You two keep my share," Alice insisted with a wave of her hand. "The porcelain I sold was going to be my wedding gift to you anyhow."

"Grams, you need that money," Georgie urged.

"Oh, I'll be fine and not another word about it!" Alice shouted in frustration and Georgie let it go while looking over at Eva and shaking his head.

"Well then, this here is Bert's five pounds and the flower women's shillings," Georgie said pulling the money out of the bag.

Margie looked up at him as she placed her teacup down onto the saucer.

"Bert said that he didn't need the five pounds back and that you and Eva are to keep the money. But I'll take the shillings for the ladies, they don't make that much as it is."

Georgie counted out the shillings and handed them to Margie.

Eva let out a loud humph.

"It seems that we came all this way to bring you the money and no one is even interested in receiving their portion," Eva said, surprised. She couldn't understand why they didn't want their money.

Alice looked up at her and smiled. "And it was a good an excuse, too, just to get the two of you back here for a visit," she said, nodding her head.

"Here, here, Alice," Margie called out in agreement.

Eva looked up at them, jaw gaping. "We would have come to visit you either way," she scoffed.

They didn't say anything in return. "Oh, well," Eva said, rolling her eyes and waving her hand.

They all had delightful conversations for the rest of the afternoon, until Georgie interrupted, saying that it was time for him and Eva to be heading to the bank before it closed.

Eva stood up sadly and everyone began saying their goodbyes to one another.

"You be sure to write and tell me how you're doing," Margie commanded.

"Yes, Mum," Eva nodded, assuring her mother and knowing that she would be thinking about her and the baby. "Please tell Bert we both give our congratulations," Eva said with a kind smile.

"Thank you for being so understanding," Margie replied, dipping her chin down and grinning widely.

They all hugged one another, then Georgie and Eva strolled out into the foyer of the lodging house. Eva stopped in the middle of the foyer, standing there she gazed around for a moment at the inside of the lodging house.

"What's the matter?" Georgie questioned.

"Next time we come to visit Alice, my mum won't be here," Eva said, shaking her head as she started crying.

Georgie pulled her into himself. "I'm sorry, Eva, I didn't think about it that way." He rubbed her back, comforting her.

Eva looked up at him. "This is where we lived right after father died. We grieved here and consoled one another. I have so many fond memories in this house with Mum and with you." Eva explained, covering her face with her hands as she began weeping.

"I know it's hard to move on, but the time is coming for us to start our own family and make our own memories," Georgie said softly, kissing the top of her head.

Eva looked up at him and Georgie wiped her tears away. She was thinking about their baby and how Georgie was right—it was time for her to move on with her own family. She took one last long look, remembering when they had first arrived at the lodging house and Georgie's family would come to visit them. Margie and Eva grew closer here, leaning on one another after Henry had passed away. Tears continued flowing down Eva's cheeks and she sucked in deep breaths, reminiscing about her mother and father being happily together. She inhaled one last breath, wiping the tears from her eyes. Then, she clasped her hand with Georgie's. Eva looked up at him, giving him a nod to let him know that she was ready to go.

Georgie gently tugged on her hand and they walked out of the lodging house together, making their way into town.

Georgie and Eva were in front of the bank and Eva asked whether she could stay outside to look at some of the store windows. Georgie reluctantly agreed, then went inside to deposit their savings without her. Eva strolled down the street, looking inside the fancy shops at all the extravagant dresses along the way. She stopped in front of one shop, recognizing its name. This was the store where Claudia had purchased their fine garments and dresses. A beautiful, lavender dress with ivory lace was sitting in the picture window, along with a matching summer hat. Eva stood there imagining what she would look like in the fashionable attire when, suddenly, she noticed a golden cane in the reflection of the store window. Eva sucked in a quick breath and almost turned around but stopped herself from doing so. She remained very still as she continued watching in the reflection of the window.

Georgie came walking out of the bank and found Eva staring into one of the store windows. "Alright, are you ready to head—"

Eva slapped him in the gut, grabbing his arm and turning him toward the store window. Georgie looked down at her, very confused.

"Shhhh!" she whispered, holding her finger up to her lips.

He stood very still, unsure of what was happening.

"I don't understand...what are we doing?" he inquired quietly while leaning into her.

She didn't glance up at him but softly spoke while staring straight at the window.

"Look at the reflection," she said softly.

Georgie peered in, taking a good look, then jerked back.

"It's Lucious," he whispered loudly.

Eva nodded her head but said nothing in return.

Georgie grabbed Eva's hand, holding it tightly.

They both continued watching closely as they saw Lucious Paddimir flirting with a young girl in the street behind them. Eva started breathing heavily and her heart was racing as she watched Lucious with the child. She stood very still, praying that he would not see them standing only a few feet away. She placed her hands on her stomach, thinking about Georgie's baby in her womb.

Lucious carefully picked up the girl's hand, kissing it gently, while passersby looked at him with funny expressions. Georgie shook his head, disgusted, as he observed Lucious coercing the young lady, much like he had done with Eva. He was probably inviting her to join her somewhere, pretending to care for her. The young girl was smiling brightly, obviously smitten with Lucious. Eva knew what the girl was thinking— how was it that this sophisticated, handsome, rich man had taken an interest in her? She wondered if she had looked like that when Lucious kissed her hand and invited her to Liberation Hall that day when they met outside of Bertram's flower shop.

Lucious finally walked away and Georgie turned around, checking to make sure that he wasn't anywhere in sight.

"I think the coast is clear," he said looking down at Eva.

Eva turned around, staring at the young girl. The young lady was still watching the place where Lucious had walked away, an excited grin upon her face. Eva remembered feeling the same way.

"I have to go warn her," Eva breathed as she started marching over to the girl.

"Wait, Eva!" Georgie said firmly, grabbing her by the hand. "What if he's watching?" Georgie questioned worriedly.

Eva looked Georgie seriously in the eyes.

"He can't hurt us anymore...but he can hurt her. I think we should warn her," Eva pleaded with him.

Georgie understood why Eva wanted to warn the young girl after what they had both been through because of Lucious, but he wasn't positive that it was a good idea. He thought about it for a moment.

"I don't know?" he said, looking around cautiously.

"Please, Georgie, we have to try and help her," Eva begged.

He inhaled deeply and sighed. "Alright, but I'm keeping a lookout while you talk with her," Georgie insisted.

They proceeded slowly toward the young girl as she began walking away.

"Excuse me!" Eva called out.

The girl didn't know that Eva was speaking to her and Eva gently touched the girl on the shoulder.

"Excuse me," she said softly.

The girl turned around quickly, looking at Eva, startled by her touch.

"Yes?" she questioned.

"That man you were speaking with a moment ago, you know, the one with the golden cane?" the girl nodded her head while listening to Eva.

"I wanted to let you know that he is a very dangerous man," Eva said directly.

The young girl leaned back, glaring at her. "How do ya know he's a dangerous man? He's only been kind to me!" The girl spoke defensively.

Eva sighed shaking her head. "Yes, that's what he does… but then, he turns on you and hurts you in ways you never thought were possible."

The girl was taken aback by Eva's comment.

"May I ask your name?" Eva inquired, but the girl didn't reply. Eva looked into her eyes. "I wish I'd listened when someone had warned me about Lucious Paddimir," Eva said sorrowfully.

The girl jolted back, surprised that Eva knew his name. She looked up at Eva, wide-eyed, tilting her head but continued to say nothing in return. Eva realized that the girl was uncomfortable with her questions and decided it was best to leave her alone.

"I'm sorry, I won't bother you any longer," Eva said turning around sadly, thinking how maybe she shouldn't have said anything.

"My name's Prissy," she called out.

Eva quickly turned around to look at her. "Oh Prissy, you seem like a very clever girl…and I know it's not my place to tell you what to do…but, I beg you Prissy, do not go anywhere with that man. He's very dangerous," Eva warned adamantly, giving the girl a pleading expression.

Prissy said nothing for a moment, then nodded. "I'll think about it," she replied, peering at Eva.

Eva's heart dropped. She hadn't convinced the young girl to stay away from Lucious, but she knew there was nothing more that she could do.

Eva sadly nodded her head as Prissy turned around and walked away. Then, Eva lifted her head once more, calling out, "Prissy!"

The girl rapidly turned around, looking back at Eva expectantly. Eva walked up to her slowly, bending down as she gazed directly into the girl's eyes.

"If you do decide to go with Lucious, whatever you do, Prissy, don't drink the juice," Eva warned and then released another sigh. She turned back around, facing Georgie. She had a sorrowful look in her eyes. Eva didn't know what little Prissy was going to do, but she hoped that the girl would listen to her, unlike she had done when she had been warned.

Georgie looked down at Eva solemnly. "Are you alright?" he asked, concerned.

"Yes, I am," she said softly, nodding. "I just hope that she makes the right decision." She turned back one last time to look at the girl.

Georgie raised his eyebrows and nodded in agreement. "Let's go to the train station," he said, taking Eva's hand; together, they began making their way to the station.

Georgie and Eva would always know that Lucious was out there, roaming around the city and seeking his next victim, but they would no longer allow him to have an impact on their lives.

"Eva, I want to start a life with you, a new life—free of the pain of what happened." Georgie said solemnly.

He noticed tears welling up in Eva's eyes. He turned toward her and placed his hand on the right side of her face.

"If we don't forgive Lucious, we can never be free and at peace. It doesn't mean that what he did was right, it means that we no longer let it define who we are."

"I... I love you, Georgie Thornber" Eva replied, with a quivering voice.

She knew he was right, as difficult as it sounded, she wanted to forgive Lucious Paddimir. She wanted to see herself as Georgie saw her—free of the past.

Leaving London that day, they decided together to leave the past behind them. They pardoned Lucious in their hearts for the awful things he had done in order to free themselves of his sins and crimes. The freedom they felt deep within by relinquishing Lucious was far more liberating than holding onto bitterness leftover from the trials that they had faced and pain that they had endured because of him.

Forty-Three

E va had blindfolded Georgie and was leading him through the soft, wavy field onto the very top of the magistrate's property. Today was Georgie's birthday and she had planned a very special picnic for the two of them. They were both given the afternoon off to celebrate and Eva had spread a large blanket in the field at the highest point on the property, knowing that this was Georgie's favorite spot, from which he liked to take in the serene surroundings.

"Where are you taking me, Mrs. Thornber?" he asked, laughing as he continued tripping over himself while climbing up the side of the hill blindfolded.

"You'll find out soon enough, when we get there," Eva teased, wagging her finger.

She had filled a large basket with sandwiches, cheeses, fruit, and some lemonade, along with two glasses. The cook had helped Eva prepare Georgie's favorite cake, which was a white cake with white frosting. Eva only hoped that the animals hadn't beaten them to their late afternoon lunch.

"We're almost there," she said enticingly. She went on, muttering, "just a little further, a little more," as she continued leading the way. "Alright, we're here," Eva stated, stopping at once while Georgie continued to walk over to her, causing them both to stumble to the ground and land on the edge of a picnic blanket. They were both laughing as they gracefully landed on the ground.

"Alright, now, may I please take this off?" Georgie pleaded, realizing that Eva was having too much fun at his expense on his birthday.

Eva crawled over to Georgie. Leaning in, she kissed him while he was still blindfolded. Georgie's insides began to swell and he grabbed Eva, pulling her down on top of him and kissing her for a few moments longer. He was envisioning Eva in her wedding dress once again as he kissed her mouth fervidly. She slowly pulled away, smiling at Georgie as he continued to lie in the field blindfolded.

Eva carefully removed the blindfold from his face and said, "*Voilà!*"

She waved her arms as she presented him with the picnic.

Georgie gazed around, seeing where they were located. "Aw, Eva, this is perfect!" he stated happily, sitting up and leaning back on his elbows with his legs straight out.

Eva poured them both a glass of lemonade and handed one of the glasses to Georgie.

"Thank you," he said as he gazed across the beautiful landscape. "This a great Eva, really," he spoke while his eyes twinkled and he inhaled the fresh country air. "If I were going to build a house," Georgie said with a pleased look on his face, "I would build right here."

They both finished his sentence in unison and Georgie looked over at Eva, shaking his head as they chuckled. He made that same comment every time they walked to the top of the hill.

Eva took a sip of lemonade and released a sigh of relief, the sweet-tart flavor easing her churning in her tummy. She smiled brightly, watching Georgie look so happy and content. Eva reached over to the picnic basket.

"Would you like a sandwich?" she offered.

Georgie took the sandwich from her hand and started eating away. "Aren't you going to have one?" he asked, looking over at her.

"Um, I'm still not feeling very well," she said, making a distasteful face.

Georgie sat up on the blanket with her. "Come on Eva, you have to eat something, it's my birthday," he begged as Eva gave him a pout. Georgie reached over into the basket, pulling out a bright, ruby-red strawberry. "You won't even take a bite of a strawberry? They're you're favorite," he enticed while holding the strawberry up her mouth, gently grazing it along her lips.

Eva looked up at him pretending to be slightly annoyed. She took a quick bite of the juicy strawberry that was resting between his fingers. "There, are you happy?" she asked sarcastically while chewing the strawberry with a smirk on her face.

"Yes, I am." He started leaning in and kissing Eva, tasting the strawberry on her lips. "Very happy."

Eva felt kindled by her husband's kisses and she grabbed his shirt and brought him down on top of her. Georgie leaned over Eva, kissing her passionately while feelings of exhilaration soared through his body from the touch of her lips against his own.

After a few moments, he pulled away. "I love you so much, Eva Thornber."

Eva smiled widely. "I love you, George Thornber…Happy Birthday!" she said breathily, pulling him back down to kiss him when Georgie quickly turned his head away from her. "What's wrong?" she questioned.

Georgie had a dumbfounded look on his face. "Eva, I don't think you've ever called me George in my entire life!" he said, looking at her in astonishment.

Eva gazed at him coyly, leaning in closer and spoke, "Well, maybe that's because there's possibly another little Georgie on the way?" she said smiling while she rubbed her tummy.

He stared at her for a moment as his eyes grew large. "Do you mean to tell me that you're…" Eva nodded, smiling blissfully up at him. "Eva!" he cried out. Georgie took Eva into his arms, embracing her tightly as he rapidly kissed her with one short kiss after another, covering her entire face.

"I'm going to be a father!" he exclaimed excitedly. "Oh, Eva, this is the greatest birthday present you could've ever given me!" He was ecstatic.

"Well, you did play a part in it, George," she said smiling up at him.

"Does this mean that you're going to call me George from now on?" he asked, looking concerned. "Because I really love that you call me by my childhood name from when we first met." He looked down at her.

"Alright, Georgie," she said. "But what happens if we have a boy?" she inquired. "I would like to name him after you and my father." She squinted at him to see whether he liked the name.

"George Henry is a fine name," he said nodding. "And if there is a little Georgie, then, I suppose, you can call me George...only sometimes, that is," he added smiling. "But, what if we have a girl?" he asked.

"Well, I was thinking about the name Claudia," she said, dipping her chin down, unsure of how he would respond.

Georgie looked at her for a moment, contemplating the name.

"Yes, I like Claudia, very much...it's a pretty name," he agreed with her.

"Well, it's settled then—George Henry or Claudia Elizabeth, after your mother," Eva added, looking at him affectionately.

Georgie gazed down upon her, caressing her forehead with his fingers and moving away the blonde tendrils that had fallen against her face.

"Eva, you have made me the happiest man in the entire world," he said, leaning down and kissing his wife tenderly on the lips.

Eva smiled radiantly as the sun illuminated her face.

"Come on...let's go for a walk through the fields," he suggested. Georgie stood up and pulled Eva onto her feet and they began strolling through the serene countryside, together, both hand in hand and step in step. The warm sunlight beat down on their skin and a soft wind blew all around them.

Eva and Georgie spent the rest of the afternoon daydreaming, laughing, and kissing passionately, making plans for their future. A future that abounded in friendship, truth, and unconditional love. A love that expelled every fear, comforted every pain, and healed every wound that they would face. A love that was so strong that not even the toughest evils nor the greatest powers of darkness could ever penetrate to separate them. A love so relentless—saturated in purity and perfect unity—that it would last through all eternity.

THE END

About the Author

Author Taran A. Schilg is a wife and mother of four boys from central Ohio. A lover of both history and romance, she has been creating stories and characters in their own colorful worlds for as long as she can remember. With a passion for understanding the power of true love in relationships, her writings reflect this sentiment in a way that seeks to bring hope and strength to voices that may have faded. When she is not writing she enjoys a good mystery, traveling, singing and songwriting, spending time with her family, and encouraging young women.

Made in the USA
Monee, IL
07 July 2020

36068360R00329